Praise for *The Lincoln Highway*

"Remarkably buoyant . . . Permeated with light, wit, youth . . . Towles has snipped off a minuscule strand of existence—ten wayward days—and when we look through his lens we see that this brief interstice teems with stories, grand as legends."

—*The New York Times Book Review*

"Set over the course of ten riveting days, the story of these four boys unfolds, refolds, tears, and is taped back together. When you aren't actually reading the book, you'll be worrying about the characters, so you might as well stay in your chair and keep reading."

—Ann Patchett, author of *The Dutch House*

"[A] real joyride . . . There's so much to enjoy in this generous novel packed with fantastic characters . . . and filled with digressions, magic tricks, sorry sagas, retributions, and the messy business of balancing accounts."

—*NPR*

"An enthralling odyssey."

—*People*

"Stories can bring us back to ourselves, Towles seems to say, if only we are open to receiving their power. . . . Anyone who follows *The Lincoln Highway* will relish the trip."

—*Los Angeles Times*

"Captivating . . . *The Lincoln Highway* has suspense, humor, philosophy, and a strong sense of time and place, moving quickly and surely toward a satisfying conclusion. . . . Like the intercontinental route that it is named for, *The Lincoln Highway* is long and filled with intriguing detours. In the hands of a master wordsmith like Towles, it is definitely worth the trip."

—*St. Louis Post-Dispatch*

"[A] reason to rejoice."   —*The Millions*

"[A] bracing, heroic adventure . . . Towles plays stylishly with elements of the picaresque, the coming-of-age novel, and the epic quest. . . . The indelible final scene, which I did not see coming, perfectly encapsulates the theme of inheritance, and what choices the characters make about what they are given, to determine their own fates."
—*The Seattle Times*

"*The Lincoln Highway* is a road novel that celebrates the mythos of an era via a cross-country highway. . . . Readers . . . will delight in this travelogue's touchstones."   —(Minneapolis) *Star-Tribune*

"Once again, I was wowed by Towles's writing—especially because *The Lincoln Highway* is so different from *A Gentleman in Moscow* in terms of setting, plot, and themes. Towles is not a one-trick pony. Like all the best storytellers, he has range."   —Bill Gates

"Magnificent . . . Towles is a supreme storyteller, and this one-of-a-kind kind of novel isn't to be missed."
—*Publishers Weekly* (starred review)

"Towles's third novel is even more entertaining than his much-acclaimed *A Gentleman in Moscow*. . . . A remarkable blend of sweetness and doom, [*The Lincoln Highway*] is packed with revelations about the American myth, the art of storytelling, and the unrelenting pull of history. An exhilarating ride through Americana."
—*Kirkus Reviews* (starred review)

© Dmitri Kasterine

PENGUIN BOOKS

THE LINCOLN HIGHWAY

Amor Towles is the author of the *New York Times* bestsellers *Rules of Civility* and *A Gentleman in Moscow*. The two novels have collectively sold more than four million copies and have been translated into more than thirty languages. Towles lives in Manhattan with his wife and two children.

Reading groups looking for special materials should visit amortowles.com

Penguin Reading Group Discussion Guide available online at penguinrandomhouse.com.

ALSO BY AMOR TOWLES

A Gentleman in Moscow
Rules of Civility

THE

LINCOLN HIGHWAY

Amor Towles

PENGUIN BOOKS

PENGUIN BOOKS
An imprint of Penguin Random House LLC
First published in the United States of America by Viking, an imprint of
Penguin Random House LLC, 2021
Published in Penguin Books 2023

CREDITS
Pages viii–ix: Map based on an original design by Alex Coulter.
Page 268: Photo by Edward Hausner/The New York Times/Redux.

ISBN 9780735222366 (paperback)

THE LIBRARY OF CONGRESS HAS CATALOGED THE HARDCOVER EDITION AS FOLLOWS:
Names: Towles, Amor, author.
Title: The Lincoln highway / Amor Towles.
Description: [New York] : Viking, [2021]
Identifiers: LCCN 2021024465 (print) | LCCN 2021024466 (ebook) |
ISBN 9780735222359 (hardcover) | ISBN 9780735222373 (ebook) |
ISBN 9780593489338 (international edition)
Classification: LCC PS3620.O945 L56 2021 (print) |
LCC PS3620.O945 (ebook) | DDC 813/.6—dc23
LC record available at https://lccn.loc.gov/2021024465
LC ebook record available at https://lccn.loc.gov/2021024466

Printed in the United States of America
1st Printing

Designed by Amanda Dewey

For
My brother Stokley
And
My sister Kimbrough

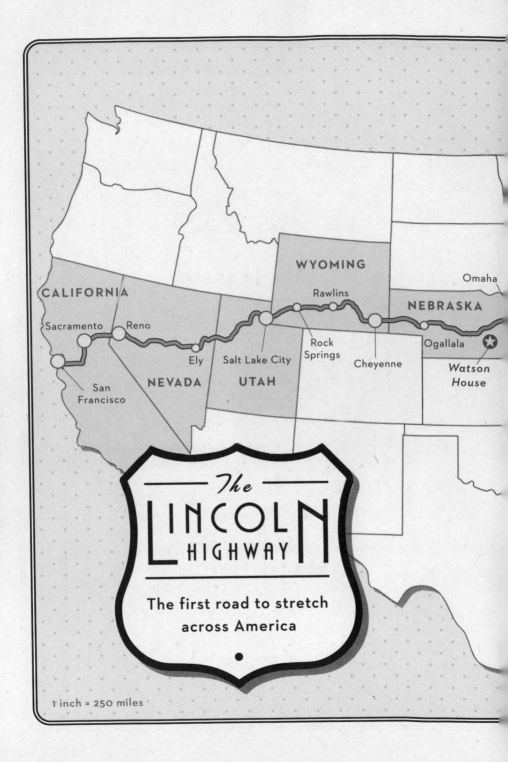

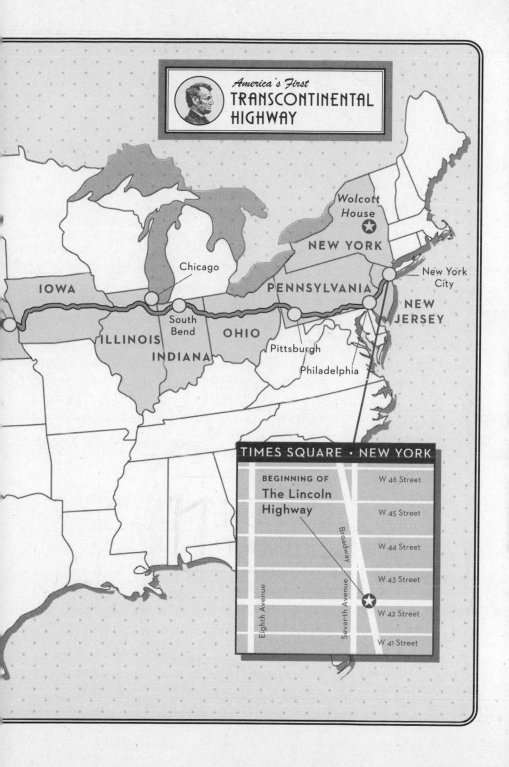

America's First
TRANSCONTINENTAL HIGHWAY

Wolcott House ⭐

NEW YORK

Chicago

IOWA

PENNSYLVANIA

New York City

NEW JERSEY

South Bend

OHIO

ILLINOIS

INDIANA

Pittsburgh

Philadelphia

TIMES SQUARE · NEW YORK

BEGINNING OF
The Lincoln Highway

W 46 Street

W 45 Street

Broadway

W 44 Street

W 43 Street

Eighth Avenue

Seventh Avenue

⭐ W 42 Street

W 41 Street

Evening and the flat land,
Rich and somber and always silent;
The miles of fresh-plowed soil,
Heavy and black, full of strength and harshness;
The growing wheat, the growing weeds,
The toiling horses, the tired men;
The long empty roads,
Sullen fires of sunset, fading,
The eternal, unresponsive sky.
Against all this, Youth . . .

—O *Pioneers!*, Willa Cather

TEN
—.—

Emmett

JUNE 12, 1954—The drive from Salina to Morgen was three hours, and for much of it, Emmett hadn't said a word. For the first sixty miles or so, Warden Williams had made an effort at friendly conversation. He had told a few stories about his childhood back East and asked a few questions about Emmett's on the farm. But this was the last they'd be together, and Emmett didn't see much sense in going into all of that now. So when they crossed the border from Kansas into Nebraska and the warden turned on the radio, Emmett stared out the window at the prairie, keeping his thoughts to himself.

When they were five miles south of town, Emmett pointed through the windshield.

—You take that next right. It'll be the white house about four miles down the road.

The warden slowed his car and took the turn. They drove past the McKusker place, then the Andersens' with its matching pair of large red barns. A few minutes later they could see Emmett's house standing beside a small grove of oak trees about thirty yards from the road.

To Emmett, all the houses in this part of the country looked like they'd been dropped from the sky. The Watson house just looked like it'd had a rougher landing. The roof line sagged on either side of the chimney and the window frames were slanted just enough that half the windows wouldn't quite open and the other half wouldn't quite shut. In another moment, they'd be able to see how the paint had been shaken right off the clapboard. But when they got within a hundred feet of the driveway, the warden pulled to the side of the road.

—Emmett, he said, with his hands on the wheel, before we drive in there's something I'd like to say.

That Warden Williams had something to say didn't come as much of a surprise. When Emmett had first arrived at Salina, the warden was a Hoosier named Ackerly, who wasn't inclined to put into words a piece of advice that could be delivered more efficiently with a stick. But Warden Williams was a modern man with a master's degree and good intentions and a framed photograph of Franklin D. Roosevelt hanging behind his desk. He had notions that he'd gathered from books and experience, and he had plenty of words at his disposal to turn them into counsel.

—For some of the young men who come to Salina, he began, whatever series of events has brought them under our sphere of influence is just the beginning of a long journey through a life of trouble. They're boys who were never given much sense of right or wrong as children and who see little reason for learning it now. Whatever values or ambitions we try to instill in them will, in all likelihood, be cast aside the moment they walk out from under our gaze. Sadly, for these boys it is only a matter of time before they find themselves in the correctional facility at Topeka, or worse.

The warden turned to Emmett.

—What I'm getting at, Emmett, is that you are not one of them. We haven't known each other long, but from my time with you I can tell that that boy's death weighs heavily on your conscience. No one imagines what happened that night reflects either the spirit of malice or an expression of your character. It was the ugly side of chance. But as a civilized society, we ask that even those who have had an unintended hand in the misfortune of others pay some retribution. Of course, the payment of the retribution is in part to satisfy those who've suffered the brunt of the misfortune—like this boy's family. But we also require that it be paid for the benefit of the young man who was the *agent* of misfortune. So that by having the opportunity to pay his debt, he too can find some solace, some sense of atonement, and thus begin the process of renewal. Do you understand me, Emmett?

—I do, sir.

—I'm glad to hear it. I know you've got your brother to care for now and the immediate future may seem daunting; but you're a bright young man and you've got your whole life ahead of you. Having paid your debt in full, I just hope you'll make the most of your liberty.

—That's what I intend to do, Warden.

And in that moment, Emmett meant it. Because he agreed with most of what the warden said. He knew in the strongest of terms that his whole life was ahead of him and he knew that he needed to care for his brother. He knew too that he had been an agent of misfortune rather than its author. But he didn't agree that his debt had been paid in full. For no matter how much chance has played a role, when by your hands you have brought another man's time on earth to its end, to prove to the Almighty that you are worthy of his mercy, that shouldn't take any less than the rest of your life.

The warden put the car in gear and turned into the Watsons'. In the clearing by the front porch were two cars—a sedan and a pickup. The warden parked beside the pickup. When he and Emmett got out of the car, a tall man with a cowboy hat in his hand came out the front door and off the porch.

—Hey there, Emmett.

—Hey, Mr. Ransom.

The warden extended his hand to the rancher.

—I'm Warden Williams. It was nice of you to take the trouble to meet us.

—It was no trouble, Warden.

—I gather you've known Emmett a long time.

—Since the day he was born.

The warden put a hand on Emmett's shoulder.

—Then I don't need to explain to you what a fine young man he is. I was just telling him in the car that having paid his debt to society, he's got his whole life ahead of him.

—He does at that, agreed Mr. Ransom.

The three men stood without speaking.

The warden had lived in the Midwest for less than a year now, but he knew from standing at the foot of other farmhouse porches that at this point in a conversation you were likely to be invited inside and offered something cool to drink; and when you received the invitation, you should be ready to accept because it would be taken as rude if you were to decline, even if you did have a three-hour drive ahead of you. But neither Emmett nor Mr. Ransom made any indication of asking the warden in.

—Well, he said after a moment, I guess I should be heading back.

Emmett and Mr. Ransom offered a final thanks to the warden, shook his hand, then watched as he climbed in his car and drove away. The warden was a quarter mile down the road when Emmett nodded toward the sedan.

—Mr. Obermeyer's?

—He's waiting in the kitchen.

—And Billy?

—I told Sally to bring him over a little later, so you and Tom can get your business done.

Emmett nodded.

—You ready to go in? asked Mr. Ransom.

—The sooner the better, said Emmett.

They found Tom Obermeyer seated at the small kitchen table. He was wearing a white shirt with short sleeves and a tie. If he was also wearing a suit coat, he must have left it in his car because it wasn't hanging on the back of the chair.

When Emmett and Mr. Ransom came through the door, they seemed to catch the banker off his guard, because he abruptly scraped back the chair, stood up, and stuck out his hand all in a single motion.

—Well, hey now, Emmett. It's good to see you.

Emmett shook the banker's hand without a reply.

Taking a look around, Emmett noted that the floor was swept, the counter clear, the sink empty, the cabinets closed. The kitchen looked cleaner than at any point in Emmett's memory.

—Here, Mr. Obermeyer said, gesturing to the table. Why don't we all sit down.

Emmett took the chair opposite the banker. Mr. Ransom remained standing, leaning his shoulder against the doorframe. On the table was a brown folder thick with papers. It was sitting just out of the banker's reach, as if it had been left there by somebody else. Mr. Obermeyer cleared his throat.

—First of all, Emmett, let me say how sorry I am about your father. He was a fine man and too young to be taken by illness.

—Thank you.

—I gather when you came for the funeral that Walter Eberstadt had a chance to sit down with you and discuss your father's estate.

—He did, said Emmett.

The banker nodded with a look of sympathetic understanding.

—Then I suspect Walter explained that three years ago your father took out a new loan on top of the old mortgage. At the time, he said it was to upgrade his equipment. In actuality, I suspect a good portion of that loan went to pay some older debts since the only new piece of farm equipment we could find on the property was the John Deere in the barn. Though I suppose that's neither here nor there.

Emmett and Mr. Ransom seemed to agree that this was neither here nor there because neither made any effort to respond. The banker cleared his throat again.

—The point I'm getting to is that in the last few years the harvest wasn't what your father had hoped; and this year, what with your father's passing, there isn't going to be a harvest at all. So we had no choice but to call in the loan. It's an unpleasant bit of business, I know, Emmett, but I want you to understand that it was not an easy decision for the bank to make.

—I should think it would be a pretty easy decision for you to make by now, said Mr. Ransom, given how much practice you get at making it.

The banker looked to the rancher.

—Now, Ed, you know that's not fair. No bank makes a loan in hopes of foreclosing.

The banker turned back to Emmett.

—The nature of a loan is that it requires the repayment of interest and principal on a timely basis. Even so, when a client in good standing falls behind, we do what we can to make concessions. To extend terms and defer collections. Your father is a perfect example. When he began falling behind, we gave him some extra time. And when he got sick, we gave him some more. But sometimes a man's bad luck becomes too great to surmount, no matter how much time you give him.

The banker reached out his arm to lay a hand on the brown folder, finally claiming it as his own.

—We could have cleared out the property and put it up for sale a month ago, Emmett. It was well within our rights to do so. But we didn't. We waited so that you could complete your term at Salina and come home to sleep in your own bed. We wanted you to have a chance to go through the house with your brother in an unhurried fashion, to organize your personal effects. Hell, we even had the power company leave on the gas and electricity at our own expense.

—That was right kind of you, said Emmett.

Mr. Ransom grunted.

—But now that you are home, continued the banker, it's probably best for everyone involved if we see this process through to its conclusion. As the executor of your father's estate, we'll need you to sign a few papers. And within a few weeks, I'm sorry to say, we'll need you to make arrangements for you and your brother to move out.

—If you've got something that needs signing, let's sign it.

Mr. Obermeyer took a few documents from the folder. He turned them around so that they were facing Emmett and peeled back pages, explaining the purpose of individual sections and subsections, translating the terminology, pointing to where the documents should be signed and where initialed.

—You got a pen?

Mr. Obermeyer handed Emmett his pen. Emmett signed and initialed the papers without consideration, then slid them back across the table.

—That it?

—There is one other thing, said the banker, after returning the documents safely to their folder. The car in the barn. When we did the routine inventory of the house, we couldn't find the registration or the keys.

—What do you need them for?

—The second loan your father took out wasn't for specific pieces of agricultural machinery. It was against any new piece of capital equipment purchased for the farm, and I'm afraid that extends to personal vehicles.

—Not to that car it doesn't.

—Now, Emmett . . .

—It doesn't because that piece of capital equipment isn't my father's. It's mine.

Mr. Obermeyer looked to Emmett with a mixture of skepticism and sympathy—two emotions that in Emmett's view had no business being on the same face at the same time. Emmett took his wallet from his pocket, withdrew the registration, and put it on the table.

The banker picked it up and reviewed it.

—I see that the car is in your name, Emmett, but I'm afraid that if it was purchased by your father on your behalf . . .

—It was not.

The banker looked to Mr. Ransom for support. Finding none, he turned back to Emmett.

—For two summers, said Emmett, I worked for Mr. Schulte to earn the money to buy that car. I framed houses. Shingled roofs. Repaired porches. As a matter of fact, I even helped install those new cabinets in your kitchen. If you don't believe me, you're welcome to go ask Mr. Schulte. But either way, you're not touching that car.

Mr. Obermeyer frowned. But when Emmett held out his hand for the registration, the banker returned it without protest. And when he left with his folder, he wasn't particularly surprised that neither Emmett nor Mr. Ransom bothered seeing him to the door.

When the banker was gone, Mr. Ransom went outside to wait for Sally and Billy, leaving Emmett to walk the house on his own.

Like the kitchen, Emmett found the front room tidier than usual—with the pillows propped in the corners of the couch, the magazines in a neat little stack on the coffee table, and the top of his father's desk rolled down. Upstairs in Billy's room, the bed was made, the collections of bottle caps and bird feathers were neatly arranged on their shelves, and one of the windows had been opened to let in some air. A window must have been opened on the other side of the hall too because there was enough of a draft to stir the fighter planes hanging over Billy's bed: replicas of a Spitfire, a Warhawk, and a Thunderbolt.

Emmett smiled softly to see them.

He had built those planes when he was about Billy's age. His mother had given him the kits back in 1943 when all Emmett or his friends could talk about were the battles unfolding in the European and Pacific theaters, about Patton at the head of the Seventh Army storming the beaches of Sicily, and Pappy Boyington's Black Sheep Squadron taunting the enemy over the Solomon Sea. Emmett had assembled the models on the kitchen table with all the precision of an engineer. He had painted the insignias and serial numbers on the fuselages with four tiny bottles of enamel paint and a fine-haired brush. When they were done, Emmett had lined them up on his bureau in a diagonal row just like they would have been on the deck of a carrier.

From the age of four, Billy had admired them. Sometimes when Emmett would come home from school, he would find Billy standing on a chair beside the bureau talking to himself in the language of a fighter pilot. So when Billy turned six, Emmett and his father hung the planes from the ceiling over Billy's bed as a birthday surprise.

Emmett continued down the hall to his father's room, where he found the same evidence of tidiness: the bed made, the photographs on the bureau dusted, the curtains tied back with a bow. Emmett approached one of the windows and looked out across his father's land. After being plowed and planted for twenty years, the fields had been left untended for just one season and you could already see the tireless advance of nature—the sagebrush and ragwort and ironweed establishing themselves among the prairie grasses. If left untended for another few years, you wouldn't be able to tell that anyone had ever farmed these acres at all.

Emmett shook his head.

Bad luck . . .

That's what Mr. Obermeyer had called it. A bad luck that was too great to surmount. And the banker was right, up to a point. When it came to bad luck, Emmett's father always had plenty to spare. But Emmett knew that wasn't the extent of the matter. For when it came to bad judgment, Charlie Watson had plenty of that to spare too.

Emmett's father had come to Nebraska from Boston in 1933 with his new wife and a dream of working the land. Over the next two decades, he had tried to grow wheat, corn, soy, even alfalfa, and had been thwarted at every turn. If the crop he chose to grow one year needed plenty of water, there were two years of drought. When he switched to a crop that needed plenty of sun, thunderclouds gathered in the west. Nature is merciless, you might counter. It's indifferent and unpredictable. But a farmer who changes the crop he's growing every two or three years? Even as a boy, Emmett knew that was a sign of a man who didn't know what he was doing.

Out behind the barn was a special piece of equipment imported from Germany for the harvesting of sorghum. At one point deemed essential, it was soon unnecessary, and now no longer of use—because his father hadn't had the good sense to resell it once he'd stopped growing sorghum. He just let it sit in the clearing behind the barn exposed to the rain and snow. When Emmett was Billy's age and his friends would come over from the neighboring farms to play—boys who, at the height of the war, were eager to climb on any piece of machinery and pretend it was a tank—they wouldn't even set foot on the harvester, sensing instinctively that it was some kind of ill omen, that within its rusting hulk was a legacy of failure that one should steer clear of whether from politeness or self-preservation.

So one evening when Emmett was fifteen and the school year nearly over, he had ridden his bike into town, knocked on Mr. Schulte's door, and asked for a job. Mr. Schulte was so bemused by Emmett's request that he sat him down at the dinner table and had him brought a slice of pie. Then he asked Emmett why on earth a boy who was raised on a farm would want to spend his summer pounding nails.

It wasn't because Emmett knew Mr. Schulte to be a friendly man, or because he lived in one of the nicest houses in town. Emmett went to Mr. Schulte because he figured that no matter what happened, a carpenter would always have work. No matter how well you build them, houses run down. Hinges loosen, floorboards wear, roof seams separate. All you had to do was stroll through the Watson house to witness the myriad ways in which time can take its toll on a homestead.

In the months of summer, there were nights marked by the roll of thunder or the whistle of an arid wind on which Emmett could hear his father stirring in the next room, unable to sleep—and not without reason. Because a farmer with a mortgage was like a man walking on the railing of a bridge with his arms outstretched and his eyes closed. It was a way of life in which the difference between abundance and ruin could be measured by a few inches of rain or a few nights of frost.

But a carpenter didn't lie awake at night worrying about the weather. He *welcomed* the extremes of nature. He welcomed the blizzards and downpours and tornadoes. He welcomed the onset of mold and the onslaughts of insects. These were the natural forces that slowly but inevitably undermined the integrity of a house, weakening its foundations, rotting its beams, and wilting its plaster.

Emmett didn't say all of this when Mr. Schulte asked his question. Putting his fork down, he simply replied:

—The way I figure it, Mr. Schulte, it was Job who had the oxen, and Noah who had the hammer.

Mr. Schulte gave a laugh and hired Emmett on the spot.

For most of the farmers in the county, if their eldest came home one night with news that he'd taken a job with a carpenter, they would have given him a talking-to he wouldn't soon forget. Then, for good measure, they would have driven over to the carpenter's house and given him a few words—a few words to remember the next time he had the inclination to interfere with the upbringing of another man's son.

But the night Emmett came home and told his father he had secured a job with Mr. Schulte, his father hadn't grown angry. He had listened carefully. After a moment of reflection, he said that Mr. Schulte was a good man and carpentry a useful skill. And on the first day of summer, he made Emmett a hearty breakfast and packed him a lunch, then sent him off with his blessing to another man's trade.

And maybe that was a sign of bad judgment too.

—·—

When Emmett came back downstairs, he found Mr. Ransom sitting on the porch steps with his forearms on his knees and his hat still in his hand. Emmett sat beside him and they both looked out across the unplanted fields. Half a mile in the distance, you could just make out the fence that marked the beginning of the older man's ranch. By Emmett's last accounting, Mr. Ransom had over nine hundred head of cattle and eight men in his employ.

—I want to thank you for taking in Billy, Emmett said.

—Taking in Billy was the least we could do. Besides, you can imagine how much it pleased Sally. She's about had it with keeping house for me, but caring for your brother's another matter. We've *all* been eating better since Billy arrived.

Emmett smiled.

—Just the same. It made a big difference to Billy; and it was a comfort to me knowing that he was in your home.

Mr. Ransom nodded, accepting the younger man's expression of gratitude.

—Warden Williams seems like a good man, he said after a moment.

—He is a good man.

—Doesn't seem like a Kansan. . . .

—No. He grew up in Philadelphia.

Mr. Ransom turned his hat in his hand. Emmett could tell that something was on his neighbor's mind. He was trying to decide how to say it, or whether to say it. Or maybe he was just trying to pick the right moment to say it. But sometimes the moment is picked for you, as when a cloud of dust a mile up the road signaled his daughter's approach.

—Emmett, he began, Warden Williams was right to say that you've paid your debt—as far as society is concerned. But this here's a small town, a lot smaller than Philadelphia, and not everyone in Morgen is going to see it the way the warden does.

—You're talking about the Snyders.

—I am talking about the Snyders, Emmett, but not just the Snyders. They've got cousins in this county. They've got neighbors and old family friends. They've got people they do business with and members of their congregation. We all know that whatever trouble Jimmy Snyder happened to find himself in was generally of Jimmy's own making. In his seventeen years, he was the engineer of a lifetime of shit piles. But that don't make any difference to his brothers. Especially after they lost Joe, Jr., in the war. If they were none too pleased that you got just eighteen months in Salina, they were in a state of righteous fury when they learned you'd be let out a few months early because of your father's passing. They're likely to make you feel the brunt of that fury as much and as often as they can. So while you do have your whole life in front of you, or rather, because you have your whole life in front of you, you may want to consider starting it somewhere other than here.

—You've no need to worry about that, said Emmett. Forty-eight hours from now, I don't expect Billy and me to be in Nebraska.

Mr. Ransom nodded.

—Since your father didn't leave much behind, I'd like to give you two a little something to help you get started.

—I couldn't take your money, Mr. Ransom. You've done enough for us already.

—Then consider it a loan. You can pay it back once you get yourself situated.

—For the time being, observed Emmett, I think the Watsons have had their fill of loans.

Mr. Ransom smiled and nodded. Then he stood and put his hat on his head as the old pickup they called Betty roared into the driveway with Sally behind the wheel and Billy in the passenger seat. Before she had skidded to a stop with a backfire out of the exhaust, Billy was opening the door and jumping to the ground. Wearing a canvas backpack that reached from his shoulders to the seat of his pants, he ran right past Mr. Ransom and wrapped his arms around Emmett's waist.

Emmett got down on his haunches so he could hug his little brother back.

Sally was approaching now in a brightly colored Sunday dress with a baking dish in her hands and a smile on her face.

Mr. Ransom took in the dress and the smile, philosophically.

—Well now, she said, look who's here. Don't you squeeze the life out of him, Billy Watson.

Emmett stood and put a hand on his brother's head.

—Hello, Sally.

As was her habit when nervous, Sally got right down to business.

—The house has been swept and all the beds have been made and there's fresh soap in the bathroom, and butter, milk, and eggs in the icebox.

—Thank you, said Emmett.

—I suggested the two of you should join us for supper, but Billy insisted you have your first meal at home. But seeing as you're just back, I made the two of you a casserole.

—You didn't have to go to all that trouble, Sally.

—Trouble or not, here it is. All you have to do is put it in the oven at 350° for forty-five minutes.

As Emmett took the casserole in hand, Sally shook her head.

—I should have written that down.

—I think Emmett will be able to remember the instructions, said Mr. Ransom. And if he doesn't, Billy surely will.

—You put it in the oven at 350° for forty-five minutes, said Billy.

Mr. Ransom turned to his daughter.

—I'm sure these boys are eager to catch up, and we've got some things to see to at home.

—I'll just go in for a minute to make sure that everything—

—Sally, Mr. Ransom said in a manner that broached no dissent.

Sally pointed at Billy and smiled.

—You be good, little one.

Emmett and Billy watched as the Ransoms climbed into their trucks and drove back up the road. Then Billy turned to Emmett and hugged him again.

—I'm glad you're home, Emmett.

—I'm glad to be home, Billy.

—You don't have to go back to Salina this time, do you?

—No. I never have to go back to Salina. Come on.

Billy released Emmett, and the brothers went into the house. In the kitchen, Emmett opened the icebox and slid the casserole onto a lower shelf. On the top shelf were the promised milk and eggs and butter. There was also a jar of homemade applesauce and another of peaches in syrup.

—You want something to eat?

—No, thank you, Emmett. Sally made me a peanut butter sandwich just before we came over.

—How about some milk?

—Sure.

As Emmett brought the glasses of milk to the table, Billy took off his backpack and set it on an empty chair. Unbuckling the uppermost flap, he carefully removed and unfolded a little package wrapped in aluminum foil. It was a stack of eight cookies. He put two on the table, one for Emmett and one for himself. Then he closed the foil, put the rest of the cookies back in his backpack, rebuckled the flap, and returned to his seat.

—That's quite a pack, Emmett said.

—It's a genuine US Army backpack, said Billy. Although it's what they call an army surplus backpack because it never actually made it to the war. I bought it at Mr. Gunderson's store. I also got a surplus flashlight and a surplus compass and this surplus watch.

Billy held out his arm to show the watch hanging loosely on his wrist.

—It even has a second hand.

After expressing his admiration for the watch, Emmett took a bite of the cookie.

—Good one. Chocolate chip?

—Yep. Sally made them.

—You help?

—I cleaned the bowl.

—I bet you did.

—Sally actually made us a whole batch, but Mr. Ransom said she was overdoing it, so she told him that she would just give us four, but secretly she gave us eight.

—Lucky for us.

—Luckier than just getting four. But not as lucky as getting the whole batch.

As Emmett smiled and took a sip of milk, he sized up his brother over the rim of the glass. He was about an inch taller and his hair was shorter, as it would be in the Ransom house, but otherwise he seemed the same in body and spirit. For Emmett, leaving Billy had been the hardest part of going to Salina, so he was happy to find him so little changed. He was happy to be sitting with him at the old kitchen table. He could tell that Billy was happy to be sitting there too.

—School year end all right? Emmett asked, setting down his glass.

Billy nodded.

—I got a hundred and five percent on my geography test.

—A hundred and five percent!

—Usually, there's no such thing as a hundred and five percent, Billy explained. Usually, one hundred percent of anything is as much as you can get.

—So how'd you wrangle another five percent out of Mrs. Cooper?

—There was an extra-credit question.

—What was the question?

Billy quoted from memory.

—*What is the tallest building in the world.*

—And you knew the answer?

—I did.

. . .

—Aren't you going to tell me?

Billy shook his head.

—That would be cheating. You have to learn it for yourself.

—Fair enough.

After a moment of silence, Emmett realized that he was staring into his milk. He was the one now with something on his mind. He was the one trying to decide how, or whether, or when to say it.

—Billy, he began, I don't know what Mr. Ransom's told you, but we're not going to be able to live here anymore.

—I know, said Billy. Because we're foreclosed.

—That's right. Do you understand what that means?

—It means the Savings and Loan owns our house now.

—That's right. Even though they're taking the house, we could stay in Morgen. We could live with the Ransoms for a while, I could go back to work for Mr. Schulte, come fall you could go back to school, and eventually we could afford to get a place of our own. But I've been thinking that this might be a good time for you and me to try something new . . .

Emmett had thought a lot about how he would put this, because he was worried that Billy would be disconcerted by the notion of leaving Morgen, especially so soon after their father's death. But Billy wasn't disconcerted at all.

—I was thinking the same thing, Emmett.

—You were?

Billy nodded with a hint of eagerness.

—With Daddy gone and the house foreclosed, there's no need for us to stay in Morgen. We can pack up our things and drive to California.

—I guess we're in agreement, said Emmett with a smile. The only difference is that I think we should be moving to Texas.

—Oh, we can't be moving to Texas, said Billy, shaking his head.

—Why's that?

—Because we've got to be moving to California.

Emmett started to speak, but Billy had already gotten up from his chair and gone to his backpack. This time, he opened the front pocket, removed a small manila envelope, and returned to his seat. As he carefully unwound the red thread that sealed the envelope's flap, he began to explain.

—After Daddy's funeral, when you went back to Salina, Mr. Ransom sent Sally and me over to the house to look for important papers. In the bottom drawer of Daddy's bureau, we found a metal box. It wasn't locked, but it was the kind of box you *could* lock if you wanted to. Inside it were important papers, just as Mr. Ransom had said there'd be—like our birth certificates and Mom and Dad's marriage license. But at the bottom of the box, at the very bottom, I found these.

Billy tipped the envelope over the table and out slid nine postcards.

Emmett could tell from the condition of the cards that they weren't exactly old and weren't exactly new. Some of them were photographs and some were illustrations, but all were in color. The one on top was a picture of the Welsh Motor Court in Ogallala, Nebraska—a modern-looking lodge with white cabanas and roadside plantings and a flagpole flying the American flag.

—They're postcards, Billy said. To you and me. From Mom.

Emmett was taken aback. Nearly eight years had passed since their mother had tucked the two of them in bed, kissed them goodnight, and walked out the door—and they hadn't heard a word from her since. No phone calls. No letters. No neatly wrapped packages arriving just in time for Christmas. Not even a bit of gossip from someone who'd happened to hear something from somebody else. At least, that's what Emmett had understood to be the case, until now.

Emmett picked up the card of the Welsh Motor Court and turned it over. Just as Billy had said, it was addressed to the two of them in their mother's elegant script. In the manner of postcards, the text was limited to a few lines. Together, the sentences expressed how much she already missed them despite having only been gone for a day. Emmett picked up another card from the pile. In the upper left-hand corner was a cowboy on the back of a horse. The lariat that he was spinning extended into the foreground and spelled out *Greetings from Rawlins, Wyoming—the Metropolis of the Plains*. Emmett turned the card over. In six sentences, including one that wrapped around the lower right-hand corner, their mother wrote that while she had yet to see a cowpoke with a lasso in Rawlins, she had seen plenty of cows. She concluded by expressing once again how much she loved and missed them both.

Emmett scanned the other cards on the table, taking in the names of the various towns, the motels and restaurants, sights and landmarks, noting that all but one of the pictures promised a bright blue sky.

Conscious that his brother was watching him, Emmett maintained an unchanged expression. But what he was feeling was the sting of resentment—resentment toward their father. He must have intercepted the cards and hidden them away. No matter how angry he had been with his wife, he had no right to keep them from his sons, certainly not from Emmett, who had been old enough to read them for himself. But Emmett felt the sting for no more than a moment. Because he knew that his father had done the only sensible thing. After all, what good could come from the occasional reception of a few sentences written on the back of a three-by-five card by a woman who had willfully abandoned her own children?

Emmett put the postcard from Rawlins back on the table.

—You remember how Mom left us on the fifth of July? asked Billy.

—I remember.

—She wrote us a postcard every day for the next nine days.

Emmett picked up the card from Ogallala again and looked just above the spot where their mother had written *Dearest Emmett and Billy*, but there was no date.

—Mom didn't write down the dates, Billy said. But you can tell from the postmarks.

Taking the Ogallala card from Emmett's hand, Billy turned all the cards over, spread them on the table, and pointed from postmark to postmark.

—July fifth. July sixth. There was no July seventh, but there are two July eighths. That's because in 1946, July seventh was on a Sunday and the post office is closed on Sunday, so she had to mail two of the cards on Monday. But look at this.

Billy went back to the front pocket of his backpack and took out something that looked like a pamphlet. When he unfolded it on the table, Emmett could see it was a road map of the United States from a Phillips 66. Cutting all the way across the middle of the map was a roadway that had been scored by Billy in black ink. In the western half of the country, the names of nine towns along the route had been circled.

—This is the Lincoln Highway, explained Billy, pointing to the long black line. It was invented in 1912 and was named for Abraham Lincoln and was the very first road to stretch from one end of America to the other.

Starting on the Atlantic Seaboard, Billy began following the highway with his fingertip.

—It starts in Times Square in New York City and it ends three thousand three hundred and ninety miles away in Lincoln Park in

San Francisco. And it passes right through Central City, just twenty-five miles from our house.

Billy paused to move his finger from Central City to the little black star that he had drawn on the map to represent their home.

—When Mom left us on the fifth of July, this is the way she went . . .

Taking up the postcards, Billy turned them over and began laying them across the lower half of the map in a westward progression, placing each card under its corresponding town.

Ogallala.

Cheyenne.

Rawlins.

Rock Springs.

Salt Lake City.

Ely.

Reno.

Sacramento.

Until the last card, which showed a large, classical building rising above a fountain in a park in San Francisco.

Billy gave an exhale of satisfaction to have the cards laid out in order on the table. But the whole collection made Emmett uneasy, like the two of them were looking at someone else's private correspondence—something they had no business seeing.

—Billy, he said, I'm not sure that we should be going to California. . . .

—We have to go to California, Emmett. Don't you see? That's why she sent us the postcards. So that we could follow her.

—But she hasn't sent a postcard in eight years.

—Because July thirteenth was when she stopped moving. All we have to do is take the Lincoln Highway to San Francisco and that's where we'll find her.

Emmett's immediate instinct was to say something to his brother that was sensible and dissuasive. Something about how their mother didn't necessarily stop in San Francisco; how she could easily have continued on, and most likely had; and that while she might have been thinking of her sons on those first nine nights, all evidence suggested that she hadn't been thinking of them since. In the end, he settled for pointing out that even if she were in San Francisco, it would be virtually impossible for them to find her.

Billy nodded with the expression of one who had already considered this dilemma.

—Remember how you told me that Mom loved fireworks so much, she took us all the way to Seward on the Fourth of July just so we could see the big display?

Emmett did not remember telling this to his brother, and all things considered, he couldn't imagine having ever had the inclination to do so. But he couldn't deny it was true.

Billy reached for the last postcard, the one with the classical building and the fountain. Turning it over, he ran his finger along their mother's script.

—*This is the Palace of the Legion of Honor in San Francisco's Lincoln Park and every year on the Fourth of July it has one of the biggest fireworks displays in all of California!*

Billy looked up at his brother.

—That's where she'll be, Emmett. At the fireworks display at the Palace of the Legion of Honor on the Fourth of July.

—Billy . . . , Emmett began.

But Billy, who could already hear the skepticism in his brother's voice, began shaking his head, vigorously. Then looking back down at the map on the table, he ran his finger along their mother's route.

—Ogallala to Cheyenne, Cheyenne to Rawlins, Rawlins to Rock Springs, Rock Springs to Salt Lake City, Salt Lake City to Ely, Ely to Reno, Reno to Sacramento, and Sacramento to San Francisco. That's the way we go.

Emmett sat back in his chair and considered.

He had not chosen Texas at random. He had thought about the question of where he and his brother should go, carefully and systematically. He had spent hours in the little library at Salina turning through the pages of the almanac and the volumes of the encyclopedia until the question of where they should go had become perfectly clear. But Billy had been pursuing his own line of thinking just as carefully, just as systematically, and he could see his own answer to the question with just as much clarity.

—All right, Billy, I'll tell you what. Why don't you put those back in their envelope and let me take a little time to think about what you've said.

Billy began nodding now.

—That's a good idea, Emmett. That's a good idea.

Gathering the postcards together in their east-to-west order, Billy slipped them into their envelope, spun the red thread until they were securely sealed, and returned them to his pack.

—You take a little time to think about it, Emmett. You'll see.

—·—

Upstairs, while Billy occupied himself in his room, Emmett took a long, hot shower. When he was done, he picked his clothes off the floor—the clothes that he'd worn both to and from Salina—removed the pack of cigarettes from the shirt pocket, and threw the heap in the trash. After a moment, he threw the cigarettes away too, being sure to tuck them under the clothes.

In his room he dressed in a fresh pair of jeans and denim shirt along with his favorite belt and boots. Then he reached into his top bureau drawer and took out a pair of socks tucked into a ball. Unfolding the socks, he gave one of them a shake until out came the keys to his car. Then he crossed the hall and stuck his head into his brother's room.

Billy was sitting on the floor beside his backpack. In his lap was the old blue tobacco tin with the portrait of George Washington on it, while on the rug were all his silver dollars laid out in columns and rows.

—Looks like you found a few more while I was away, said Emmett.

—Three, Billy answered while carefully putting one of the dollars in its place.

—How many more to go?

With his index finger Billy poked at the empty spots in the grid.

—1881. 1894. 1895. 1899. 1903.

—You're getting pretty close.

Billy nodded in agreement.

—But 1894 and 1895 will be very hard to find. I was lucky to find 1893.

Billy looked up at his brother.

—Have you been thinking about California, Emmett?

—I have been thinking about it, but I need to think about it a little bit more.

—That's okay.

As Billy turned his attention back to the silver dollars, Emmett looked around his brother's room for the second time that day, once again taking in the collections that were neatly arranged on their shelves and the planes that hung over the bed.

—Billy . . .

Billy looked up again.

—Whether we end up going to Texas or California, I think it may be best if we plan to travel light. Since we'll be making something of a fresh start.

—I was thinking the same thing, Emmett.

—You were?

—Professor Abernathe says that the intrepid traveler often sets out with what little he can fit in a kit bag. That's why I bought my backpack at Mr. Gunderson's store. So that I'd be ready to leave as soon as you got home. It already has everything in it that I need.

—Everything?

—Everything.

Emmett smiled.

—I'm headed out to the barn to check on the car. You want to come?

—Now? asked Billy in surprise. Hold on! Wait a second! Don't go without me!

Having carefully laid out the silver dollars in chronological order, Billy now swept them up and began pouring them back into the tobacco tin as quickly as he could. Closing the lid, he put the tin back in his backpack and the backpack back on his back. Then he led the way downstairs and out the door.

As they crossed the yard, Billy looked over his shoulder to report that Mr. Obermeyer had put a padlock on the barn doors, but Sally had broken it off with the crowbar she kept in the back of her truck.

Sure enough, at the barn door they found the bracket—with the padlock still secured to it—hanging loosely on its screws. Inside, the air was warm and familiar, smelling of cattle though there hadn't been cattle on the farm since Emmett was a boy.

Emmett paused to let his eyes adjust. Before him was the new John Deere and behind that a battered old combine. Proceeding to the back of the barn, Emmett stopped before a large, sloping object draped with canvas.

—Mr. Obermeyer took off the cover, said Billy, but Sally and I put it back.

Gripping the canvas by the corner, Emmett pulled with both hands until it was piled at his feet, and there, waiting just where he'd left it fifteen months ago, was a powder-blue, four-door hardtop—his 1948 Studebaker Land Cruiser.

After running his palm along the surface of the hood, Emmett opened the driver's door and climbed inside. For a moment, he sat with his hands on the steering wheel. When he'd bought her, she already had 80,000 miles on the odometer, dents in the hood, and cigarette burns in the seat covers, but she ran smoothly enough. Inserting and turning the key, he pushed the starter, ready for the soothing rumble of the engine—but there was silence.

Billy, who had been keeping his distance, approached, tentatively.

—Is it broken?

—No, Billy. The battery must be dead. It happens when you leave a car idle for too long. But it's an easy thing to fix.

Looking relieved, Billy sat down on a hay bale and took off his backpack.

—You want another cookie, Emmett?

—I'm fine. But you go right ahead.

As Billy opened his backpack, Emmett climbed out of the car, stepped to the rear, and opened the trunk. Satisfied that the upright lid blocked his brother's view, Emmett pulled back the felt that covered the recess in which the spare tire rested and gently ran his hand around its outer curve. At the top, he found the envelope with his name on it, right where his father had said it would be. Inside was a note in his father's script.

Another handwritten missive from another ghost, thought Emmett.

> Dear Son,
>
> By the time you read this, I imagine the farm will be in the hands of the bank. You may be angry or disappointed with me as a result, and I wouldn't blame you for being so.
>
> It would shock you to know how much my father left me when he died, how much my grandfather left my father, and how much my great-grandfather left him. Not simply stocks and bonds, but houses and paintings. Furniture and tableware. Memberships in clubs and societies. All three of those men were

*devoted to the Puritan tradition of finding favor in the eyes of
the Lord by leaving more to their children than had been
left to them.*

*In this envelope, you will find all that I have to leave
you—two legacies, one great, one small, both a form of sacrilege.*

*As I write this, it shames me some to know that in leading
my life as I have, I have broken the virtuous cycle of thrift
established by my forebears. But at the same time, it fills me with
pride to know that you will undoubtedly achieve more with this
small remembrance than I could have achieved with a fortune.*

With love and admiration,

Your father, Charles William Watson

Attached to the letter by a paper clip was the first of the two
legacies—a single page torn from an old book.

Emmett's father wasn't one to lash out at his children in anger even
when they deserved it. In fact, the only time Emmett could remember
his father expressing unmitigated ire toward him was when he was sent
home from school for defacing a textbook. As his father made painfully
clear that night, to deface the pages of a book was to adopt the manner
of a Visigoth. It was to strike a blow against that most sacred and noble
of man's achievements—the ability to set down his finest ideas and
sentiments so that they might be shared through the ages.

For his father to tear a page from any book was a sacrilege. What
was even more shocking was that the page was torn from Ralph Waldo
Emerson's *Essays*—that book which his father held in greater esteem
than any other. Near the bottom, his father had carefully underlined
two sentences in red ink.

There is a time in every man's education when he
arrives at the conviction that envy is ignorance; that
imitation is suicide; that he must take himself for better,
for worse, as his portion; that though the wide universe

is full of good, no kernel of nourishing corn can come to him but through his toil bestowed on that plot of ground which is given to him to till. The power which resides in him is new in nature, and none but he knows what that is which he can do, nor does he know until he has tried.

Emmett recognized immediately that this passage from Emerson represented two things at once. First, it was an excuse. It was an explication of why, against all good sense, his father had left behind the houses and paintings, the memberships in clubs and societies in order to come to Nebraska and till the soil. Emmett's father offered this page from Emerson as evidence—as if it were a divine decree—that he had had no choice.

But if, on the one hand, it was an excuse, on the other, it was an exhortation—an exhortation for Emmett that he should feel no remorse, no guilt, no hesitation in turning his back on the three hundred acres to which his father had dedicated half his life, as long as he abandoned them in order to pursue without envy or imitation his own portion, and in so doing discover that which he alone was capable of.

Tucked in the envelope behind the page of Emerson was the second legacy, a stack of brand-new twenty-dollar bills. Running his thumb over the crisp, clean edges, Emmett figured there were about 150 in all, amounting to some three thousand dollars.

If Emmett could understand why his father considered the torn page a sacrilege of sorts, he couldn't accept that the bills were. Presumably, his father characterized the money as a sacrilege because he was bestowing it behind the backs of his creditors. In so doing, he had gone against both his legal obligation and his own sense of what was right and wrong. But after meeting the interest payments on his mortgage for twenty years, Emmett's father had paid for the farm two times over. He had paid for it again with hard labor and disappointment, with his marriage, and finally with his life. So, no, the setting aside of three thousand dollars was not a sacrilege in Emmett's eyes. As far as he was concerned, his father had earned every penny.

Taking one of the bills for his pocket, Emmett returned the envelope to its spot above the tire and laid the felt back in place.

—Emmett . . . , said Billy.

Emmett closed the trunk and looked to Billy, but Billy wasn't looking at him. He was looking at the two figures in the doorway of the barn. With the late afternoon light behind them, Emmett couldn't tell who they were. At least not until the wiry one on the left stretched out his arms and said:

—Ta-da!

Duchess

YOU SHOULD HAVE SEEN the look on Emmett's face when he realized who was standing in the door. From his expression, you would've thought we'd popped out of thin air.

Back in the early forties, there was an escape artist who went by the name of Kazantikis. Some of the wisecrackers on the circuit liked to call him the half-wit Houdini from Hackensack, but that wasn't totally fair. While the front half of his act was a little shaky, the finale was a gem. Right before your eyes, he'd get bound up in chains, locked in a trunk, and sunk to the bottom of a big glass tank. A good-looking blonde would wheel out a giant clock as the emcee reminded the audience that the average human being can only hold his breath for two minutes, that deprived of oxygen most grow dizzy after four and unconscious after six. Two officers of the Pinkerton Detective Agency were present to ensure that the padlock on the trunk was secure, and a priest from the Greek Orthodox Church—complete with a long black cassock and long white beard—was on hand should it prove necessary to administer the last rites. Down into the water the trunk would go and the blonde would start the clock. At two minutes, the members of the audience would whistle and jeer. At five minutes, they would ooh and aah. But at eight minutes, the Pinkertons would exchange worried glances. At ten, the priest would cross himself and recite an indecipherable prayer. At the twelfth minute, as the blonde burst into tears, two stagehands would rush from behind the curtains to help the Pinkertons hoist the trunk from the tank. It would be dropped to the stage with a thump as water gushed across the footlights and into the orchestra pit. When one of the Pinkertons fumbled with his keys, the other would brush him aside, draw his pistol, and shoot off the lock. He would rip open the lid and tip over the trunk, only to discover . . . it was empty. At which point, the orthodox priest would pluck off his beard revealing that he was none other than Kazantikis, his hair still wet, as every single member of the audience looked on in holy amazement. That's how Emmett Watson looked when he realized who was standing in the door. Of all the people in the world, he just couldn't believe it was us.

—Duchess?

—In the flesh. And Woolly too.

He still looked dumbfounded.

—But how . . . ?

I laughed.

—That's the question, right?

I put a hand to the side of my mouth and lowered my voice.

—We hitched a ride with the warden. While he was signing you out, we slipped into the trunk of his car.

—You can't be serious.

—I know. It's not what you'd call first-class travel. What with it being a hundred degrees in there and Woolly complaining every ten minutes about having to go to the bathroom. And when we crossed into Nebraska? I thought I was going to get a concussion from the divots in the road. Someone should write a letter to the governor!

—Hey, Emmett, said Woolly, like he'd just joined the party.

You've got to love that about Woolly. He's always running about five minutes late, showing up on the wrong platform with the wrong luggage just as the conversation is pulling out of the station. Some might find the trait a little exasperating, but I'd take a guy who runs five minutes late over a guy who runs five minutes early, any day of the week.

Out of the corner of my eye I had been watching as the kid, who'd been sitting on a hay bale, began edging his way in our direction. When I pointed, he froze like a squirrel on the grass.

—Billy, right? Your brother says you're as sharp as a tack. Is that true?

The kid smiled and edged a little closer until he was standing at Emmett's side. He looked up at his brother.

—Are these your friends, Emmett?

—Of course we're his friends!

—They're from Salina, Emmett explained.

I was about to elaborate when I noticed the car. I'd been so focused on the charms of the reunion that I hadn't seen it hiding behind the heavy equipment.

—Is that the Studebaker, Emmett? What do they call that? Baby blue?

Objectively speaking, it looked a little like a car that your dentist's wife would drive to bingo, but I gave it a whistle anyway. Then I turned to Billy.

—Some of the boys in Salina would pin a picture of their girl back home on the bottom of the upper bunk so they could stare at it before lights out. Some of them had a photo of Elizabeth Taylor or Marilyn Monroe. But your brother, he pinned up an advertisement torn from an old magazine with a full-color picture of his car. I'll be honest with you, Billy. We gave your brother a lot of grief about that. Getting all moon-eyed over an automobile. But now that I see her up close . . .

I shook my head in a show of appreciation.

—Hey, I said, turning to Emmett. Can we take her for a spin?

Emmett didn't answer because he was looking at Woolly—who was looking at a spider web without a spider.

—How are you doing, Woolly? he asked.

Turning, Woolly thought about it for a moment.

—I'm all right, Emmett.

—When was the last time you had something to eat?

—Oh, I don't know. I guess it was before we got in the warden's car. Isn't that right, Duchess?

Emmett turned to his brother.

—Billy, you remember what Sally said about supper?

—She said to cook it at 350° for forty-five minutes.

—Why don't you take Woolly back to the house, put the dish in the oven, and set the table. I need to show Duchess something, but we'll be right behind you.

—Okay, Emmett.

As we were watching Billy and Woolly walk back toward the house, I wondered what Emmett wanted to show me. But when he turned in my direction, he didn't look himself. As a matter of fact, he seemed out of sorts. I guess some people are like that when it comes to surprises. Me, I love surprises. I love it when life pulls a rabbit out of a hat. Like when the blue-plate special is turkey and stuffing in the middle of May. But some people just don't like being caught off guard—even by good news.

—Duchess, what are you doing here?

Now it was me who looked surprised.

—What are we doing here? Why, we've come to see you, Emmett. And the farm. You know how it is. You hear enough stories from a buddy about his life back home and eventually you want to see it for yourself.

To make my point, I gestured toward the tractor and the hay bale and the great American prairie that was waiting right outside the door, trying its best to convince us that the world was flat, after all.

Emmett followed my gaze, then turned back.

—I'll tell you what, he said. Let's go have something to eat, I'll give you and Woolly a quick tour, we'll get a good night's sleep, then in the morning, I'll drive you back to Salina.

I gave a wave of my hand.

—You don't need to drive us back to Salina, Emmett. You just got home yourself. Besides, I don't think we're going back. At least not yet.

Emmett closed his eyes for a moment.

—How many months do you have left on your sentences? Five or six? You're both practically out.

—That's true, I agreed. That's perfectly true. But when Warden Williams took over for Ackerly, he fired that nurse from New Orleans. The one who used to help Woolly get his medicine. Now he's down to his last few bottles, and you know how bluesy he gets without his medicine. . . .

—It's not his medicine.

I shook my head in agreement.

—One man's toxin is another man's tonic, right?

—Duchess, I shouldn't have to spell this out for you, of all people. But the longer you two are AWOL and the farther you get from Salina, the worse the consequences are going to be. And you both turned eighteen this winter. So if they catch you across state lines, they may not send you back to Salina. They may send you to Topeka.

Let's face it: Most people need a ladder and a telescope to make sense of two plus two. That's why it's usually more trouble than it's worth to explain yourself. But not Emmett Watson. He's the type of guy who can see the whole picture right from the word go—the grander scheme and all the little details. I put up both of my hands in surrender.

—I'm with you one hundred percent, Emmett. In fact, I tried to tell Woolly the very same thing in the very same words. But he wouldn't listen. He was dead set on jumping the fence. He had a whole plan. He was going to split on a Saturday night, hightail it into town, and steal a car. He even pilfered a knife when he was on kitchen duty. Not a paring knife, Emmett. I'm talking about a butcher knife. Not that Woolly would ever hurt a soul. You and I know that. But the cops don't know it. They see a fidgety stranger with a drifty look in his eye and a butcher knife in his hand, and they'll put him down like a dog. So I told him if he put the knife back where he'd found it, I'd help him get out of Salina safe and sound. He put back the knife, we slipped into the trunk, presto chango, here we are.

And all of this was true.

Except the part about the knife.

That's what you'd call an embellishment—a harmless little exaggeration in the service of emphasis. Sort of like the giant clock in Kazantikis's act, or the shooting of the padlock by the Pinkerton. Those little elements that on the surface seem unnecessary but that somehow bring the whole performance home.

—Look, Emmett, you know me. I could have done my stretch and then done Woolly's. Five months or five years, what's the difference. But given Woolly's state of mind, I don't think he could have done five more days.

Emmett looked off in the direction that Woolly had walked.

We both knew that his problem was one of plenty. Raised in one of those doorman buildings on the Upper East Side, Woolly had a house in the country, a driver in the car, and a cook in the kitchen. His grandfather was friends with Teddy *and* Franklin Roosevelt, and his father was a hero in the Second World War. But there's something about all that good fortune that can become too much. There's a tender sort of soul who, in the face of such abundance, feels a sense of looming trepidation, like the whole pile of houses and cars and Roosevelts is going to come tumbling down on top of him. The very thought of it starts to spoil his appetite and unsettle his nerves. It becomes hard for him to concentrate, which affects his reading, writing, and arithmetic. Having been asked to leave one boarding school, he gets sent to another. Then maybe another. Eventually, a guy like that is going to need *something* to hold the world at bay. And who can blame him? I'd be the first to tell you that rich people don't deserve two minutes of your sympathy. But a bighearted guy like Woolly? That's a different story altogether.

I could see from Emmett's expression that he was going through a similar sort of calculus, thinking about Woolly's sensitive nature and wondering if we should send him back to Salina or help him safely on his way. As a quandary it was pretty hard to parse. But then I guess that's why they call it a quandary.

—It's been a long day, I said, putting a hand on Emmett's shoulder. What say we go back to the house and break bread? Once we've had something to eat, we'll all be in a better frame of mind to weigh the whys and wherefores.

—·—

Country cooking . . .

You hear a lot about it back East. It's one of those things that people revere even when they've never had any firsthand experience with it. Like justice and Jesus. But unlike most things that people admire from afar, country cooking deserves the admiration. It's twice as tasty as anything you'd find at Delmonico's and without all the folderol. Maybe it's because they're using the recipes their great-great-grandmas perfected on the wagon trail. Or maybe it's all those hours they've spent in the company of pigs and potatoes. Whatever the reason, I didn't push back my plate until after the third helping.

—That was some meal.

I turned to the kid—whose head wasn't too far over the tabletop.

—What's the name of that pretty brunette, Billy? The one in the flowery dress and work boots whom we have to thank for this delectable dish?

—Sally Ransom, he said. It's a chicken casserole. Made from one of her own chickens.

—One of her own chickens! Hey, Emmett, what's that folksy saying? The one about the fastest way to a young man's heart?

—She's a neighbor, said Emmett.

—Maybe so, I conceded. But I've had a lifetime supply of neighbors, and I've never had one who brought me a casserole. How about you, Woolly?

Woolly was making a spiral in his gravy with the tines of his fork.

—What's that?

—Have you ever had a neighbor bring you a casserole? I asked a little louder.

He thought about it for a second.

—I've never had a casserole.

I smiled and raised my eyebrows at the kid. He smiled and raised his eyebrows back.

Casserole or no casserole, Woolly suddenly looked up like he'd had a timely thought.

—Hey, Duchess. Did you get a chance to ask Emmett about the escapade?

—The escapade? asked Billy, poking his head a little higher over the table.

—That's the other reason we came here, Billy. We're about to set off on a little escapade and we were hoping your brother would come along.

—An escapade . . . , said Emmett.

—We've been calling it that for lack of a better word, I said. But it's a good deed, really. A sort of mitzvah. In fact, it's the fulfillment of a dying man's wish.

As I began to explain, I looked from Emmett to Billy and back again since the two seemed equally intrigued.

—When Woolly's grandfather died, he left some money for Woolly in what they call a trust fund. Isn't that right, Woolly?

Woolly nodded.

—Now, a trust fund is a special investment account that's set up for the benefit of a minor with a trustee who makes all the decisions until the minor comes of age, at which point the minor can do with the money as he sees fit. But when Woolly turned eighteen, thanks to a little bit of fancy jurisprudence, the trustee—who happens to be Woolly's brother-in-law—had Woolly declared temperamentally unfit. Wasn't that the term, Woolly?

—Temperamentally unfit, Woolly confirmed with an apologetic smile.

—And in so doing, his brother-in-law extended his authority over the trust until such a time as Woolly should improve his temperament, or in perpetuity, whichever comes first.

I shook my head.

—And they call that a *trust* fund?

—That sounds like Woolly's business, Duchess. What does it have to do with you?

—With us, Emmett. What does it have to do with us.

I pulled my chair a little closer to the table.

—Woolly and his family have a house in upstate New York—

—A camp, said Woolly.

—A camp, I amended, where the family gathers from time to time. Well, during the Depression, when the banks began failing, Woolly's great-grandfather decided he could never entirely trust the American banking system again. So, just in case, he put a hundred and fifty thousand dollars in cash in a wall safe at the camp. But what's particularly interesting here—even fateful, you might say—is that the value of Woolly's trust today is almost exactly a hundred and fifty thousand dollars.

I paused to let that sink in. Then I looked at Emmett directly.

—And because Woolly's a man who's big of heart and modest of needs, he has proposed that if you and I accompany him to the Adirondacks to help him claim what is rightfully his, he will divvy up the proceeds in three equal parts.

—One hundred and fifty thousand dollars divided by three is fifty thousand dollars, said Billy.

—Exactly, I said.

—All for one and one for all, said Woolly.

As I leaned back in my chair, Emmett stared at me for a moment. Then he turned to Woolly.

—This was your idea?

—It was my idea, Woolly acknowledged.

—And you're not going back to Salina?

Woolly put his hands in his lap and shook his head.

—No, Emmett. I'm not going back to Salina.

Emmett gave Woolly a searching look, as if he were trying to formulate one more question. But Woolly, who was naturally disinclined to the answering of questions and who'd had plenty of practice in avoiding them, began clearing the plates.

In a state of hesitation, Emmett drew a hand across his mouth. I leaned across the table.

—The one hitch is that the camp always gets opened up for the last weekend in June, which doesn't give us a lot of time. I've got to make a quick stop in New York to see my old man, but then we're heading straight for the Adirondacks. We should have you back in Morgen by Friday—a little road weary, maybe, but on the sunny side of fifty grand. Think about that for a second, Emmett. . . . I mean, what could you do with fifty grand? What *would* you do with fifty grand?

There is nothing so enigmatic as the human will—or so the headshrinkers would have you believe. According to them, the motivations of a man are a castle without a key. They form a multilayered labyrinth from which individual actions often emerge without a readily discernible rhyme or reason. But it's really not so complicated. If you want to understand a man's motivations, all you have to do is ask him: *What would you do with fifty thousand dollars?*

When you ask most people this question, they need a few minutes to think about it, to sort through the possibilities and consider their options. And that tells you everything you need to know about them. But when you pose the question to a man of substance, a man who merits your consideration, he will answer in a heartbeat—and with specifics. Because he's already thought about what he would do with fifty grand. He's thought about it while he's been digging ditches, or pushing paper, or slinging hash. He's thought about it while listening to his wife, or tucking in the kids, or staring at the ceiling in the middle of the night. In a way, he's been thinking about it all his life.

When I put the question to Emmett, he didn't respond, but that wasn't because he didn't have an answer. I could see from the expression on his face that he knew *exactly* what he'd do with fifty thousand dollars, nickel for nickel and dime for dime.

As we sat there silently, Billy looked from me to his brother and back again; but Emmett, he looked straight across the table like he and I were suddenly the only people in the room.

—Maybe this was Woolly's idea and maybe it wasn't, Duchess. Either way, I don't want any part of it. Not the stop in the city, not the trip to the Adirondacks, not the fifty thousand dollars. Tomorrow, I need to take care of a few things in town. But on Monday morning, first thing, Billy and I are going to drive you and Woolly to the Greyhound station in Omaha. From there you can catch a bus to Manhattan or the Adirondacks or anywhere you like. Then Billy and I will get back in the Studebaker and go on about our business.

Emmett was serious as he delivered this little speech. In fact, I've never seen a guy so serious. He didn't raise his voice, and he didn't take his eyes off me once—not even to glance at Billy, who was listening to every word with a look of wide-eyed wonder.

And that's when it hit me. The blunder I'd made. I had laid out all the specifics right in front of the kid.

Like I said before, Emmett Watson understands the whole picture better than most. He understands that a man can be patient, but only up to a point; that it's occasionally necessary for him to toss a monkey wrench in the workings of the world in order to get his God-given due. But Billy? At the age of eight, he probably hadn't set foot out of the state of Nebraska. So you couldn't expect him to understand all the intricacies of modern life, all the subtleties of what was and wasn't fair. In fact, you wouldn't *want* him to understand it. And as the kid's older brother, as his guardian and sole protector, it was Emmett's job to spare Billy from such vicissitudes for as long as he possibly could.

I leaned back in my chair and gave the nod of common understanding.

—Say no more, Emmett. I read you loud and clear.

—·—

After supper, Emmett announced that he was walking over to the Ransoms to see if his neighbor would come jump his car. As the house was a mile away, I offered to keep him company, but he thought it best that Woolly and I stay out of sight. So I remained at the kitchen table, chatting with Billy while Woolly did the dishes.

Given what I've already told you about Woolly, you'd probably think he wasn't cut out for doing dishes—that his eyes would glaze over and his mind would wander and he'd generally go about the business in a slipshod fashion. But Woolly, he washed those dishes like his life depended on it. With his head bent at a forty-five-degree angle and the tip of his tongue poking between his teeth, he circled the sponge over the surface of the plates with a tireless intention, removing some spots that had been there for years and others that weren't there at all.

It was a wonder to observe. But like I said, I love surprises.

When I turned my attention back to Billy, he was unwrapping a little package of tinfoil that he'd taken from his knapsack. From inside the tinfoil he carefully withdrew four cookies and put them on the table—one cookie in front of each chair.

—Well, well, well, I said. What do we have here?

—Chocolate chip cookies, said Billy. Sally made them.

While we chewed in silence, I noticed that Billy was staring rather shyly at the top of the table, as if he had something he wanted to ask.

—What's on your mind, Billy?

—All for one and one for all, he said a little tentatively. That's from *The Three Musketeers*, isn't it?

—Exactly, *mon ami*.

Having successfully identified the source of the quotation, you might have imagined the kid would be pleased as punch, but he looked despondent. Positively despondent. And that's despite the fact that the mere mention of *The Three Musketeers* usually puts a smile on a young boy's face. So Billy's disappointment rather mystified me. That is until I was about to take another bite, and I recalled the all-for-one-and-one-for-all arrangement of the cookies on the table.

I put my cookie down.

—Have you seen *The Three Musketeers*, Billy?

—No, he admitted, with a hint of the same despondency. But I have read it.

—Then you should know better than most just how misleading a title can be.

Billy looked up from the table.

—Why is that, Duchess?

—Because, in point of fact, *The Three Musketeers* is a story about *four* musketeers. Yes, it opens with the delightful camaraderie of Orthos and Pathos and Artemis.

—Athos, Porthos, and Aramis?

—Exactly. But the central *business* of the tale is the means by which the young adventurer . . .

—D'Artagnan.

— . . . by which D'Artagnan joins the ranks of the swashbuckling threesome. And by saving the honor of the queen, no less.

—That's true, said Billy, sitting up in his chair. In point of fact, it is a story about four musketeers.

In honor of a job well done, I popped the rest of my cookie in my mouth and brushed the crumbs from my fingers. But Billy was staring at me with a new intensity.

—I sense that something else is on your mind, young William.

He leaned as far forward as the table would allow and spoke a little under his breath.

—Do you want to hear what I would do with fifty thousand dollars?

I leaned forward and spoke under my breath too.

—I wouldn't miss it for the world.

—I would build a house in San Francisco, California. It would be a white house just like this one with a little porch and a kitchen and a front room. And upstairs, there would be three bedrooms. Only instead of a barn for the tractor, there would be a garage for Emmett's car.

—I love it, Billy. But why San Francisco?

—Because that's where our mother is.

I sat back in my chair.

—You don't say.

Back at Salina, whenever Emmett mentioned his mother—which wasn't very often, to be sure—he invariably used the past tense. But he didn't use it in a manner suggesting that his mother had gone to California. He used it in a manner suggesting that she had gone to the great beyond.

—We're leaving right after we take you and Woolly to the bus station, added Billy.

—Just like that, you're going to pack up the house and move to California.

—No. We're not going to pack up the house, Duchess. We're going to take what little we can fit in a kit bag.

—Why would you do that?

—Because Emmett and Professor Abernathe agree that's the best way to make a fresh start. We're going to drive to San Francisco on the Lincoln Highway, and once we get there, we'll find our mother and build our house.

I didn't have the heart to tell the kid that if his mother didn't want to live in a little white house in Nebraska, she wasn't going to want to live in a little white house in California. But setting the vagaries of motherhood aside, I figured the kid's dream was about forty thousand dollars under budget.

—I love your plan, Billy. It's got the sort of specificity that a heart-felt scheme deserves. But are you sure you're dreaming big enough? I mean, with fifty thousand dollars you could go a hell of a lot further. You could have a pool and a butler. You could have a four-car garage.

Billy shook his head with a serious look on his face.

—No, he said. I don't think we will need a pool and a butler, Duchess.

I was about to gently suggest that the kid shouldn't jump to con-clusions, that pools and butlers weren't so easy to come by, and those who came by them were generally loath to give them up, when sud-denly Woolly was standing at the table with a plate in one hand and a sponge in the other.

—No one needs a pool or a butler, Billy.

You never know what's going to catch Woolly's attention. It could be a bird that settles on a branch. Or the shape of a footprint in the snow. Or something someone said on the previous afternoon. But whatever gets Woolly thinking, it's always worth the wait. So as he took the seat next to Billy, I quickly went to the sink, turned off the water, and returned to my chair, all ears.

—No one needs a four-car garage, Woolly continued. But I think what you will need is a few more bedrooms.

—Why is that, Woolly?

—So that friends and family can come visit for the holidays.

Billy nodded in acknowledgment of Woolly's good sense, so Woolly continued making suggestions, warming to his subject as he went along.

—You should have a porch with an overhanging roof so that you can sit under it on rainy afternoons, or lie on top of it on warm summer nights. And downstairs there should be a study, and a great room with a fireplace big enough so that everyone can gather around it when it snows. And you should have a secret hiding place under the staircase, and a special spot in the corner for the Christmas tree.

There was no stopping Woolly now. Asking for paper and pencil, he swung his chair around next to Billy's and began drawing a floor plan in perfect detail. And this wasn't some back-of-the-napkin sort of sketch. As it turned out, Woolly drew floor plans like he washed dishes. The rooms were rendered to scale with walls that were parallel and corners at perfect right angles. It gave you a zing just to see it.

Setting aside the merits of a covered porch versus a four-car garage, you had to give Woolly credit on the dreaming front. The place he imagined on Billy's behalf was three times the size of the one the kid had imagined on his own, and it must have struck a chord. Because when Woolly was done with the picture, Billy asked him to add an arrow pointing north and a big red star to mark the spot where the Christmas tree should go. And when Woolly had done that, the kid carefully folded the floor plan and stowed it away in his pack.

Woolly looked satisfied too. Although, when Billy had cinched the straps nice and tight and returned to his chair, Woolly gave him his sad sort of smile.

—I wish I didn't know where my mother is, he said.

—Why is that, Woolly?

—So that I could go and look for her just like you.

—.—

Once the dishes were clean and Billy had taken Woolly upstairs to show him where he could shower, I did some poking around.

It was no secret that Emmett's old man had gone bust. But all you had to take was one look around the place to know it wasn't from drinking. When the man of the house is a drunk, you can tell. You can tell from the look of the furniture and the look of the front yard. You can tell from the look on the faces of the kids. But even if Emmett's old man was a teetotaler, I figured there had to be a drink of something somewhere—like maybe a bottle of apple brandy or peppermint schnapps tucked away for special occasions. In this part of the country, there usually was.

I started with the kitchen cabinets. In the first, I found the plates and bowls. In the second, the glasses and mugs. In the third, I found the usual assortment of foodstuffs, but no sign of a bottle, not even hiding behind the ten-year-old jar of molasses.

There wasn't any hooch in the hutch either. But in the lower compartment was a jumble of fine china covered in a thin layer of dust. Not just dinner plates, you understand. There were soup bowls, salad plates, dessert plates, and teetering towers of coffee cups. I counted twenty settings in all—in a house without a dining-room table.

I seemed to remember Emmett telling me his parents had been raised in Boston. Well, if they were raised in Boston, it must have been on the top of Beacon Hill. This was the sort of stuff that is given to a Brahmin bride with every expectation it will be handed down from one generation to the next. But the whole collection could barely fit in the cupboard, so it certainly wasn't going to fit in a kit bag. Which sort of made you wonder . . .

In the front room, the only place to stow a bottle was in the big old desk in the corner. I sat in the chair and rolled up the top. The writing surface had the normal accessories—scissors, a letter opener, a pad and pencil—but the drawers were cluttered with all sorts of things that had no business being there, like an old alarm clock, a half a deck of cards, and a scattering of nickels and dimes.

After scraping up the loose change (waste not, want not), I opened the bottom drawer with my fingers crossed, knowing it to be a classic stowing spot. But there was no room for a bottle in there, because the drawer was filled to the brim with mail.

It didn't take more than a glance to know what this mess was all about: unpaid bills. Bills from the power company and the phone company, and whoever else had been foolish enough to extend Mr. Watson credit. At the very bottom would be the original notices, then the reminders, while here at the top, the cancellations and threats of legal action. Some of those envelopes hadn't even been opened.

I couldn't help but smile.

There was something sort of sweet in how Mr. Watson kept this assortment in the bottom drawer—not a foot away from the trash can. It had taken him just as much effort to stuff the bills inside his desk as it would have to consign them to oblivion. Maybe he just couldn't bring himself to admit that he was never going to pay them.

My old man certainly wouldn't have gone to the trouble. As far as he was concerned, an unpaid bill couldn't find its way into the garbage fast enough. In fact, he was so allergic to the very paper on which bills were printed, he would go to some lengths to ensure that they never caught up with him in the first place. That's why the incomparable Harrison Hewett, who was something of a stickler when it came to the English language, was occasionally known to misspell his own address.

But waging a war with the Post Office is no small affair. They have entire fleets of trucks at their disposal, and an army of foot soldiers whose sole purpose in life is to make sure that an envelope with your name on it finds its way into your mitts. Which is why the Hewetts were occasionally known to arrive by the lobby and depart by the fire escape, usually at five in the morning.

Ah, my father would say, pausing between the fourth and third floors and gesturing toward the east. *Rosy-fingered dawn! Count yourself lucky to be of its acquaintance, my boy. There are kings who never laid eyes upon it!*

Outside, I heard the wheels of Mr. Ransom's pickup turning into the Watsons' drive. The headlights briefly swept the room from right to left as the truck passed the house and headed toward the barn. I closed the bottom drawer of the desk so that the whole pile of notices could remain safe and sound until the final accounting.

Upstairs, I stuck my head into Billy's room, where Woolly was already stretched out on the bed. He was humming softly and staring at the airplanes hanging from the ceiling. He was probably thinking about his father in the cockpit of his fighter plane at ten thousand feet. That's where Woolly's father would always be for Woolly: somewhere between the flight deck of his carrier and the bottom of the South China Sea.

I found Billy in his father's room, sitting Indian style on the bedcovers with his knapsack at his side and a big red book in his lap.

—Hey there, gunslinger. What're you reading?

—*Professor Abacus Abernathe's Compendium of Heroes, Adventurers, and Other Intrepid Travelers.*

I whistled.

—Sounds impressive. Is it any good?

—Oh, I've read it twenty-four times.

—Then *good* may not be big enough a word.

Entering the room, I took a little stroll from corner to corner as the kid turned the page. On top of the bureau were two framed photographs.

The first was of a standing husband and seated wife in turn-of-the-century garb. The Watsons of Beacon Hill, no doubt. The other was of Emmett and Billy from just a few years back. They were sitting on the same porch that Emmett and his neighbor had sat on earlier that day. There was no picture of Billy and Emmett's mother.

—Hey, Billy, I said, putting the photograph of the brothers back on the bureau. Can I ask you a question?

—Okay, Duchess.

—When exactly did your mother go to California?

—On the fifth of July 1946.

—That's pretty exactly. So she just up and left, huh? Never to be heard from again?

—No, said Billy, turning another page. She was heard from again. She sent us nine postcards. That's how we know that she's in San Francisco.

For the first time since I'd entered the room, he looked up from his book.

—Can I ask you a question, Duchess?

—Fair's fair, Billy.

—How come they call you that?

—Because I was born in Dutchess County.

—Where is Dutchess County?

—About fifty miles north of New York.

Billy sat up straight.

—You mean the city of New York?

— None other.

—Have you ever been to the city of New York?

—I've been to hundreds of cities, Billy, but I've been to the city of New York more than I've been to anywhere else.

—That's where Professor Abernathe is. Here, look.

Turning to one of the first pages, he offered up his book.

—Small print gives me a headache, Billy. Why don't you do the honors.

Looking down, he began reading with the help of a fingertip.

—*Dearest Reader, I write to you today from my humble office on the fifty-fifth floor of the Empire State Building at the junction of Thirty-Fourth Street and Fifth Avenue on the isle of Manhattan in the city of New York at the northeastern edge of our great nation—the United States of America.*

Billy looked up with a certain level of expectation. I responded with a look of inquiry.

—Have you ever met Professor Abernathe? he asked.

I smiled.

—I've met a lot of people in our great nation and many of them from the isle of Manhattan, but to the best of my knowledge, I have never had the pleasure of meeting your professor.

—Oh, said Billy.

He was quiet for a moment, then his little brow furrowed.

—Something else? I asked.

—Why have you been to hundreds of cities, Duchess?

—My father was a thespian. Although we were generally based in New York, we spent a good part of the year traveling from town to town. We'd be in Buffalo one week and Pittsburgh the next. Then Cleveland or Kansas City. I've even spent some time in Nebraska, believe it or not. When I was about your age, I lived for a stretch on the outskirts of a little city called Lewis.

—I know Lewis, said Billy. It's on the Lincoln Highway. Halfway between here and Omaha.

—No kidding.

Billy set his book aside and reached for his knapsack.

—I have a map. Would you like to see?

—I'll take your word for it.

Billy let go of the knapsack. Then his brow furrowed again.

—When you were moving from town to town, how did you go to school?

—Not all worth knowing can be found between the covers of compendiums, my boy. Let's simply say that my academy was the thoroughfare, my primer experience, and my instructor the fickle finger of fate.

Billy seemed to consider this for a moment, apparently unsure of whether he should be willing to accept the principle as an article of faith. Then, after nodding twice to himself, he looked up with a touch of embarrassment.

—Can I ask you something else, Duchess?

—Shoot.

—What is a thespian?

I laughed.

—A thespian is a man of the stage, Billy. An actor.

Extending a hand, I looked into the distance and intoned:

She should have died hereafter.
There would have been a time for such a word.
Tomorrow, and tomorrow, and tomorrow
Creeps in this petty pace from day to day
To the last syllable of recorded time;
And all our yesterdays have lighted fools
The way to dusty death. . . .

It was a pretty good delivery, if I do say so myself. Sure, the pose was a little hackneyed, but I put a world of weariness into the *tomorrows*, and I hit that old *dusty death* with an ominous flare.

Billy gave me his patented wide-eyed look.

—William Shakespeare from the Scottish play, I said. Act five, scene five.

—Was your father a Shakespearean actor?

—Very Shakespearean.

—Was he famous?

—Oh, he was known by name in every saloon from Petaluma to Poughkeepsie.

Billy looked impressed. But then his brow furrowed once again.

—I have learned a little about William Shakespeare, he said. Professor Abernathe calls him the greatest adventurer to have never set sail on the seas. But he never mentions the Scottish play. . . .

—Not surprisingly. You see, the Scottish play is how theater folk refer to *Macbeth*. Some centuries ago, it was determined that the play was cursed, and that to speak of it by name can only bring misfortune upon the heads of those who dare perform it.

—What sorts of misfortune?

—The worst sorts. At the very first production of the play back in the sixteen hundreds, the young actor cast as Lady Macbeth died right before going onstage. About a hundred years ago, the two greatest Shakespearean actors in the world were an American named Forrest and a Brit named Macready. Naturally, the American audience was partial to the talents of Mr. Forrest. So when Macready was cast in the role of Macbeth at the Astor Place Opera House—on the isle of Manhattan—a riot broke out in which ten thousand clashed and many were killed.

Needless to say, Billy was enthralled.

—But why is it cursed?

—Why is it cursed! Have you never heard the tale of Macbeth? The black-hearted Thane of Glamis? What? No? Well then, my boy, make some room, and I shall bring you into the fraternity!

Professor Applenathe's *Compendium* was set aside. And as Billy got under the covers, I switched off the light—just as my father would have when he was about to tell a dark and grisly tale.

Naturally enough, I began on the fen with the three witches bubbling, bubbling, toil and troubling. I told the kid how, spurred by the ambitions of the Missus, Macbeth honored the visit of his king with a dagger through the heart; and how this cold-blooded act of murder begot another, which in turn begot a third. I told him how Macbeth became tormented by ghostly visions, and his wife began sleepwalking the halls of Cawdor while wiping the specter of blood from her hands. Oh, I stuck the courage to the sticking place, all right!

And once the trees of Birnam Wood had climbed the hill of Dunsinane, and Macduff, that man of no woman born, had left the regicide slain upon the fields, I tucked Billy in with a wish of pleasant dreams. And as I retreated down the hall, I took a bow with a gentle flourish when I noted that young Billy had gotten out of bed to switch the light back on.

—·—

Sitting on the edge of Emmett's bed, what struck me immediately about his room was all that wasn't in it. While there was a chip in the plaster where a nail had once been lodged, there were no pictures hanging, no posters or pennants. There was no radio or record player. And while there was a curtain rod above the window, there were no curtains. If there had been a cross on the wall, it could well have been the cell of a monk.

I suppose he could have cleared it out right before going to Salina. Putting his childish ways behind him, and what have you, by dumping all his comic books and baseball cards in the trash. Maybe. But something told me this was the room of someone who had been preparing to walk out of his house with nothing but a kit bag for a long, long time.

The beams from Mr. Ransom's headlights swept across the wall again, this time from left to right as the truck passed the house on its way to the road. After the screen door slammed, I heard Emmett turn off the lights in the kitchen, then the lights in the front room. When he climbed the stairs, I was waiting in the hall.

—Up and running? I asked.

—Thankfully.

He looked genuinely relieved, but a little worn out too.

—I feel terrible putting you out of your room. Why don't you take your bed and I'll sleep downstairs on the couch. It may be a little short, but it's bound to be more comfortable than the mattresses at Salina.

In saying this, I didn't expect Emmett to take me up on the offer. He wasn't the type. But I could tell he appreciated the gesture. He gave me a smile and even put a hand on my shoulder.

—That's all right, Duchess. You stay put and I'll join Billy. I think we could all use a good night's sleep.

Emmett continued down the hall a few steps, then stopped and turned back.

—You and Woolly should switch out of those clothes. He can find something in my father's closet. They were about the same size. I've already packed things for Billy and me, so you can take what you want from mine. There's also a pair of old book bags in there that you two can use.

—Thanks, Emmett.

As he continued down the hall, I went back into his room. From behind the closed door, I could hear him washing up, then going to join his brother.

Lying down on his bed, I stared at the ceiling. Over my head were no model airplanes. All I had was a crack in the plaster that turned a lazy curve around the ceiling lamp. But at the end of a long day, maybe a crack in the plaster is all you need to trigger fanciful thoughts. Because the way that little imperfection curved around the fixture was suddenly very reminiscent of how the Platte River bends around Omaha.

Oh, Omaha, I remember thee well.

It was in August of 1944, just six months after my eighth birthday. That summer, my father was part of a traveling revue claiming to raise money for the war effort. Though the show was billed as *The Greats of Vaudeville*, it might just as well have been called *The Cavalcade of Has-Beens*. It opened with a junkie juggler who'd get the shakes in the second half of his act, followed by an eighty-year-old comedian who could never remember which jokes he had already told. My father's bit was to perform a medley of Shakespeare's greatest monologues—or, as he put it: *A lifetime supply of wisdom in twenty-two minutes.* Wearing the beard of a Bolshevik and a dagger in his belt, he would lift his gaze slowly from the footlights in search of that realm of sublime ideas located somewhere in the upper right-hand corner of the balcony, and thence wouldst commence: *But soft, what light through yonder window breaks . . .* and *Once more unto the breach, dear friends . . .* and *O reason not the need! . . .*

From Romeo to Henry to Lear. A tailor-made progression from the moonstruck youth, to the nascent hero, to the doddering old fool.

As I recall, that tour began at the Majestic Theatre in glamorous Trenton, New Jersey. From there, we headed west, hitting all the bright lights of the interior from Pittsburgh to Peoria.

The last stop was a one-week residence at the Odeon in Omaha. Tucked somewhere between the railway station and the red-light district, it was a grand old Deco spot that hadn't had the good sense to turn itself into a movie theater when it still had the chance. Most of the time while we were on the road, we stayed with the other performers in the hotels that were suited to our kind—the ones frequented by fugitives and Bible salesmen. But whenever we reached the final stop on a tour—that stop from which there would be no forwarding address—my father would check us into the fanciest hotel in town. Sporting the walking stick of Winston Churchill and the voice of John Barrymore, he would saunter up to the front desk and ask to be shown to his room. Discovering that the hotel was fully booked and had no record of his reservation, he would express the outrage appropriate to a man of his station. *What's that! No reservation! Why, it was none other than Lionel Pendergast, the general manager of the Waldorf Astoria (and a close personal friend), who, having assured me that there was no other place in Omaha to spend the night, called your offices in order to book my room!* When the management would eventually admit that the presidential suite was available, Pops would concede that, though he was a man of simple needs, the presidential suite would do very nicely, thank you.

Once ensconced, this man of simple needs would take full advantage of the hotel's amenities. Every stitch of our clothing would be sent to the laundry. Manicurists and masseuses would be summoned to our rooms. Bell boys would be sent out for flowers. And in the lobby bar every night at six, drinks would be ordered all round.

It was on a Sunday in August, the morning after his last performance, that my father proposed an excursion. Having been hired for a run at the Palladium in Denver, he suggested we celebrate by having a picnic on the bank of a meandering river.

As we carried our luggage down the hotel's back stairs, my father wondered whether perhaps we should augment our festivities by bringing along a representative of the gentler sex. Say, Miss Maples, that delightful young lady whom Mephisto, the cross-eyed magician, had been sawing in half every night in the second act. And who should we find standing in the alley with her suitcase in hand, but the buxom blonde we'd just been discussing.

—Tallyho! said my father.

Ah, what a delightful day that turned out to be.

With me in the rumble seat and Miss Maples up front, we drove to a large municipal park on the edge of the Platte River, where the grass was lush, the trees were tall, and the sunshine glistened on the surface of the water. The night before, my father had ordered a picnic of fried chicken and cold corn on the cob. He had even stolen a tablecloth right out from under our breakfast plates (try that one, Mephisto!).

Miss Maples, who couldn't have been more than twenty-five,

seemed to delight in my old man's company. She laughed at all his jokes and warmly expressed her gratitude whenever he refilled her glass with wine. She even blushed at some of the compliments he had stolen from the Bard.

She had brought along a portable record player, and I was put in charge of picking the records and cuing the needle as the two of them danced uncertainly on the grass.

It has been observed that that which comforts the stomach dullens the wits. And surely, no truer words have ever been said. For after we had tossed the wine bottles into the river, packed the phonograph into the trunk, and put the car in gear, when my father mentioned that we needed to make a quick stop in a nearby town, I thought nothing of it. And when we pulled up to an old stone building on top of a hill and he asked me to wait with a young nun in one room while he spoke to an older nun in another, I still thought nothing of that. In fact, it was only when I happened to glance through the window and spied my father speeding down the driveway with Miss Maples's head on his shoulder that I realized I'd been had.

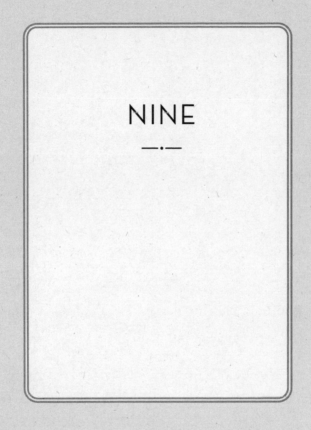

NINE

Emmett

Emmett woke to the smell of bacon frying in a pan. He couldn't remember the last time he'd woken to the smell of bacon. For over a year, he'd been waking to the complaint of a bugle and the stirring of forty boys at six fifteen in the morning. Rain or shine they had forty minutes to shower, dress, make their beds, eat their breakfast, and line up for duty. To wake on a real mattress under clean cotton sheets with the smell of bacon in the air had become so unfamiliar, so unexpected, it took Emmett a moment to wonder where the bacon had come from and who was cooking it.

He turned over and saw that Billy was gone and the clock on the bedside table read 9:45. Swearing softly, he climbed out of bed and dressed. He had hoped to get in and out of town before church let out.

In the kitchen, he found Billy and Duchess sitting across from each other—and Sally at the stove. In front of the boys were plates of bacon and eggs, in the middle of the table a basket of biscuits and a jar of strawberry preserves.

—Boy are you in for a treat, said Duchess when he saw Emmett.

Pulling up a chair, Emmett looked toward Sally, who was picking up the percolator.

—You didn't have to make breakfast for us, Sally.

By way of reply, she set down a mug on the table in front of him.

—Here's your coffee. Your eggs will be ready in a minute.

Then she turned on her heels and went back to the stove.

Duchess, who had just taken a second bite from a biscuit, was shaking his head in appreciation.

—I've traveled all around America, Sally, but I've never had anything like these biscuits. What's your secret recipe?

—There's nothing secret about my recipe, Duchess.

—If there isn't, there should be. And Billy tells me you made the jelly too.

—Those are preserves, not jelly. But yes, I make them every July.

—It takes her a whole day, said Billy. You should see her kitchen. There are baskets of berries on every counter and a five-pound bag of sugar and four different pots simmering on the stove.

Duchess whistled and shook his head again.

—It may be an old-fashioned endeavor, but from where I sit, it's worth the effort.

Sally turned from the stove and thanked Duchess, with a touch of ceremony. Then she looked at Emmett.

—You ready yet?

Without waiting for an answer, she brought over his serving.

—You really didn't have to go to all this trouble, Emmett said. We could have seen to our own breakfast, and there was plenty of jam in the cabinet.

—I'll be sure to keep that in mind, Sally said, setting down his plate. Then she went to the sink and began scrubbing the skillet.

Emmett was staring at her back when Billy addressed him.

—Did you ever go to the Imperial, Emmett?

Emmett turned to his brother.

—What's that, Billy? The Imperial?

—The movie theater in Salina.

Emmett directed a frown at Duchess, who quickly set the record straight.

—Your brother never went to the Imperial, Billy. That was just me and a few of the other boys.

Billy nodded, looking like he was thinking something over.

—Did you have to get special permission to go to the movies?

—You didn't need permission, so much as . . . initiative.

—But how did you get out?

—Ah! A reasonable question under the circumstances. Salina wasn't exactly like a prison, Billy, with guard towers and searchlights. It was more like boot camp in the army—a compound in the middle of nowhere with a bunch of barracks and a mess hall and some older guys in uniform who yelled at you for moving too fast when they weren't yelling at you for moving too slow. But the guys in uniform—our sergeants, if you will—didn't sleep with us. They had their own barracks, with a pool table, and a radio, and a cooler full of beer. So after lights-out on Saturday, while they were drinking and shooting pool, a few of us would slip out the bathroom window and make our way into town.

—Was it far?

—Not too far. If you jogged across the potato fields, in about twenty minutes you'd come to a river. Most of the time, the river was only a few feet deep, so you could wade across in your skivvies and make it downtown in time for the ten o'clock show. You could have a bag of popcorn and a bottle of pop, watch the feature from the balcony, and be back in bed by one in the morning, leaving no one the wiser.

—Leaving no one the wiser, repeated Billy, with a hint of awe. But how did you pay for the movies?

—Why don't we change the subject, suggested Emmett.

—Why not! said Duchess.

Sally, who had been drying the skillet, set it down on the stovetop with a bang.

—I'll go make the beds, she said.

—You don't have to make the beds, said Emmett.

—They won't make themselves.

Sally left the kitchen and they could hear her marching up the stairs.

Duchess looked at Billy and raised his eyebrows.

—Excuse me, said Emmett, pushing back his chair.

As he headed upstairs, Emmett could hear Duchess and his brother launching into a conversation about the Count of Monte Cristo and his miraculous escape from an island prison—the promised change of subject.

When Emmett got to his father's room, Sally was already making the bed with quick, precise movements.

—You didn't mention that you were having company, she said, without looking up.

—I didn't know I was having company.

Sally fluffed the pillows by giving them a punch on either end, then set them against the headboard.

—Excuse me, she said, squeezing past Emmett in the doorway as she went across the hall to his room.

When Emmett followed, he found her staring at the bed—because Duchess had already made it. Emmett was a little impressed by Duchess's effort, but Sally wasn't. She pulled back the quilt and sheet and began tucking them back in with the same precise movements. When she turned her attention to the punching of pillows, Emmett glanced at the bedside clock. It was almost ten fifteen. He really didn't have time for this, whatever this was.

—If something's on your mind, Sally . . .

Sally stopped abruptly and looked him in the eye for the first time that morning.

—What would be on my mind?

—I'm sure I don't know.

—That sounds about right.

She straightened her dress and made a move toward the door, but he was standing in her way.

—I'm sorry if I didn't seem grateful in the kitchen. All I was trying to say was—

—I know what you were trying to say because you said it. That I didn't need to go to the trouble of skipping church so that I could make you breakfast this morning; just like I didn't need to go to the trouble of making you dinner last night. Which is fine and dandy. But for your information, telling someone they didn't have to go to the trouble of doing something is not the same as showing gratitude for it. Not by a long shot. No matter how much store-bought jam you have in the cabinet.

—Is that what this is about? The jam in the cabinet? Sally, I did not mean to slight your preserves. Of course they're better than the jam in the cabinet. But I know how much effort it takes for you to make them, and I didn't want you to feel you had to waste a jar on us. It's not like it's a special occasion.

—It may interest you to know, Emmett Watson, that I am quite happy to have my preserves eaten by friends and family when there is no occasion to speak of. But maybe, just maybe, I thought you and Billy might like to enjoy one last jar before you packed up and moved to California without saying so much as a word.

Emmett closed his eyes.

—Come to think of it, she continued, I guess I should thank my lucky stars that your friend Duchess had the presence of mind to inform me of your intentions. Otherwise, I might have come over tomorrow morning and made pancakes and sausage only to find there was no one here to eat them.

—I'm sorry I haven't had the chance to mention that to you, Sally. But it wasn't like I was trying to hide it. I talked about it with your father yesterday afternoon. In fact, he was the one who brought it up—saying it might be best if Billy and I were to pull up stakes and make a fresh start somewhere else.

Sally looked at Emmett.

—My father said that. That you should pull up stakes and make a fresh start.

—In so many words . . .

—Well, doesn't that just sound delightful.

Pushing past Emmett, Sally continued into Billy's room, where Woolly was lying on his back and blowing at the ceiling, trying to stir the airplanes.

Sally put her hands on her hips.

—And who might you be?

Woolly looked up in shock.

—I'm Woolly.

—Are you Catholic, Woolly?

—No, I'm Episcopalian.

—Then what are you still doing in bed?

—I'm not sure, admitted Woolly.

—It's after ten in the morning and I've got plenty to do. So at the count of five, I'm going to make that bed, whether you're in it or not.

Woolly jumped out from under the covers in his boxer shorts and watched in a state of amazement as Sally went about the business of making the bed. While scratching the top of his head, he noticed Emmett on the threshold.

—Hey, Emmett!

—Hey, Woolly.

Woolly squinted at Emmett for a moment, then his face lit up.

—Is that bacon?

—Ha! said Sally.

And Emmett, he headed down the stairs and out the door.

—·—

It was a relief for Emmett to be alone behind the wheel of the Studebaker.

Since leaving Salina, he'd barely had a moment to himself. First there was the drive with the warden, then Mr. Obermeyer in the kitchen and Mr. Ransom on the porch, then Duchess and Woolly, and now Sally. All Emmett wanted, all he needed, was a chance to clear his head so that, wherever he and Billy decided to go, whether to Texas or California or someplace else altogether, he could set out in the right frame of mind. But as he turned onto Route 14, what Emmett found himself dwelling on was not where he and Billy might go, it was his exchange with Sally.

I'm sure I don't know.

That's how he'd replied when she had asked him what might be on her mind. And in the strictest sense, he hadn't known.

But he could have made a pretty good guess.

He understood well enough what Sally had come to expect. At one time, he may even have given her cause for expecting it. That's the sort of thing young people do: fan the flames of each other's expectations— until the necessities of life begin to make themselves known. But Emmett hadn't given her much cause for expectations since he went to Salina. When she had sent him those packages—with the homemade cookies and hometown news—he had not replied with a word of thanks. Not on the phone and not in a note. And in advance of coming home, he had not sent her word of his pending arrival or asked her to tidy the house. He hadn't asked her to sweep or make beds or put soap in the bathroom or eggs in the icebox. He hadn't asked her to do a thing.

Was he grateful to discover that she had chosen to do these things on his and Billy's behalf? Of course he was. But being grateful was one thing, and being beholden, that was another thing altogether.

As Emmett drove, he saw the intersection with Route 7 approaching. Emmett knew that if he took a right and circled back on 22D, he could reach town without having to pass the fairgrounds. But what would be the point of that? The fairgrounds would still be there whether he passed them or not. They'd still be there whether he went to Texas or California or someplace else altogether.

No, taking the long route wouldn't change a thing. Except maybe letting one imagine for a moment that what had happened already hadn't happened at all. So not only did Emmett continue straight through the intersection, he slowed the car to twenty miles an hour as he approached the fairgrounds, then pulled over on the opposite shoulder where he had no choice but to give it a good hard look.

For fifty-one weeks of the year, the fairgrounds were exactly like they were right now—four empty acres scattered with hay to hold down the dust. But in the first week of October, they would be anything but empty. They would be filled with music and people and lights. There would be a carousel and bumper cars and colorful booths where one could try one's hand at pitching or riflery. There would be a great striped tent where, with an appropriate sense of ceremony, judges would convene, confer, and bestow blue ribbons for the largest pumpkin and the tastiest lemon meringue pie. And there would be a corral with bleachers where they would hold the tractor pull and calf roping, and where more ribbons would be awarded by more judges. And back there, just beyond the food concessions, would be a spot-lit stage for the fiddling contest.

It was right by the cotton-candy vendor, of all places, on the last night of the fair that Jimmy Snyder had chosen to pick his fight.

When Jimmy called out his first remark, Emmett thought he must be talking to someone else—because he barely knew Jimmy. A year younger, Emmett wasn't in any of Jimmy's classes and didn't play on any of his teams, so he had little reason to interact with him.

But Jimmy Snyder didn't have to know you. He liked running people down whether he knew them or not. And it didn't matter for what. It could have been for the clothes you were wearing, or the food you were eating, or the way your sister crossed the street. Yes, sir, it could have been about anything, as long as it was something that got under your skin.

Stylistically speaking, Jimmy was one for framing his insults as inquiries. Looking curious and mild, he'd ask his first question to no one in particular. And if that didn't hit a sore spot, he'd answer the first question himself, then ask another, circling ever inward.

Isn't that cute? was the question he'd posed when he'd seen Emmett holding Billy's hand. *I mean, isn't that the cutest thing you ever saw?*

When Emmett realized that Jimmy was referring to him, he brushed it off. What did he care if he was seen holding his younger brother's hand at the county fair. Who wouldn't be holding the hand of a six-year-old boy in the middle of a large crowd at eight in the evening?

So Jimmy tried again. Shifting gears, as it were, he wondered out loud whether the reason Emmett's father hadn't fought in the war was because he'd been 3-C, the Selective Service classification that allowed farmers to defer. This struck Emmett as an odd taunt given how many men in Nebraska had received the 3-C designation. It struck him as so odd that he couldn't help but stop and turn around—which was his first mistake.

Now that Jimmy had Emmett's attention, he answered the query himself.

No, he said, *Charlie Watson wouldn't have been 3-C. 'Cause he couldn't grow grass in the Garden of Eden. He must have been 4-F.*

Here, Jimmy turned a finger around his ear to imply Charlie Watson's incapacity to reason.

Granted, these were juvenile taunts, but they had begun to make Emmett grit his teeth. He could feel the old heat rising to the surface of his skin. But he could also feel that Billy was tugging at his hand—maybe for the simple reason that the fiddling contest was about to begin, or maybe because, even at the age of six, Billy understood that no good could come from engaging with the likes of Jimmy Snyder. But before Billy could tug Emmett away, Jimmy took one more crack at it.

No, he said, *it couldn't have been because he was 4-F. He's too simple to be crazy. I suppose if he didn't fight, it must have been because he was 4-E. What they call a conscientious—*

Before Jimmy could say the word *objector*, Emmett had hit him. He had hit him without even letting go of his brother's hand, extending his fist from his shoulder in one clean jab, breaking Jimmy's nose.

It wasn't the broken nose that killed him, of course. It was the fall. Jimmy was so used to speaking with impunity that he wasn't prepared for the punch. It sent him stumbling backward, arms flailing. When his heel caught on a braid of cables, Jimmy fell straight back, hitting his head on a cinderblock that was bracing the stake of a tent.

According to the medical examiner, Jimmy landed with such force that the corner of the cinderblock dug a triangular hole an inch deep into the back of his skull. It put him in a coma that left him breathing, but that was slowly sapping his strength. After sixty-two days, it finally drained the life out of him altogether, as his family sat at his bedside in their fruitless vigil.

Like the warden said: *The ugly side of chance.*

Sheriff Petersen was the one who brought the news of Jimmy's death to the Watsons' doorstep. He had held off on pressing charges, waiting to see how Jimmy would fare. In the meantime, Emmett had maintained his silence, seeing no virtue in rehashing the events while Jimmy was fighting for his life.

But Jimmy's pals did not maintain their silence. They talked about the fight often and at length. They talked about it in the schoolhouse, at the soda fountain, and in the Snyders' living room. They told of how the four of them had been on their way to the cotton-candy stand when Jimmy bumped into Emmett by mistake; and how before Jimmy even got the chance to apologize, Emmett had punched him in the face.

Mr. Streeter, Emmett's attorney, had encouraged him to take the stand and tell his own version of events. But whatever version prevailed, Jimmy Snyder was still going to be dead and buried. So Emmett told Mr. Streeter that he didn't need a trial. And on March 1, 1953, at a hearing before Judge Schomer in the county courthouse, after freely admitting his guilt, Emmett was sentenced to eighteen months at a special juvenile reform program on a farm in Salina, Kansas.

In another ten weeks, the fairgrounds wouldn't be empty, thought Emmett. The tent would be raised and the stage rebuilt and the people would gather once again in anticipation of the contests and food and music. As Emmett put the Studebaker in gear, he took little comfort from the fact that when the festivities commenced he and Billy would be more than a thousand miles away.

— · —

Emmett parked along the lawn at the side of the courthouse. As it was Sunday, only a few stores were open. He made quick stops at Gunderson's and the five-and-dime, where he spent the twenty dollars from his father's envelope on sundries for the journey west. Then after putting his bags in the car, he walked up Jefferson to the public library.

At the front of the central room, a middle-aged librarian sat at a V-shaped desk. When Emmett asked where he could find the almanacs and encyclopedias, she led him to the reference section and pointed to various volumes. As she was doing so, Emmett could tell that she was scrutinizing him through her glasses, giving him a second look, as if maybe she recognized him. Emmett hadn't been in the library since he was a boy, but she could have recognized him for any number of reasons, not least of which was that his picture had been on the front page of the town paper more than once. Initially, it was his school portrait set alongside Jimmy's. Then it was Emmett Watson being taken into the station house to be formally charged, and Emmett Watson descending the courthouse steps in the minutes after his hearing. The girl at Mr. Gunderson's had given him a similar look.

—Can I help you find anything in particular? the librarian asked after a moment.

—No, ma'am. I'm all set.

When she retreated to her desk, Emmett pulled the volumes he needed, brought them to one of the tables, and took a seat.

For much of 1952, Emmett's father had been wrestling with one illness or another. But it was a flu he couldn't shake in the spring of '53 that prompted Doc Winslow to send him to Omaha for some tests. In the letter Emmett's father sent to Salina a few months later, he assured his son that he was *back on his feet* and *well on the road to recovery*. Nonetheless, he had agreed to make a second trip to Omaha so that the specialists could do a few more tests, *as specialists are wont to do*.

Reading the letter, Emmett wasn't fooled by his father's folksy assurances or his wry remark on the penchants of medical professionals. His father had been using mollifying words for as long as Emmett could remember. Mollifying words to describe how the planting had gone, how the harvest was coming, and why their mother was suddenly nowhere to be found. Besides, Emmett was old enough to know that the road to recovery was rarely lined with repeat visits to specialists.

Any doubts as to Mr. Watson's prognosis were swept aside one morning in August when he stood up from the breakfast table and fainted right before Billy's eyes, prompting a third trip to Omaha, this one in the back of an ambulance.

That night—after Emmett had received the call from Doc Winslow in the warden's office—a plan began to take shape. Or to be more accurate, it was a plan that Emmett had been toying with for months in the back of his mind, but now it was in the forefront, presenting itself in a series of variations that differed in timing and scope, but which always took place somewhere other than Nebraska. As his father's condition deteriorated over the fall, the plan became sharper; and when he died that April, it was clear as could be—as if Emmett's father had surrendered his own vitality to ensure the vitality of Emmett's intentions.

The plan was simple enough.

As soon as Emmett was out of Salina, he and Billy were going to pack their things and head to some metropolitan area—somewhere without silos or harvesters or fairgrounds—where they could use what little remained of their father's legacy to buy a house.

It didn't have to be a grand house. It could be a three- or four-bedroom with one or two baths. It could be colonial or Victorian, clapboard or shingled. What it had to be was in disrepair.

Because they wouldn't be buying this house to fill it with furniture and tableware and art, or with memories, for that matter. They'd be buying the house to fix it up and sell it. To make ends meet, Emmett would get a job with a local builder, but in the evenings while Billy was doing his schoolwork, Emmett would be setting the house right, inch by inch. First, he'd do whatever work was needed on the roof and windows to ensure the house was weather tight. Then he'd shift his attention to the walls, doors, and flooring. Then the moldings and banisters and cabinets. Once the house was in prime condition, once the windows opened and closed and the staircase didn't creak and the radiators didn't rattle, once every corner looked finished and fine, then and only then would they sell.

If he played his cards right, if he picked the right house in the right neighborhood and did the right amount of work, Emmett figured he could double his money on the first sale—allowing him to invest the proceeds in two more run-down houses, where he could start the process over again. Only this time, when the two houses were finished, he would sell one and rent out the other. If Emmett maintained his focus, within a few years he figured he'd have enough money to quit his job and hire a man or two. Then he'd be renovating two houses and collecting rent from four. But at no time, under any circumstances, would he ever borrow a dime.

Other than his own hard work, Emmett figured there was only one thing essential to his success, and that was to pursue his plan in a metropolitan area that was big and getting bigger. With that in mind, he had visited the little library at Salina, and with volume eighteen of the *Encyclopedia Britannica* open on the table, he had written down the following:

Population of Texas

1920	4,700,000
1930	5,800,000
1940	6,400,000
1950	7,800,000
1960E	9,600,000

When Emmett had the Texas entry in front of him, he hadn't even bothered to read the opening paragraphs—the ones that summarized the state's history, its commerce, culture, and climate. When he saw that between 1920 and 1960 the population would more than double, that was all he needed to know.

But by the same logic, he should be open to considering any large growing state in the Union.

As he sat in the Morgen library, Emmett removed the scrap of paper from his wallet and set it on the table. Then he opened volume three of the encyclopedia and added a second column.

Population of Texas		Population of California	
1920	4,700,000	1920	3,400,000
1930	5,800,000	1930	5,700,000
1940	6,400,000	1940	6,900,000
1950	7,800,000	1950	10,600,000
1960E	9,600,000	1960E	15,700,000

Emmett was so surprised by California's growth that this time he read the opening paragraphs. What he learned was that its economy was expanding on multiple fronts. Long an agricultural giant, the war had turned the state into a leading builder of ships and airplanes; Hollywood had become the manufacturer of dreams for the world; and taken together, the ports of San Diego, Los Angeles, and San Francisco amounted to the single largest gateway for trade into the US of A. In the 1950s alone, California was projected to grow by more than five million citizens, at a rate of close to fifty percent.

The notion that he and his brother would find their mother seemed as crazy as it had the day before, if not crazier, given the growth of the state's population. But if Emmett's intention was to renovate and sell houses, the case for California was indisputable.

Emmett returned the scrap to his wallet and the encyclopedia to its shelf. But having slid the third volume back in its slot, Emmett removed the twelfth. Without sitting down, he turned to the entry on Nebraska and scanned the page. With a touch of grim satisfaction, Emmett noted that from 1920 to 1950 its population had hovered around 1.3 million people, and that in the current decade it wasn't expected to increase by a soul.

Emmett replaced the volume and headed for the door.

—Did you find what you were looking for?

Having passed the reference desk, Emmett turned to face the librarian. With her eyeglasses now resting on her head, Emmett saw that he had been wrong about her age. She was probably no older than thirty-five.

—I did, he said. Thank you.

—You're Billy's brother, aren't you?

—I am, he said, a little surprised.

She smiled and nodded.

—I'm Ellie Matthiessen. I could tell because you look so much like him.

—Do you know my brother well?

—Oh, he's spent a lot of time here. At least, since you've been away. Your brother loves a good story.

—He does at that, agreed Emmett with a smile.

Although as he went out the door, he couldn't help but add to himself: *for better or worse*.

—.—

There were three of them standing by the Studebaker when Emmett returned from the library. He didn't recognize the tall one on the right in the cowboy hat, but the one on the left was Jenny Andersen's older brother, Eddie, and the one in the middle was Jacob Snyder. From the way that Eddie was kicking at the pavement, Emmett could tell that he didn't want to be there. Seeing Emmett approach, the tall stranger nudged Jake in the side. When Jake looked up, Emmett could tell that he didn't want to be there either.

Emmett stopped a few feet away with his keys in his hand and nodded to the two men he knew.

—Jake. Eddie.

Neither replied.

Emmett considered offering Jake an apology, but Jake wasn't there for an apology. Emmett had already apologized to Jake and the rest of the Snyders. He'd apologized in the hours after the fight, then at the station house, and finally on the courthouse steps. His apologies hadn't done the Snyders any good then, and they weren't going to do them any good now.

—I don't want any trouble, said Emmett. I just want to get in my car and go home.

—I can't let you do that, said Jake.

And he was probably right. Though Emmett and Jake had only been talking for a minute, there were already people gathering around. There were a few farmhands, the Westerly widows, and two boys who had been biding their time on the courthouse lawn. If the Lutheran or Congregational church let out, the crowd would only grow. Whatever happened next was sure to get back to old man Snyder, and that meant there was only one way that Jake could let the encounter come to its conclusion.

Emmett put his keys in his pocket, leaving his hands at his side.

It was the stranger who spoke up first. Leaning against the door of the Studebaker, he tilted back his hat and smiled.

—Seems like Jake here's got some unfinished business with you, Watson.

Emmett met the gaze of the stranger, then turned back to Jake.

—If we've got unfinished business, Jake, let's finish it.

Jake looked like he was struggling with how to begin, like the anger that he'd expected to feel—that he was *supposed* to feel—after all these months was suddenly eluding him. Taking a page from his brother's book, he started with a question.

—You think of yourself as quite a fighter, don't you, Watson?

Emmett didn't reply.

—And maybe you are something of a fighter—as long as you get to hit a man unprovoked.

—It wasn't unprovoked, Jake.

Jake took half a step forward, feeling something closer to anger now.

—Are you saying Jimmy tried to hit you first?

—No. He didn't try to hit me.

Jake nodded with his jaw clenched, then took another half step.

—Seeing as you like to take the first swing so much, why don't you take the first swing at me?

—I'm not going to take a swing at you, Jake.

Jake stared at Emmett for a moment, then looked away. He didn't look at his two friends. He didn't look at the townspeople who had gathered behind him. He turned his gaze in order to look at nothing in particular. And when he turned back, he hit Emmett with a right cross.

Given that Jake hadn't been looking at Emmett when he went into motion, his fist glanced off the top of Emmett's cheek rather than hitting him squarely in the jaw. But he made enough contact that Emmett stumbled to his right.

Everyone took a step forward now. Eddie and the stranger, the onlookers, even the woman with the stroller who had just joined the crowd. Everyone, that is, but Jake. He remained where he was standing, watching Emmett.

Emmett returned to the spot where he'd been the moment before, his hands back at his side.

Jake was red in the face with some combination of exertion and anger and maybe a hint of embarrassment too.

—Put up your fists, he said.

Emmett didn't move.

—Put up your goddamn fists!

Emmett raised his fists high enough to be in the stance of a fighter, but not so high as to defend himself effectively.

This time, Jake hit him in the mouth. Emmett stumbled three steps back, tasting blood on his lips. He regained his footing and advanced the three steps that would bring him back within Jake's reach. As he heard the stranger egging Jake on, Emmett halfway raised his fists and Jake knocked him to the ground.

Suddenly, the world was out of kilter, sloping away at a thirty-degree angle. To get onto his knees, Emmett had to support himself with both hands on the pavement. As he pushed himself upward, he could feel the heat of the day rising up from the concrete through his palms.

On all fours, Emmett waited for his head to clear, then he began to stand.

Jake took a step forward.

—Don't you get up again, he said, his voice thick with emotion. Don't you get up again, Emmett Watson.

When Emmett reached his full height, he started to raise his fists, but he hadn't been ready to stand, after all. The earth reeled and angled upward, and Emmett landed back on the pavement with a grunt.

—That's enough, someone called out. That's enough, Jake.

It was Sheriff Petersen pushing through the onlookers.

The sheriff instructed one of his deputies to pull Jake aside and the other to disperse the crowd. Then he got down on his haunches to assess Emmett's condition. He even reached out and turned Emmett's head so he could get a better look at the left side of his face.

—Doesn't seem like anything's broken. You gonna be all right, Emmett?

—I'm gonna be all right.

Sheriff Petersen stayed on his haunches.

—You gonna want to press charges?

—For what.

The sheriff signaled to a deputy that he could let Jake go, then turned back to Emmett, who was sitting on the pavement now, wiping the blood from his lip.

—How long have you been back?

—Since yesterday.

—Didn't take long for Jake to find you.

—No, sir, it didn't.

—Well, I can't say as I'm surprised.

The sheriff was quiet for a moment.

—You staying out at your place?

—Yes, sir.

—All right then. Let's get you cleaned up before we send you home.

The sheriff took Emmett's hand in order to help him off the ground. But as he did so, he took the opportunity to look at Emmett's knuckles.

The sheriff and Emmett were driving through town in the Studebaker with Emmett in the passenger seat and the sheriff behind the wheel, moving at a nice easy pace. Emmett was checking his teeth with the tip of his tongue when the sheriff, who had been whistling a Hank Williams song, interrupted himself.

—Not a bad car. How fast can she go?

—About eighty without shaking.

—No kidding.

But the sheriff kept driving at his easy pace, taking wide lazy turns as he whistled his tune. When he drove past the turnoff to the station house, Emmett gave him a quizzical glance.

—I thought I'd take you to our place, the sheriff explained. Let Mary have a look at you.

Emmett didn't protest. He had appreciated the chance to get cleaned up before heading home, but he had no desire to revisit the station house.

After they'd come to a stop in the Petersens' driveway, Emmett was about to open the passenger-side door when he noted that the sheriff wasn't making a move. He was sitting there with his hands on the wheel—just like the warden had the day before.

As Emmett waited for the sheriff to say whatever was on his mind, he looked out the windshield at the tire swing hanging from the oak tree in the yard. Though Emmett didn't know the sheriff's children, he knew they were grown, and he found himself wondering whether the swing was a vestige of their youth, or the sheriff had hung it for the benefit of his grandchildren. Who knows, thought Emmett; maybe it had been hanging there since before the Petersens owned the place.

—I only arrived at the tail end of your little skirmish, the sheriff began, but from the look of your hand and Jake's face, I'd have to surmise you didn't put up much of a fight.

Emmett didn't respond.

—Well, maybe you thought you had it coming to you, continued the sheriff in a tone of reflection. Or maybe, having been through what you've been through, you've decided that your fighting days are be-hind you.

The sheriff looked at Emmett as if he were expecting Emmett to

say something, but Emmett remained silent, staring through the windshield at the swing.

—You mind if I smoke in your car? the sheriff asked after a moment.
Mary doesn't let me smoke in the house anymore.

—I don't mind.

Sheriff Petersen took a pack from his pocket and tapped two cigarettes out of the opening, offering one to Emmett. When Emmett
accepted, the sheriff lit both cigarettes with his lighter. Then out of
respect for Emmett's car, he rolled down the window.

—The war's been over almost ten years now, he said after taking a
drag and exhaling. But some of the boys who came back act like they're
still fighting it. You take Danny Hoagland. Not a month goes by without me getting a call on his account. One week he's at the roadhouse
in a brawl of his own making, a few weeks later he's in the aisle of the
supermarket giving the back of his hand to that pretty young wife
of his.

The sheriff shook his head as if mystified by what the pretty young
woman saw in Danny Hoagland in the first place.

—And last Tuesday? I got hauled out of bed at two in the morning
because Danny was standing in front of the Iversons with a pistol in
his hand, shouting about some old grievance. The Iversons' didn't know
what he was talking about. Because, as it turned out, Danny's grievance
wasn't with the Iversons. It was with the Barkers. He just wasn't standing in front of the right house. Come to think of it, he wasn't on the
right block.

Emmett smiled in spite of himself.

—Now at the other end of the spectrum, said the sheriff, pointing
his cigarette at some unknown audience, were those boys who came
back from the war swearing that they would never again lay a hand on
their fellow men. And I have a lot of respect for their position. They've
certainly earned the right to have it. The thing of it is, when it comes

to drinking whiskey, those boys make Danny Hoagland look like a deacon of the church. I never get called out of bed on their account. Because they're not out in front of the Iversons' or the Barkers' or anybody else's at two in the morning. At that hour, they're sitting in their living room working their way to the bottom of a bottle in the dark. All I'm saying, Emmett, is I'm not sure either of these approaches works that well. You can't keep fighting the war, but you can't lay down your manhood either. Sure, you can let yourself get beat up a time or two. That's your prerogative. But eventually, you're going to have to stand up for yourself like you used to.

The sheriff looked at Emmett now.

—You understand me, Emmett?

—Yes, sir, I do.

—I gather from Ed Ransom you might be leaving town. . . .

—We're headed out tomorrow.

—All right then. After we get you cleaned up, I'll take a ride over to the Snyders' and make sure they keep out of your way in the interim. While I'm at it, are there any other people who've been giving you trouble?

Emmett rolled down his window and tossed out the cigarette.

—Mostly, he said, what people have been giving me is advice.

Duchess

WHENEVER I COME TO a new town, I like to get my bearings. I want to understand the layout of the streets and the layout of the people. In some cities this can take you days to accomplish. In Boston, it can take you weeks. In New York, years. The great thing about Morgen, Nebraska, is it only took a few minutes.

The town was laid out in a geometric grid with the courthouse right in the middle. According to the mechanic who'd given me a lift in his tow truck, back in the 1880s the town elders spent a whole week deliberating how best to christen the streets before deciding—with an eye to the future—that the east-west streets would be named for presidents and the north-south streets for trees. As it turned out, they could have settled on seasons and suits because seventy-five years later the town was still only four blocks square.

—Howdy, I said to the two ladies coming in the opposite direction, neither of whom said howdy back.

Now, don't get me wrong. There's a certain charm to a town like this. And there's a certain kind of person who would rather live here than anywhere else—even in the twentieth century. Like a person who wants to make some sense of the world. Living in the big city, rushing around amid all that hammering and clamoring, the events of life can begin to seem random. But in a town this size, when a piano falls out of a window and lands on a fellow's head, there's a good chance you'll know why he deserved it.

At any rate, Morgen was the sort of town where when something out of the ordinary happens, a crowd is likely to gather. And sure enough, when I came around the courthouse, there was a semicircle of citizens ready to prove the point. From fifty feet away I could tell they were a representative sample of the local electorate. There were hayseeds in hats, dowagers with handbags, and lads in dungarees. Fast approaching was even a mother with a stroller and a toddler at her side.

Tossing the rest of my ice cream cone in the trash, I walked over to get a closer look. And who did I find at center stage? None other than Emmett Watson—being taunted by some corn-fed kid with a corn-fed grievance.

The people who had gathered to watch seemed excited, at least in a midwestern sort of way. They weren't shouting or grinning, but they were glad to have happened along at just the right moment. It would be something they could talk about in the barbershop and hair salon for weeks to come.

For his part, Emmett looked fantastic. He was standing with his eyes open and his arms at his sides, neither eager to be there nor in a hurry to leave. It was the taunter who looked anxious. He was shifting back and forth and sweating through his shirt, despite the fact that he'd brought along two cronies to back him up.

—Jake, I don't want any trouble, Emmett was saying. I just want to get in my car and go home.

—I can't let you do that, replied Jake, though it looked like that's exactly what he wanted Emmett to do.

Then one of the wingmen—the tall one in the cowboy hat—tossed in his two cents.

—Seems like Jake here's got some unfinished business with you, Watson.

I had never seen this cowboy before, but from the tilt of his hat and the smile on his face, I knew exactly who he was. He was the guy who's started a thousand fights without ever throwing a punch.

So what did Emmett do? Did he let the cowboy unsettle him? Did he tell him to shut up and mind his own business? He didn't even deign to respond. He just turned to Jake and said:

—If we've got unfinished business, let's finish it.

Pow!

If we've got unfinished business, let's finish it.

You could wait your whole life to say a sentence like that and not have the presence of mind to say it when the time comes. That sort of level-headedness isn't the product of upbringing or practice. You're either born with it or you're not. And mostly, you're not.

But here comes the best part.

It turned out that this Jake was the brother of the Snyder kid whom Emmett put out of commission back in 1952. I could tell because he started talking some nonsense about how Jimmy had been sucker-punched, as if Emmett Watson would ever stoop to hitting a man with his guard down.

When the prodding didn't work, Mr. Fair Fight here looked off in the distance as if he were lost in thought, then, without any warning, hit Emmett in the face. After stumbling to his right, Emmett shook off the blow, straightened up, and started moving back in Jake's direction.

Here we go is what everybody in the crowd was thinking. Because Emmett could clearly beat this guy to a pulp, even if he was ten pounds lighter and two inches shorter. But much to the crowd's dismay, Emmett didn't keep coming. He stopped on the very spot where he'd been standing the moment before.

Which really got to Jake. His face turned as red as his union suit, and he started yelling that Emmett should raise his fists. So Emmett raised them, more or less, and Jake took another crack at it. This time, he hit Emmett right in the kisser. Emmett stumbled again, but didn't topple. Bleeding from the lip, he regained his footing and came back for another helping.

Meanwhile, the cowboy—who was still leaning dismissively on the door of Emmett's car—shouted, *You show him, Jake,* as if Jake were about to teach Emmett a lesson. But the cowboy had it upside down. It was Emmett who was teaching the lesson.

Alan Ladd in *Shane.*

Frank Sinatra in *From Here to Eternity.*

Lee Marvin in *The Wild One.*

You know what these three have in common? They all took a beating. I don't mean getting a pop in the nose or having the wind knocked out of them. I mean a *beating.* Where their ears rang, and their eyes watered, and they could taste the blood on their teeth. Ladd took his at Grafton's Saloon from Ryker's boys. Sinatra took his in the stockade from Sergeant Fatso. And Marvin, he took his at the hands of Marlon Brando in the street of a little American town just like this one, with another crowd of honest citizens gathered around to watch.

The willingness to take a beating: That's how you can tell you're dealing with a man of substance. A man like that doesn't linger on the sidelines throwing gasoline on someone else's fire; and he doesn't go home unscathed. He presents himself front and center, undaunted, prepared to stand his ground until he can't stand at all.

It was Emmett who was teaching the lesson, all right. And he wasn't just teaching it to Jake. He was teaching it to the whole goddamn town.

Not that they understood what they were looking at. You could tell by the expressions on their faces that the whole point of the instruction was going right over their heads.

Jake, who was beginning to tremble, was probably thinking that he couldn't keep it up much longer. So this time, he tried to make it count. Finally getting his aim and his anger into alignment, he let one loose that knocked Emmett clear off his feet.

The whole crowd gave a little gasp, Jake breathed a sigh of relief, and the cowboy let out a snicker of satisfaction, like he was the one who'd thrown the punch. Then Emmett started getting up again.

Man, I wish I'd had a camera. I could've taken a picture and sent it to *Life* magazine. They would've put it on the cover.

It was beautiful, I tell you. But it was too much for Jake. Looking like he might burst into tears, he stepped forward and began shouting at Emmett that he should not get up. That he should not get up, so help him God.

I don't know if Emmett even heard him, given that his senses were probably rattled. Though whether he heard Jake or not didn't make much difference. He was going to do the same thing either way. Stepping a little uncertainly, he moved back within range, stood to his full height, and raised his fists. Then the blood must have rushed from his head because he staggered and fell to the ground.

Seeing Emmett on his knees was an unwelcome sight, but it didn't worry me. He just needed a moment to gather his wits so he could get up and return to the hitting spot. That he would do so was as certain as sunrise. But before he got the chance, the sheriff spoiled the show.

—That's enough, he said, pushing his way through the gawkers. That's enough.

At the sheriff's instruction, a deputy began dispersing the crowd, waving his arms and telling everyone it was time to move along. But there was no need for the deputy to disperse the cowboy. Because the cowboy had dispersed himself. The second the authorities appeared on the scene, he had lowered the brim of his hat and started ambling around the courthouse like he was headed to the hardware store for a can of paint.

I ambled after him.

When the cowboy reached the other side of the building, he crossed one of the presidents and headed up a tree. So eager was he to put some distance between himself and his handiwork, he walked right past an old lady with a cane who was trying to put a grocery bag in the back of her Model T.

—Here you go, ma'am, I said.

—Thank you, young man.

By the time granny was climbing behind the wheel, the cowboy was half a block ahead of me. When he took a right down the alley beyond the movie theater, I actually had to run to catch up, despite the fact that running is something I generally avoid on principle.

Now, before I tell you what happened next, I think I should give you a little context by taking you back to when I was about nine and living in Lewis.

When my old man dropped me off at St. Nicholas's Home for Boys, the nun in charge was a woman of certain opinions and uncertain age named Sister Agnes. It stands to reason that a strong-minded woman who finds herself in an evangelical profession with a captive audience would be likely to avail herself of every opportunity to share her point of view. But not Sister Agnes. Like a seasoned performer, she knew how to choose her moments. She could make an unobtrusive entrance, remain at the back of the stage, wait until everyone had delivered their lines, then steal the show with five minutes in the spotlight.

Her favorite time to impart her wisdom was just before bed. Coming into the dormitory, she would quietly watch as the other sisters scurried about in their habits instructing one kid to fold his clothes, another to wash his face, and everyone to say their prayers. Then when we had all climbed under the covers, Sister Agnes would pull up a chair and deliver her lesson. As you might imagine, Sister Agnes was partial to a biblical grammar, but she spoke with such a sympathetic inflection that her words would silence the intermittent chatter and linger in our ears long after the lights were out.

One of her favorite lessons was something she referred to as the

Chains of Wrongdoing. *Boys*, she would begin in her motherly way, *in your time you shall do wrong unto others and others shall do wrong unto you. And these opposing wrongs will become your chains. The wrongs you have done unto others will be bound to you in the form of guilt, and the wrongs that others have done unto you in the form of indignation. The teachings of Jesus Christ Our Savior are there to free you from both. To free you from your guilt through atonement and from your indignation through forgiveness. Only once you have freed yourself from both of these chains may you begin to live your life with love in your heart and serenity in your step.*

At the time, I didn't understand what she was talking about. I didn't understand how your movements could be hampered by a little wrong-doing, since in my experience those who were prone to wrongdoing were always the first ones out the door. I didn't understand why when someone had done wrong unto you, you had to carry a burden on their behalf. And I certainly didn't understand what it meant to have seren-ity in your step. But as Sister Agnes also liked to say: *What wisdom the Lord does not see fit to endow us with at birth, He provides through the gift of experience.* And sure enough, as I grew older, experience began to make some sense of Sister Agnes's sermon.

Like when I first arrived at Salina.

It was the month of August, when the air was warm, the days were long, and the first crop of potatoes had to be dug from the earth. Old Testament Ackerly would have us working from dawn till dusk, such that when dinner was over, the only thing we wanted was a good night's sleep. And yet, once the lights were out, I would often find myself stewing over how I'd come to be at Salina in the first place, reviewing every bitter detail until the rooster crowed. On other nights, I would imagine being called to the warden's office, where he would solemnly deliver the news of a car crash or a hotel fire in which my old man had lost his life. And while such visions would appease for the moment, they would badger me for the rest of the night with a sense of shameful remorse. So there they were: indignation and guilt. Two contradictory forces so sure to confound, I resigned myself to the possibility I might never sleep soundly again.

But when Warden Williams took over for Ackerly and initiated his era of reform, he instituted a program of afternoon classes designed to prepare us for lives of upright citizenship. To that end, he had a civics teacher come talk about the three branches of government. He had a selectman instruct us on the scourge of Communism and the importance of every man's vote. Pretty soon, we were all wishing we could get back to the potato fields.

Then a few months ago, he arranged to have a certified public accountant explain the basics of personal finance. After describing the interplay between assets and liabilities, this CPA approached the chalkboard and in a few quick strokes demonstrated the balancing of accounts. And right then, while sitting in the back row of that hot little classroom, I finally understood what Sister Agnes had been talking about.

In the course of our lives, she had said, we may do wrong unto others and others may do wrong unto us, resulting in the aforementioned chains. But another way to express the same idea was that through our misdeeds we put ourselves in another person's debt, just as through their misdeeds they put themselves in ours. And since it's these debts—those we've incurred and those we're owed—that keep us stirring and stewing in the early hours, the only way to get a good night's sleep is to balance the accounts.

Emmett wasn't much better than me at listening in class, but he didn't need to pay heed to this particular lesson. He had learned it long before coming to Salina. He had learned it firsthand by growing up under the shadow of his father's failure. That's why he signed those foreclosure papers without a second thought. That's why he wouldn't accept the loan from Mr. Ransom or the china from the bottom of the cabinet. And that's why he was perfectly happy to take the beating.

Just like the cowboy said, Jake and Emmett had some unfinished business. Regardless of who had been provoked by who, or whom by whom, when Emmett hit the Snyder kid at the county fair, he took on a debt just as surely as his father had when he had mortgaged the family farm. And from that day forward, it hung over Emmett's head— keeping *him* up at night—until he satisfied the debt at the hands of his creditor and before the eyes of his fellow men.

But if Emmett had a debt to repay to Jake Snyder, he didn't owe a goddamn thing to the cowboy. Not a shekel, not a drachma, not one red cent.

—Hey, Tex, I called as I jogged after him. Hold up!

The cowboy turned and looked me over.

—Do I know you?

—You know me not, sir.

—Then what do you want?

I held up my hand to catch my breath before I replied.

—Back there at the courthouse, you suggested that your friend Jake had some unfinished business with my friend Emmett. For what it's worth, I think I could just as easily argue that it was Emmett who had unfinished business with Jake. But either way, whether Jake had the business with Emmett or Emmett had the business with Jake, I think we can both agree it was no business of yours.

—Buddy, I don't know what you're talking about.

I tried to be more clear.

—What I'm saying is that even though Jake may have had good reason to give Emmett a beating, and Emmett may have had good reason to take one, you had no cause for all that goading and gloating. Given time, I suspect you'll come to regret the role you played in today's events, and you'll find yourself wishing you could make amends—for your own peace of mind. But since Emmett's leaving town tomorrow, by then it'll be too late.

—You know what I suspect, said the cowboy. I suspect you can go fuck yourself.

Then he turned and began walking away. Just like that. Without even saying goodbye.

I admit, I felt a little deflated. I mean, here I was trying to help a stranger understand a burden of his own making, and he gives me the back of his shirt. It's the sort of reception that could turn you off charitable acts forever. But another of Sister Agnes's lessons was that when one is doing the work of the Lord, one should be willing to have patience. For just as surely as the righteous will meet setbacks on the road to justice, the Lord will provide them the means to prevail.

And lo and behold, what suddenly appeareth before me but the movie theater's dumpster filled to the brim with the previous night's trash. And poking out from among the Coca-Cola bottles and popcorn boxes was a two-foot length of two-by-four.

—Hey! I called once more while skipping down the alley. Hold on a second!

The cowboy turned on his heels and from the look on his face I could tell that he had something priceless to say, something that was likely to bring smiles to the faces of all the boys at the bar. But I guess we'll never know, because I hit him before he could speak.

The blow was a good crack along the left side of his head. His hat, which went lofting in the air, did a somersault before alighting on the other side of the alley. He dropped right where he'd been standing like a marionette whose strings have been cut.

Now, I had never hit anybody in my life. And to be perfectly honest, my first impression was how much it hurt. Shifting the two-by-four to my left hand, I looked at my right palm, where two bright-red lines had been left behind by the edges of the wood. Tossing it on the ground, I rubbed my palms together to take out the sting. Then I leaned over the cowboy to get a better look. His legs were folded under him and his left ear was split down the middle, but he was still conscious. Or conscious enough.

—Can you hear me, Tex? I asked.

Then I spoke a little louder to make sure he could.

—Consider your debt repaid in full.

As he looked back at me, his eyelashes fluttered for a moment. But then he gave a little smile, and I could tell from the way his eyelids closed that he was going to sleep like a baby.

Walking out of the alley, I became conscious not simply of a welling sense of moral satisfaction, but that my footfall felt a little lighter and my stride a little jauntier.

Well, what do you know, I thought to myself with a smile. There's serenity in my step!

And it must have showed. Because when I emerged from the alley and said howdy to the two old men passing by, they both said howdy back. And though on the way into town, ten cars had passed me before the mechanic picked me up, on the way back to the Watsons', the first car that came along pulled over to offer me a ride.

Woolly

THE FUNNY THING ABOUT A STORY, thought Woolly—while Emmett was in town, and Duchess was on a walk, and Billy was reading aloud from his big red book—the funny thing about a story is that it can be told in all sorts of lengths.

The first time Woolly heard *The Count of Monte Cristo*, he must have been younger than Billy. His family was spending the summer at the camp in the Adirondacks, and every night his sister Sarah would read him a chapter before he went to bed. But what his sister was reading from was the original book by Alexander Dumas, which was a thousand pages long.

The thing about hearing a story like *The Count of Monte Cristo* from the one-thousand-page version is that whenever you sense an exciting part is coming, you have to wait and wait and wait for it to actually arrive. In fact, sometimes you have to wait so long for it to arrive you forget that it's coming altogether and let yourself drift off to sleep. But in Billy's big red book, Professor Abernathe had chosen to tell the entire story over the course of eight pages. So in his version, when you sensed an exciting part was coming, it arrived lickety-split.

Like the part that Billy was reading now—the part when Edmond Dantès, convicted of a crime he didn't commit, is carted off to spend the rest of his life in the dreaded Château d'If. Even as he is being led in chains through the prison's formidable gates, you just know that Dantès is bound to escape. But in Mr. Dumas's telling, before he regains his freedom you have to listen to so many sentences spread across so many chapters that it begins to feel like *you* are the one who is in the Château d'If! Not so with Professor Abernathe. In his telling, the hero's arrival at the prison, his eight years of solitude, his friendship with the Abbé Faria, and his miraculous escape all occur on the very same page.

Woolly pointed at the solitary cloud that was passing overhead.

—That's what I imagine the Château d'If looked like.

Carefully marking his place with his finger, Billy looked up to where Woolly was pointing and readily agreed.

—With its straight rock walls.

—And the watchtower in the middle.

Woolly and Billy both smiled to see it, but then Billy's expression grew rather more serious.

—Can I ask you a question, Woolly?

—Of course, of course.

—Was it hard to be at Salina?

As Woolly considered the question, far overhead the Château d'If transformed itself into an ocean liner—with a giant smokestack where the watchtower once had been.

—No, said Woolly, it wasn't so hard, Billy. Certainly not like the Château d'If was for Edmond Dantès. It's just that . . . It's just that every day at Salina was an every-day day.

—What's an every-day day, Woolly?

Woolly took another moment to consider.

—When we were at Salina, every day we would get up at the same time and get dressed in the same clothes. Every day we had breakfast at the same table with the same people. And every day we did the same work in the same fields before going to sleep at the same hour in the same beds.

Though Billy was just a boy, or maybe because he was just a boy, he seemed to understand that while there is nothing wrong with waking up or getting dressed or having breakfast, per se, there is something fundamentally disconcerting about doing these things in the exact same fashion day in and day out, especially in the one-thousand-page version of one's own life.

After nodding, Billy found his place and began to read again.

What Woolly did not have the heart to tell Billy was that while this was unquestionably the way of life at Salina, it was also the way of life in many other places. It was certainly the way of life at boarding school. And not simply at St. George's, where Woolly had most recently been enrolled. At all three boarding schools that Woolly had attended, every day they would wake up at the same time, get dressed in the same clothes, and have breakfast at the same table with the same people before heading off to attend the same classes in the same classrooms.

Woolly had often wondered about that. Why did the heads of boarding schools choose to make every day an every-day day? After some reflection, he came to suspect that they did so because it made things easier to manage. By turning every day into an every-day day, the cook would always know when to cook breakfast, the history teacher when to teach history, and the hall monitor when to monitor the halls.

But then Woolly had an epiphany.

It was in the first semester of his second junior year (the one at St. Mark's). On his way from physics down to the gymnasium, he happened to notice the dean of students getting out of a taxi in front of the schoolhouse. As soon as he saw the taxi, it occurred to Woolly what a pleasant surprise it would be were he to pay a visit to his sister, who had recently bought a big white house in Hastings-on-Hudson. So, jumping in the back of the cab, Woolly gave the address.

You mean in New York? the driver asked in surprise.

I mean in New York! Woolly confirmed, and off they went.

When he arrived a few hours later, Woolly found his sister in the kitchen on the verge of peeling a potato.

Hallo, Sis!

Were Woolly to pay a surprise visit to any other member of his family, they would probably have greeted him with an absolute slew of whos, whys, and whats (especially when he needed 150 dollars for the taxi driver, who was waiting outside). But after paying the driver, Sarah just put the kettle on the stove, some cookies on a plate, and the two of them had a grand old time—sitting at her table and discussing all the various topics that happened to pop into their heads.

But after an hour or so, Woolly's brother-in-law, "Dennis," walked through the kitchen door. Woolly's sister was seven years older than Woolly, and "Dennis" was seven years older than Sarah, so mathematically speaking "Dennis" had been thirty-two at the time. But "Dennis" was also seven years older than himself, which made him almost forty in spirit. That is why, no doubt, he was already a vice president at J.P. Morgan & Sons & Co.

When "Dennis" discovered Woolly at the kitchen table, he was a little upset on the grounds that Woolly was supposed to be someplace else. But he was even more upset when he discovered the half-peeled potato on the counter.

When is dinner? he asked Sarah.

I'm afraid I haven't started preparing it yet.

But it's half past seven.

Oh, for heaven's sake, Dennis.

For a moment, "Dennis" looked at Sarah in disbelief, then he turned to Woolly and asked if he could speak to Sarah in private.

In Woolly's experience, when someone asks if they can speak to someone else in private, it is difficult to know what to do with yourself. For one thing, they generally don't tell you how long they're going to be, so it's hard to know how deeply you should involve yourself in some new endeavor. Should you take the opportunity to visit the washroom? Or start a jigsaw puzzle that depicts a sailboat race with fifty spinnakers? And how *far* should you go? You certainly need to go far enough so that you can't hear them talking. That was the whole point of their asking you to leave in the first place. But it often sounds like they may want you to come back a bit later, so you need to be close enough to hear them when they call.

Doing his best to split the hair down the muddle, Woolly went into the living room, where he discovered an unplayed piano and some unread books and an unwound grandfather clock—which, come to think of it, was very aptly named since it once had belonged to their grandfather! But as it turned out, given how upset "Dennis" had become, the living room wasn't far enough away, because Woolly could hear every word.

You were the one who wanted to move out of the city, "Dennis" was saying. *But I'm the one who has to get up at the crack of dawn in order to catch the 6:42 so that I can be at the bank in time for the investment committee meeting at 8:00. For most of the next ten hours, while you're here doing God knows what, I am working like a dog. Then, if I run to Grand Central and I'm lucky enough to catch the 6:14, I just might make it home by half past seven. After a day like that, is it really so much to ask that you have dinner waiting on the table?*

That's the moment the epiphany came. Standing there before his grandfather's clock listening to his brother-in-law, it suddenly occurred to Woolly that maybe, just maybe, St. George's and St. Mark's and St. Paul's organized every day to be an every-day day not because it made things easier to manage, but because it was the best possible means by which to prepare the fine young men in their care to catch the 6:42 so that they would always be on time for their meetings at 8:00.

At the very moment that Woolly concluded the recollection of his epiphany, Billy reached the point in the story when Edmond Dantès, having successfully escaped from prison, was standing in the secret cave on the isle of Monte Cristo before a magnificent pile of diamonds, pearls, rubies, and gold.

—You know what would be magnificent, Billy? You know what would be absotively magnificent?

Marking his place, Billy looked up from his book.

—What, Woolly? What would be absotively magnificent?

—A one-of-a-kind kind of day.

Sally

AT LAST WEEK'S SUNDAY SERVICE, Reverend Pike read a parable from the Gospels in which Jesus and His disciples, having arrived in a village, are invited by a woman into her home. Having made them all comfortable, this woman, Martha, retreats into her kitchen to fix them something to eat. And all the while she's cooking and generally seeing to everyone's needs by filling empty glasses and getting second helpings, her sister, Mary, is sitting at Jesus's feet.

Eventually, Martha has had enough and she lets her feelings be known. *Lord*, she says, *can't you see that my idler of a sister has left me to do all the work? Why don't you tell her to lend me a hand?* Or something to that effect. And Jesus, He replies: *Martha, you are troubled by too many things when only one thing is needful. And it is Mary who has chosen the better way.*

Well, I'm sorry. But if ever you needed proof that the Bible was written by a man, there you have it.

I am a good Christian. I believe in God, the Father almighty, creator of heaven and earth. I believe that Jesus Christ, His only begotten Son, was born of the Virgin Mary and suffered under Pontius Pilate, was crucified, died, was buried, and on the third day rose again. I believe that having ascended to heaven, He will come again to judge the quick and the dead. I believe that Noah built an ark and herded every manner of living thing up the gangplank two by two before it rained for forty days and forty nights. I am even willing to believe that Moses was spoken to by a burning bush. But I am *not* willing to believe that Jesus

Christ Our Savior—who at the drop of a hat would heal a leper or restore sight to the blind—would turn his back on a woman who was taking care of a household.

So I don't blame Him.

Whom I blame is Matthew, Mark, Luke, and John, and every other man who's served as priest or preacher since.

From a man's point of view, the one thing that's *needful* is that you sit at his feet and listen to what he has to say, no matter how long it takes for him to say it, or how often he's said it before. By his figuring, you have plenty of time for sitting and listening because a meal is something that makes itself. The manna, it falls from heaven, and with a snap of the fingers, the water can be turned into wine. Any woman who's gone to the trouble of baking an apple pie can tell you that's how a man sees the world.

To bake an apple pie, you've first got to make the dough. You've got to cut the butter into the flour, gather it with a beaten egg and a few tablespoons of ice water, let it bind overnight. The next day, you've got to peel and core the apples, cut them into wedges, and toss them with cinnamon sugar. You've got to roll out the crust and assemble the pie. Then you bake it at 425° for fifteen minutes and 350° for another forty-five. Finally, when supper's over, you carefully plate a slice and set it on the table where, in midsentence, a man will fork half of it into his mouth and swallow without chewing, so that he can get right back to saying what he was saying without the chance of being interrupted.

And strawberry preserves? Don't you get me started on strawberry preserves!

As young Billy pointed out so rightly, making preserves is a *time-consuming* venture. Just picking the berries takes you half a day. Then you have to wash and stem the fruit. You have to sterilize the lids and jars. Once you combine the ingredients, you have to set them on simmer and watch them like a hawk, never letting yourself stray more than a few feet from the stove to make sure they don't overcook. When they're ready, you pour the preserves, seal the jars, and lug them into the pantry one tray at a time. Only then can you start the process of cleaning up, which is a job in itself.

And yes, as Duchess pointed out, the canning of preserves is a little *old-fashioned*, hearkening back to the era of root cellars and wagon trains. I suppose the very word *preserves* is bygone when compared to the blunt precision of *jam*.

And as Emmett pointed out, it is, above all else, *unnecessary*. Thanks to Mr. Smucker, at the grocery there are fifteen varieties of jam selling for nineteen cents a jar, season in and season out. In fact, jam has become so readily available, you can practically buy it at the hardware store.

So yes, the making of strawberry preserves is time-consuming, old-fashioned, and unnecessary.

Then why, you might ask, do I bother to do it?

I do it *because* it's time-consuming.

Whoever said that something worthwhile shouldn't take time? It took months for the Pilgrims to sail to Plymouth Rock. It took years for George Washington to win the Revolutionary War. And it took decades for the pioneers to conquer the West.

Time is that which God uses to separate the idle from the industrious. For time is a mountain and upon seeing its steep incline, the idle will lie down among the lilies of the field and hope that someone passes by with a pitcher of lemonade. What the worthy endeavor requires is planning, effort, attentiveness, and the willingness to clean up.

I do it *because* it's old-fashioned.

Just because something's new doesn't mean it's better; and often enough, it means it's worse.

Saying *please* and *thank you* is plenty old-fashioned. Getting married and raising children is old-fashioned. Traditions, the very means by which we come to know who we are, are nothing if not old-fashioned.

I make preserves in the manner that was taught to me by my mother, God rest her soul. She made preserves in the manner that was taught to her by her mother, and Grandma made preserves in the manner that was taught to her by hers. And so on, and so forth, back through the ages all the way to Eve. Or, at least as far as Martha.

And I do it *because* it's unnecessary.

For what is kindness but the performance of an act that is both beneficial to another and unrequired? There is no kindness in paying a bill. There is no kindness in getting up at dawn to slop the pigs, or milk the cows, or gather the eggs from the henhouse. For that matter, there is no kindness in making dinner, or in cleaning the kitchen after your father heads upstairs without so much as a word of thanks.

There is no kindness in latching the doors and turning out the lights, or in picking up the clothes from the bathroom floor in order to put them in the hamper. There is no kindness in taking care of a household because your only sister had the good sense to get herself married and move to Pensacola.

Nope, I said to myself while climbing into bed and switching off the light, there is no kindness in any of that.

For kindness begins where necessity ends.

Duchess

HAVING COME UPSTAIRS AFTER SUPPER, I was about to flop down on Emmett's bed when I noticed the smoothness of the covers. After freezing in place for a moment, I leaned over the mattress to get a closer look.

There was no question about it. She had remade it.

I thought I'd done a pretty good job, if I do say so myself. But Sally had done a better one. There wasn't a ripple on the surface. And where the sheet gets folded at the top of the blanket, there was a four-inch-high rectangle of white running from one edge of the bed to the other as if she had measured it with a ruler. While at the base, she had tucked in the covers so tightly that you could see the corners of the mattress through the surface of the blanket, the way you can see Jane Russell through the surface of her sweater.

It was such a thing of beauty, I didn't want to disturb it until I was ready to go to bed. So I sat on the floor, leaned against the wall, and gave some thought to the Watson brothers, as I waited for everyone else to fall asleep.

Earlier that day when I had gotten back to the house, Woolly and Billy were still lying out on the grass.

—How was your walk? asked Woolly.

—Rejuvenating, I replied. What have you two been up to?

—Billy has been reading me some of the stories from Professor Abernathe's book.

—Sorry I missed that. Which ones?

Billy was in the middle of running down the list when Emmett pulled into the drive.

Speaking of stories, I thought to myself . . .

In another moment, Emmett was going to emerge from his car a little worse for wear. He was certainly going to have a fat lip and some bruises; he might even have the beginnings of a shiner. The question was how was he going to explain them? Did he trip on a crack in the sidewalk? Did he tumble down a set of stairs?

In my experience, the best explanations make use of the unexpected. Like: *I was crossing the lawn of the courthouse admiring the sight of a whip-poor-will perched on the branch of a tree when a football hit me in the face.* With an explanation like that, your listener is so focused on the whip-poor-will up in the tree, they never see the football coming.

But when Emmett walked over and a wide-eyed Billy asked what had happened, Emmett said that he'd run into Jake Snyder while in town, and Jake had hit him. Just like that.

I turned to Billy, expecting an expression of shock or maybe outrage, but he was nodding his head and looking thoughtful.

—Did you hit him back? he asked after a moment.

—No, said Emmett. Instead, I counted to ten.

Then Billy smiled at Emmett, and Emmett smiled right back.

Truly, Horatio, there are more things in heaven and Earth, than are dreamt of in your philosophy.

—·—

Shortly after midnight, I poked my head into Woolly's room. From the sound of his breathing, I could tell that he was lost in his dreams. I crossed my fingers that he hadn't taken too much of his medicine before going to bed since I was going to have to roust him soon enough.

The Watson brothers were sound asleep too, Emmett flat on his back and Billy curled on his side. In the moonlight I could see the kid's book on the foot of the bed. If he happened to stretch his legs, it might drop to the floor, so I moved it to the spot on the bureau where his mother's picture should have been.

I found Emmett's pants hanging over the back of a chair—with all of its pockets empty. Tiptoeing around the bed, I squatted at the bed-side table. The drawer wasn't more than a foot from Emmett's face, so I had to ease it open inch by inch. But the keys weren't there either.

—Harrumph, I said to myself.

I had already looked for them in the car and in the kitchen before coming upstairs. Where in the hell could he have put them?

As I was mulling this over, the beam from a set of headlights swept across the room as a vehicle pulled into the Watsons' drive and rolled to a stop.

Quietly, I headed down the hall and paused at the top of the stairs. Outside I heard the door of the vehicle open. After a moment, there were footsteps on and off the porch, then the door closed and the vehicle drove away.

When I was sure that no one had woken, I went down into the kitchen, opened the screen door, and stepped out onto the porch. In the distance I could see the lights of the vehicle headed back up the road. It took me a moment to notice the shoebox at my feet with big black letters scrawled across the top.

I may be no scholar, but I know my own name when I see it, even by the light of the moon. Getting down on my haunches, I gently lifted the lid, wondering what in God's name could be inside.

—Well, I'll be damned.

EIGHT

—.—

Emmett

WHEN THEY PULLED OUT of the driveway at five thirty in the morning, Emmett was in good spirits. The night before, with the help of Billy's map, he had laid out an itinerary. The route from Morgen to San Francisco was a little over fifteen hundred miles. If they averaged forty miles an hour for ten hours a day—leaving time enough to eat and sleep—they could make the trip in four days.

Of course there was plenty to see between Morgen and San Francisco. As their mother's postcards attested, there were motor courts and monuments, rodeos and parks. If you were willing to drive out of your way, there were Mount Rushmore, Old Faithful, and the Grand Canyon. But Emmett didn't want to waste time or money on the journey west. The sooner they got to California, the sooner he could get to work; and the more money they had in hand when they got there, the better a house they would be able to buy. If they began frittering away what little they had while in transit, they'd have to settle for buying a marginally worse house in a marginally worse neighborhood, which, when the time came to sell, would result in a marginally worse profit. As far as Emmett was concerned, the faster they crossed the country the better.

Emmett's primary worry when he'd gone to bed had been that he wouldn't be able to rouse the others, that he'd waste the first hours of daylight getting them up and out the door. But he needn't have worried. When he rose at five, Duchess was already in the shower and he could hear Woolly humming down the hall. Billy had gone so far as to sleep in his clothes so he wouldn't have to get dressed when he woke. By the time Emmett took his place behind the wheel and retrieved his keys from above the visor, Duchess was already in the passenger seat and Billy was sitting beside Woolly in the back with his map in his lap. And when, shortly before dawn, they turned out of the driveway, not one of them cast a backward glance.

Maybe they all had reasons for wanting to make an early start, thought Emmett. Maybe they all were ready to be someplace else.

As Duchess was sitting in front, Billy asked if he wanted to hold the map. When Duchess declined on the grounds that reading in cars made him queasy, Emmett felt a little relieved, recognizing that Duchess didn't always pay the closest attention to details, while Billy was practically born to navigate. Not only did he have his compass and pencils at the ready, he had a ruler so he could calculate mileage off the one-inch scale. But when Emmett signaled a right-hand turn onto Route 34, he found himself wishing that Duchess had taken on the job, after all.

—You don't need to switch on your signal yet, said Billy. We need to go straight for a little longer.

—I'm turning onto Route 34, Emmett explained, because that's the fastest way to Omaha.

—But the Lincoln Highway goes to Omaha.

Emmett pulled onto the shoulder and looked back at his brother.

—It does, Billy. But it takes us a little out of the way.

—A little out of the way of what? asked Duchess with a smile.

—A little out of the way of where we're going, said Emmett.

Duchess looked into the back seat.

—Just how far is it to the Lincoln Highway, Billy?

Billy, who already had his ruler on the map, said it was seventeen and a half miles.

Woolly, who had been quietly looking at the scenery, turned to Billy with an awakened curiosity.

—What's the Lincoln Highway, Billy? Is it a special highway?

—It was the first highway to cross America.

—The first highway to cross America, repeated Woolly in awe.

—Come on, Emmett, prodded Duchess. What's seventeen and a half miles?

It's seventeen and a half miles, Emmett wanted to reply, on top of the hundred and thirty that we're already going out of our way in order to take you to Omaha. But at the same time, Emmett knew that Duchess was right. The added distance wasn't much to speak of, especially given how disappointed Billy would be if he insisted on taking Route 34.

—All right, he said. We'll go by way of the Lincoln Highway.

As he pulled back onto the road, he could almost hear his brother nodding in affirmation that this was a good idea.

For the next seventeen and a half miles, no one said a word. But when Emmett took the right at Central City, Billy looked up from his map in excitement.

—This is it, he said. This is the Lincoln Highway.

Billy began leaning forward to see what was coming, then looking over his shoulder to see what they'd passed. Central City may only have been a city in name, but having dreamed for months about the journey to California, Billy was taking satisfaction from the handful of restaurants and motels, pleased to find they were not unlike the ones on their mother's postcards. That he was headed in the wrong direction didn't seem to make much difference.

Woolly was sharing in Billy's excitement, looking at the roadside services with new appreciation.

—So this road stretches from coast to coast?

—It stretches almost from coast to coast, corrected Billy. It goes from New York City to San Francisco.

—That sounds pretty coast-to-coast, said Duchess.

—Except that the Lincoln Highway doesn't begin or end at the water. It begins in Times Square and ends at the Palace of the Legion of Honor.

—Is it named for *Abraham* Lincoln? Woolly asked.

—It is, said Billy. And there are statues of him all along the way.

—All along the way?

—Boy Scout troops raised money to commission them.

—There's a bust of Abraham Lincoln on my great-grandfather's desk, said Woolly with a smile. He was a great admirer of President Lincoln.

—How long has this highway been around? asked Duchess.

—It was invented by Mr. Carl G. Fisher in 1912.

—Invented?

—Yes, said Billy. Invented. He believed the American people should be able to drive from one end of the country to the other. He built the first sections in 1913, with the help of donations.

—People *gave* him money to build it? asked Duchess in disbelief.

Billy nodded in earnest.

—Including Thomas Edison and Teddy Roosevelt.

—Teddy Roosevelt! exclaimed Duchess.

—Bully, said Woolly.

As they made their way eastward—with Billy dutifully naming every town they passed—Emmett took satisfaction that at least they were making good time.

Yes, the trip to Omaha was going to take them out of their way, but having gotten an early start, Emmett figured they could drop Duchess and Woolly at the bus station, turn the car around, and easily make Ogallala before dark. Maybe they'd even make it as far as Cheyenne. After all, at this point in June they would have eighteen hours of light. As a matter of fact, thought Emmett, if they were willing to drive twelve hours a day and averaged fifty miles an hour, they could make the whole trip in under three days.

But that's when Billy pointed to a water tower in the distance with the name Lewis painted across it.

—Look, Duchess. It's Lewis. Isn't that the city where you lived?

—You lived in Nebraska? Emmett asked, looking at Duchess.

—For a couple of years when I was a kid, Duchess confirmed.

Then he sat up a little in his seat and began looking around with heightened interest.

—Hey, he said to Emmett after a moment. Can we swing by? I'd love to get a look at the place. You know, for old times' sake.

—Duchess . . .

—Oh, come on. Please? I know you said you wanted to be in Omaha by eight, but it seems like we've been making pretty good time.

—We're twelve minutes ahead of schedule, said Billy after looking at his surplus watch.

—There. See?

—All right, said Emmett. We can swing by. But just for a look.

—That's all I'm asking.

When they reached the edge of the city, Duchess took over the navigation, nodding at the passing landmarks.

—Yes. Yes. Yes. There! Take that left by the fire station.

Emmett took the left, which led into a residential neighborhood with fine houses on nicely groomed lots. After a few miles, they passed a high-steepled church and a park.

—You take that next right, said Duchess.

The right led them onto a wide, curving road interspersed with trees.

—Pull over up there.

Emmett pulled over.

They were at the bottom of a grassy hill on the top of which was a large stone building. Three stories high with turrets on either end, it looked like a manor.

—Was this your house? asked Billy.

—No, said Duchess with a laugh. It's a school of sorts.

—A boarding school? asked Woolly.

—More or less.

For a moment they all admired its grandeur, then Duchess turned to Emmett.

—Can I go in?

—For what?

—To say hi.

—Duchess, it's six thirty in the morning.

—If no one's up, I'll leave a note. They'll get a kick out of it.

—A note for your teachers? asked Billy.

—Exactly. A note for my teachers. What do you say, Emmett. It'll only take a few minutes. Five minutes tops.

Emmett glanced at the clock in the dash.

—All right, he said. Five minutes.

Grabbing the book bag at his feet, Duchess climbed out of the car and jogged up the hill toward the building.

In the back seat, Billy began explaining to Woolly why he and Emmett needed to be in San Francisco by the Fourth of July.

Turning off the engine, Emmett stared through the windshield, wishing he had a cigarette.

Duchess's five minutes came and went.

Then another five.

Shaking his head, Emmett chastised himself for letting Duchess go into the building. No one drops in anywhere for five minutes, whatever the time of day. Certainly no one who liked to talk as much as Duchess.

Emmett got out of the car and walked around to the passenger side. Leaning against the door, he looked up at the school, noting that it was made from the same red limestone that they had used to build the courthouse in Morgen. The stone probably came from one of the quarries in Cass County. In the late 1800s, it had been used to build city halls, libraries, and courthouses in every town for two hundred miles. Some of the buildings were so similar in appearance that when you went from one town to the next it felt like you hadn't gone anywhere at all.

Even so, there was something that didn't seem quite right about this building. It took Emmett a few minutes to realize that what was odd was that there wasn't a prominent entrance. Whether it had originally been designed as a manor house or school, a building this grand would have had a fitting approach. There would have been a tree-lined drive leading up to an impressive front door.

It occurred to Emmett that they must be parked at the back of the building. But why hadn't Duchess directed them to drive up to the front?

And why had he taken the book bag?

—I'll be right back, he said to Billy and Woolly.

—Okay, they replied, without looking up from Billy's map.

Climbing the hill, Emmett made his way toward a door that was in the center of the building. As he walked, he was feeling a growing sense of irritation, almost looking forward to the dressing down he would be giving Duchess once he found him. Telling him, in no uncertain terms, that they didn't have time for this sort of nonsense. That his uninvited appearance was already an imposition and that the trip to Omaha was taking them two and a half hours out of their way. Five hours when you accounted for there and back. But these thoughts went out of Emmett's head as soon as he saw the broken pane—the one closest to the doorknob. Easing the door open, Emmett stepped inside, shards of glass crunching under the soles of his boots.

Emmett found himself in a large kitchen with two metal sinks, a ten-burner stove, and a walk-in refrigerator. Like most institutional kitchens, it had been put in order the night before—its counters cleared, its cabinets closed, and all of its pots hung on their hooks.

The only sign of disorder, other than the broken glass, was in a pantry area at the other side of the kitchen, where several drawers had been pulled open and spoons were scattered on the floor.

Passing through a swinging door Emmett entered a paneled dining room with six long tables like you'd expect to find in a monastery. Adding to the religious aura was a large stained-glass window that was casting patterns of yellow, red, and blue on the opposite wall. The window depicted the moment that Jesus, risen from the dead, displayed the wounds in His hands—only, in this depiction, the amazed disciples were accompanied by children.

Exiting the dining room's main doors, Emmett stepped into a grand entrance hall. To his left was the impressive front door that he'd expected, while to his right was a staircase made of the same polished oak. Under different circumstances, Emmett would have liked to linger in order to study the carvings on the door panels and the balusters of the staircase, but even as he was noting the quality of the workmanship, he heard sounds of commotion coming from somewhere overhead.

Taking the steps two at a time, Emmett passed over an additional scattering of spoons. On the second-floor landing, hallways led in opposite directions, but from the one on the right came the unmistakable sound of children in turmoil. So that's the way he went.

The first door Emmett came to opened on a dormitory. While the beds were arranged in two perfect rows, their linens were in disarray and they were empty. The next door led to a second dormitory with two more rows of beds and more linens in disarray. But in this room, sixty boys in blue pajamas were clustered in six raucous groups at the center of each of which was a jar of strawberry preserves.

In some of the groups, the boys were dutifully taking turns, while in others they were fighting for access, stabbing their spoons into the jam and transferring the contents into their mouths as quickly as possible, so they could get another crack at the jar before it was empty.

For the first time, it occurred to Emmett that this wasn't a boarding school. It was an orphanage.

As Emmett was taking in the disorder, a ten-year-old boy with glasses who had noticed him, tugged at the sleeve of one of the older boys. Looking up at Emmett, the older boy signaled a peer. Without exchanging a word, the two advanced shoulder to shoulder in order to place themselves between Emmett and the others.

Emmett raised both of his hands in peace.

—I'm not here to bother you. I'm just looking for my friend. The one who brought the jam.

The two older boys stared at Emmett in silence, but the boy with the glasses pointed in the direction of the hallway.

—He went the way he came.

Emmett left the room and doubled back to the landing. He was about to head down the stairs when from the opposite hallway he heard the muted sound of a woman shouting, followed by the pounding of a fist on wood. Emmett paused, then proceeded to the hallway, where he found two doors with tilted chairs tucked under the knobs. The shouting and pounding were coming from behind the first one.

—Open this door right this minute!

When Emmett removed the chair and opened the door, a woman in her forties wearing a long white nightgown nearly fell into the hallway. Behind her, Emmett could see another woman sitting on a bed weeping.

—How dare you! the pounder shouted, once she had regained her footing.

Emmett ignored her and went to the second door to remove the second chair. Inside this room was a third woman kneeling beside her bed in prayer and an older woman sitting peacefully in a high-back chair smoking a cigarette.

—Ah! she said when she saw Emmett. How good of you to open the door. Come in, come in.

As the older woman tamped out her cigarette in the ashtray that was in her lap, Emmett took a step forward uncertainly. But even as he did so, the sister from the first room came in behind him.

—How dare you! she shouted again.

—Sister Berenice, said the older woman. Why are you raising your voice at this young man? Can't you see that he is our liberator?

The weeping sister now came into the room still in tears, and the older woman turned to address the one who was kneeling.

—Compassion before prayers, Sister Ellen.

—Yes, Sister Agnes.

Sister Ellen rose from her place beside the bed and took the weeping sister in her arms, saying, *Hush hush hush*, while Sister Agnes turned her attention back to Emmett.

—What is your name, young man?

—Emmett Watson.

—Well, Emmett Watson, perhaps you can illuminate us as to what has been transpiring here at St. Nicholas's this morning.

Emmett felt a strong inclination to turn and walk out the door, but his inclination to answer Sister Agnes was stronger.

—I was driving a friend to the bus station in Omaha and he asked me to stop. He said he used to live here. . . .

All four sisters were looking at Emmett keenly now, the crying sister no longer crying and the hushing sister no longer hushing. The shouting sister was no longer shouting, but she took a threatening step toward Emmett.

—*Who* used to live here?

—His name is Duchess. . . .

—Ha! she exclaimed, turning to Sister Agnes. Didn't I tell you we hadn't seen the last of him! Didn't I say that he would return some day to perpetrate some final act of mischief!

Ignoring Sister Berenice, Sister Agnes looked toward Emmett with an expression of gentle curiosity.

—But tell me, Emmett, why did Daniel lock us in our rooms? To what end?

Emmett hesitated.

—Well?! demanded Sister Berenice.

Shaking his head, Emmett gestured in the direction of the dormitories.

—As best as I can tell, he got me to stop so that he could bring the boys some jars of strawberry jam.

Sister Agnes let out a sigh of satisfaction.

—There. You see, Sister Berenice? What our little Daniel has returned to perpetrate is an act of charity.

Whatever Duchess was perpetrating, thought Emmett, this little diversion had already set them back thirty minutes; and he sensed that if he hesitated now, they might be stuck here for hours.

—Well then, he said as he backed toward the door, if everything's all right . . .

—No, wait, said Sister Agnes, extending her hand.

Once in the hallway, Emmett moved quickly to the landing. With the voices of the sisters rising behind him, he dashed down the staircase, back through the dining room, and out the kitchen door, feeling a general sense of relief.

He was halfway down the hillside before he noticed that Billy was sitting on the grass with his backpack at his side and his big red book in his lap—while Duchess, Woolly, and the Studebaker were nowhere to be seen.

—Where's the car? Emmett said breathlessly, when he reached his brother.

Billy looked up from his book.

—Duchess and Woolly borrowed it. But they're going to bring it back.

—Bring it back after what?

—After they go to New York.

For a moment Emmett stared at his brother, at once dumbfounded and irate.

Sensing that something was wrong, Billy offered his assurance.

—Don't worry, he said. Duchess promised they'd be back by the eighteenth of June, leaving us plenty of time to get to San Francisco by the Fourth of July.

Before Emmett could respond, Billy was pointing at something behind him.

—Look, he said.

Turning, Emmett saw the figure of Sister Agnes descending the hill, the hem of her long black habit billowing behind her as if she were floating on air.

—·—

—You mean the Studebaker?

Emmett was standing alone in Sister Agnes's office talking to Sally on the phone.

—Yes, he said. The Studebaker.

—And Duchess took it?

—Yes.

There was silence on the other end of the line.

—I don't understand, she said. Took it where?

—To New York.

—New York, New York?

—Yes. New York, New York.

. . .

—And you're in Lewis.

—Nearly.

—I thought you were going to California. Why are you nearly in Lewis? And why is Duchess on his way to New York?

Emmett was beginning to regret having called Sally. But what choice had he had?

—Look, Sally, none of that matters right now. What matters is that I've got to get my car back. I called the depot in Lewis and apparently an eastbound train stops there later today. If I catch it, I can beat Duchess to New York, retrieve the car, and be back in Nebraska by Friday. The reason I'm calling is that in the meantime I need someone to take care of Billy.

—Then why didn't you say so.

After giving Sally directions and hanging up Sister Agnes's phone, Emmett looked out the window and found himself thinking of the day that he'd been sentenced.

Before heading into the courthouse with his father, Emmett had taken his brother aside to explain that he had waived his right to a trial. He explained that while he had intended Jimmy no serious harm, he had let his anger get the best of him, and he was ready to accept the consequences for his actions.

While Emmett was explaining this, Billy didn't shake his head in disagreement or argue that Emmett was making a mistake. He seemed to understand that what Emmett was doing was the right thing to do. But if Emmett was going to plead guilty without a hearing, then Billy wanted him to promise one thing.

—What's that, Billy?

—Promise me that whenever you feel like hitting someone in anger, first you'll count to ten.

And not only had Emmett promised to do so, they had shaken on it.

Nonetheless, Emmett suspected that if Duchess were there right now, ten might not be a high-enough number to do the trick.

—·—

By the time Emmett entered the dining hall, it was filled with the clamor of sixty boys talking all at once. Any dining hall crowded with boys was likely to be loud, but Emmett guessed this one was louder than usual as they relived the events of the morning: the sudden appearance of a mysterious confederate who delivered jars of jam after locking the sisters in their rooms. From his time in Salina, Emmett knew that the boys weren't simply reliving the events in service of their excitement. They were reliving the events in order to establish them in lore—to settle upon all the key particulars of this story that was sure to be told in the halls of the orphanage for decades to come.

Emmett found Billy and Sister Agnes sitting beside each other in the middle of one of the long monastic tables. A half-eaten plate of French toast had been pushed aside to make room for Billy's big red book.

—I should have thought, Sister Agnes was saying as she laid a finger on a page, that your Professor Abernathe would have included Jesus in place of Jason. For surely He was one of the most intrepid travelers of all. Don't you agree, William? Ah! Here is your brother!

Emmett took the chair opposite Sister Agnes since the chair opposite Billy was occupied by his backpack.

—Can we offer you some French toast, Emmett? Or perhaps some coffee and eggs?

—No, thank you, sister. I'm fine.

She gestured to the backpack.

—I don't think you've had the opportunity to tell me where you two were headed when you chanced into our company.

Chanced into our company, thought Emmett with a frown.

—We were just taking Duchess—or Daniel—and another friend to the bus station in Omaha.

—Ah, yes, said Sister Agnes. I think you did mention that.

—But the trip to the station was just a detour, said Billy. We are actually on our way to California.

—California! exclaimed Sister Agnes, looking at Billy. How exciting. And why are you headed to California?

So Billy explained to Sister Agnes about their mother leaving home when they were young, and their father dying of cancer, and the post-cards in the box in the bureau—the ones their mother had mailed from nine different stops along the Lincoln Highway on her way to San Francisco.

—And that's where we're going to find her, concluded Billy.

—Well, said Sister Agnes with a smile, that does sound like an adventure.

I don't know about an adventure, said Emmett. The reality is that the bank foreclosed on the farm. We needed to make a fresh start and it seemed sensible to do so in a place where I can find work.

—Yes, of course, said Sister Agnes in a more measured manner.

She studied Emmett for a moment, then looked at Billy.

—Are you finished with your breakfast, Billy? Why don't you clear your things. The kitchen is right over there.

Sister Agnes and Emmett watched as Billy placed his silverware and glass on his plate and carried them carefully away. Then she turned her attention back to Emmett.

—Is something wrong?

Emmett was a little surprised by the question.

—What do you mean?

—A moment ago, you seemed a little put out when I echoed your brother's enthusiasm over your journey west.

—I suppose I'd rather you hadn't encouraged him.

—And why is that?

—We haven't heard from our mother in eight years and have no idea where she is. As you've probably sensed, my brother has a strong imagination. So when possible, I try to help him steer clear of disappointments—rather than heap on cause for more.

As Sister Agnes studied Emmett, he could feel himself shifting in his chair.

Emmett had never liked ministry. Half the time it seemed like a preacher was trying to sell you something you didn't need; and the other half he was selling you something you already had. But when it came to people of the cloth, Sister Agnes unnerved him more than most.

—Did you happen to notice the window behind me? she asked finally.

—I did.

She nodded, then gently closed Billy's book.

—When I first came to St. Nicholas's in 1942, I found that window to have a rather mysterious effect on me. There was something about it that captured my attention, but in a manner I couldn't quite pin down. Some afternoons, when things were quiet, I would sit with a cup of coffee—about where you're sitting now—and stare at it, simply to take it in. Then one day, I realized what it was that had been affecting me so. It was the difference between the expressions on the faces of the disciples and the faces of the children.

Sister Agnes turned a little in her chair so that she could look up at the window. Almost reluctantly, Emmett followed her gaze.

—If you look at the faces of the disciples, you can tell that they remain quite skeptical about what they have just seen. *Surely*, they are thinking to themselves, *this must be some kind of hoax or vision, for with our own eyes we witnessed His death on the Cross, and with our own hands we carried His body into the tomb*. But if you look at the faces of the children, there isn't a hint of skepticism. They look upon this miracle with awe and wonder, yes, but without disbelief.

Emmett knew that Sister Agnes was well intentioned. And given that she was a woman in her sixties who had devoted her life not only in service to the Church, but in service to orphans, Emmett knew when she began her story that she deserved his full attention. But as she spoke, Emmett couldn't help noting that the yellow, red, and blue patterns from the very window she was describing had moved from the wall to the surface of the table, marking the progress of the sun and the loss of another hour.

—·—

— . . . Then he went up the hill with Emmett's book bag and broke the window to the kitchen door!

Like one of the boys in the orphanage, Billy was recounting the morning's events in a state of excitement as Sally maneuvered Betty through traffic.

—He broke the window?

—Because the door was locked! And then he went into the kitchen and got a fistful of spoons and carried them upstairs to the dormitories.

—What did he want with a fistful of spoons?

—He wanted the spoons because he was bringing them your strawberry preserves!

Sally looked over at Billy with an expression of shock.

—He gave them a jar of my strawberry preserves?

—No, said Billy. He gave them six. Isn't that what you said, Emmett?

Both Billy and Sally turned to Emmett, who was looking out the passenger-side window.

—That sounds about right, he replied without looking back.

—I don't understand, said Sally, almost to herself.

Leaning forward over the steering wheel, she accelerated in order to pull around a sedan.

—I only *gave* him six jars. They might have lasted him from now until Christmas. Why on earth would he hand over the whole batch to a bunch of strangers?

—Because they are orphans, explained Billy.

Sally considered this.

—Yes, of course, Billy. You're absolutely right. Because they are orphans.

As Sally nodded her head in acknowledgment of Billy's reasoning and Duchess's charity, Emmett couldn't help but note that she'd been plenty more indignant about the fate of her jam than she had been about the fate of his car.

—There, said Emmett pointing to the station.

In order to make the turn, Sally cut in front of a Chevy. When she skidded to a stop, the three of them climbed from the cab. But as Emmett was glancing at the entrance of the station, Billy went to the bed of the truck, grabbed his backpack, and began swinging it onto his back.

Seeing this, Sally exhibited a moment of surprise, then she looked toward Emmett with the narrowed eyes of castigation.

—You haven't told him? she asked under her breath. Well, don't expect me to!

Emmett took his brother aside.

—Billy, he began, you don't need to put your backpack on right now.

—It's okay, Billy said, while tightening the shoulder straps. I can take it off when we get on the train.

Emmett got down on his haunches.

—You're not coming on the train, Billy.

—What do you mean, Emmett? Why aren't I coming on the train?

—It makes more sense for you to go with Sally while I get the car. But as soon as I've got it, I'm coming right back to Morgen to pick you up. It shouldn't take me more than a few days.

But even as Emmett was explaining this, Billy was shaking his head.

—No, he said. No. I can't go back with Sally, Emmett. We have already left Morgen and we are on our way to San Francisco.

—That's true, Billy. We are on our way to San Francisco. But right now, the car is on its way to New York. . . .

When Emmett said this, Billy's eyes opened wide with revelation.

—New York is where the Lincoln Highway begins, he said. After we take the train and find the Studebaker, we can drive to Times Square and start our journey from there.

Emmett looked to Sally for support.

She took a step forward and put a hand on Billy's shoulder.

—Billy, she said in her no-nonsense tone, you are absolutely right.

Emmett closed his eyes.

Now it was Sally he was taking aside.

—Sally . . . , he began, but she cut him off.

—Emmett, you know that there is nothing I would rather do than keep Billy at my side for another three days. As God is my witness, I would be happy to keep him for another three years. But he has already spent fifteen months waiting for you to return from Salina. And in the meanwhile, he's lost his father and his home. At this juncture, Billy's place is at your side, and he knows it. And I imagine, by now, he thinks that you should know it too.

What Emmett actually knew was that he needed to get to New York and find Duchess as quickly as possible, and that having Billy along wasn't going to make the job any easier.

But in one important respect, Billy had been right: They had already left Morgen. Having buried their father and packed their bags, they had put that part of their lives behind them. It would be something of a comfort for both of them to know that whatever happened next, they wouldn't have to go back.

Emmett turned to his brother.

—All right, Billy. We'll go to New York together.

Billy nodded in acknowledgment that this was the sensible thing to do.

After waiting for Billy to retighten the straps on his pack, Sally gave him a hug, reminding him to mind his manners and his brother. Then without giving a hug to Emmett, she climbed in her truck. But once she had turned the ignition, she beckoned him to her window.

—There's one more thing, she said.

—What's that?

—If you want to chase your car to New York that's your own

business. But I have no intention of spending the next few weeks waking up in the middle of the night in a state of worry. So a few days from now, you need to give me a call and let me know that you're safe.

Emmett began to express the impracticality of Sally's request—that once in New York, their focus would be on finding the car, that he didn't know where they'd be staying, or whether they'd have access to a phone . . .

—You didn't seem to have any trouble finding the means to call me at seven this morning so I could drop whatever I was doing and drive all the way to Lewis. I have no doubt that in a city as big as New York, you'll be able to find another telephone and the time to use it.

—Okay, said Emmett. I'll call.

—Good, said Sally. When?

—When what?

—When will you call?

—Sally, I don't even—

—Friday then. You can call me on Friday at two thirty.

Before Emmett could respond, Sally put the truck in gear and pulled to the depot's exit, where she idled, waiting for a break in the traffic.

Earlier that morning when they had been preparing to leave the orphanage, Sister Agnes had bestowed on Billy a pendant on a chain saying it was the medallion of Christopher, the patron saint of travelers. When she turned to Emmett, he worried that she was about to bestow a medallion on him too. Instead, she said there was something she wanted to ask him, but before doing so, she had another story to tell: the story of how Duchess had come into her care.

One afternoon in the summer of 1944, she said, a man of about fifty had appeared at the orphanage door with a scrawny little eight-year-old at his side. Once the man was alone with Sister Agnes in her office, he explained that his brother and sister-in-law had died in a car crash, and that he was the boy's only surviving relative. Of course, he wanted nothing more than to care for his nephew, especially at such an impressionable age; but as an officer in the armed forces, he was due to ship out for France at the end of the week, and he didn't know when he would return from the war or, for that matter, if he would return at all. . . .

—Now, I didn't believe a word this man had to say. Never mind that his unkempt hair was hardly befitting an officer in the armed forces and that he had a lovely young girl waiting in the passenger seat of his convertible car. It was plain enough that he was the boy's father. But it is not my calling to concern myself with the duplicity of unscrupulous men. It is my calling to concern myself with the welfare of forsaken boys. And let there be no doubt about it, Emmett, young Daniel was forsaken. Yes, his father reappeared two years later to reclaim Daniel, when it suited him to do so, but Daniel didn't know to expect that. Most of the boys who come into our care are truly orphans. We have boys whose parents died together of influenza or in fires, whose mothers died in childbirth and fathers died at Normandy. And it is a terrible trial for these children who must come of age without the love of their parents. But imagine becoming an orphan not by calamity, but by your father's preference—by his determination that you have become an inconvenience.

Sister Agnes let that sink in for a moment.

—I have no doubt that you are angry with Daniel for taking liberties with your car. But we both know that there is goodness in him, a goodness that has been there from the beginning, but which has never had the chance to fully flourish. At this critical time in his life, what he needs more than anything else is a friend who will stand reliably at his side; a friend who can steer him clear of folly and help him find the way to fulfilling his Christian purpose.

—Sister, you said you were going to ask me something. You didn't say you were going to ask something of me.

The nun studied Emmett for a second, then smiled.

—You are absolutely right, Emmett. I am not asking you this. I'm asking it of you.

—I have someone to watch over already. Someone who is my own flesh and blood and who is an orphan in his own right.

She looked at Billy with an affectionate smile, but then turned back to Emmett with undiminished intent.

—Do you count yourself a Christian, Emmett?

—I'm not the churchgoing sort.

—But do you count yourself a Christian?

—I was raised to be one.

—Then I imagine you know the parable of the Good Samaritan.

—Yes, sister, I know the parable. And I know that a good Christian helps a man in need.

—Yes, Emmett. A good Christian shows compassion toward those who are in difficulty. And that is an important part of the parable's meaning. But an equally important point that Jesus is making is that we do not always get to *choose* to whom we should show our charity.

When Emmett had come to the end of his driveway shortly before dawn, he had turned onto the road knowing that he and Billy were unencumbered—free of any debts or obligations as they began their life anew. And now, having traveled just sixty miles from home headed in the wrong direction, he had made two promises in as many hours.

Once the traffic finally subsided and Sally took a left out of the station, Emmett expected her to turn and wave. But leaning forward over her wheel, Sally punched the gas, Betty backfired, and they both headed west without a glance in his direction.

Only as they sped out of sight did Emmett realize he didn't have any money.

Duchess

WHAT A DAY, WHAT A DAY, what a day! Emmett's car may not have been the fastest one on the road, but the sun was high, the skies were blue, and everyone we passed had a smile on their face.

After leaving Lewis, for the first one hundred and fifty miles we had seen more grain elevators than human beings. And most of the towns we passed through seemed to be limited to one of everything by local decree: one movie theater and one restaurant; one cemetery and one savings and loan; in all likelihood, one sense of right and wrong.

But for most people, it doesn't matter where they live. When they get up in the morning, they're not looking to change the world. They want to have a cup of coffee and a piece of toast, put in their eight hours, and wrap up the day with a bottle of beer in front of the TV set. More or less, it's what they'd be doing whether they lived in Atlanta, Georgia, or Nome, Alaska. And if it doesn't matter for most people where they live, it certainly doesn't matter where they're going.

That's what gave the Lincoln Highway its charm.

When you see the highway on a map, it looks like that Fisher guy Billy was talking about took a ruler and drew a line straight across the country, mountains and rivers be damned. In so doing, he must have imagined it would provide a timely conduit for the movement of goods and ideas from sea to shining sea, in a final fulfillment of manifest destiny. But everyone we passed just seemed to have a satisfied sense of their own lack of purpose. *Let the road rise up to meet you,* say the Irish, and that's what was happening to the intrepid travelers on the Lincoln Highway. It was rising up to meet each and every one of them, whether they were headed east, headed west, or going around in circles.

—It was awfully nice of Emmett to loan us his car, said Woolly.

—It was at that.

He smiled for a moment, then his brow furrowed just like Billy's.

—Do you think they had any trouble getting home?

—No, said I. I'll bet you Sally came racing over in that pickup of hers, and the three of them are already back in her kitchen eating biscuits and jelly.

—You mean biscuits and preserves.

—Exactly.

I did feel a little bad about Emmett having to make the journey to Lewis and back. If I'd known he kept his keys above the visor, I could have saved him the trip.

The irony is that when we set out from Emmett's house, I had no intention of borrowing the car. By then I was looking forward to taking the Greyhound. And why not? On the bus you get to sit back and relax. You can take a nap, or make a little conversation with the shoe-leather salesman across the aisle. But just as we were about to make the turn toward Omaha, Billy piped up about the Lincoln Highway, and next thing you know, we were on the outskirts of Lewis. Then when I came out of St. Nick's, there was the Studebaker sitting by the curb with the key in its slot and the driver's seat empty. It was as if Emmett and Billy had planned the whole thing. Or the Good Lord. Either way, destiny seemed to be announcing itself pretty loud and clear—even if Emmett had to make the round trip.

—The good news, I said to Woolly, is that if we keep up this pace, we should be in New York by Wednesday morning. We can see my old man, zip out to the camp, and be back with Emmett's share before he misses us. And given the size of the house that you and Billy cooked up, I think Emmett's going to be glad to have a little extra cabbage when he lands in San Francisco.

Woolly smiled at the mention of Billy's house.

—Speaking of our pace, I said, how long until we get to Chicago?

The smile left Woolly's face.

In Billy's absence, I had given him the job of navigating. Since Billy wouldn't let us borrow his map, we had to get one of our own (from a Phillips 66, of course). And just like Billy, Woolly had carefully marked our route with a black line that followed the Lincoln Highway all the way to New York. But once we were under way, he acted like he couldn't get that map into the glove compartment fast enough.

—You want me to calculate the distance? he asked with an unmistakable sense of foreboding.

—I'll tell you what, Woolly: Why don't you forget about Chicago and find us a little something to listen to on the radio.

And just like that, the smile was back.

Presumably, the dial was normally set to Emmett's favorite station, but we had left that signal somewhere back in Nebraska. So when Woolly turned on the radio, all that came through the speaker was static.

For a few seconds, Woolly gave it his full attention, as if he wanted to identify exactly what kind of static it was. But as soon as he began to turn the tuner, I could tell that here was another of Woolly's hidden talents—like the dishes and the floor plan. Because Woolly didn't just spin the dial and hope for the best. He turned it like a safecracker. With his eyes narrowed and his tongue between his teeth, he moved that little orange needle slowly across the spectrum until he could hear the faintest hint of a signal. Then slowing even further, he would let the signal gain in strength and clarity until he suddenly came to a stop at the incidence of perfect reception.

The first signal Woolly landed on was a country music station. It was playing a number about a cowboy on the range who'd either lost his woman or his horse. Before I could figure out which, Woolly had turned the dial. Next up was a crop report coming live to us all the way from Iowa City, then the fiery sermon of a Baptist preacher, then a bit of Beethoven with all the edges sanded down. When he didn't even stop for *Sh-boom, sh-boom*, I began to wonder if anything on the radio was going to be good enough. But when he tuned into 1540, a commercial for a breakfast cereal was just beginning. Letting go of the knob, Woolly stared at the radio, giving the advertisement the sort of attention that one would normally reserve for a physician or fortune-teller. And so it began.

Oh, how this kid loved a commercial. Over the next hundred miles, we must have listened to fifty. And they could have been for anything. For a Coupe DeVille or the new Playtex bra. It didn't seem to matter. Because Woolly wasn't looking to buy anything. What captivated him was the drama.

At the beginning of a commercial, Woolly would listen gravely as the actor or actress articulated their particular dilemma. Like the tepid flavor of their menthol cigarettes or the grass stains on their children's pants. From Woolly's expression, you could see that he not only shared in their distress, he had a looming suspicion that *all* quests for happiness were doomed to disappointment. But as soon as these beleaguered souls decided to try the new brand of this or that, Woolly's expression would brighten, and when they discovered that the product in question had not only removed the lumps from their mashed potatoes but the lumps from their life, Woolly would break into a smile, looking uplifted and reassured.

A few miles west of Ames, Iowa, the commercial that Woolly happened upon introduced us to a mother who has just learned—to her utter dismay—that each of her three sons has arrived for supper with a guest. At the revelation of this setback, Woolly let out an audible gasp. But suddenly we heard the twinkling of a magic wand and who should appear but Chef Boy-Ar-Dee with his big puffy hat and even puffier accent. With another wave of the wand, six cans of his Spaghetti Sauce with Meat appeared lined up on the counter ready to save the day.

—Doesn't that sound delicious, Woolly sighed, as the boys on the radio dug into their dinner.

—Delicious! I exclaimed in horror. It comes out of a can, Woolly.

—I know. Isn't that amazing?

—Whether it's amazing or not, that is no way to eat an Italian dinner.

Woolly turned to me with a look of genuine curiosity.

—What is the way to eat an Italian dinner, Duchess?

Oh, where to begin.

—Have you ever heard of Leonello's? I asked. Up in East Harlem?

—I don't think so.

—Then you'd better pull up a chair.

Woolly made a good faith effort to do so.

—Leonello's, I began, is a little Italian place with ten booths, ten tables, and a bar. The booths are lined with red leather, the tables are draped with red and white cloths, and Sinatra's playing on the jukebox, just like you'd expect. The only hitch is that if you walked in off the street on a Thursday night and asked for a table, they wouldn't let you sit down for supper—even if the place was empty.

As one who always loves a conundrum, Woolly's expression brightened up.

—Why won't they let you sit down for supper, Duchess?

—The reason they won't let you sit down, Woolly, is because all the tables are taken.

—But you just said the whole place was empty.

—And so it is.

—Then taken by whom?

—Ay, my friend, there's the rub. You see, the way that Leonello's works is that every table in the place is reserved in perpetuity. If you're one of Leonello's customers, you might have the table for four by the jukebox on Saturdays at eight. And you pay for that table every Saturday night, whether you show up or not, so no one else can use it.

I looked over at Woolly.

—You with me so far?

—I'm with you, he said.

And I could tell he was.

—Let's say you're not a customer of Leonello's, but you're lucky enough to have a friend who is, and this friend has given you the use of his table when he's out of town. When Saturday night rolls around, you put on your best duds and head up to Harlem with your three closest friends.

—Like you and Billy and Emmett.

—Exactly. Like me and Billy and Emmett. But once we're all settled and we've ordered a drink, don't bother asking for menus.

—Why not?

—Because at Leonello's, they don't have them.

I really had Woolly with that one. I mean, he let out a bigger gasp than he had during the Chef Boy-Ar-Dee commercial.

—How can you order dinner without a menu, Duchess?

—At Leonello's, I explained, once you've taken your seat and ordered your drinks, the waiter will drag a chair over to your table, spin it around, and sit with his arms on its back so that he can tell you exactly what they're serving that night. *Welcome to Leonello's*, he'll say. *Tonight for starters we got stuffed artichokes, mussels marinara, clams oreganata, and calamari fritti. For the first course we got linguine with clams, spaghetti carbonara, and penne Bolognese. And for the main course, chicken cacciatore, veal scallopini, veal Milanese, and osso buco.*

I took a quick glance at my copilot.

—I can see from your expression that you're a little daunted by all this variety, Woolly, but worry not. Because the only dish that you have to order at Leonello's is the one the waiter hasn't mentioned:

Fettuccine Mio Amore, the specialty of the house. A fresh-made pasta that's tossed in a sauce of tomatoes, bacon, caramelized onions, and pepper flakes.

—But why doesn't the waiter mention it, if it's the specialty of the house?

—He doesn't mention it *because* it's the specialty of the house. That's the way it goes with *Fettuccine Mio Amore*. Either you know enough to order it, or you don't deserve to eat it.

I could tell from the smile on Woolly's face that he was enjoying his night at Leonello's.

—Did your father have a table at Leonello's? he asked.

I laughed.

—No, Woolly. My old man didn't have a table anywhere. But for six glorious months, he was the maître d', and I was allowed to hang out in the kitchen, as long as I didn't get in the way.

I was about to tell Woolly about Lou, the chef, when a truck driver came barreling around us with a shake of the fist.

Normally, I would have replied with a bite of the thumb, but when I looked up to do so, I realized I had gotten so wrapped up in the telling of my tale, I had let our speed drop to thirty miles an hour. No wonder the trucker was out of joint.

But when I punched the accelerator, the little orange needle in the speedometer dropped from twenty-five to twenty. When I pushed the pedal to the floor, we slowed to fifteen, and when I pulled onto the shoulder, we rolled to a stop.

Turning the key off and on, I counted to three and pushed the starter to no effect.

Fucking Studebaker, I muttered to myself. It's probably the battery again. But even as I thought this, I realized the radio was still playing, so it couldn't be the battery. Maybe it had something to do with the spark plug . . . ?

—Are we out of gas? asked Woolly.

After looking at Woolly for a second, I looked at the fuel gauge. It too had a thin orange needle, and sure enough, the needle was sitting on the bottom.

—So it would seem, Woolly. So it would seem.

As luck would have it, we were still in the Ames city limits, and not far up the road I could see the flying red horse of a Mobil station. Putting my hands in my pockets, I withdrew what change was left from Mr. Watson's desk drawer. After accounting for the hamburger and ice cream cone I'd purchased back in Morgen, it amounted to seven cents.

—Woolly, you wouldn't happen to have any money on you?

—Money? he replied.

Why is it, I wondered, that people born with money are always the ones who say the word like it's in a foreign language?

Getting out of the car, I looked up and down the road. Across the street was a diner beginning to get busy with the lunch crowd. Next was a laundromat with two cars in the lot. But farther up the way was a liquor store that didn't look like it had opened yet.

In New York City, no liquor store owner worth his salt would leave cash on the premises overnight. But we weren't in New York City. We were in the heartland, where most of the people who read *In God We Trust* on a silver dollar took the words literally. But on the off chance there wasn't any money sitting in the till, I figured I could grab a case of whiskey and offer a few bottles to the gas station attendant in exchange for filling the tank.

The only problem was how to get in.

—Hand me the keys, would you?

Leaning over, Woolly removed the keys from the ignition and passed them through the window.

—Thanks, I said, turning toward the trunk.

—Duchess?

—Yeah, Woolly?

—Do you think it's possible . . . ? Do you think I might . . . ?

Generally, I don't like to tinker with another man's habits. If he wants to get up early and go to mass, let him get up early and go to mass; and if he wants to sleep until noon wearing last night's clothes, let him sleep until noon wearing last night's clothes. But given that Woolly was down to his last few bottles of medicine and I needed help with the navigation, I had asked him to forgo his midmorning dose.

I took another glance at the liquor store. I had no idea how long it was going to take for me to get in and out. So in the meantime, it was probably just as well if Woolly was lost in his thoughts.

—All right, I said. But why don't you keep it to a drop or two.

He was already reaching for the glove compartment as I headed to the back of the car.

When I opened the trunk, I had to smile. Because when Billy had said that he and Emmett were heading for California with what little they could fit in a kit bag, I figured he was speaking figuratively. But there was nothing figurative about it. It was a kit bag, all right. Setting it aside, I folded back the felt that covered the spare. Nesting beside the tire, I found the jack and handle. The handle was about the width of a candy cane, but if it was strong enough to crank up a Studebaker, I figured it would be strong enough to open a country door.

Picking up the handle with my left hand, I went to fold the felt back in place with my right. And that's when I saw it: a little corner of paper sticking up from behind the black of the tire, looking as white as an angel's wing.

Emmett

IT TOOK EMMETT HALF AN HOUR to find his way to the gates of the freight yard. While the passenger and freight lines were adjacent, they had their backs to each other. So even though their respective terminals were just a few hundred yards apart, to get from the entrance of one to the entrance of the other, you had to walk a circumventing mile. The route initially took Emmett along a well-groomed thoroughfare of shops, but then over the tracks and into a zone of foundries, scrapyards, and garages.

As he followed the wire fence that bordered the rail yard, Emmett began to sense the enormity of the task before him. For while the passenger terminal was just large enough to accommodate the few hundred travelers who arrived or departed from this midsized city in a day—the freight yard sprawled. Fanning out over twenty acres, it encompassed a receiving yard, a switching yard, wheelhouses, offices, and maintenance areas, but most of all, boxcars. Hundreds of them. Rectilinear and rust-colored, they were lined end to end and row by row for almost as far as the eye could see. And whether they were slotted to head east or west, north or south, laden or empty, they were exactly as common sense should have told him they would be: anonymous and interchangeable.

The entrance to the yard was on a wide street lined with warehouses. As Emmett approached, the only person in sight was a middle-aged man in a wheelchair positioned near the gates. Even from a distance, Emmett could see that both of his legs had been cut off above the knee—a casualty of the war, no doubt. If the veteran's intention was to profit from the kindness of strangers, thought Emmett, he would have been better off in front of the passenger terminal.

In order to assess the situation, Emmett took up a position across the street from the gates, in the doorway of a shuttered building. Not far behind the fencing he could see a two-story brick building in relatively good repair. That's where the command center would be—the room with the manifests and timetables. Naively, Emmett had imagined that he would be able to slip into the building sight unseen and cull the information he needed from a schedule posted on a wall. But just beyond the gates was a small building that looked very much like a guardhouse.

Sure enough, as Emmett was studying it, a truck pulled into the entrance and a man in uniform emerged from the house with a clipboard in order to clear the truck for admission. There wasn't going to be any slipping or culling, thought Emmett. He would have to wait for the information to come to him.

Emmett glanced at the dial of the army surplus watch, which Billy had loaned him. It was quarter past eleven. Figuring he would get his chance when the lunch hour came, Emmett leaned back in the shadows of the doorway and bided his time, his thoughts returning to his brother.

When Emmett and Billy had entered the passenger terminal, Billy was all eyes, taking in the high ceilings and ticket windows, the coffee shop and shoe shine and newsstand.

—I've never been in a train station before, he said.

—Is it different than you expected?

—It's just as I expected.

—Come on, said Emmett with a smile. Let's sit over here.

Emmett led his brother through the main waiting area to a quiet corner with an empty bench.

Removing his backpack, Billy sat down and slid over to make room for Emmett, but Emmett didn't sit.

—I need to go find out about the trains to New York, Billy. But it might take a little while. Until I get back, I want you to promise you'll stay put.

—Okay, Emmett.

—And keep in mind, this isn't Morgen. There's going to be plenty of people coming and going, all of them strangers. It's probably for the best if you keep to yourself.

—I understand.

—Good.

—But if you want to find out about the trains to New York, why don't you ask at the information window? It's right there under the clock.

When Billy pointed, Emmett looked back toward the information window, then he joined his brother on the bench.

—Billy, we're not going to be taking one of the passenger trains.

—Why not, Emmett?

—Because all of our money is in the Studebaker.

Billy thought about this, then reached for his backpack.

—We can use my silver dollars.

With a smile, Emmett stayed his brother's hand.

—We can't do that. You've been collecting those for years. And you only have a few more to go, right?

—Then what are we going to do, Emmett?

—We're going to hitch a ride on one of the freight trains.

For most people, Emmett figured, rules were a necessary evil. They were an inconvenience to be abided for having the privilege of living in an orderly world. And that's why most people, when left to their own devices, were willing to stretch the boundaries of a rule. To speed on an empty road or liberate an apple from an untended orchard. But when it came to rules, Billy wasn't simply an abider. He was a stickler. He made his bed and brushed his teeth without needing to be asked. He insisted that he be at school fifteen minutes before the first bell, and he always raised his hand in class before speaking. As a result, Emmett had thought a lot about how he was going to put this, eventually settling on the phrase *hitch a ride* in the hope it might diminish any qualms his brother was sure to have. From Billy's expression, Emmett could see that he had chosen well.

—Like stowaways, Billy said, a little wide-eyed.

—That's right. Like stowaways.

Patting his brother on the knee, Emmett rose from the bench and turned to go.

—Like Duchess and Woolly in the warden's car.

Emmett paused and turned back.

—How do you know about that, Billy?

—Duchess told me. Yesterday after breakfast. We were talking about *The Count of Monte Cristo* and how Edmond Dantès, imprisoned unjustly, escaped from the Château d'If by stitching himself into the sack that was meant for the body of Abbé Faria, so that the unwitting guards would carry him out of the prison gates. Duchess explained how he and Woolly had done almost the exact same thing. How, unjustly imprisoned, they had hidden in the trunk of the warden's car and the warden had unwittingly driven them right through the gates. Only Duchess and Woolly weren't tossed in the sea.

As Billy related this, he spoke with the same excitement that he had shown when describing for Sally the incident at the orphanage— with the broken window and fistful of spoons.

Emmett sat down again.

—Billy, you seem to like Duchess.

Billy looked back in perplexity.

—Don't you like Duchess, Emmett?

—I do. But just because I like someone doesn't mean I like everything they happen to do.

—Like when he gave away Sally's preserves?

Emmett laughed.

—No. I'm all right with that one. I meant other things. . . .

As Billy continued to stare back at him, Emmett searched for an appropriate example.

—You remember Duchess's story about going to see the movies?

—You mean when he would sneak out the bathroom window and jog across the potato fields.

—Right. Well, there's a little more to that story than Duchess related. He wasn't just a participant when it came to sneaking into town, he was the instigator. He's the one who came up with the idea and who would rally a few of the others whenever he wanted to see a movie. And for the most part, it was like he said. If they slipped out on a Saturday night around nine, they could be back by one in the morning, leaving no one the wiser. But one night, Duchess was eager to see some new western with John Wayne. Since it had been raining all week and it looked as if it might rain some more, the only one he could convince to go was my bunkmate, Townhouse. They weren't halfway across the fields when it started to pour. Though they were getting drenched and their boots were getting stuck in the mud, they pushed on. But when they finally got to the river, which was riding high because of the rain, Duchess just sat down and quit. He said he was too cold, too wet, too tired to go farther. Townhouse figured he'd come that far, he wasn't turning back. So he swam across, leaving Duchess behind.

Billy was nodding as Emmett spoke, his brow furrowed in concentration.

—All of this would have been fine, continued Emmett, but after Townhouse left, Duchess decided he was too wet, too cold, and too tired to walk all the way back to the barracks. So he went to the near-est road, flagged down a passing pickup, and asked if he could get a lift to a diner up the way. The only problem was that the driver of the pickup was an off-duty cop. Instead of taking Duchess to the diner, he took him to the warden. And when Townhouse returned at one in the morning, the guards were waiting.

—Was Townhouse punished?

—He was, Billy. And pretty severely, at that.

What Emmett didn't tell his brother was that Warden Ackerly had two simple rules when it came to *willful infractions*. The first rule was that you could pay the piper in weeks or strokes. You get in a fight in the mess hall and that's either three weeks tacked onto your sentence or three lashes on your back. His second rule was that since Negro boys were only half as suited to learning as white boys, their lessons had to be twice as long. So while Duchess took four extra weeks tacked onto his sentence, Townhouse received eight strokes from the switch— right there in front of the mess hall with everyone lined up to watch.

—The point is, Billy, that Duchess is full of energy and enthusiasm and good intentions too. But sometimes, his energy and enthusiasm get in the way of his good intentions, and when that happens the con-sequences often fall on someone else.

Emmett had hoped this recollection would be a little sobering for Billy, and from Billy's expression it seemed to have hit the mark.

—That is a sad story, he said.

—It is, said Emmett.

—It makes me feel sorry for Duchess.

Emmett looked at his brother in surprise.

—Why for Duchess, Billy? He's the one who got Townhouse in trouble.

—That only happened because Duchess wouldn't cross the river when it was riding high.

—That's true. But why would that make you feel sorry for him?

—Because he must not know how to swim, Emmett. And he was too ashamed to admit it.

—·—

Just as Emmett anticipated, shortly after noon some of the railyard's employees began walking through the gates on their way to get lunch. As he watched, Emmett noted that he couldn't have been more wrong about where the vet positioned himself. Nearly every man who exited had something for him—be it a nickel, a dime, or a friendly word.

Emmett understood that the men who emerged from the administrative building were most likely to have the information he needed. Responsible for scheduling and dispatching, they would know which boxcars were to be attached to which trains at which times and where they would be headed. But Emmett didn't approach them. Instead, he waited for the others: the brakemen and loaders and mechanics—the men who worked with their hands and were paid by the hour. Instinctively, Emmett knew that these men would be more likely to see in him a version of themselves and, if not exactly overcome with sympathy, at least reasonably indifferent to whether the railroad collected another fare. But if instinct told Emmett that these were the men he should approach, reason told him that he should wait for a straggler, because even though a working man might be open to bending the rules on behalf of a stranger, he'd be less likely to do so in the company of others.

Emmett had to wait almost half an hour for his first opportunity— a lone workman in jeans and a black tee shirt who looked no more than twenty-five. As the young man paused to light a cigarette, Emmett crossed the street.

—Excuse me, he said.

Waving out his match, the young man gave Emmett a once-over but didn't reply. Emmett forged ahead with the story he had fashioned, explaining that he had an uncle from Kansas City who was an engineer, who was scheduled to stop in Lewis sometime that afternoon on a freight train headed for New York, but Emmett couldn't remember which train it was, or when it would arrive.

When Emmett had first seen this young man, he'd imagined their proximity in ages would play to his advantage. But as soon as he began speaking, he realized he'd been wrong about that too. The young man's expression was as dismissive of Emmett as only a young man's expression can be.

—No kidding, he said with a slanted smile. An uncle from Kansas City. Imagine that.

The young man took a drag and flicked his unfinished cigarette into the street.

—Why don't you do yourself a favor, kid, and head on home. Your momma's wondering where you've gotten to.

As the young man sauntered away, Emmett made eye contact with the panhandler, who had watched the entire exchange. Emmett shifted his gaze to the guardhouse to see if the guard had been watching too, but he was leaning back in his chair reading a newspaper.

An older man in a jumpsuit came through the gates now and stopped to exchange a few friendly words with the panhandler. The man had a cap pushed so far back on his head, it made you wonder why he wore it at all. When he began walking away, Emmett approached.

If proximity in age had proven a liability with the first man, Emmett decided he'd make the most of the difference in age with the second.

—Excuse me, sir, he said, with deference.

Turning, the man looked at Emmett with a friendly smile.

—Hey there, son. What can I do you for?

As Emmett repeated the story about his uncle, the man in the jumpsuit listened with interest, even leaning a little forward as if he didn't want to miss a word. But once Emmett finished, he shook his head.

—I'd love to help ya, fella, but I just fix 'em. I don't ask where they're headed.

As the mechanic continued down the street, Emmett began to accept that he needed a whole new plan of action.

—Hey there, someone called.

Emmett turned to find it was the panhandler.

—I'm sorry, Emmett said, drawing the pockets out of his pants. I've got nothing for you.

—You're misunderstandin', friend. It's me who's got somethin' for you.

As Emmett hesitated, the panhandler wheeled himself closer.

—You're lookin' to hop a freight train headed for New York. That about it?

Emmett exhibited a little surprise.

—I lost my legs, not my ears! But listen: If you're tryin' to hop a train, you're askin' the wrong guys. Jackson wouldn't stomp on your foot if your toes were on fire. And like Arnie says, he just fixes 'em. Which is no small matter, mind you, but it's got everythin' to do with how a train is runnin', and nothin' to do with where it's goin'. So there's no point in askin' Jackson or Arnie. No, sirree. If you want to know how to hop a train to New York, the guy you should be talkin' to is me.

Emmett must have betrayed incredulity, because the panhandler grinned and pointed a thumb to his chest.

—I worked for the railroads for twenty-five years. Fifteen as a brakeman and ten in the switchin' yard right here in Lewis. How do you think I lost my legs?

He pointed to his lap with another smile. Then he looked Emmett over, though in a more generous manner than the young workman had.

—What are you—eighteen?

—That's right, said Emmett.

—Believe it or not, I started ridin' the rails when I was a few years younger than you. Back in the day, they'd take you on if you was six-teen; maybe fifteen, if you was tall for your age.

The panhandler shook his head with a nostalgic smile, then he leaned back like an old man who was sitting in his favorite living room chair, making himself comfortable.

—I got my start on the Union Pacific lines and worked the south-west corridor for seven years. I spent another eight workin' for the Pennsylvania Railroad—the largest in the nation. In those days, I spent more time in motion than I spent standin' still. It got so when I was home, when I'd get out of bed in the mornin' it would feel like the whole house was rollin' under my feet. I'd have to hold on to the furniture just to make my way to the bathroom.

The panhandler laughed and shook his head again.

—Yep. The Pennsylvania. The Burlington. The Union Pacific and Great Northern. I know all the lines.

Then he was quiet.

—You were talking about a train to New York, Emmett prompted gently.

—Righto, he replied. The Big Apple! But are you sure about New York? The thing about a freight yard is you can get to anywhere you've thought of, and plenty of places you haven't. Florida. Texas. California. How about Santa Fe? You been there? Now that's a town. This time of year, it's warm durin' the day and cool at night, and it's got some of the friendliest *señoritas* you'll ever meet.

As the panhandler began laughing, Emmett worried he was losing the thread of their conversation again.

—I'd love to go to Santa Fe at some point, Emmett said, but for the time being, I need to go to New York.

The panhandler stopped laughing and adopted a more serious ex-pression.

—Well, that's life in a nutshell, ain't it. Lovin' to go to one place and havin' to go to another.

The panhandler looked left and right, then he wheeled a little closer.

—I know you were askin' Jackson about an afternoon train to New York. Now that would be the Empire Special, which leaves at one fifty-five, and she's a beauty. Runnin' at ninety miles an hour and stoppin' only six times, she can make it to the city in under twenty hours. But if you want to *get* to New York, then you don't want to ride the Empire Special. 'Cause when she reaches Chicago, she takes on a carload of bearer bonds headed for Wall Street. She never has fewer than four armed guards, and when they decide to remove you from the train, they don't wait for it to come into a station.

The panhandler looked up in the air.

—Now, the West Coast Perishables, she comes through Lewis at six o'clock. And she ain't a bad ride. But this time of year, she'll be filled to the brim and you'd have to board her in broad daylight. So you don't want the Perishables neither. What you want is the Sunset East, which will be comin' through Lewis shortly after midnight. And I can tell you exactly how to board her, but before I do, you'll have to answer me a question.

—Go ahead, said Emmett.

The panhandler grinned.

—What's the difference between a ton of flour and a ton of crackers?

—.—

When Emmett returned to the passenger terminal, he was relieved to find Billy just where he'd left him—sitting on the bench with his backpack at his side and his big red book in his lap.

When Emmett joined him, Billy looked up with some excitement.

—Did you figure out which train we're going to hitch a ride on, Emmett?

—I did, Billy. But it doesn't go until shortly after midnight.

Billy nodded to express his approval, as if shortly after midnight was exactly when it should go.

—Here, said Emmett, taking off his brother's watch.

—No, said Billy. You wear it for now. You need to keep track of the time.

While strapping the watch back on, Emmett saw that it was nearly two.

—I'm starving, he said. Maybe I'll take a look around and see if I can scrounge up something for us to eat.

—You don't have to scrounge up something, Emmett. I have our lunch.

Billy reached into his backpack and took out his canteen, two paper napkins, and two sandwiches wrapped in wax paper with tight creases and sharp corners. Emmett smiled, noting that Sally wrapped her sandwiches as neatly as she made her beds.

—One is roast beef and one is ham, Billy said. I couldn't remember if you liked roast beef more than ham, or ham more than roast beef, so we decided on one of each. They both have cheese, but only the roast beef has mayonnaise.

—I'll take the roast beef, said Emmett.

The brothers unwrapped their sandwiches and both took healthy bites.

—God bless, Sally.

Billy looked up in agreement with Emmett's sentiment, but apparently curious as to the timing of the remark. By way of explanation, Emmett held his sandwich in the air.

—Oh, said Billy. These aren't from Sally.

—They're not?

—They're from Mrs. Simpson.

Emmett froze for a moment with his sandwich in the air, while Billy took another bite.

—Who is Mrs. Simpson, Billy?

—The nice lady who sat beside me.

—Sat beside you here?

Emmett pointed to the spot on the bench where he was sitting.

—No, said Billy pointing to the empty spot on his right. Sat beside me here.

—She made these sandwiches?

—She bought them in the coffee shop, then brought them back because I told her I had to stay put.

Emmett set his sandwich down.

—You shouldn't be accepting sandwiches from strangers, Billy.

—But I didn't accept the sandwiches when we were strangers, Emmett. I accepted them when we were friends.

Emmett closed his eyes for a moment.

—Billy, he said as gently as he could, you can't become friends with someone just by talking to them in a train station. Even if you spent an hour together sitting on a bench, you would hardly know anything about them.

—I know a lot about Mrs. Simpson, Billy corrected. I know that she was raised outside Ottumwa, Iowa, on a farm just like ours, although they only grew corn and it never got foreclosed. And she has two daughters, one who lives in St. Louis and one who lives in Chicago. And the one who lives in Chicago, whose name is Mary, is about to have a baby. Her first. And that's why Mrs. Simpson was here in the station. In order to take the Empire Special to Chicago so that she could help Mary with the care of the baby. Mr. Simpson couldn't go because he's the president of the Lions Club and is presiding over a dinner on Thursday night.

Emmett held up his hands.

—All right, Billy. I can see that you've learned a lot about Mrs. Simpson. So the two of you may not be strangers, exactly. You've been getting acquainted with each other. But that still doesn't make you friends. To become friends doesn't take just an hour or two. It takes a bit longer. Okay?

—Okay.

Emmett picked up his sandwich and took another bite.

—How much? asked Billy.

Emmett swallowed.

—How much?

—How much longer do you need to talk to a stranger before they become your friend?

For a moment, Emmett considered wading into the intricacies of how relationships evolve over time. Instead, he said:

—Ten days.

Billy thought about this for a moment, then shook his head.

—Ten days seems like a very long time to have to wait to become a friend, Emmett.

—Six days? suggested Emmett.

Billy took a bite and chewed as he considered, then nodded his head with satisfaction.

—Three days, he said.

—All right, said Emmett. We'll agree that it takes at least three days for someone to become a friend. But before that we'll think of them as strangers.

—Or acquaintances, said Billy.

—Or acquaintances.

The brothers went back to eating.

Emmett gestured with his head toward the big red book, which Billy had set down in the spot where Mrs. Simpson had been.

—What is this book you've been reading?

—*Professor Abacus Abernathe's Compendium of Heroes, Adventurers, and Other Intrepid Travelers.*

—Sounds compelling. Can I take a look?

With a touch of concern, Billy looked from the book to his brother's hands and back again.

Setting his sandwich down on the bench, Emmett carefully wiped his hands on his napkin. Then Billy passed him the book.

Knowing his brother as he did, Emmett did not simply open the book to some random page. He began at the beginning—the *very* beginning—by opening to the endpapers. And it was a good thing he had. For while the book's cover was solid red with a golden title, the endpapers were illustrated with a detailed map of the world criss-crossed by an array of dotted lines. Each of the different lines was identified by a letter of the alphabet and presumably indicated the route of a different adventurer.

Billy, who had put down his sandwich and wiped his hands on his own napkin, moved a little closer to Emmett so that they could study the book together—just as he had when he was younger and Emmett would read to him from a picture book. And just as in those days, Emmett looked to Billy to see if he was ready to continue. At Billy's nod, Emmett turned to the title page, where he was surprised to find an inscription.

> *To the Intrepid Billy Watson,*
> *With wishes for all manner of travels and adventures,*
> *Ellie Matthiessen*

Though the name seemed vaguely familiar, Emmett couldn't re-member who Ellie Matthiessen was. Billy must have sensed his broth-er's curiosity, because he gently put a finger on her signature.

—The librarian.

Of course, thought Emmett. The one with the glasses who had spoken so fondly of Billy.

Turning the page, Emmett came to the table of contents.

Achilles
Boone
Caesar
Dantès
Edison
Fogg

Galileo
Hercules
Ishmael
Jason
King Arthur
Lincoln
Magellan
Napoleon
Orpheus
Polo
Quixote
Robin Hood
Sinbad
Theseus
Ulysses
da Vinci
Washington
Xenos
You
Zorro

—They're in alphabetical order, said Billy.

After a moment, Emmett turned back to the endpapers to compare the heroes' names with the letters attached to the various dotted lines. Yes, he thought, there was Magellan sailing from Spain to the East Indies, and Napoleon marching into Russia, and Daniel Boone exploring the wilds of Kentucky.

Having glanced briefly at the introduction, Emmett began turning through the book's twenty-six chapters, each of which was eight pages long. While each offered a glimpse of the hero's boyhood, the primary focus was on his exploits, achievements, and legacy. Emmett could understand why his brother could return to this book again and again, because each chapter had an array of maps and illustrations designed to fascinate: like the blueprint of da Vinci's flying machine and the plan of the labyrinth in which Theseus fought the Minotaur.

As he neared the end of the book, Emmett came to a stop on two pages that were blank.

—Looks like they forgot to print a chapter.

—You missed a page.

Reaching over, Billy turned the page back. Here again the leaves were blank except that at the top of the left-hand page was the chapter title: *You*.

Billy touched the empty page with a hint of reverence.

—This is where Professor Abernathe invites you to set down the story of your own adventure.

—I guess you haven't had your adventure yet, said Emmett with a smile.

—I think we're on it now, said Billy.

—Maybe you can make a start of setting it down while we're waiting for the train.

Billy shook his head. Then he turned all the way back to the very first chapter and read the opening sentence:

—*It is fitting that we begin our adventures with the story of Swift-Footed Achilles, whose ancient exploits were forever immortalized by Homer in his epic poem* The Iliad.

Billy looked up from his book to explain.

—The causes of the Trojan War began with the Judgment of Paris. Angered that she was not invited to a banquet on Olympus, the goddess of discord threw a golden apple on the table with the inscription *For the Fairest*. When Athena, Hera, and Aphrodite each claimed the apple as their own, Zeus sent them to earth, where Paris, a Trojan prince, was chosen to resolve the dispute.

Billy pointed to an illustration of three loosely clad women gathered around a young man sitting under a tree.

—To influence Paris, Athena offered him wisdom, Hera offered him power, and Aphrodite offered him the most beautiful woman in the world, Helen of Sparta, the wife of King Menelaus. When Paris chose Aphrodite, she helped him spirit Helen away, resulting in Menelaus's outrage and the declaration of war. But Homer didn't begin his story at the beginning.

Billy moved his finger to the third paragraph and pointed to a three-word phrase in Latin.

—Homer began his story *in medias res*, which means *in the middle of the thing*. He began in the ninth year of the war with the hero, Achilles, nursing his anger in his tent. And ever since then, this is the way that many of the greatest adventure stories have been told.

Billy looked up at his brother.

—I am pretty sure that we are on our adventure, Emmett. But I won't be able to make a start of setting it down until I know where the middle of it is.

Duchess

WOOLLY AND I WERE lying on our beds in a HoJo's about fifty miles west of Chicago. When we had passed the first one, right after crossing the Mississippi into Illinois, Woolly had admired the orange roof and blue steeple. When we passed the second one, he did a double take—like he was worried that he was seeing things, or that I had somehow lost my bearings.

—No need to fret, I said. It's just a Howard Johnson's.

—A Howard Who's?

—It's a restaurant and motor lodge, Woolly. They're everywhere you go, and they always look like that.

—All of them?

—All of them.

By the time Woolly was sixteen, he had been to Europe at least five times. He'd been to London and Paris and Vienna, where he'd wandered the halls of museums and attended the opera and climbed to the top of the Eiffel Tower. But while on his native soil, Woolly had spent most of his time shuttling between an apartment on Park Avenue, the house in the Adirondacks, and the campuses of three New England prep schools. What Woolly didn't know about America would fill the Grand Canyon.

Woolly looked back over his shoulder as we passed the entrance to the restaurant.

—Twenty-eight flavors of ice cream, he quoted in some amazement.

So when it was growing late and we were tired and hungry and Woolly saw a bright blue steeple rising above the horizon, there was just no escaping it.

Woolly had spent plenty of nights in hotels, but never in one like a Howard Johnson's. When we came into the room, he examined it like a private detective from another planet. He opened the closets, startled to find an ironing board and iron. He opened the bedside drawer, startled to find a Bible. And when he went into the bathroom, he came right back out holding up two little bars of soap.

—They're individually wrapped!

Once we had settled in, Woolly turned on the television. When the signal came up, there was the Lone Ranger, wearing a hat even bigger and whiter than Chef Boy-Ar-Dee's. He was talking to a young gunslinger, giving him a lecture on truth, justice, and the American way. You could tell the gunslinger was losing his patience, but just when he was about to reach for his six-shooter, Woolly turned the channel.

Now it was Sergeant Joe Friday in a suit and fedora giving the exact same speech to a delinquent working on his motorcycle. The delinquent was losing his patience too. But just when it looked like he was going to hurl his ratchet at Sergeant Friday's head, Woolly turned the channel.

Here we go again, I thought.

Sure enough, Woolly kept switching the channel until he found a commercial. Then after lowering the volume all the way, he propped his pillows and made himself comfortable.

Wasn't that classic Woolly? In the car he was mesmerized by the sound of advertisements without their pictures. Now he wanted to watch the pictures of advertisements without their sounds. When the commercial break was over, Woolly turned off his light and slid down so he could lie with his hands behind his head and stare at the ceiling.

Woolly had taken a few more drops of medicine after dinner and I figured they'd be working their magic right about now. So I was a little surprised when he addressed me.

—Hey, Duchess, he said, still looking at the ceiling.

—Yeah, Woolly?

—On the Saturday night at eight when you and me and Emmett and Billy are sitting at the table by the jukebox, who else will be there?

Lying back, I looked up at the ceiling too.

—At Leonello's? Let's see. On a Saturday night you'd have a few of the top dogs from city hall. A boxer and some mobsters. Maybe Joe DiMaggio and Marilyn Monroe, if they happen to be in town.

—They would all be at Leonello's on the same night?

—That's the way it goes, Woolly. You open a place that no one can get into, and everybody wants to be there.

Woolly thought about this for a minute.

—Where are they sitting?

I pointed to a spot on the ceiling.

—The gangsters are in the booth next to the mayor. The boxer is over by the bar eating oysters with some chantoosie. And the DiMaggios are at the table next to ours. But here's the most important part, Woolly. Over there in the booth by the kitchen door is a small balding man in a pinstripe suit sitting all by himself.

—I see him, said Woolly. Who is he?

—Leonello Brandolini.

. . .

—You mean the owner?

—None other.

—And he sits by himself?

—Exactly. At least, in the early part of the evening. Usually, he settles in around six o'clock before anyone else is in the place. He'll have a little something to eat and a glass of Chianti. He'll go over the books and maybe take a call on one of those phones with the long cord that they can bring right to your table. But then around eight, when the place is starting to hum, he'll polish off a double espresso and make his way from table to table. *How is everybody tonight?* he'll say, while patting a customer's shoulder. *It's good to see you again. You hungry? I hope so. 'Cause there's gonna be plenty to eat.* After giving the ladies a few compliments, he'll signal the bartender. *Hey, Rocko. Another round over here for my friends.* Then he'll move on to the next table, where there'll be more shoulder patting, more compliments for the ladies, and another round of drinks. Or maybe this time, it's a plate of calamari, or some cannoli. Either way, it's on the house. And when Leonello's finished making his rounds, everybody in the place—and I mean everybody from the mayor to Marilyn Monroe—will feel like tonight is something special.

Woolly was silent, giving the moment its due. Then I told him something I had never told anyone before.

—That's what I would do, Woolly. That's what I would do, if I had fifty grand.

I could hear him roll over on his side so he could look at me.

—You'd get a table at Leonello's?

I laughed.

—No, Woolly. I'd open *my own* Leonello's. A little Italian place with red leather booths and Sinatra on the box. A place where there are no menus and every table is spoken for. In the booth by the kitchen, I'd have a little dinner and take some calls. Then around eight, after a double espresso, I'd go from table to table greeting the customers and telling the bartender to send them another round of drinks—on the house.

I could tell that Woolly liked my idea almost as much as he liked Billy's, because after he rolled on his back he was smiling at the ceiling, imagining what the whole scene would look like almost as clearly as I could. Maybe even more so.

Tomorrow, I thought, I'll get him to draw me a floor plan.

—Where would it be? he asked after a moment.

—I don't know yet, Woolly. But once I've decided, you'll be the first to know.

And he smiled at that too.

A few minutes later, he was in Slumberland. I could tell because when his arm slipped off the edge of the bed, he left it hanging there with his fingers grazing the carpet.

Getting up, I returned his arm to his side and covered him with the blanket from the bottom of the bed. Then I filled a glass with water and placed it on the nightstand. Though Woolly's medicine always left him thirsty in the morning, he never seemed to remember to put a glass of water within reach before drifting off to sleep.

When I had turned off the TV, undressed, and climbed under my own covers, what I found myself wondering was *Where would it be?*

From the beginning, I had always imagined that when I had my own place it would be in the city—probably down in the Village on MacDougal or Sullivan Street, in one of those little spots around the corner from the jazz clubs and cafés. But maybe I was on the wrong track. Maybe what I should be doing is opening in a state where they don't have a Leonello's yet. A state like . . . California.

Sure, I thought. California.

After we had picked up Woolly's trust and driven back to Nebraska, we wouldn't even have to get out of the car. It would be just like this morning with Woolly and Billy in the back seat, and me and Emmett up front, only now the arrow on Billy's compass would be pointed west.

The problem was that I wasn't so sure about San Francisco.

Don't get me wrong. Frisco's a town with plenty of atmosphere—what with the fog drifting along the wharf, and the winos drifting through the Tenderloin, and the giant paper dragons drifting down the streets of Chinatown. That's why in the movies someone's always getting murdered there. And yet, despite all its atmosphere, San Francisco didn't seem to warrant a spot like Leonello's. It just didn't have the panache.

But Los Angeles?

The city of Los Angeles has so much panache it could bottle it and sell it overseas. It's where the movie stars have lived since the beginning of movie stars. More recently, it's where the boxers and mobsters were setting up shop. Even Sinatra had made the move. And if Ol' Blue Eyes could trade in the Big Apple for Tinseltown, so could we.

Los Angeles, I thought to myself, where it's summer all winter long, every waitress is a starlet in the making, and the street names have long since run out of presidents and trees.

Now that's what I call a fresh start!

But Emmett was right about the kit bag. Making a fresh start isn't just a matter of having a new address in a new town. It isn't a matter of having a new job, or a new phone number, or even a new name. A fresh start requires the cleaning of the slate. And that means paying off all that you owe, and collecting all that you're due.

By letting go of the farm and taking his beating in the public square, Emmett had already balanced his accounts. If we were going to head out west together, then maybe it was time for me to balance mine.

It didn't take me long to do the math. I'd spent more than enough nights in my bunk at Salina thinking about my unsettled debts, so the big ones rose right to the surface, three of them in all: One I would have to make good on, and two I would have to collect.

Emmett

EMMETT AND BILLY MOVED quickly through the scrub at the base of the embankment, headed west. It would have been easier going were they to walk on the tracks, but the notion of doing so struck Emmett as reckless even in the moonlight. Stopping, he looked back at Billy, who was doing his best to keep up.

—Are you sure you don't want me to carry your backpack?

—I've got it, Emmett.

As Emmett resumed his pace, he glanced at Billy's watch and saw that it was quarter to twelve. They had left the station at quarter past eleven. Though the walking had been harder than Emmett had anticipated, it seemed like they should have been at the pine grove by now, so he breathed a sigh of relief when he finally saw the pointed silhouettes of evergreens up ahead. Reaching the grove, they took a few steps into its shadows and waited in silence, listening to the owls overhead and smelling the scent of the pine needles underfoot.

Glancing again at Billy's watch, Emmett saw that it was now eleven fifty-five.

—Wait here, he said.

Climbing the embankment, Emmett looked down the tracks. In the distance he could see the pinpoint of light that emanated from the front of the locomotive. As Emmett rejoined his brother in the shadows, he was glad they hadn't walked on the tracks. For even though to Emmett's eye the locomotive had seemed a mile away, by the time he reached his brother, the long chain of boxcars was already flashing past.

Whether from excitement or anxiety, Billy took Emmett's hand.

Emmett guessed that fifty cars raced by before the train began to slow. When it finally rolled to a stop, the last ten cars were right in front of where Emmett and Billy were standing, just as the panhandler had said they would be.

So far, everything had happened as the panhandler had said it would.

What's the difference between a ton of flour and a ton of crackers? That's what the panhandler had asked Emmett back at the freight yard. Then with a wink he had answered his own riddle: *A few hundred cubic feet.*

A company that has freight traveling back and forth along the same route—he went on to explain in his good-natured way—was generally better off if they had their own capacity so they weren't exposed to fluctuations in price. Since Nabisco's facility in Manhattan received weekly deliveries of flour from the Midwest and sent weekly deliveries of finished goods back to the region, it was sensible for them to own their own cars. The only problem was that there are few things more dense than a bag of flour, and few things less so than a box of crackers. So while all of the company's cars were full when they headed west, on the way back to New York there were always five or six that were empty and that no one bothered to secure.

From the free-rider's perspective, the panhandler pointed out, the fact that the empty cars were hitched at the back of the train was particularly fortuitous, because when the engine of the Sunset East arrived in Lewis a few minutes after twelve, its caboose would still be a mile from the station.

Once the train had stopped, Emmett quickly scaled the embankment and tried the doors of the closest cars, finding the third one unlocked. After beckoning Billy and giving him a boost, Emmett climbed inside and pulled the door shut with a loud clack—throwing the car into darkness.

The panhandler had said that they could leave the hatch in the roof open for light and air—as long as they were sure to close it when they were approaching Chicago, where an open hatch was unlikely to go unnoticed. But Emmett hadn't thought to open the hatch before he closed the boxcar's door, or even to make note of where it was. Reaching out his hands, he felt for the latch so that he could open the door again, but the train jolted forward, sending him stumbling back against the opposite wall.

In the darkness he could hear his brother moving.

—Stay put, Billy, he cautioned, while I find the hatch.

But suddenly there was a beam of light shining in his direction.

—Do you want to use my flashlight?

Emmett smiled.

—Yes, Billy, I would. Or better yet, why don't you train the beam on that ladder in the corner.

Climbing the ladder, Emmett threw the hatch open, letting in moonlight and a welcome rush of air. Having been exposed to the sun all day, the boxcar's interior must have been eighty degrees.

—Why don't we stretch out over here, Emmett said, leading Billy to the other end of the car, where they wouldn't be so easily seen were someone to look through the hatch.

Taking two shirts from his backpack, Billy handed one to Emmett, explaining that if they folded them over, they could use them as pillows, just like soldiers. Then having refastened the straps, Billy lay down with his head on his folded shirt and was soon sound asleep.

Though Emmett was almost as exhausted as his brother, he knew that he wouldn't be able to fall asleep so quickly. He was too keyed up from the day's events. What he really wanted was a cigarette. He would have to settle for a drink of water.

Quietly picking up Billy's backpack, Emmett carried it to a spot beneath the hatch, where the air was a little cooler, and sat with his back to the wall. Unfastening the backpack's straps, he removed Billy's canteen, twisted off the cap, and took a drink. Emmett was so thirsty he could easily have emptied it, but they might not have a chance to get more water until they arrived in New York, so he took a second swallow, returned the canteen to the pack, and securely refastened the straps just as his brother would. Emmett was about to set the backpack down when he noticed the outer pocket. Glancing at Billy, he undid the flap and removed the manila envelope.

For a moment Emmett sat with the envelope in his hands as if he were trying to weigh it. After taking a second glance at his brother, he unwound the red thread and poured his mother's postcards into his lap.

As a boy, Emmett would never have described his mother as unhappy. Not to another person and not to himself. But at some point, at an unspoken level he had come to know that she was. He had come to know it not by tears or open laments, but by the sight of unfinished tasks in the early afternoon. Coming downstairs into the kitchen, he might find a dozen carrots lying on the cutting board beside the chopping knife, six of them sliced and six of them whole. Or returning from the barn, he might find half of the laundry flapping on the line and the other half damp in a basket. Looking for where his mother had gotten to, he would often find her sitting on the front steps with her elbows on her knees. When quietly, almost tentatively, Emmett would say, *Mom?*, she would look up as if pleasantly surprised. Making room for him on the step, she would put her arm over his shoulder or tousle his hair, then go back to looking at whatever it was that she had been looking at before—something somewhere between the front porch steps and the horizon.

Because young children don't know how things are supposed to be done, they will come to imagine that the habits of their household are the habits of the world. If a child grows up in a family where angry words are exchanged over supper, he will assume that angry words are exchanged at every kitchen table; while if a child grows up in a family where no words are exchanged over supper at all, he will assume that all families eat in silence. And yet, despite the prevalence of this truth, the young Emmett knew that chores left half done in the early afternoon were a sign of something amiss—just as he would come to know a few years later that the shifting of crops from one season to the next was the sign of a farmer who's at a loss what to do.

Holding the postcards up to the moonlight, Emmett revisited them one by one in their westward order—Ogallala, Cheyenne, Rawlins, Rock Springs, Salt Lake City, Ely, Reno, Sacramento, San Francisco—scanning the pictures from corner to corner and reading the messages word for word, as if he were an intelligence officer looking for a coded communication from an agent in the field. But if tonight he studied the cards more closely than he had at the kitchen table, he studied none more closely than he studied the last.

This is the Palace of the Legion of Honor in San Francisco's Lincoln Park, it read, *and every year on the Fourth of July it has one of the biggest fireworks displays in all of California.*

Emmett had no recollection of telling Billy about their mother's love of fireworks, but it was uncontestably so. When she was growing up in Boston, his mother would spend her summers in a little town on Cape Cod. While she hadn't spoken much about her time there, she had described with an old excitement how the volunteer fire department would sponsor a fireworks display over the harbor every Fourth of July. When she was a child, she and her family would watch from the end of their pier. But once she got older, she was allowed to row out among the sailboats that were swinging on their moorings so she could watch the pyrotechnics while lying alone in the bottom of her boat.

When Emmett was eight, his mother learned from Mr. Cartwright at the hardware store that the town of Seward—a little more than an hour from Morgen—had quite a little celebration on the Fourth of July, with a parade in the afternoon and fireworks after dark. Emmett's mother wasn't interested in the parade. So after an early supper, Emmett and his parents got in their truck and made the journey.

When Mr. Cartwright had said it was *quite a little celebration*, Emmett's mother had imagined it would be like any other small-town festivity, with banners made by the schoolchildren and refreshments sold off folding tables by the women of the parish. But when they arrived, she was stunned to discover that the Fourth of July in Seward put to shame any Fourth of July that she had ever seen. It was a celebration that the township prepared for all year and to which people came from as far away as Des Moines. By the time the Watsons arrived, the only parking was a mile from the center of town, and when they finally walked into Plum Creek Park, where the fireworks display was to take place, every square inch of lawn had been claimed by families on blankets eating their picnic dinners.

The following year, his mother had no intention of making the same mistake. At breakfast on the Fourth, she announced they would be leaving for Seward right after lunch. But once she had prepared their picnic dinner and opened the cutlery drawer to take out some forks and knives, she stopped and stared. Then turning around, she walked out of the kitchen and up the stairs with Emmett close on her heels. Moving a chair from her bedroom, she climbed up on it and reached for a short length of string that was hanging from the ceiling. When she pulled the string, a hatch dropped down with a sliding ladder that led to an attic.

Wide-eyed, Emmett was prepared for his mother to tell him that he should wait right there, but she was so intent upon her purpose she mounted the ladder without pausing to deliver a cautionary remark. And when he climbed up the narrow steps after her, she was so engaged in moving boxes she didn't bother to send him back down.

As his mother went about her search, Emmett surveyed the attic's strange inventory: an old wireless that was almost as tall as he was, a broken rocking chair, a black typewriter, and two large trunks covered in colorful stickers.

—Here we are, his mother said.

Giving Emmett a smile, she held up what looked like a small suitcase. Only instead of leather, it was made of wicker.

Back in the kitchen, his mother put the suitcase on the table.

Emmett could see that she was perspiring from the warmth of the attic, and when she wiped her brow with the back of her hand, she left a streak of dust on her skin. After throwing the clasps on the case, she smiled at Emmett again, then opened the lid.

Emmett knew well enough that a suitcase stored in an attic was likely to be empty, so he was startled to find that not only was this one packed, it was packed to perfection. Neatly arranged inside was everything you could possibly need to have a picnic. Under one strap there was a stack of six red plates, while under another, a tower of six red cups. There were long narrow troughs holding forks, knives, and spoons, and a shorter one for a wine opener. There were even two specially shaped indentations for salt and pepper shakers. And in the recess of the lid, there was a red-and-white-checkered tablecloth held in place by two leather straps.

In all his life, Emmett had never seen anything so ingeniously put together—with nothing missing, nothing extra, and everything in its place. He wouldn't see anything quite like it again, until at the age of fifteen, when he saw the worktable in Mr. Schulte's shed with its orderly arrangement of slots, pegs, and hooks to hold his various tools.

—Golly, Emmett had said, and his mother had laughed.

—It was from your great aunt Edna.

Then she shook her head.

—I don't think I've opened it since the day we were married. But we're going to put it to use tonight!

That year they arrived in Seward at two in the afternoon and found a spot right in the center of the lawn to spread out their checkered cloth. Emmett's father, who had expressed some reluctance about going so early in the day, showed no signs of impatience once they were there. In fact, as something of a surprise, he produced a bottle of wine from his bag. And as Emmett's parents drank, Emmett's father told stories about his penny-pinching aunt Sadie and his absent-minded uncle Dave and all his other crazy relatives back East, making Emmett's mother laugh in a way she rarely laughed.

As the hours passed, the lawn filled with more blankets and baskets, with more laughter and good feelings. When night had finally fallen, and the Watsons lay on their checkered cloth with Emmett in the middle, and the first of the fireworks whistled and popped, his mother had said: *I wouldn't have missed this for the world.* And driving home that night, it had seemed to Emmett that the three of them would be attending Seward's Fourth of July celebration for the rest of their lives.

But the following February—in the weeks after Billy was born—his mother was suddenly not herself. Some days she was so tired she couldn't even start the chores that she used to leave half done. Other days she didn't get out of bed.

When Billy was three weeks old, Mrs. Ebbers—whose children had children of their own—began to come every day to help keep house and see to Billy's needs while Emmett's mother tried to regain her strength. By April, Mrs. Ebbers was coming just in the mornings, and by June, she wasn't coming at all. But over dinner on the first of July, when Emmett's father asked with some enthusiasm what time they should head out for Seward, Emmett's mother said she wasn't sure she wanted to go.

Looking across the table, Emmett didn't think he had ever seen his father so heartbroken. But as was his way, Emmett's father pushed ahead, buoyed by a confidence that wasn't overly inclined to learn from experience. On the morning of the Fourth, Emmett's father made the picnic dinner. He pulled down the hatch and climbed the narrow ladder in order to retrieve the basket from the attic. He put Billy in the bassinet and brought the truck around to the front door. And when at one o'clock he came inside and called, *Come on, everybody! We don't want to lose our favorite spot!* Emmett's mother agreed to go.

Or rather, she acquiesced.

She climbed in the truck and didn't say a word.

None of them said a word.

But once they arrived in Seward and had made their way to the center of the park and his father had billowed out the checkered cloth and begun to take the forks and knives from their troughs, Emmett's mother said:

—Here, let me help.

And in that moment, it was as if a great weight had been lifted from them all.

After putting out the red plastic cups, she laid out the sandwiches that her husband had made. She fed Billy the apple sauce that her husband had thought to pack, and rocked Billy's bassinet back and forth until he fell asleep. As they drank the wine that her husband had remembered to bring, she asked him to tell some of those stories about his crazy uncles and aunts. And when, shortly after nightfall, the first salvo exploded over the park in a great distending spray of colored sparks, she reached out in order to squeeze her husband's hand, and gave him a tender smile as tears ran down her face. And when Emmett and his father saw her tears, they smiled in return, for they could tell that these were tears of gratitude—gratitude that rather than relenting to her initial lack of enthusiasm, her husband had persisted so that the four of them could share in this grand exhibition on this warm summer night.

When the Watsons got home, as Emmett's father brought in the bassinet and the picnic basket, Emmett's mother led him upstairs by the hand, tucked him tightly under his covers, and gave him a kiss on the forehead, before going down the hallway to do the same for Billy.

That night Emmett slept as soundly as any night in his life. And when he woke in the morning, his mother was gone.

With a final look at the Palace of the Legion of Honor, Emmett returned the postcards to their envelope. He spun the thin red thread to seal them inside, and stowed them in Billy's backpack, being sure to tightly cinch the straps.

That first year had been a hard one for Charlie Watson, Emmett remembered as he took his place beside his brother. The trials of weather continued unabated. Financial difficulties loomed. And the people of the town, they gossiped freely about Mrs. Watson's sudden departure. But what weighed on his father the most—what weighed on them both—was the realization that when Emmett's mother had gripped her husband's hand as the fireworks began, it hadn't been in gratitude for his persistence, for his fealty and support, it had been in gratitude that by gently coaxing her from her malaise in order to witness this magical display, he had reminded her of what joy could be, if only she were willing to leave her daily life behind.

SEVEN

Duchess

IT'S A MAP! exclaimed Woolly in surprise.

—So it is.

We were sitting in a booth at the HoJo's waiting for our breakfast. In front of each of us was a paper place mat that was also a simplified map of the state of Illinois showing major roads and towns along with some out-of-scale illustrations of regional landmarks. In addition, there were sixteen Howard Johnson's, each with its little orange roof and little blue steeple.

—This is where we are, Woolly said, pointing to one of them.

—I'll take your word for it.

—And here's the Lincoln Highway. And look at this!

Before I could look over to see what *this* was, our waitress—who couldn't have been more than seventeen—set our plates down on top of our place mats.

Woolly frowned. After watching her retreat, he nudged his plate to the right so that he could continue studying the map while he pretended to eat.

It was ironic to see how little attention Woolly paid to his breakfast, given how much attention he had paid to ordering it. When our waitress had handed him the menu, he looked a little unnerved by its size. Taking a breath, he set about reading the descriptions of every single item out loud. Then, to make sure he hadn't missed anything, he went

back to the beginning and read them again. When our waitress returned to take our order, he reported with self-assurance that he was
going to have waffles—or make that scrambled eggs—only to switch
to the hotcakes when she was turning to go. But when his hotcakes
arrived, having decorated them with an elaborate spiral of syrup,
Woolly ignored them at his bacon's expense. I, on the other hand, who
hadn't even bothered to glance at the menu, made quick business of
my corned beef hash and sunny-side ups.

Having cleaned my plate, I sat back and took a look around, thinking if Woolly wanted to get a sense of what my restaurant was going
to be like, he need look no further than a Howard Johnson's. Because
in every respect it was going to be the opposite.

From the standpoint of ambience, the good people at Howard Johnson's had decided to carry the colors of their well-known rooftop into
the restaurant by dressing the booths in bright orange and the waitresses in bright blue—despite the fact that the combination of orange
and blue hasn't been known to stimulate an appetite since the beginning of time. The definitive architectural element of the space was an
uninterrupted chain of picture windows, which gave everyone an un-
impeded view of the parking lot. The cuisine was a gussied-up version
of what you'd find in a diner, and the defining characteristic of the
clientele was that with a single glance you could tell more about them
than you wanted to know.

Take the red-faced fellow in the next booth who was wiping up his
yolk with a corner of whole wheat toast. A traveling salesman, if ever
I saw one—and I've seen a lifetime supply. On the family tree of un-
memorable middle-aged men, traveling salesmen are the first cousins
of the has-been performers. They go to the same towns in the same
cars and stay at the same hotels. In fact, the only way you can tell
them apart is that the salesmen wear more sensible shoes.

As if I needed any proof, after watching him use his command of percentages to tally his waitress's tip, I saw him annotate the receipt, fold it in two, and stow it in his wallet for the boys back in accounting.

As the salesman stood to go, I noticed from the clock on the wall that it was already half past seven.

—Woolly, I said, the whole point of getting up early is to get an early start. So why don't you tackle some of those hotcakes while I go to the john. Then we can pay the bill and hit the road.

—Sure thing, said Woolly, while pushing his plate another few inches to the right.

Before going to the men's room, I got some change from the cashier and slipped into a phone booth. I knew that Ackerly had retired to Indiana, I just didn't know where. So I had the operator look up the number for Salina and put me through. Given the hour, it rang eight times before someone finally answered. I think it was Lucinda, the brunette with the pink glasses who guarded the warden's door. Taking a page from my father's book, I gave her the old King Lear. That's what my father would use whenever he needed a little help from someone on the other end of the line. Naturally, it entailed a British accent, but with a touch of befuddlement.

Explaining that I was Ackerly's uncle from England, I told her that I wanted to send him a card on Independence Day in order to assure him there were no hard feelings, but I seemed to have misplaced my address book. Was there any way that she could see to helping a forgetful old soul? A minute later, she returned with the answer: 132 Rhododendron Road in South Bend.

With a whistle on my lips, I traveled from the phone booth to the men's room, and who should I find standing at the urinals but the red-faced fellow from the neighboring booth. When I finished doing my business and joined him at the sinks, I gave him a quick smile in the mirror.

—You, sir, strike me as a salesman.

A little impressed, he looked back at me in the reflection.

—I am in sales.

I nodded my head.

—You've got that friendly man-of-the-world look about you.

—Why, thanks.

—Door-to-door?

—No, he said, a little offended. I'm an account man.

—Of course you are. In what line, if you don't mind me asking.

—Kitchen appliances.

—Like refrigerators and dishwashers?

He winced a little, as if I'd hit a sore spot.

—We specialize in the smaller electric conveniences. Like blenders and hand mixers.

—Small but essential, I pointed out.

—Oh, yes, indeed.

—So tell me, how do you do it? When you go into an account, I mean, how do you make a sale? Of your blender, for instance?

—Our blender sells itself.

From the way he delivered the line, I could tell that he had done so ten thousand times before.

—You're too modest, I'm sure. But seriously, when you speak of your blender versus the competitions', how do you . . . differentiate it?

At the word *differentiate*, he grew rather grave and confidential. Never mind that he was talking to an eighteen-year-old kid in the bathroom of a Howard Johnson's. He was gearing up for the pitch now and couldn't stop himself even if he wanted to.

—I was only half kidding, he began, when I remarked that our blender sells itself. Because, you see, it wasn't so long ago that all the leading blenders came with three settings: low, medium, and high. Our company was the first to differentiate its blender buttons by the *type* of blending: mix, beat, and whip.

—Ingenious. You must have the market to yourself.

—For a time, we did, he admitted. But soon enough our competitors were following suit.

—So you've got to keep one step ahead.

—Precisely. That's why this year, I'm proud to say, we became the first blender manufacturer in America to introduce a fourth stage of blending.

—A fourth stage? After mix, beat, and whip?

The suspense was killing me.

—Puree.

—Bravo, I said.

And in a way, I meant it.

I gave him another once-over, this one in admiration. Then I asked him if he had fought in the war.

—I didn't have the honor of doing so, he said, also for the ten thousandth time.

I shook my head in sympathy.

—What a hoopla when the boys came home. Fireworks and parades. Mayors pinning medals on lapels. And all the good-looking dames lining up to kiss any putz in a uniform. But you know what I think? I think the American people should pay a little more homage to the traveling salesmen.

He couldn't tell if I was having him on or not. So I put a hint of emotion into my voice.

—My father was a traveling salesman. Oh, the miles he logged. The doorbells he rang. The nights he spent far from the comforts of home. I say to you that traveling salesmen are not simply hardworking men, they are the foot soldiers of capitalism!

I think he actually blushed at that one. Though it was hard to tell given his complexion.

—It's an honor to meet you, sir, I said, and I stuck out my hand even though I hadn't dried it yet.

. . .

When I came out of the bathroom, I saw our waitress and flagged her down.

—Do you need something else? she asked.

—Just the check, I replied. We've got places to go and people to see.

At the phrase *places to go*, she looked a little wistful. I do believe if I had told her we were headed for New York and offered her a ride, she would have hopped into the back seat without taking the time to change out of her uniform—if for no other reason than to see what happens when you drive off the edge of the place mat.

—I'll bring it right over, she said.

As I headed to our booth, I regretted making fun of our neighbor for his attention to receipts. Because it suddenly occurred to me that we should be doing something similar on Emmett's behalf. Since we were using the money from his envelope to cover our expenses, he had every right to expect a full accounting upon our return—so that he could be reimbursed before we divvied up the trust.

The night before, I'd left Woolly to pay the dinner bill while I checked into the hotel. I was going to ask him how much it ended up costing, but when I got to our booth, there was no Woolly.

Where could he have gotten to, I wondered, with a roll of the eyes. He couldn't be in the bathroom, since that's where I had just come from. Knowing him to be an admirer of shiny and colorful things, I looked over at the ice cream counter, but there were just two little kids pressing their noses against the glass, wishing it wasn't so early in the morning. With a growing sense of foreboding, I turned to the plate-glass windows.

Out I looked into the parking lot, moving my gaze across the shimmering sea of glass and chrome to the very spot in which I had parked the Studebaker, and in which the Studebaker was no longer. Taking a step to my right—in order to see around a pair of beehive hairdos—I looked toward the parking lot's entrance just in time to see Emmett's car taking a right onto the Lincoln Highway.

—Jesus fucking shitting Christ.

Our waitress, who happened to arrive with the check at that very moment, turned pale.

—Excuse my French, I said.

Then glancing at the check, I gave her a twenty from the envelope.

As she hurried off for the change, I slumped down in my seat and stared across the table to where Woolly should have been. On his plate, which was back where it had started, the bacon was gone, along with a narrow wedge of hotcakes.

As I was admiring the precision with which Woolly had removed such a slender little slice from the stack, I noticed that under the white ceramic of his plate was the Formica surface of the table. Which is to say, the place mat was gone.

Shoving my plate aside, I picked up my own place mat. As I said before, it was a map of Illinois, with major roads and towns. But in the lower right-hand corner there was an inset with a map of the local downtown area, at the center of which was a little green square, and rising from the middle of that little green square, looking as large as life, was a statue of Abraham Lincoln.

Woolly

H UM DE-DUM DE-DUM, Woolly hummed as he took another look at the map in his lap. *Performance is sweeter, nothing can beat her, life is completer* . . . Oh, hum de-dum de-dum.

—Get out of the road! someone yelled as they passed the Studebaker with a triple honk of the horn.

—Apologies, apologies, apologies! replied Woolly in reciprocal triplicate, with a friendly wave of the hand.

As he angled back into his lane, Woolly acknowledged that it probably wasn't advisable to drive with a map in your lap, what with all the looking up and looking down. So keeping the steering wheel in his left hand, he held the map up in his right. That way he could look at the map out of one eye and the road out of the other.

The day before, when Duchess had secured the Phillips 66 Road Map of America at the Phillips 66 gas station, he handed it to Woolly, saying that since he was driving, Woolly would have to navigate. Woolly had accepted this responsibility with a touch of unease. When a gas station map is handed to you, it's almost the perfect size—like a playbill at the theater. But in order to read a gas station map, you have to unfold and unfold and unfold it until the Pacific Ocean is up against the gear shift and the Atlantic Ocean is lapping at the passenger-side door.

Once a gas station map is open all the way, just the sight of it is likely to make you woozy, because it is positutely crisscrossed from top to bottom and side to side by highways and byways and a thousand little roads, each of which is marked with a tiny little name or tiny little number. It reminded Woolly of the textbook for a biology class that he had taken while at St. Paul's. Or was it St. Mark's? Either way, early in this volume, on a left-hand page was a picture of a human skeleton. After looking carefully at this skeleton with all of the various bones in their proper places, when you turned to the next page fully expecting the skeleton to disappear, the skeleton was still there—because the next page was made of see-through paper! It was made of see-through paper so that you could study the nervous system right on top of the skeleton. And when you turned the page after that, you could study the skeleton, the nervous system, *and* the circulatory system with all of its little blue and red lines.

Woolly knew that this multilayered illustration was meant to make things perfectly clear, but he found it very unnerving. Was it a picture of a man or a woman, for instance? Old or young? Black or white? And how did all the blood cells and nerve impulses that were traveling along these complicated networks know where they were supposed to go? And once they got there, how did they find their way home? That's what the Phillips 66 road map was like: an illustration with hundreds of arteries, veins, and capillaries branching ever outward until no one traveling along any one of them could possibly know where they were going.

But this was hardly the case with the place-mat map from Howard Johnson's! It didn't have to be unfolded at all. And it wasn't covered with a confusion of highways and byways. It had exactly the right amount of roads. And those that were named were named clearly, while those that weren't named clearly weren't named at all.

The other highly commendable characteristic of the Howard Johnson's map was the illustrations. Most mapmakers are particularly good at shrinking things. The states, the towns, the rivers, the roads, every single one of them is shrunk to a smaller dimension. But on the

Howard Johnson's place mat, after reducing the towns, rivers, and roads, the mapmaker added back a selection of illustrations that were *bigger* than they were supposed to be. Like a big scarecrow in the lower left-hand corner that showed you where the cornfields were. Or the big tiger in the upper right-hand corner that showed you the Lincoln Park Zoo.

It was just the way the pirates used to draw their treasure maps. They shrunk down the ocean and the islands until they were very small and simple, but then they added back a big ship off the coast, and a big palm tree on the beach, and a big rock formation on a hill that was in the shape of a skull and was exactly fifteen paces from the X that marked the spot.

In the box that was in the lower right-hand corner of the place mat, there was a map within the map, which showed the center of town. According to this map, if you took a right on Second Street and drove an inch and a half, you would arrive at Liberty Park, in the middle of which would be a great big statue of Abraham Lincoln.

Suddenly, out of his left eye, Woolly saw the sign for Second Street. Without a moment to spare, he took a sharp right turn to the tune of another honking horn.

—Apologies, he called.

Leaning toward the windshield, he caught a glimpse of greenery.

—Here we go, he said. Here we go.

A minute later he was there.

Pulling to the curb, he opened his door and it was nearly taken off by a passing sedan.

—Whoops!

Closing the door, Woolly skootched over the seat, climbed out the passenger side, waited for a break in traffic, and dashed across the street.

In the park, it was a bright and sunny day. The trees were in leaf, the bushes in bloom, and the daisies sprouting up on both sides of the path.

—Here we go, he said again as he went zipping along.

But suddenly the daisy-lined path was intersected by another path, presenting Woolly with three different options: go left, go right, or go straight ahead. Wishing he'd thought to bring the place-mat map, Woolly looked in each direction. To his left were trees and shrubs and dark-green benches. To his right were more trees, shrubs, and benches, as well as a man in a baggy suit and floppy hat who looked vaguely familiar. But straight ahead, if Woolly squinted, he could just make out a fountain.

—Aha! he shouted.

For in Woolly's experience, statues were often found in the vicinity of fountains. Like the statue of Garibaldi that was near the fountain in Washington Square Park, or the statue of the angel on top of that big fountain in Central Park.

With heightened confidence, Woolly ran to the lip of the fountain and paused in the refreshing mist to get his bearings. What he discovered from a quick survey was that the fountain was an epicenter from which eight different paths emanated (if you included the one that he'd just come zipping along). Fending off discouragement, Woolly slowly began working his way clockwise around the fountain's circumference, peering down each of the individual paths with a hand over his eyes like a captain at sea. And there, at the end of the sixth path, was Honest Abe himself.

Rather than zip down this path, out of respect for the statue Woolly walked in long Lincolnian strides until he came to a stop a few feet away.

What a wonderful likeness, thought Woolly. Not only did it capture the president's stature, it seemed to suggest his moral courage. While for the most part, this Lincoln was depicted as one might expect, with his Shenandoah beard and his long black coat, the sculptor had made one unusual choice: In his right hand, the president was holding his hat lightly by the brim, as if he had just removed it upon meeting an acquaintance in the street.

Taking a seat on a bench in front of the statue, Woolly turned his thoughts to the day before, when Billy was explaining the history of the Lincoln Highway in the back of Emmett's car. Billy had mentioned that when it was first being constructed (in nineteen something-something), enthusiasts had painted red, white, and blue stripes on barns and fenceposts all along the route. Woolly could picture this perfectly, because it reminded him of how on the Fourth of July his family would hang red, white, and blue streamers from the rafters of the great room and the rails of the porch.

Oh, how his great-grandfather had loved the Fourth of July.

On Thanksgiving, Christmas, and Easter, Woolly's great-grandfather hadn't cared whether his children chose to celebrate the holiday with him or went off to celebrate with somebody else. But when it came to Independence Day, he did not abide absenteeism. He made it perfectly clear that every child, grandchild, and great-grandchild was expected in the Adirondacks no matter how far they had to travel.

And gather they did!

On the first of July, family members would start to pull up in the driveway, or arrive at the train station, or land at the little airstrip that was twenty miles away. By the afternoon of the second, every sleeping spot in the house was taken—with the grandparents, uncles, and aunts in the bedrooms, the younger cousins on the sleeping porch, and all the cousins who were lucky enough to be older than twelve in the tents among the pines.

When the Fourth arrived, there was a picnic lunch on the lawn, followed by canoe races, swim races, the riflery and archery contests, and a great big game of capture the flag. At six o'clock on the dot there were cocktails on the porch. At half past seven the bell would be rung and everyone would make their way inside for a supper of fried chicken, corn on the cob, and Dorothy's famous blueberry muffins. Then at ten, Uncle Bob and Uncle Randy would row out to the raft in the middle of the lake in order to launch the fireworks that they had bought in Pennsylvania.

How Billy would have loved it, thought Woolly with a smile. He would have loved the streamers on the fence rail and the tents among the trees and the baskets of blueberry muffins. But most of all, he would have loved the fireworks, which always started with whistles and pops, but would grow bigger and bigger until they seemed to fill the sky.

But even as Woolly was having this wonderful memory, his expression grew somber, for he had almost forgotten what his mother would refer to as *The Reason We're All Here*: the recitations. Every year on the Fourth of July, once all the food had been set out, in lieu of grace, the youngest child older than sixteen would take his or her place at the head of the table and recite from the Declaration of Independence.

When in the course of human events, and *We hold these truths to be self-evident*, and so forth.

But, as Woolly's great-grandfather liked to observe, if Messrs. Washington, Jefferson, and Adams had the vision to found the Republic, it was Mr. Lincoln who had the courage to perfect it. So, when the cousin who had recited from the Declaration had resumed his or her seat, the youngest child older than ten would take his or her place at the head of the table in order to recite the Gettysburg Address in its entirety.

When that was completed, the speaker would take a bow and the room would erupt into an ovation that was almost as loud as the one that followed the finale of the fireworks. Then the platters and baskets would go zipping around the table to the sound of laughter and good cheer. It was a moment that Woolly always looked forward to.

Looked forward to, that is, until the sixteenth of March 1944, the day that he turned ten.

Right after his mother and sisters had sung Happy Birthday on his behalf, his oldest sister, Kaitlin, had felt it necessary to note that come the Fourth of July, it would be Woolly's turn to stand at the head of the table. Woolly was so unnerved by this bit of news that he could barely finish his piece of chocolate cake. Because if Woolly knew anything by the age of ten, it was that he wasn't any good at rememorizing.

Sensing Woolly's concern, his sister Sarah—who seven years before had given a flawless recitation—offered to serve as his coach.

—Memorizing the Address is well within your grasp, she said to Woolly with a smile. After all, it's only ten sentences.

Initially, this assurance heartened Woolly. But when his sister showed him the actual text of the speech, Woolly discovered that while at first glance it might *seem* to be only ten sentences, the very last sentence was actually three different sentences disguised as one.

—For all intents and porpoises (as Woolly used to say), there are twelve sentences, not ten.

—Even so, Sarah replied.

But just to be sure, she suggested they start their preparations well in advance. In the first week of April, Woolly would learn to recite the first sentence word for word. Then in the second week of April, he would learn the first and second sentences. Then in the third week, the first three sentences, and so on, until twelve weeks later, just as the month of June was drawing to a close, Woolly would be able to recite the entire speech without a hitch.

And that's exactly how they prepared. Week by week, Woolly learned one sentence after another until he could recite the speech in its entirety. In fact, by the first of July he had recited it from beginning to end, not only in front of Sarah, but by himself in front of the mirror, at the kitchen sink while helping Dorothy do the dishes, and once in a canoe in the middle of the lake. So when the fateful day arrived, Woolly was ready.

After his cousin Edward had recited from the Declaration of

Independence and received a friendly round of applause, Woolly assumed the privileged spot.

But just as he was about to begin, he discovered the first problem with his sister's plan: the people. For while Woolly had recited the Address many times in front of his sister and often by himself, he had never recited it in front of anybody else. And this wasn't even anybody else. It was thirty of his closest relatives lined up on opposite sides of a table in two attentive rows, with none other than his great-grandfather seated at the opposite end.

Casting a glance at Sarah, Woolly received a nod of encouragement, which bolstered his confidence. But just as he was about to begin, Woolly discovered the second problem with his sister's plan: the attire. For while Woolly had previously recited the Address in his corduroys, his pajamas, and his bathing suit, not once had he recited it in an itchy blue blazer with a red-and-white tie gripping at his throat.

As Woolly pulled at his collar with a crooked finger, some of his younger cousins began to giggle.

—Shh, said his grandmother.

Woolly looked back to Sarah, who gave him another friendly nod.

—Go ahead, she said.

Just as she had taught, Woolly stood up straight, took two deep breaths, and began:

—*Four score and seven years*, he said. *Four score and seven years ago.*

There was more sniggering from the younger cousins, followed by another shush from his grandmother.

Remembering that Sarah had said if he got nervous he should look over the heads of the family, Woolly raised his eyes to the moose head on the wall. But finding the gaze of the moose unsympathetic, he tried looking instead at his shoes.

—*Four score and seven years ago . . .*, he began again.

—*Our fathers brought forth*, Sarah softly prompted.

—*Our fathers brought forth*, Woolly said looking up at his sister. *Our fathers brought forth on this countenance.*

—*On this continent . . .*

—*On this continent a new nation. A new nation . . .*

— *. . . Conceived in Liberty*, said a friendly voice.

Only it wasn't Sarah's voice. It was the voice of cousin James, who had graduated from Princeton a few weeks before. And this time, when Woolly renewed his recital, Sarah and James joined in.

—*Conceived in Liberty*, the three of them said together, *and dedicated to the proposition that all men are created equal.*

Then other relatives who in their time had been tasked with reciting Mr. Lincoln's Address added their voices. Then joining the chorus were members of the family who had never been required to recite the Address, but who had heard it so many times before that they too knew it by heart. Soon, everyone at the table—including Great-grandpa—was reciting; and when all together they said those grand and hopeful words that the *government of the people, by the people, for the people, shall not perish from the earth*, the family burst into a round of cheering like the room had never heard.

Surely, this was the way that Abraham Lincoln had meant his Address to be recited. Not as a little boy standing alone at the head of a table in an itchy coat, but as four generations of a family speaking together in unison.

Oh, if only his father could have been there, thought Woolly, wiping a tear from his cheek with the flat of his hand. If only his father could be here now.

—·—

After Woolly had battled away the blues and finished paying his respects to the president, he went back the way he'd come. This time, when he reached the fountain, he was careful to walk *counterclockwise* around its circumference until he reached the sixth path.

No path looks quite the same in both directions, so as Woolly progressed, he began to wonder if he'd made a mistake. Perhaps he had miscounted the number of paths when he had counterclockwised the fountain. But just as he was considering retracing his steps, he saw the man in the floppy hat.

When Woolly gave him the smile of recognition, the man gave him the smile of recognition back. But when Woolly gave him a little wave, the man didn't return it. Instead, he reached into the baggy pockets of his baggy jacket. Then he formed a circle with his arms by placing the fist of his right hand on his left shoulder and the fist of his left hand on his right shoulder. Intrigued, Woolly watched as the man began moving his hands down the length of the opposing arms leaving little white objects at every consecutive inch.

—It's popcorn, Woolly said in amazement.

Once the pieces of popcorn extended from the top of his shoulders to the top of his wrists, ever so slowly the man began to open his arms until they were stretching out at his sides like . . . like . . .

Like a scarecrow! Woolly realized. That's why the man in the floppy hat had seemed so familiar. Because he looked exactly like the scarecrow in the bottom left-hand corner of the place-mat map.

Only, this man wasn't a scarecrow. He was the opposite of a scarecrow. For once his arms were fully extended, all the little sparrows which had been milling about began to flutter in the air and hover near his arms.

As the sparrows pecked at the popcorn, two squirrels that had been hiding under a bench scurried to the gentleman's feet. His eyes wide, Woolly thought for a moment that they were going to climb him like a tree. But the squirrels, who knew their business, waited for the sparrows to knock the occasional piece of popcorn from the gentleman's arms to the ground.

I must remember to tell Duchess all about this, thought Woolly as he hurried along.

For the Birdman of Liberty Park seemed just like one of those old vaudevillians that Duchess liked to tell them about.

But as Woolly emerged onto the street, the joyful image of the Birdman standing with his arms outstretched was replaced by the much less joyful image of a police officer standing behind Emmett's car with a ticket book in hand.

Emmett

EMMETT WOKE WITH A vague awareness that the train was no longer moving. Glancing at Billy's watch, he could see it was shortly after eight. They must have already reached Cedar Rapids.

Quietly, so as not to wake his brother, Emmett rose, climbed the ladder, and stuck his head through the hatch in the roof. Looking back, he could see that the train, which was now on a siding, had been lengthened by at least twenty cars.

Standing on the ladder, his face exposed to the cool morning air, Emmett was no longer stirred by thoughts of the past. What stirred him now was hunger. All he had eaten since leaving Morgen was the sandwich his brother had given him in the station. Billy, at least, had had the good sense to eat breakfast at the orphanage when it was offered to him. By Emmett's estimation, they still had another thirty hours before reaching New York, and all they had in Billy's backpack was a canteen of water and the last of Sally's cookies.

But when the panhandler had told Emmett that they would stop for a few hours on a private siding outside of Cedar Rapids, he'd said it was so that General Mills could hitch some of their cars to the back of the train—cars stacked from floor to ceiling with boxes of cereal.

Emmett went down the ladder and gently woke his brother.

—The train's going to be stopped here for a bit, Billy. I'm going to see if I can find us something to eat.

—Okay, Emmett.

As Billy went back to sleep, Emmett climbed up the ladder and out the hatch. Seeing no signs of life up or down the line, he began working his way to the rear of the train. As the General Mills cars were laden, Emmett knew that they were likely to be locked. He simply had to hope that one of the hatches had been left unsecured inadvertently. Figuring he had less than an hour before they were under way, he moved as quickly as he could, leaping from the top of one boxcar to the next.

But when he reached the last of the empty Nabisco cars, he came to a stop. While he could see the flat rectangular tops of the General Mills cars stretching into the distance, the two that were immediately in front of him had the curved rooftops of passenger cars.

After a moment's hesitation, Emmett climbed down onto the narrow platform and peered through the small window in the door. Most of the interior was obscured by the curtains that bordered the inside of the window, but what little Emmett could see was promising. It appeared to be the sitting room of a well-appointed private car after a night of festivities. Beyond a pair of high-back chairs with their backs to him, Emmett could see a coffee table covered with empty glasses, a champagne bottle upside down in an ice bucket, and a small buffet on which were the remnants of a meal. The passengers were presumably in the sleeping compartments of the adjacent car.

Opening the door, Emmett quietly stepped inside. As he took his bearings, he could see that what festivities there had been had left the room in disarray. Strewn across the floor were feathers from a busted pillow along with bread rolls and grapes, as if they'd been used as ammunition in a fight. The glass front of a grandfather clock was open, the hands missing from its face. And sound asleep on a couch by the buffet was a man in his midtwenties wearing a soiled tuxedo and the bright red stripes of an Apache on his cheeks.

Emmett considered backing out of the car and continuing over the roof, but he wasn't going to get a better chance than this. Keeping his eyes on the sleeping figure, Emmett passed between the high-back chairs and advanced cautiously. On the buffet were a bowl of fruit, loaves of bread, hunks of cheese, and a half-eaten ham. There was also an overturned jar of ketchup, no doubt the source of the war paint. At his feet, Emmett found the case of the busted pillow. Loading it quickly with enough food for two days, he spun it around by the neck to cinch it. Then he took one last look at the sleeper and turned toward the door.

—Oh, steward . . .

Slumped in one of the high-back chairs was a second man in a tuxedo.

With his attention trained on the sleeper, Emmett had walked right by this one without noticing him—which was all the more surprising given his size. He must have been nearly six feet tall and two hundred pounds. He wasn't wearing war paint, but he had a slice of ham sticking neatly out of his breast pocket, as if it were a handkerchief.

With his eyes half open, the reveler raised a hand and slowly unfolded a finger in order to point at something on the floor.

—If you would be so kind. . . .

Looking in the indicated direction, Emmett saw a half-empty bottle of gin lying on its side. Setting down the pillowcase, Emmett retrieved the gin and handed it to the reveler, who received it with a sigh.

—For the better part of an hour, I have had my eye on this bottle, sorting through the various stratagems by which it might be delivered into my possession. One by one, I had to discard them as ill conceived, ill advised, or defying the laws of gravity. Eventually, I turned to the last recourse of a man who wants something done and who has exhausted every option short of doing it himself—which is to say, I prayed. I prayed to Ferdinand and Bartholomew, the patron saints of Pullman cars and toppled bottles. And an angel of mercy hath descended upon me.

Looking to Emmett with a grateful smile, he suddenly expressed surprise.

—You aren't the steward!

—I'm one of the brakemen, said Emmett.

—My thanks all the same.

Turning to his left, the reveler picked up a martini glass that was on a small round table and began carefully filling it with gin. As he did so, Emmett noted that the olive in the bottom of the glass had been speared with the minute hand of the clock.

Having filled the glass, the reveler looked to Emmett.

—Could I interest you . . . ?

—No, thank you.

—On duty, I suppose.

Raising his drink briefly toward Emmett, he emptied the glass at a toss, then considered it, ruefully.

—You were wise to decline. This gin is unnaturally tepid. Criminally so, you might say. Nonetheless . . .

Refilling the glass, he raised it once again to his lips, but this time stopped short with a look of concern.

—You wouldn't happen to know where we are?

—Outside Cedar Rapids.

—Iowa?

—Yes.

—And the time?

—About half past eight.

—In the morning?

—Yes, said Emmett. In the morning.

The reveler began to tilt his glass, but stopped again.

—Not *Thursday* morning?

—No, said Emmett trying to contain his impatience. It's Tuesday.

The reveler exhaled in relief, then leaned toward the man who was sleeping on the couch.

—Did you hear that, Mr. Packer?

When Packer didn't respond, the reveler set down his glass, took a bread roll from a jacket pocket, and threw it at Packer's head, accurately.

—I say: Did you hear that?

—Hear what, Mr. Parker?

—It's not Thursday yet.

Rolling onto his side, Packer faced the wall.

—Wednesday's child is full of woe, but Thursday's child has far to go.

Parker stared at his companion thoughtfully, then leaned toward Emmett.

—Between us, Mr. Packer is also unnaturally tepid.

—I heard that, said Packer to the wall.

Parker ignored him and continued confiding in Emmett.

—Normally, I am not one to fret over such things as the days of the week. But Mr. Packer and I are bound by a sacred trust. For sound asleep in the next cabin is none other than Alexander Cunningham the Third, the beloved grandson of the owner of this delightful car. And we have vowed that we will have Mr. Cunningham back in Chicago at the doors of the Racquet Club (that's racquet with a *q*, mind you), by Thursday night at six, so that we can deliver him safely—

—Into the hands of his captors, said Packer.

—Into the hands of his bride-to-be, corrected Parker. Which is a duty not to be taken lightly, Mr. Brakeman. For Mr. Cunningham's grandfather is the largest operator of refrigerated boxcars in America and the bride's grandfather is the largest producer of sausage links. So I think you can see the importance of our getting Mr. Cunningham to Chicago on time.

—The future of breakfast in America depends upon it, said Packer.

—Indeed, it does, agreed Parker. Indeed, it does.

Emmett was raised to hold no man in disdain. To hold another man in disdain, his father would say, presumed that you knew so much about his lot, so much about his intentions, about his actions both public and private that you could rank his character against your own without fear of misjudgment. But as he watched the one called Parker empty another glass of tepid gin and then draw the olive off the minute hand with his teeth, Emmett couldn't help but measure the man and find him wanting.

Back in Salina, one of the stories that Duchess liked to tell—when they were working in the fields or biding time in the barracks—was about a performer who called himself Professor Heinrich Schweitzer, Master of Telekinesis.

When the curtain rose on the professor, he would be sitting in the middle of the stage at a small table with a white tablecloth, a single dinner setting, and an unlit candle. From offstage a waiter would appear, serve the professor a steak, pour a glass of wine, and light the candle. When the waiter left, in an unhurried manner the professor would eat some of the steak, drink some of the wine, and stick his fork upright in the meat—all without saying a word. After wiping his lips with his napkin, he would hold a parted thumb and finger in the air. As he slowly closed them together, the flame of the candle would sputter, then expire, leaving a thin trail of smoke. Next, the professor would stare at his wine until it boiled over the rim. When he turned his attention to his plate, the top half of the fork would bend until it was at a ninety-degree angle. At this point, the audience, which had been warned to maintain a perfect silence, was rumbling with expressions of amazement or disbelief. With a raised hand, the professor would quiet the house. Closing his eyes, he would point his palms toward the table. As he concentrated, the table would begin to tremble to such a degree that you could hear its legs knocking against the surface of the stage. Then reopening his eyes, the professor would suddenly swipe his hands to the right, and the tablecloth would shoot into the air, leaving the dinner plate, wine glass, and candle undisturbed.

The whole act was a hoax, of course. An elaborate illusion achieved through the use of invisible wires, electricity, and jets of air. And

Professor Schweitzer? According to Duchess, he was a Pole from Pough-keepsie who hadn't enough mastery over telekinesis to drop a hammer on his own foot.

No, thought Emmett with a touch of bitterness, the Schweitzers of this world were in no position to move objects with a glance or a wave of the hand. That power was reserved for the Parkers.

In all probability, no one had ever told Parker that he had the power of telekinesis; but they hadn't needed to. He had learned it through experience, starting from the days of his childhood, when he would demand a toy that was in the window of a shop or an ice cream from a vendor in the park. Experience had taught him that if he wanted something badly enough, it would eventually be delivered into his hands, even if in defiance of the laws of gravity. With what but disdain can one look upon a man who in possession of this extraordinary power uses it to retrieve the remnants of a bottle of gin from across a room without having to get up from his chair?

But even as Emmett was having this thought, there was a delicate whirring and the handless clock began to chime. Glancing at Billy's watch, Emmett saw with a flash of anxiety that it was already nine. He had completely underestimated how much time had passed. The train could be under way at any moment.

As Emmett reached for the pillowcase at his feet, Parker shifted his gaze.

—You're not leaving?

—I need to get back to the engine.

—But we were just getting to know one another. Surely there's no rush. Here, have a seat.

Reaching over, Parker pulled the empty armchair closer to his own, effectively blocking Emmett's path to the door.

In the distance Emmett heard a hiss of steam as the brakes were released and the train began to move. Shoving the empty chair aside, Emmett took a step toward the door.

—Wait! Parker shouted.

Placing his hands on the arms of his chair, he hoisted himself up. Once Parker was standing, Emmett realized he was even larger than he'd seemed. With his head nearly hitting the ceiling of the car, he swayed in place for a moment, then lurched forward with his hands extended, as if he intended to grab Emmett by the shirt.

Emmett felt a surge of adrenaline and the sickening sensation that time was replaying itself for ill. A few feet behind Parker was the coffee table with the empty glasses and the overturned champagne bottle. Given the unsteadiness of Parker's stance, Emmett knew without even thinking that if he gave Parker a single push in the sternum, he could topple him like a tree. It was another opportunity presented by chance for Emmett to upend all of his plans for the future with the action of an instant.

But with surprising agility, Parker suddenly slipped a folded five-dollar bill into the pocket of Emmett's shirt. Then he stepped back and fell into his chair.

—With the utmost gratitude, Parker called, as Emmett went out the door.

Gripping the pillowcase in one hand, Emmett scaled the ladder, moved quickly across the length of the boxcar's roof, and leapt over the gap to the next car—just as he had earlier that morning.

Only now the train was moving, lurching lightly left and right, and it was gaining speed. Emmett guessed it was traveling at only twenty miles an hour, but he had felt the force of the oncoming air when he'd made the jump between the cars. If the train reached thirty miles an hour, he would need to be moving pretty fast to clear the gap; and if it reached forty, he wasn't sure he would be able to clear the gap at all.

Emmett began to run.

He couldn't remember how many boxcars he had crossed earlier that morning before reaching the Pullman. With a growing sense of urgency, he looked up to see if he could pinpoint the car with the open hatch. What he saw instead was that half a mile ahead, the train was curving over a bend in the tracks.

While it was the bend in the tracks that was fixed and the train that was moving, from Emmett's vantage point it seemed like it was the bend that was in motion, making its way rapidly down the chain of boxcars, heading toward him inexorably, the way that slack moves along a length of a rope when one end has been whipped.

Emmett began to sprint as fast as he could in the hope of making it to the next boxcar before the curve arrived. But the curve came faster than he anticipated, passing under his feet just as he made the leap. With the boxcar swaying, Emmett landed unevenly and went hurtling forward such that a moment later he was splayed across the roof with one foot hanging off its edge.

Intent on not letting go of the pillowcase, Emmett scrambled to grab something, anything, with his free hand. Blindly, he caught hold of a metal lip and pulled himself toward the middle of the roof.

Without standing, Emmett eased his way backward toward the gap that he'd just leapt across. Finding the ladder with his feet, he slid farther back, climbed down, and collapsed on the narrow platform, heaving from the exertion and burning with self-recrimination.

What had he been thinking? Jumping from car to car at a sprint. He could easily have been thrown from the train. Then what would have happened to Billy?

The train was moving at least fifty miles an hour now. At some point in the coming hour it was sure to slow, then he would be able to make his way safely back to their car. Emmett looked down at his brother's watch to log the time, only to find that the crystal was broken and the second hand frozen in place.

Pastor John

WHEN PASTOR JOHN SAW that there was somebody asleep in the boxcar, he nearly moved along. When one has far to go, there is much to be said for companionship. The journey in a boxcar is long in hours and short in common comforts, and every man, however vagabond, has a story that may edify or entertain. But ever since Adam last saw Eden, sin has been lodged in the hearts of men such that even those predisposed to be meek and kind may of a sudden become covetous and cruel. So, when a weary traveler has in his possession a half-pint of whiskey and eighteen dollars that he has earned by the sweat of his own brow, prudency counsels that he forgo the benefits of fellowship and pass the hours in the safety of his own solicitude.

This is what Pastor John was thinking when he saw the stranger sit up, switch on a flashlight, and direct its narrow beam upon the pages of an oversize book—revealing that he was no more than a boy.

A runaway, thought Pastor John with a smile.

No doubt he'd gotten in a tiff with his parents and slipped away with his rucksack over his shoulder, setting out in the manner of Tom Sawyer—little reader that he was. By the time he reached New York, the boy would welcome the moment of his discovery, so that he could be returned by the authorities to his father's stern reproach and his mother's warm embrace.

But New York was still a day's journey, and though boys may be impetuous, inexperienced, and naïve, they are not without a certain practical intelligence. For while a grown man who storms off in the heat of anger is likely to do so with only the shirt upon his back, a boy who runs away will always have the foresight to pack a sandwich. Perhaps even a bit of his mother's fried chicken left over from the night before. And then there was the flashlight to consider. How often in the last year alone would Pastor John have found it providential to have a flashlight near at hand? More times than he could count.

—Well, hello there!

Without waiting for a response, Pastor John climbed down the ladder and brushed the dust from his knees, noting that while the boy had looked up in some surprise, he had the good manners not to train the beam of his light on a newcomer's face.

—For the foot soldiers of the Lord, began Pastor John, the hours are long and the comforts few. So I, for one, would welcome a little company. Do you mind if I join you by your fire?

—My fire? asked the boy.

Pastor John pointed to the flashlight.

—Forgive me. I was speaking in the poetical sense. It is an occupational hazard for men of the cloth. Pastor John, at your service.

When John offered his hand, the boy rose and shook it like a little gentleman.

—My name is Billy Watson.

—A pleasure to meet you, William.

Though suspicion is as old as sin, the boy didn't betray a hint of it. But he did exhibit a reasonable curiosity.

—Are you a real pastor?

Pastor John smiled.

—I do not have a steeple or bells under my command, my boy. Rather, like my namesake, John the Baptist, my church is the open road and my congregation the common man. But yes, I am as real a pastor as you are likely to meet.

—You are the second person of the cloth that I have met in two days, said the boy.

—Do tell.

—Yesterday, I met Sister Agnes at St. Nicholas's in Lewis. Do you know her?

—I have *known* many a sister in my time, the pastor said with an inward wink. But I don't believe I have had the pleasure of knowing one named Agnes.

Pastor John smiled down at the boy, then took the liberty of sitting. When the boy joined him, John expressed his admiration for the flashlight and wondered if he might take a closer look. Without a moment's hesitation, the boy handed it over.

—It's an army surplus flashlight, he explained. From the Second World War.

As if to marvel at the flashlight's beam, Pastor John used it to survey the rest of the boxcar, noting with pleasant surprise that the boy's rucksack was bigger than it first had seemed.

—The Lord's first creation, Pastor John observed in appreciation while returning the flashlight to its owner.

Once again, the boy looked at him with curiosity. By way of explanation, Pastor John quoted the verse.

—*And the Lord said,* Let there be light, *and there was light.*

—But in the very beginning, God created the heavens and the earth, said the boy. Wouldn't light be His third creation?

Pastor John cleared his throat.

—You're perfectly right, William. At least, in the technical sense. Either way, I think we can assume that the Lord takes great satisfaction from the fact that having witnessed his *third* creation be harnessed for the benefit of men at war, the device has found a second life in the service of a boy's edification.

With this satisfactory observation the boy was silenced, and Pastor John found himself glancing rather longingly at his bag.

The day before, Pastor John had been preaching the Word of the Lord at the edge of a traveling Christian revival meeting on the outskirts of Cedar Rapids. Although the pastor was not *officially* a part of the meeting, so taken were the attendees with his own special brand of fire and brimstone that he had preached from dawn till dusk without even taking time for a brief repast. In the evening, when the crew had begun to roll up the tents, Pastor John had planned to retire to a nearby tavern, where a lovely young member of a Methodist choir had agreed to join him for supper and, perhaps, a glass of wine. But it so happened that the girl's choirmaster was also her father, and one thing leading to another, Pastor John was forced to make a hastier departure than he'd intended. So when he'd taken his seat with the boy, he was quite eager to skip along to the moment when they would break bread.

But there is as much call for etiquette in an empty boxcar as there is at the table of a bishop. And what the etiquette of the road demanded was that one traveler should come to know another before expecting to share in his food. To that end, Pastor John took the initiative.

—Tell me, young man: What is that you're reading?

—*Professor Abacus Abernathe's Compendium of Heroes, Adventurers, and Other Intrepid Travelers.*

—How appropriate! May I?

Again the boy handed over one of his possessions without the slightest hesitation. A Christian through and through, thought Pastor John, while opening the book. Reaching the table of contents, John saw that it was in fact a compendium of heroes, more or less.

—No doubt, you are headed off on an adventure of your own, prompted John.

In response, the boy nodded energetically.

—Don't tell me. Let me guess.

Glancing down, Pastor John ran his finger along the list.

—Hmm. Let me see. Yes, yes.

With a smile he tapped the book, then looked up at the boy.

—I suspect you are off to circumnavigate the globe in eighty days— in the manner of Phileas Fogg!

—No, said the boy. I am not off to circumnavigate the globe.

Pastor John glanced back at the table of contents.

—You plan to sail the Seven Seas like Sinbad . . . ?

The boy shook his head again.

In the earnest silence that followed, Pastor John was reminded of how quickly one becomes bored with children's games.

—You have me, William. I give up. Why don't you tell me where your adventure is taking you.

—To California.

Pastor John raised his eyebrows. Should he tell the lad that of all the possible directions in which he might travel, he had chosen the one least likely to get him to California? The news would undoubtedly prove valuable to the boy, but it also might disconcert him. And what was to be gained by that?

—California, you say? An excellent destination. I imagine you are headed there in hopes of finding gold.

The pastor smiled encouragingly.

—No, the boy replied in his parrotlike manner, I am not headed to California in hopes of finding gold.

Pastor John waited for the boy to elaborate, but elaboration did not appear to be in his nature. At any rate, thought Pastor John, that seemed conversation enough.

—Wherever we happen to be traveling and for whatever the reasons, I count it a stroke of good fortune to find myself in the company of a young man with knowledge of Scripture and a love of adventure. Why, the only thing missing to make our journey more perfect . . .

As the pastor paused, the boy looked at him expectantly.

— . . . Would be a little something to nibble upon as we pass the time in conversation.

Pastor John gave a wistful smile. Then it was his turn to look expectantly.

But the boy didn't blink.

Hmm, thought Pastor John. Was it possible that young William was being cagey?

No. He wasn't the sort. Guileless as he was, he would share a sandwich if he had one. Unfortunately, whatever sandwich he'd had the good sense to pack had probably been eaten. For if runaway boys had the unusual foresight to pack some food, what they lacked was the self-discipline to ration it out.

Pastor John frowned.

What charity the Good Lord bestows upon the presumptuous, He does so in the form of disappointment. This was a lesson that John had taught many times under many tents to many souls and to great effect. And yet, whenever proof of the lesson emerged in the course of his own interactions, it always seemed such an unpleasant surprise.

—You should probably turn off your light, said Pastor John a little sourly. So that you don't waste the batteries.

Seeing the wisdom in the suggestion, the boy picked up his flashlight and clicked it off. But when he reached for his rucksack in order to stow it away, a delicate sound emanated from the bag.

Upon hearing it, Pastor John sat a little more upright and the frown disappeared from his face.

Was it a sound that he recognized? Why, it was a sound so familiar, so unexpected, and so welcome that it stimulated every fiber of his being—in the manner that the rustle of a field mouse in the autumn leaves will stimulate a cat. For what had emanated from the rucksack was the unmistakable jangle of coins.

As the boy tucked the flashlight away, Pastor John could see the top of a tobacco tin and hear the currency shifting musically inside it. Not pennies and nickels, mind you, which announce themselves with an appropriate poverty of sound. These were almost certainly half- or silver dollars.

Under the circumstances, Pastor John felt the urge to grin, to laugh, even to sing. But he was, above all else, a man of experience. So instead, he offered the boy the teasing smile of an old familiar.

—What's that you have there, young William? Is that tobacco I see? Don't tell me you indulge in the smoking of cigarettes?

—No, Pastor. I don't smoke cigarettes.

—Thank goodness. But why, pray tell, are you lugging about such a tin?

—It's where I keep my collection.

—A collection, you say! Oh, how I love a collection. May I see it?

The boy took the tin from his bag, but despite having been so ready to share his flashlight and book, he was visibly reluctant to exhibit his collection.

Once again, the pastor found himself wondering if young William was not quite as naïve as he pretended to be. But following the boy's gaze to the boxcar's rough and dusty floor, Pastor John realized that if the boy hesitated, it was because he didn't feel the surface a worthy one.

It was perfectly natural, conceded John, for a collector of fine china or rare manuscripts to be finicky about the surfaces on which his prized possessions were laid. But when it comes to metal currencies, surely one surface was as good as the next. After all, within its lifetime a typical coin is likely to journey from the coffers of a magnate to the palm of a beggar and back again many times over. It has found itself on poker tables and in offering plates. It has been carried into battle in the boot of a patriot and lost among the velvety cushions of a young lady's boudoir. Why, the typical coin has circumnavigated the globe *and* sailed the Seven Seas.

There was hardly any call for such finickiness. The coins would be as ready to fulfill their purpose after being spread across the floor of a boxcar as they were on the day they were struck at the mint. All the boy needed was a little encouragement.

—Here, said Pastor John, let me help.

But when Pastor John reached out, the boy—who still had his hands on his tin and his eye on the floor—pulled back.

Reflexes being what they are, the boy's sudden backward motion prompted the pastor to lurch forward.

Now they both had their hands on the tin.

The boy showed an almost admirable determination as he pulled it toward his chest, but the strength of a child is no match for that of a grown man, and a moment later the tin was in the pastor's possession. Holding it off to the side with his right hand, John held his left against the boy's chest in order to keep him at bay.

—Mind yourself, William, he cautioned.

But as it turned out, he needn't have. For the boy was no longer trying to reclaim the tin or its contents. Like one who has been taken with the Spirit of the Lord, the boy was now shaking his head and uttering incoherent phrases, seemingly unaware of his surroundings. With his rucksack pulled tightly into his lap, he was clearly agitated, but also contained.

—Now, said a satisfied Pastor John, let us see what's inside.

Opening the lid, he spilled out the contents. While the jostling of the tin had resulted in a lovely little jangle, the spilling of the contents onto the hard wooden floor recalled the sound of a Liberty Bell machine paying off. With the tips of his fingers, Pastor John gently spread the coins across the floor. There were at least forty of them and they were all silver dollars.

—Praise the Lord, said Pastor John.

For surely it was divine providence that had delivered this bounty into his hands.

Glancing quickly at William, he was pleased to find him still in his state of self-containment. It allowed John to turn his full attention upon the windfall. Picking up one of the dollars, he angled it toward the morning light that was beginning to shine through the hatch.

—Eighteen eighty-six, the pastor whispered.

Quickly, he took another from the pile. Then another, and another. 1898. 1901. 1904. 1896. 1882!

Pastor John looked at the boy with an expression of fresh appreciation, for he had not spoken lightly when he called the contents of his tin a collection. Here was not simply a country boy's savings. It was a patiently gathered sampling of American silver dollars minted in different years—some of which were likely to be valued at more than a dollar. Perhaps *much* more than a dollar.

Who knew what this little pile was worth?

Pastor John didn't, that's for sure. But once he was in New York, he would be able to find out easily enough. The Jews on Forty-Seventh Street would certainly know their worth and would probably be willing to buy them. But they could hardly be trusted to give him a fair price. Perhaps there was literature somewhere on the value of the coins. Yes, that was it. There was always literature on the value of items that collectors liked to collect. And as luck would have it, the main branch of the New York Public Library was right around the corner from where the Jews plied their trade.

The boy, who had been quietly repeating the same word over and over, was beginning to raise his voice.

—Easy now, said Pastor John, in admonition.

But when he looked at the boy—rocking in place with his rucksack in his lap, far away from home, hungry and headed in the wrong direction—Pastor John was struck by a pang of Christian sympathy. In a moment of exhilaration, he had imagined that God had sent the boy to him. But what if it was the other way around? What if God had sent *him to the boy?* Not the God of Abraham, who would sooner strike down a sinner than call him by name, but the God of Christ. Or even Christ Himself, the One who assured us that no matter how often we have strayed, we can find forgiveness and even redemption by redirecting our steps toward the path of virtue.

Perhaps he was meant to help the boy sell his collection. To bring him safely into the city and to negotiate with the Jews on his behalf to ensure that he wasn't taken advantage of. Then John would bring him to Pennsylvania Station, where he would put him on the train to California. And in exchange, all he would ask for was a nominal offering. A tithe, perhaps. But under the lofty ceiling of the station, surrounded by fellow travelers, the boy would insist they split their windfall down the middle!

Pastor John smiled at the thought of it.

But what if the boy had a change of heart . . . ?

What if in one of the shops on Forty-Seventh Street, he suddenly objected to his collection's sale. What if he were to hold the tin to his chest as tightly as he held his rucksack now, proclaiming to any who would listen that the coins were *his*. Oh, how the Jews would enjoy that! How they would relish the chance to call the police, point their fingers at a pastor, and have him carted away.

No. If the Good Lord had intervened, it was to bring the boy to him, and not the other way around.

He looked to William with an almost sympathetic shake of his head.

But as he did so, Pastor John couldn't help but take note of just how tightly the boy gripped his rucksack. Pulling it against his chest, he had wrapped both arms around it, tucked up his knees, and lowered his chin as if to make it invisible to the naked eye.

—Tell me, William. What else do you have in that bag of yours . . . ?

Without rising, the boy began to slide back across the boxcar's rough and dusty floor without letting up on his grip.

Yes, remarked the pastor. Look how he holds it to his chest even as he edges away. There is something else in that bag, and so help me, I shall know what it is.

As Pastor John rose to his feet, he heard the squeak of metal wheels as the train began to move.

Perfect, he thought. He would liberate the bag from the boy and the boy from the boxcar. Then he could travel to New York in the safety of his own solicitude with a hundred dollars or more.

With his hands extended, Pastor John took a small step forward as the boy came up against the wall. When the pastor took another step, the boy began to slide to his right, only to find himself wedged in the corner with nowhere to go.

Pastor John softened his tone from one of accusation to one of explanation.

—I can see that you do not wish me to look in your bag, William. But it is the Lord's will that I should do so.

The boy, who was still shaking his head, now closed his eyes in the manner of one who acknowledges the approach of the inevitable but who wishes not to witness its arrival.

Gently, John reached down, took hold of the rucksack, and began to lift it away. But the boy's grip was fast. So fast that when John began to lift, he found he was lifting the bag and the boy together.

Pastor John let out a little laugh at the comedy of the situation. It was something that might have occurred in one of the films of Buster Keaton.

But the more Pastor John tried to lift the bag away, the tighter the boy held on; and the tighter he held on, the more clear it became that something of value was hidden within.

—Come now, said John, in a tone that betrayed a reasonable loss of patience.

But shaking his head with his eyes tightly closed, the boy simply repeated his incantation more loudly and clearly.

—Emmett, Emmett, Emmett.

—There is no Emmett here, said John in a soothing voice, but the boy showed no signs of slackening his hold.

Having no choice, Pastor John struck him.

Yes, he struck the boy. But he struck him as a schoolmarm might strike a student, to correct his behavior and ensure his attention.

Some tears began to progress down the boy's cheeks, but he still wouldn't open his eyes or loosen his grip.

With something of a sigh, Pastor John held the rucksack tightly with his right hand and drew back his left. This time, he would strike the boy as his own father had struck him—firmly across the face with the back of the hand. Sometimes, as his father liked to say, to make an impression on a child, one must leave an impression on a child. But before Pastor John could set his hand in motion, there was a loud thump behind him.

Without letting go of the boy, John looked over his shoulder.

Standing at the other end of the boxcar, having dropped through the hatch, was a Negro six feet tall.

—Ulysses! exclaimed the pastor.

For a moment, Ulysses neither moved nor spoke. The scene before him may well have been obscured by his sudden transition from daylight into shadow. But his eyes adjusted soon enough.

—Let go of the boy, he said in his unhurried way.

But Pastor John did not have his hands on the boy. He had his hands on the bag. Without letting go, he began explaining the situation as quickly as he could.

—This little thief snuck into the car while I was sound asleep. Luckily, I woke just as he was going through my bag. In the struggle that followed, my savings spilled to the floor.

—Let go of the boy, Pastor. I won't tell you again.

Pastor John looked at Ulysses, then slowly released his grip.

—You're perfectly right. There's no need to admonish him further.

At this point, he has surely learned his lesson. I will just gather up my dollars and return them to my bag.

Fortuitously, the boy did not object.

But somewhat to Pastor John's surprise, this was not out of fear. Quite to the contrary, the boy, who was no longer shaking his head with his eyes closed, was staring at Ulysses with an expression of amazement.

Why, he has never seen a Negro, thought Pastor John.

Which was just as well. For before the boy regained his senses, Pastor John could gather up the collection. To that end he fell to his knees and began sweeping up the coins.

—Leave them be, said Ulysses.

With his hands still hovering a few inches above the windfall, Pastor John looked back at Ulysses and spoke with a hint of indignation.

—I was just going to reclaim what is rightfully—

—Not a one, said Ulysses.

The pastor shifted his tone to reason.

—I am not a greedy man, Ulysses. Though I have earned these dollars through the sweat of my own brow, may I suggest that we follow the counsel of Solomon and split the money in half?

Even as he made this suggestion, Pastor John realized with some dismay that he had gotten the lesson upside down. All the more reason to press onward.

—We could split it three ways, if you'd prefer. An equal share for you, me, *and* the boy.

But while Pastor John was making this proposal, Ulysses had turned to the boxcar's door, thrown the latch, and slid it rumbling open.

—This is where you get off, said Ulysses.

When Pastor John had first taken the boy's bag in hand, the train had been barely moving, but in the interim it had gained considerable speed. Outside, the branches of trees were flashing by in what amounted to a blur.

—Here? he replied in shock. Now?

—I ride alone, Pastor. You know that.

—Yes, I remember that to be your preference. But the journey in a boxcar is long in hours and short in common comforts; surely a little Christian fellowship—

—For more than eight years, I have been riding alone without the benefit of Christian fellowship. If for some reason I suddenly found myself in need of it, I certainly wouldn't be in need of yours.

Pastor John looked to the boy in an appeal to his sense of charity and in the hope that he might come to his defense, but the boy was still staring at the Negro in amazement.

—All right, all right, acquiesced the pastor. Every man has the right to form his own friendships, and I have no desire to impose my company upon you. I will just climb up the ladder, slip out the hatch, and make my way to another car.

—No, said Ulysses. This is the way you go.

For a moment, Pastor John hesitated. But when Ulysses made a move in his direction, he stepped toward the door.

Outside, the terrain did not look welcoming. Along the tracks was an embankment covered in a mix of gravel and scrub, while beyond that a dense and ancient wood. Who knew how far they were from the nearest town or road.

Sensing that Ulysses was now behind him, Pastor John looked back with an imploring expression, but the Negro didn't meet his gaze. He too was watching the trees flash by, watching them without remorse.

—Ulysses, he pled once more.

—With my help or without it, Pastor.

—All right, all right, Pastor John replied, while mustering up a tone of righteous indignation. I will jump. But before I do so, the least you can do is allow me a moment of prayer.

Almost imperceptibly, Ulysses shrugged.

—Psalm Twenty-Three would be appropriate, said Pastor John in a cutting manner. Yes, I should think that Psalm Twenty-Three would do very nicely.

Placing his palms together and closing his eyes, the pastor began:

—*The Lord is my shepherd; I shall not want. He maketh me to lie down in green pastures: he leadeth me beside the still waters. He restoreth my soul: he leadeth me in the paths of righteousness for his name's sake.*

The pastor began reciting the psalm slowly and quietly, in a tone of humility. But when he reached the fourth verse his voice began to rise with that sense of inner strength that is known only to the soldiers of the Lord.

—*Yea*, he intoned with an uplifted hand, as if he were waving the Good Book over the heads of his congregants. *Though I walk through the valley of the shadow of death, I will fear no evil: for thou art with me! Thy rod and thy staff they comfort me!*

There were only two verses left in the Psalm, but no two verses could be more apt. With Pastor John in full feather, having built up his oratory to an appropriate pitch, the line *Thou preparest a table before me in the presence of mine enemies* was sure to sting Ulysses to the very marrow. And he would all but tremble when Pastor John concluded: *Surely goodness and mercy shall follow me all the days of my life: and I will dwell in the house of the Lord for ever!*

But Pastor John never got the chance to ring this particular oratorical bell, for just as he was about to deliver the last two verses, Ulysses sent him sailing into the air.

Ulysses

WHEN ULYSSES TURNED FROM THE DOOR, he found the white boy looking up at him, his knapsack gripped in his arms.

Ulysses waved a hand at the dollars.

—Gather your things, son.

But the boy didn't make a move to do as he was told. He just kept staring back without a sign of trepidation.

He must be only eight or nine, thought Ulysses. Not much younger than my own boy would be by now.

—It's like you heard me tell the pastor, he continued more softly. I ride alone. That's the way it's been and that's the way it's going to stay. But in half an hour or so, there will be a steep grade and the train will slow. When we reach it, I will lower you into the grass and you won't come to harm. Do you understand?

But the boy kept on staring as if he hadn't heard a word, and Ulysses began to wonder if he was simple. But then he spoke.

—Were you in a war?

Ulysses was taken aback by the question.

—Yes, he said after a moment. I was in the war.

The boy took a step forward.

—Did you sail across a sea?

—All of us were overseas, replied Ulysses a little defensively.

The boy thought to himself, then took another step forward.

—Did you leave a wife and son behind?

Ulysses, who stepped back from no man, stepped back from the child. He stepped back so abruptly it would have appeared to an observer that the boy had touched a raw wire to the surface of his skin.

—Do we know each other? he asked, shaken.

—No. We don't know each other. But I think I know who you are named for.

—Everyone knows who I'm named for: Ulysses S. Grant, commander of the Union Army, the unwavering sword in Mr. Lincoln's hand.

—No, said the boy, shaking his head. No, it wasn't that Ulysses.

—I should think I would know.

The boy continued to shake his head, though not in a contrary way. He shook his head in the manner of patience and kinship.

—No, he said again. You must have been named for the *Great* Ulysses.

Ulysses looked at the boy with feelings of growing uncertainty, as one who has suddenly found himself in the presence of the unworldly.

For a moment the boy turned his gaze to the ceiling of the boxcar. When he looked back at Ulysses his eyes were opened wide as if he'd been struck by a notion.

—I can *show* you, he said.

Sitting down on the floor, he opened the flap of his knapsack and withdrew a large red book. He flipped to a page near the back and began to read:

> Sing to me, Oh Muse, of the great and wily wanderer
> Odysseus, or Ulysses by name
> One tall in stature and supple in mind
> Who having shown his courage on the field of battle
> Was doomed to travel this way and that
> From one strange land to the next . . .

It was Ulysses who took a step forward now.

—It's all here, said the boy, without looking up from his book. In ancient times, with utmost reluctance, the Great Ulysses left his wife and son and sailed across the sea to fight in the Trojan War. But once the Greeks were victorious, Ulysses set out for home in the company of his comrades, only to have his ship blown off course time and again.

The boy looked up.

—This must be who you were named for, Ulysses.

And though Ulysses had heard his name spoken ten thousand times before, to hear it spoken by this boy in this moment—in this boxcar somewhere west of where he was headed and east of where he had been—it was as if he were hearing it for the very first time.

The boy tilted the book so that Ulysses could see it more clearly. Then he shifted a little to his right, as one does when making room for another on a bench. And Ulysses found himself sitting beside the boy and listening to him read, as if the boy were the seasoned traveler hardened by war, and he, Ulysses, were the child.

In the minutes that followed, the boy—this Billy Watson—read of how the Great Ulysses, having trimmed his sails and trained his tiller homeward, angered the god Poseidon by blinding his one-eyed son, the Cyclops, and thus was cursed to wander unforgiving seas. He read of how Ulysses was given a bag by Aeolus, the Keeper of the Winds, to speed his progress, only to have his crewmen, who were suspicious that he was hiding gold, untie the bag, unleash the winds, and set Ulysses's ship a thousand leagues off course—at the very moment that the shores of his longed-for homeland had come into view.

And as Ulysses listened, for the first time in memory he wept. He wept for his namesake and his namesake's crew. He wept for Penelope and Telemachus. He wept for his own comrades-in-arms who had been slain on the field of battle, and for his own wife and son, whom he had left behind. But most of all, he wept for himself.

—·—

When Ulysses met Macie in the summer of 1939, they were alone in the world. In the depths of the Depression, they both had buried their parents, they both had left the states of their birth—she Alabama and he Tennessee—for the city of St. Louis. Upon arriving, they both had shifted from rooming house to rooming house and job to job without companions or kin. Such that by the time they chanced to be standing side by side at the bar near the back of the Starlight Ballroom—both more prone to listen than to dance—they had come to believe that a life of aloneness was all the heavens held in store for the likes of them.

With what joy they came to find otherwise. Talking to each other that night, how they laughed—as two who not only knew each other's foibles, but who had watched each other fashion them willfully out of their own dreams and vanities and foolhardy ways. And once he had worked up the courage to ask her to dance, she joined him on the dance floor in a manner never to be undone. Three months later, when he was hired as a lineman at the phone company making twenty dollars a week, they were married and moved into a two-room flat on Fourteenth Street, where from dawn till dusk, and a few hours more, their inseparable dance continued.

But then the troubles began overseas.

Ulysses had always imagined that, should the time come, he would answer the call of his country just as his father had in 1917. But when the Japs bombed Pearl Harbor in December of '41 and all the boys began converging on the recruitment office, Macie—who had waited in solitude for so many years—met his gaze with narrowed eyes and a slow-motion shake of the head, as much as to say: *Ulysses Dixon, don't you dare.*

As if the US government itself had been persuaded by Macie's unambiguous gaze, in early '42 it declared that all linemen with two years' experience were too essential to serve. So even as the war effort mounted, he and Macie woke in the same bed, ate breakfast at the same table, and went off to their jobs with the same lunch pails in hand. But with every day that passed, Ulysses's willingness to sidestep the conflict was being sorely tested.

It was tested by the speeches of FDR on the wireless as he assured the nation that through our shared resolve we would triumph over the forces of evil. Tested by the headlines in the papers. Tested by the neighborhood boys who were lying about their ages in order to join the fight. And most of all, it was tested by the men in their sixties who would look at him on his way to work with sideways glances, wondering what in the hell an able-bodied man was doing sitting on a trolley at eight in the morning while the rest of the world was at war. But whenever he happened to pass a new recruit in his newly issued uniform, there was Macie with her narrowed eyes to remind him of how long she had waited. So Ulysses swallowed his pride, and as the months ticked by, he rode the trolley with a downward gaze and burned his idle hours within the walls of their apartment.

Then in July of '43, Macie discovered that she was with child. As the weeks passed, no matter what the news from either front, she began to radiate an inner illumination that would not be denied. She started meeting Ulysses at his trolley stop, wearing a summer dress and a wide yellow hat, and she would hook her arm under his to stroll with him back to their apartment, nodding at friends and strangers alike. Then toward the end of November, just as she had begun to show, she persuaded him against his better judgment to put on his Sunday suit and take her to the Thanksgiving dance at the Hallelujah Hall.

As soon as Ulysses walked through the door, he knew he had made a terrible mistake. For everywhere he turned, he met the eye of a mother who had lost a son, a wife who had lost a husband, or a child who had lost a father, each individual gaze made all the more bitter by Macie's beatitude. Even worse was when he met the eyes of the other men his age. For when they saw him standing awkwardly at the edge of the dance floor, they came and shook his hand, their smiles tempered by their own manner of cowardice, their spirits relieved to find another able-bodied man to share in the brotherhood of shame.

That night when he and Macie returned to their flat, before they had even taken off their coats, Ulysses had announced his decision to enlist. Having prepared himself for the likelihood that Macie would grow angry or weep, he expressed his intentions in the manner of a foregone conclusion, a decision that broached no debate. But when he was finished with his talking, she didn't tremble or shed a tear. And when she responded, she didn't raise her voice.

—If you have to go to war, she said, then go to war. Take on Hitler and Tojo with one arm tied behind your back for all I care. But don't expect to find us here when you get back.

The next day, when he walked into the recruiting office, he feared that he'd be turned away as a man of forty-two, but ten days later he was at Camp Funston and ten months after that he was on his way to serve in the 92nd Infantry Division under the Fifth Army in the Italian campaign. All through those unforgiving days, despite the fact that he did not receive a single letter from his wife, he never imagined—or rather, never let himself imagine—that she and the child would not be waiting for him upon his return.

But when his train pulled into St. Louis on the twentieth of December 1945, they were not at the station. When he went to Fourteenth Street, they were not in the flat. And when he tracked down the landlord, and the neighbors, and her friends from work, the report was always the same: Two weeks after giving birth to a beautiful baby boy, Macie Dixon had packed up her things and left the city without leaving word of where she was headed.

Less than twenty-four hours after returning to St. Louis, Ulysses put his bag on his shoulder and walked back to Union Station. There, he boarded the very next train, unconcerned with where it was going. He rode that train as far is it went—to Atlanta, Georgia—and then without setting foot outside the station, he boarded the next train headed in a different direction and rode that one all the way to Santa Fe. That was more than eight years ago. He had been riding ever since—in the passenger cars while his money held out and in the boxcars once it was gone—back and forth across the nation, never allowing himself to spend a second night in any one spot before jumping the next train to wherever it was bound.

—·—

As the boy read on and the Great Ulysses went from landfall to landfall and trial to trial, Ulysses listened in silence, the tears falling from his eyes, unabashedly. He listened as his namesake faced the metamorphical spells of Circe, the ruthless seduction of the Sirens, and the closely knit perils of Scylla and Charybdis. But when the boy read of how Ulysses's hungry crew ignored the warnings of the seer, Tiresias, and slaughtered the sacred cattle of the sun god, Helios, prompting Zeus to besiege the hero once again with thunder and swells, Ulysses placed a hand across the pages of the young boy's book.

—Enough, he said.

The boy looked up in surprise.

—Don't you want to hear the end?

Ulysses was silent for a moment.

—There is no end, Billy. There is no end of travails for those who have angered the Almighty.

But Billy was shaking his head, once again in kinship.

—That isn't so, he said. Although the Great Ulysses angered Poseidon and Helios, he didn't wander without end. When did you set sail from your war in order to return to America?

Doubtful of what it could matter, Ulysses answered.

—On the fourteenth of November, 1945.

Gently pushing Ulysses's hand aside, the boy turned the page and pointed to a passage.

—Professor Abernathe tells us that the Great Ulysses returned to Ithaca and was reunited with his wife and son *after ten long years*.

The boy looked up.

—That means that you have almost come to the end of your

228 | AMOR TOWLES

wanderings, and that you will be reunited with your family in less than two years' time.

Ulysses shook his head.

—Billy, I don't even know where they are.

—That's okay, the boy replied. If you knew where they were, then you wouldn't have to find them.

Then the boy looked down at his book and nodded his head in satisfaction that this is how it should be.

Was it possible? wondered Ulysses.

It was true that on the field of battle he had offended the teachings of His Lord, Jesus Christ, in every possible way, offended them to such a degree that it was hard to imagine crossing the threshold of a church in good conscience ever again. But all of the men whom he had fought alongside—as well as those he'd fought against—had offended the same teachings, broken the same covenants, and ignored the same commandments. So Ulysses had come to some peace with the sins of the battlefield, recognizing them as the sins of a generation. What Ulysses had not come to peace with, what weighed upon his conscience, was his betrayal of his wife. Theirs was a covenant too, and when he betrayed it, he betrayed it alone.

Even as he was standing in that poorly lit hallway of their old apartment house in full uniform, feeling less like a hero than a fool, he understood that the consequences of what he had done *should* be irrevocable. That is what had led him back to Union Station and into the life of a vagabond—a life destined to be lived without companionship or purpose.

But maybe the boy was right . . .

Maybe by placing his own sense of shame above the sanctity of their union, by so readily condemning himself to a life of solitude, he had betrayed his wife a second time. Had betrayed his wife and son.

As he was having this thought, the boy had closed his book and begun picking up the silver dollars, dusting them off with the cuff of his sleeve and returning them to their tin.

—Here, said Ulysses, let me help.

He too began picking up the coins, polishing them on his sleeve, and dropping them in the tin.

But when the boy was about to put the last coin away, he suddenly looked over Ulysses's shoulder as if he'd heard something. Quickly packing away the tin and his big red book, the boy tightened the straps on his knapsack and swung it on his back.

—What is it? asked Ulysses, a little startled by the boy's sudden movements.

—The train is slowing, he explained, rising to his feet. We must have reached the grade.

It took Ulysses a moment to understand what the boy was talking about.

—No, Billy, he said, following the boy to the door. You don't have to go. You should stay with me.

—Are you sure, Ulysses?

—I'm sure.

Billy nodded in acceptance, but as he gazed out the door at the brush flashing by, Ulysses could tell that he was taken with a fresh concern.

—What is it, son?

—Do you think that Pastor John was hurt when he jumped from the train?

—No more than he deserved.

Billy looked up at Ulysses.

—But he was a preacher.

—In that man's heart, said Ulysses, sliding the door shut, there is more treachery than preachery.

The two walked to the other end of the car with the intention of sitting back down, but as they were about to do so, Ulysses heard a scuffing behind him as if someone had carefully stepped off the ladder.

Without waiting to hear more, Ulysses spun about with his arms outstretched, inadvertently knocking Billy to the ground.

When Ulysses had heard the scuffing, it flashed through his mind that Pastor John had somehow reboarded the train and returned to confront him with vengeance in mind. But it wasn't Pastor John. It was a white youth with contusions and a determined look. In his right hand, he had the cinched bag of a thief. Dropping the bag, he took a step forward and assumed his own fighting stance, with his arms extended.

—I don't want to fight you, said the youth.

—No one wants to fight me, said Ulysses.

They both took a step forward.

Ulysses found himself wishing that he hadn't shut the boxcar door. If it were open, he could make a cleaner business of it. He would simply have to grab hold of the youth by the arms and cast him off the train. With the door closed he would have to either knock the youth unconscious or secure him in a grip and have Billy open the door. But he didn't want to put the boy anywhere within reach of the youth. So he would pick his moment. He would keep himself between Billy and the youth, draw a little closer, and then hit him on the bruised side of his face, where it was sure to be tender.

Behind him, Ulysses could hear Billy working his way onto his feet.

—Stay back, Billy, both he and the youth said at the very same time.

Then they looked at each other bewildered but unwilling to lower their arms.

Ulysses heard Billy taking a step to the side as if to see around him.

—Hey, Emmett.

With his arms still up and one eye on Ulysses, the youth took a step to his left.

—Are you all right, Billy?

—I'm all right.

—Do you know him? asked Ulysses.

—He's my brother, said Billy. Emmett, this is Ulysses. He fought in the war like the Great Ulysses and now must wander for ten years until he's reunited with his wife and son. But you needn't worry. We're not friends yet. We're just getting acquainted.

Duchess

L OOK AT ALL THE HOUSES, said Woolly in amazement. Have you ever seen so many houses?

—It's a lot of houses, I agreed.

Earlier that day, my taxi had come around the corner just in time for me to see Woolly emerging from a park. Across the street I could see where he'd left the Studebaker—in front of a fire hydrant with the passenger-side door open and the engine running. I could also see the cop standing at the back of the car with his ticket book in hand, jotting down the number of the license plate.

—Pull over, I told the cabby.

I don't know what Woolly said to the cop by way of explanation, but by the time I'd paid the cabby, the cop was putting away his ticket book and taking out his cuffs.

I approached wearing my best approximation of a small-town smile.

—What seems to be the trouble, officer?

(They love it when you call them officer.)

—Are you two together?

—In a manner of speaking. I work for his parents.

The cop and I both looked over at Woolly, who had wandered off to get a closer look at the fire hydrant.

When the cop gave me the rundown of Woolly's infractions, including the fact that he didn't seem to have his driver's license on him, I shook my head.

—You're preaching to the choir, officer. I kept telling them if they intended to bring him back home, they'd better hire someone to keep an eye on him. But what do I know? I'm just the groundskeeper.

The cop took another look at Woolly.

—Are you implying there's something wrong with him?

—Let's just say his receiver is tuned to a different frequency than yours and mine. He has a habit of wandering off, so when his mother woke up this morning and saw that her car was missing—again—she asked me to track him down.

—How did you know where to find him?

—He's got a thing about Abraham Lincoln.

The officer looked at me with a hint of skepticism. So I showed him.

—Mr. Martin, I called. Why did you come to the park?

Woolly thought about it for a moment, then smiled.

—To see the statue of President Lincoln.

Now the officer was looking at me with a hint of uncertainty. On the one hand he had his list of infractions and his oath to maintain law and order in the state of Illinois. But what was he supposed to do? Arrest some troubled kid who'd snuck out of the house in order to pay his respects to Honest Abe?

The cop looked from me to Woolly and back again. Then he straightened his shoulders and tugged at his belt, as cops are wont to do.

—All right, he said. Why don't you see him safely home.

—I intend to, officer.

—But a young man on his *frequency* should not be driving. Maybe it's time his family put the keys to the car on a higher shelf.

—I'll let them know.

Once the cop had driven off and we were back in the Studebaker, I gave Woolly a little talking to about the meaning of all for one and one for all.

—What happens if you get yourself arrested, Woolly? And your name ends up on the blotter? Before you know it, they'd have us both on a bus back to Salina. Then we'd never make it to the camp, and Billy wouldn't get to build his house in California.

—I'm sorry, Woolly said with a look of genuine contrition—and pupils as big as flying saucers.

—How many drops of your medicine did you take this morning?

. . .

—Four?

—How many bottles do you have left?

. . .

—One?

—One! Jesus, Woolly. That stuff isn't Coca-Cola. And who knows when we can get you some more. You'd better let me hold on to the last one for now.

Sheepishly, Woolly opened the glove compartment and handed over the little blue bottle. In return, I handed him the map of Indiana that I'd bought off the cabbie. He frowned when he saw it.

—I know. It's not a Phillips 66 map, but it's the best that I could do. While I'm driving, I need you to figure out how to get to 132 Rhododendron Road in South Bend.

—What's at 132 Rhododendron Road?

—An old friend.

—·—

Having reached South Bend around half past one, we were now in the middle of a brand-new subdivision of identical homes on identical lots, presumably inhabited by identical people. It almost made me long for the roads of Nebraska.

—It's like the labyrinth in Billy's book, said Woolly with a hint of awe. The one designed so ingeniously by Daedalus that no one who entered ever came out alive. . . .

—All the more reason, I pointed out sternly, for you to keep an eye on the street signs.

—Okay, okay. I got it, I got it.

After taking a quick glance at the map, Woolly leaned toward the windshield in order to give a little more attention to where we were going.

—Left on Tiger Lily Lane, he said. Right on Amaryllis Avenue . . . Wait, wait . . . There it is!

I took the turn onto Rhododendron Road. All the lawns were green and neatly mowed, but so far the rhododendron part was strictly aspirational. Who knows. Maybe it always would be.

I slowed down so that Woolly could keep an eye on the house numbers.

—124 . . . 126 . . . 128 . . . 130 . . . 132!

As I drove past the house, Woolly looked back over his shoulder.

—It was that one, he said.

I turned the corner at the next intersection and pulled the car over to the curb. Across the street an overfed pensioner in an undershirt was watering his grass with a hose. He looked like he could have used his own dousing.

—Isn't your friend at 132?

—He is. But I want to surprise him.

Having learned my lesson, when I got out of the car I took the keys with me rather than leaving them over the visor.

—I should only be a few minutes, I said. You stay put.

—I will, I will. But Duchess . . .

—Yeah, Woolly?

—I know we're trying to get the Studebaker back to Emmett as quickly as possible, but do you think we might be able to visit my sister Sarah in Hastings-on-Hudson before we head to the Adirondacks?

Most people make a habit of asking for things. At the drop of a hat, they'll ask you for a light or for the time. They'll ask you for a lift or a loan. For a hand or a handout. Some of them will even ask you for forgiveness. But Woolly Martin rarely asked for anything at all. So when he did ask for something, you knew it was something that mattered.

—Woolly, I said, if you can get us back out of this labyrinth alive, we can visit anyone you like.

Ten minutes later, I was standing in a kitchen with a rolling pin in my hand wondering if it would do the trick. Given its shape and heft, it certainly felt better than a two-by-four. But it struck me as an implement better used for comic effect—like by a hausfrau who's chasing her hapless husband around the kitchen table.

Putting the rolling pin back in its drawer, I opened another. This one was filled with a clutter of smaller implements, like vegetable peelers and measuring spoons. The next had the larger and flimsier tools like spatulas and whisks. Tucked under a ladle I found a meat tenderizer. Being careful not to jangle the other items, I removed it from the drawer and found it to have a nice wooden handle and a rough smacking surface, but it was a little on the delicate side, fashioned more for flattening a cutlet than for pounding a side of beef.

On the counter beside the sink were all the usual modern conveniences—a can opener, a toaster, a *three*-button blender, each perfectly engineered if your desire was to open or toast or blend someone. In the cabinets above the counter, I found enough canned food for a bomb shelter. Front and center were at least ten cans of Campbell's soup. But there were also cans of beef stew, chili, and franks and beans. Which seemed to suggest that the only appliance the Ackerlys really needed was the can opener.

I couldn't help but remark on the similarity between the food in Ackerly's cabinet and the menu at Salina. We had always chalked up the prevalence of this sort of cuisine to its institutional utility, but maybe it was an expression of the warden's personal tastes. For a moment I was tempted to use the can of franks and beans in the interests of poetic justice. But if you hit someone with a can, I figured you might do as much damage to your fingers as you did to his skull.

Closing the cabinet, I put my hands on my hips like Sally would have. She'd know where to look, I thought. Trying to see the situation through her eyes, I reviewed the kitchen from corner to corner. And what did I find sitting right there on the stovetop but a skillet as black as Batman's cape. Picking it up, I weighed it in my hand, admiring its design and durability. With a gentle taper and curved edges, the handle fit so securely in your palm you could probably deliver two hundred pounds of force without losing your grip. And the bottom of the pan had a sweet spot so wide and flat you could clean someone's clock with your eyes closed.

Yep, the cast-iron skillet was perfect in just about every respect, despite the fact that there was nothing modern or convenient about it. As a matter of fact, this very pan could have been a hundred years old. It could have been used by Ackerly's great-grandmother on the wagon train and handed down until it had fried porkchops for four generations of Ackerly men. With a tip of the hat to the westward pioneers, I picked up the pan and carried it into the living room.

It was a lovely little room with a television in the spot where the fireplace should have been. The drapes, a chair, and the couch were upholstered in a matching floral print. In all likelihood, Mrs. Ackerly wore a dress cut from the same fabric, so that if she sat on the couch quietly enough, her husband wouldn't know she was there.

Ackerly was still right where I had found him—stretched out on his BarcaLounger, sound asleep.

You could tell from the smile on his face that he loved that lounger. During his tenure at Salina, whenever Ackerly was dispensing strokes of the switch, he must have been dreaming about the day when he could own a lounger like this one in which to fall asleep at two in the afternoon. In fact, after all those years of anticipation, he was probably *still* dreaming about sleeping in a BarcaLounger, even though that's exactly what he was doing.

—To sleep, perchance to dream, I quoted quietly while raising the skillet over his head.

But something on the side table caught my eye. It was a recent photograph of Ackerly standing between two young boys, each with the Ackerly beak and brow. The boys were wearing Little League uniforms and Ackerly was wearing a matching cap, suggesting that he had come to a game to cheer his grandsons on. Naturally, he had a big, fat smile on his face, but the boys were smiling too, like they were glad to know that Grandpa had been in the stands. I felt a surge of tender feelings for the old man in a manner that made my hands sweat. But if the Bible tells us that the sons shall not have to bear the iniquity of the fathers, then it stands to reason that the fathers should not get to bear the innocence of the sons.

So I hit him.

When I made contact, his body gave a jolt, like a shot of electricity had gone through it. Then he slumped a little lower in the chair and his khaki pants grew dark at the groin as his bladder relaxed.

I gave an appreciative nod at the skillet, thinking here was an object that had been carefully designed for one purpose, yet was perfectly suited to another. An added benefit of using the skillet—versus the meat tenderizer, or the toaster, or the can of franks and beans—was that when it made contact, it emitted a harmonious *clong*. It was like the toll of a church bell calling the devoted to prayer. In fact, the sound was so satisfying, I was tempted to hit him again.

But I had taken the time to do my arithmetic with care, and I was pretty confident that Ackerly's debt to me would be satisfied with one solid whack on the crown. To hit him a second time would just put me in *his* debt. So I returned the skillet to the stovetop and slipped out the kitchen door, thinking: *One down, two to go.*

Emmett

REALIZING THAT HE HAD *been frittering away not only the fortune his father had left him, but the more valuable treasure of time, the young Arabian sold what few possessions he had left, joined the ranks of a merchant vessel, and set sail into the great unknown . . .*

Here we go again, thought Emmett.

That afternoon—while Emmett had been laying out the bread and ham and cheese that he'd secured from the Pullman car—Billy had asked Ulysses if he wanted to hear another story about someone who had traveled the seas. When Ulysses said that he would, Billy took out his big red book, sat at the black man's side, and began reading of Jason and the Argonauts.

In that story, the young Jason, who is the rightful king of Thessaly, is told by his usurping uncle that the throne is his to reclaim if he can sail to the kingdom of Colchis and return with the Golden Fleece.

In the company of fifty adventurers—including Theseus and Hercules in the years before their fame—Jason sets course for Colchis with the winds at his back. In the untold days that follow, he and his band travel from trial to trial, variously facing a colossus made of bronze, the winged harpies, and the *spartoi*—a battalion of warriors who spring from the soil fully armed when the teeth of a dragon have been sown. With the help of the sorceress Medea, Jason and his Argonauts eventually overcome their adversaries, secure the Fleece, and make their way safely back to Thessaly.

So enthralled was Billy with the telling of the tale and Ulysses with the hearing of it, when Emmett handed them the sandwiches that he'd made on their behalf, they hardly seemed to notice they were eating them.

As he sat on the other side of the boxcar eating his own sandwich, Emmett found himself mulling over Billy's book.

For the life of him, Emmett could not understand why this so-called professor had chosen to mix Galileo Galilei, Leonardo da Vinci, and Thomas Alva Edison—three of the greatest minds of the scientific age—with the likes of Hercules, Theseus, and Jason. Galileo, da Vinci, and Edison were not heroes of legend. These were men of flesh and blood who had the rare ability to witness natural phenomena without superstition or prejudice. They were men of industry who with patience and precision studied the inner workings of the world and, having done so, turned what knowledge they'd gained in solitude toward practical discoveries in the service of mankind.

What good could possibly come from mixing the lives of these men with stories of mythical heroes setting sail on fabled waters to battle fantastical beasts? By tossing them together, it seemed to Emmett, Abernathe was encouraging a boy to believe that the great scientific discoverers were not exactly real and the heroes of legend not exactly imagined. That shoulder to shoulder they traveled through the realms of the known and unknown making the most of their intelligence and courage, yes, but also of sorcery and enchantment and the occasional intervention of the gods.

Wasn't it hard enough in the course of life to distinguish between fact and fancy, between what one witnessed and what one wanted? Wasn't it the challenge of making this very distinction that had left their father, after twenty years of toil, bankrupt and bereft?

And now, as the day was drawing to a close, Billy and Ulysses had turned their attention to Sinbad, a hero who set sail seven different times on seven different adventures.

—I'm going to bed, Emmett announced.

—Okay, the two responded.

Then, so as not to disturb his brother, Billy lowered his voice, and Ulysses lowered his head, the two looking more like conspirators than strangers.

As Emmett lay down, trying not to listen to the murmured saga of the Arabian sailor, he understood perfectly well that when Ulysses had happened upon their boxcar it had been a stroke of extraordinary luck; but it had been humbling too.

After Billy had made introductions, in his excited way he had recounted everything that had happened from the moment of Pastor John's appearance to his timely departure from the train. When Emmett expressed his gratitude to Ulysses, the stranger had dismissed the thanks as unnecessary. But the first chance he got—when Billy was retrieving his book from his backpack—Ulysses had taken Emmett aside and given him a thorough schooling. *How could he be such a fool as to leave his brother alone like that? Just because a boxcar has four walls and a ceiling doesn't make it safe, not remotely so. And make no mistake: The pastor wasn't simply going to give Billy the back of his hand. He had every intention of throwing him from the train.*

When Ulysses had turned back to Billy and sat down at his side, ready to hear about Jason, Emmett had felt the sting of the reprimand burning on his cheeks. He felt the heat of indignation too, indignation that this man whom he had only just met should take the liberty of scolding him as a parent scolds a child. But at the same time, Emmett understood that his taking umbrage at being treated like a child was childish in itself. Just as he knew that it was childish to feel resentment that Billy and Ulysses hadn't lingered over their sandwiches, or to feel jealous over their sudden confederacy.

Trying to calm the roiling waters of his own temperament, Emmett turned his attention away from the events of the day toward the challenges that lay ahead.

When they had all been seated together at the kitchen table in Morgen, Duchess had said that before going to the Adirondacks, he and Woolly were going to stop in Manhattan to see his father.

From Duchess's stories it was clear that Mr. Hewett rarely had a steady address. But on Townhouse's last day in Salina, Duchess had encouraged Townhouse to look him up in the city—by contacting one of his father's booking agencies. *Even if a has-been is on the run from creditors, wanted by the cops, and living under an assumed name,* Duchess had said with a wink, *he'll always leave word of where he can be found with the agencies. And in New York City, all the biggest bookers of has-beens have offices in the same building at the bottom of Times Square.*

The only problem was that Emmett couldn't remember the name of the building.

He was fairly certain it began with an *S*. As he lay there, he tried to jog his memory by going through the alphabet and systematically sounding out all the possible combinations of the first three letters of the building's name. Beginning with Sa, he would say to himself: Sab, sac, sad, saf, sag, and so on. Then it was the combinations flowing from Sc and Se and Sh.

Maybe it was the sound of Billy whispering, or his own murmuring of alphabetical triplets. Or maybe it was the warm, wooden smell of the boxcar after its long day in the sun. Whatever the cause, instead of recalling the name of a building at the bottom of Times Square, Emmett was suddenly nine years old in the attic of his house with the hatch pulled up, building a fort with his parents' old trunks—the ones that once had traveled to Paris and Venice and Rome and that hadn't traveled anywhere since—which in turn brought memories of his mother wondering where he could have gotten to and the sound of her voice calling out his name as she went from room to room to room.

SIX

—.—

Duchess

WHEN I KNOCKED ON THE DOOR of room 42, I heard a groan and a labored movement on the bedsprings as if the sound of my rapping had woken him from a deep sleep. Given it was nearly noon, that was right on schedule. After a moment, I could hear him put his hungover feet on the floor. I could hear him look around the room as he tried to get his bearings, taking in the cracked plaster of the ceiling and the peeling wallpaper with a hint of bewilderment, as if he couldn't quite grasp what he was doing in a room like this, couldn't quite believe it, even after all these years.

Ah, yes, I could almost hear him say.

Ever so politely, I knocked again.

Another groan—this time a groan of effort—then the release of the bedsprings as he rose to his feet and began moving slowly toward the door.

—Coming, a muffled voice called.

As I waited, I found myself genuinely curious as to how he would look. Barely two years had gone by, but at his age with his lifestyle, two years could do a lot of damage.

But when the door creaked open, it wasn't my old man.

—Yes?

Somewhere in his seventies, room 42's occupant had a genteel bearing and the accent to go with it. At one time, he could have been the master of an estate, or served the man who was.

—Is there something I can do for you, young man? he asked, as I glanced over his shoulder.

—I was looking for someone who used to live here. My father, actually.

—Oh, I see. . . .

His shaggy eyebrows drooped a little, as if he were actually sorry to have been the cause of a stranger's disappointment. Then his eyebrows rose again.

—Perhaps he left a forwarding address downstairs?

—More likely an unpaid bill, but I'll ask on my way out. Thanks.

He nodded in sympathy. But when I turned to go, he called me back.

—Young man. By any chance, was your father an actor?

—He was known to call himself one.

—Then wait a moment. I believe he may have left something behind.

As the old gent shuffled his way to the bureau, I scanned the room, curious as to his weakness. At the Sunshine Hotel, for every room there was a weakness, and for every weakness an artifact bearing witness. Like an empty bottle that has rolled under the bed, or a feathered deck of cards on the nightstand, or a bright pink kimono on a hook. Some evidence of that one desire so delectable, so insatiable that it overshadowed all others, eclipsing even the desires for a home, a family, or a sense of human dignity.

Given how slow the old man moved I had plenty of time to look, and the room was only ten by ten, but if evidence of his weakness was present, for the life of me I couldn't spot it.

—Here we are, he said.

Shuffling back, he handed me what he'd rummaged from the bureau's bottom drawer.

It was a black leather case about twelve inches square and three inches tall with a small, brass clasp—like a larger version of what might hold a double strand of pearls. The similarity wasn't a coincidence, I suppose. Because at the knee-high height of my father's fame, when he was a leading man in a small Shakespearean troupe performing to half-filled houses, he had six of these cases and they were his prized possessions.

Though the gold embossing on this one was chipped and faint, you could still make out the O of *Othello*. Throwing the clasp, I opened the lid. Inside were four objects resting snuggly in velvet-lined indentations: a goatee, a golden earring, a small jar of blackface, and a dagger.

Like the case, the dagger had been custom made. The golden hilt, which had been fashioned to fit perfectly in my old man's grasp, was adorned with three large jewels in a row: one ruby, one sapphire, one emerald. The stainless steel blade had been forged, tempered, and burnished by a master craftsman in Pittsburgh, allowing my father in act three to cut a wedge from an apple and stick the dagger upright into the surface of a table, where it would remain ominously as he nursed his suspicions of Desdemona's infidelity.

But while the steel of the blade was the real McCoy, the hilt was gilded brass and the jewels were paste. And if you pressed the sapphire with your thumb, it would release a catch, so that when my old man stabbed himself in the gut at the end of act five, the blade would retract into the hilt. As the ladies in the loge gasped, he would take his own sweet time staggering back and forth in front of the footlights before finally giving up his ghost. Which is to say, the dagger was as much a gimmick as he was.

When the set of six cases was still complete, each had its own label embossed in gold: *Othello, Hamlet, Henry, Lear, Macbeth*, and—I kid you not—*Romeo*. Each case had its own velvet-lined indentations holding its own dramatic accessories. For Macbeth these included a bottle of fake blood with which to smear his hands; for Lear a long gray beard; for Romeo a vial of poison, and a small jar of blush that could no more obscure the ravages of time on my old man's face than the crown could obscure the deformities of Richard III.

Over the years, the collection of my father's cases had slowly diminished. One had been stolen, another misplaced, another sold. Hamlet was lost in a game of five-card stud in Cincinnati, appropriately to a pair of kings. But it was not a coincidence that Othello was the last of the six, for it was the one my old man prized most. This was not simply because he had received some of his best reviews for his performance as the Moor, but because on several occasions the jar of blackface had secured him a timely exit. Sporting the uniform of a bellhop and the face of Al Jolson, he would carry his own luggage off the elevator and through the lobby, right past the debt collectors, or angry husbands, or whoever happened to be waiting among the potted palms. To have left the Othello case behind, my old man must have been in quite a hurry. . . .

—Yes, I said while closing the lid, this is my father's. If you don't mind my asking, how long have you been in the room?

—Oh, not long.

—It would be a great help if you could remember more precisely.

—Let's see. Wednesday, Tuesday, Monday . . . Since Monday, I believe. Yes. It was Monday.

In other words, my old man had pulled up stakes the day after we left Salina—having received, no doubt, a worrisome call from a worried warden.

—I do hope you find him.

—Of that I can assure you. Anyway, sorry for the bother.

—It wasn't a bother at all, the old gent replied, gesturing toward his bed. I was only reading.

Ah, I thought, seeing the corner of the book poking out from the folds of his sheets. I should have known. The poor old chap, he suffers from the most dangerous addiction of all.

As I was headed back toward the stairs, I noticed a slice of light on the hallway floor, suggesting that the door to room 49 was ajar.

After hesitating, I passed the stairwell and continued down the hall. When I reached the room, I stopped and listened. Hearing no sounds within, I nudged the door with a knuckle. Through the gap, I could see that the bed was empty and unmade. Guessing the occupant was in the bathroom at the other end of the hall, I opened the door the rest of the way.

When my old man and I first came to the Sunshine Hotel in 1948, room 49 was the best one in the house. Not only did it have two windows at the back of the building, where it was quiet, in the center of the ceiling was a Victorian light fixture with a fan—the only such amenity in the whole hotel. Now all that hung from the ceiling was a bare bulb on a wire.

In the corner, the little wooden desk was still there. It was another amenity that added to the value of the room in the eyes of the tenants, despite the fact that no one had written a letter in the Sunshine Hotel in over thirty years. The desk chair was there too, looking as old and upright as the gentleman down the hall.

It may have been the saddest room that I had ever seen.

—•—

Down in the lobby I made sure that Woolly was still waiting in one of the chairs by the window. Then I went to the front desk, where a fat man with a thin moustache was listening to the ball game on the radio.

—Any rooms available?

—For the night or by the hour? he asked, after glancing at Woolly with a knowing look.

It never ceased to amaze me how a guy working in a place like this could still imagine that he knows anything at all. He was lucky I didn't have a frying pan.

—*Two* rooms, I said. For the night.

—Four bucks in advance. Another two bits if you want towels.

—We'll take the towels.

Removing Emmett's envelope from my pocket, I thumbed slowly through the stack of twenties. That wiped the smirk off his face faster than the frying pan would have. Finding the change that I'd received at the HoJo's, I took out a five and put it on the counter.

—We've got two nice rooms on the third floor, he said, suddenly sounding like a man of service. And my name's Bernie. If there's anything you want while you're here—booze, broads, breakfast—don't hesitate to ask.

—I don't think we'll be needing any of that, but you might be able to help me in another way.

I took another two bucks from the envelope.

—Sure, he said, with a lick of the lips.

—I'm looking for someone who was staying here until recently.

—Which someone?

—The someone in room 42.

—You mean Harry Hewett?

—None other.

—He checked out earlier this week.

—So I gather. Did he say where he was headed?

Bernie struggled to think for a moment, and I do mean struggled, but to no avail. I began to put the bills back from whence they came.

—Wait a second, he said. Wait a second. I don't know where Harry went. But there's a guy who used to live here who was very tight with him. If anyone would know where Harry is now, he would.

—What's his name?

—FitzWilliams.

—Fitzy FitzWilliams?

—That's the guy.

—Bernie, if you tell me where I can find Fitzy FitzWilliams, I'll give you a fin. If you'll loan me your radio for the night, I'll make it two.

—·—

Back in the 1930s when my father first became friends with Patrick "Fitzy" FitzWilliams, Fitzy was a third-rate performer on vaudeville's secondary circuit. A reciter of verses, he was generally shoved out onstage in between acts in order to keep the audience in their seats with a few choice stanzas in the patriotic or pornographic vein, sometimes both.

But Fitzy was a genuine man of letters and his first love was the poetry of Walt Whitman. Realizing in 1941 that the fiftieth anniversary of the poet's death was right around the corner, he decided to grow a beard and buy a floppy hat in the hope of convincing stage managers to let him honor the anniversary by bringing the words of the poet to life.

Now, there are all manner of beards. There's the Errol Flynn and the Fu Manchu, the Sigmund Freud and the good old Amish underneck. But as luck would have it, Fitzy's beard came in as white and woolly as Whitman's, so with the floppy hat on his head and his milky blue eyes, he was every bit the song of himself. And when he premiered his impersonation at a low-budget theater in Brooklyn Heights— singing of the immigrants continually landing, of the ploughmen ploughing and the miners mining, of the mechanics toiling away in the numberless factories—the working-class crowd gave Fitzy the first standing ovation of his life.

In a matter of weeks, every institution from Washington, DC, to Portland, Maine, that had planned on marking the anniversary of Whitman's death wanted Fitzy. He was traveling the Northeast Corridor in first-class cars, reciting in Grange halls, liberty halls, libraries, and historical societies, making more money in six months than Whitman made in his life.

Then in November 1942, when he returned to Manhattan for an encore performance at the New-York Historical Society, one Florence Skinner happened to be in attendance. Mrs. Skinner was a prominent socialite who prided herself on giving the most talked-about parties in town. That year she was planning to open the Christmas season with a glamorous affair on the first Thursday in December. When she saw Fitzy, it struck her like a bolt of lightning that with his big white beard and soft blue eyes, he would be the perfect Santa Claus.

Sure enough, a few weeks later when Fitzy appeared at her party with his bowl full of jelly and rattled off *The Night Before Christmas*, the crowd brimmed over with the joys of the season. The Irish in Fitzy tended to make him thirsty for a dram whenever he had to be on his feet, a fact that proved something of a liability in the theater world. But the Irish in him also made his cheeks go red when he drank, which turned out to be an asset at Mrs. Skinner's soirée because it provided the perfect polish to his Old Saint Nick.

The day after Mrs. Skinner's, the phone on the desk of Ned Mosely—Fitzy's booking agent—rang from dawn till dusk. The Van Whozens, Van Whyzens, and Van Whatsits were all planning holiday parties and they all just *had* to have Fitzy. Mosely may have been a third-rate agent, but he knew a golden goose when he was sitting on one. With only three weeks left until Christmas, he priced access to Fitzy on an accelerating scale. It was three hundred dollars for an appearance on the tenth of December and fifty bucks more for every day that followed. So if you wanted him to come down your chimney on Christmas Eve, it would cost an even grand. But if you threw in an extra fifty, the children were allowed to tug on his beard just to put their pesky suspicions to rest.

Needless to say, when it came to celebrating the birth of Jesus in this circle, money was no object. Fitzy was often booked for three appearances on a single night. Walt Whitman was sent to the showers, and Fitzy went ho-ho-ho-ing all the way to the bank.

Fitzy's stature as the uptown Santa grew from year to year, such that by the end of the war—despite working only for the month of December—he lived in a Fifth Avenue apartment, wore three-piece suits, and carried a cane that was topped with the silver head of a reindeer. What's more, it turned out that there was a whole class of young socialites whose pulse would quicken whenever they saw Saint Nick. So it wasn't particularly surprising to Fitzy when after performing at a Park Avenue party, the shapely daughter of an industrialist asked if she could call on him a few nights hence.

When she appeared at Fitzy's apartment, she was wearing a dress that was as provocative as it was elegant. But it turned out that romance was not on her mind. Declining a drink, she explained that she was a member of the Greenwich Village Progressive Society and that they were planning a large event for the first of May. When she had seen Fitzy's performance, it had occurred to her that with his big white beard, he would be the perfect man to open the gathering by reciting a few passages from the works of Karl Marx.

No doubt Fitzy was taken by the young woman's allure, swayed by her flattery, and influenced by the promise of a significant fee. But he was also an artist through and through, and he was game to take on the challenge of bringing the old philosopher to life.

When the first of May rolled around and Fitzy was standing backstage, it felt like any other night on the boards. That is, until he peeked from behind the curtain. For not only was the room packed to capacity, it was filled with hardworking men and women. Here were the plumbers and welders and longshoremen, the seamstresses and housemaids who in that dingy hall in Brooklyn Heights all those years ago had given Fitzy his first standing ovation. With a deep sense of gratitude and a surge of populist affection, Fitzy stepped through the gap in the curtain, assumed his place on the podium, and gave the performance of his life.

His monologue was drawn straight from *The Communist Manifesto*, and as he spoke he had that audience stirred to the soul. So much so, when he reached his fiery conclusion, they would have leapt to their feet and broken into thunderous applause—had not every door of the auditorium suddenly burst open to admit a small battalion of police officers blowing whistles and wielding billy clubs under the pretext of a fire code violation.

On the following morning, the headline in the *Daily News* read:

PARK AVENUE SANTA DOUBLES
AS COMMIE PROVOCATEUR

And that was the end of the high life for Fitzy FitzWilliams.

Having tripped over the end of his own beard, Fitzy tumbled down the stairs of good fortune. The Irish whiskey that had once put the jovial blush in his yuletide cheeks assumed command over his general welfare by emptying his coffers and severing his connections to clean clothes and polite society. By 1949, Fitzy was reciting dirty limericks on the subways with his hat in his hand and living in room 43 of the Sunshine Hotel—right across the hall from me and my old man.

I was looking forward to seeing him.

Emmett

I N THE LATE AFTERNOON as the train began to slow, Ulysses raised his head briefly out of the hatch, then came back down the ladder.

—This is where we get off, he said.

After helping Billy put on his backpack, Emmett took a step toward the door by which he and his brother had entered, but Ulysses gestured to the other side of the car.

—This way.

Emmett had imagined that they would be disembarking into a sprawling freight yard—like the one in Lewis, only larger—situated somewhere on the outskirts of the city, with the skyline marking the horizon. He imagined they would need to slip from the car with caution in order to make their way past railwaymen and security guards. But when Ulysses slid the door open, there was no sign of a freight yard, no sign of other trains or other people. Instead, what filled the doorway was the city itself. They appeared to be on a narrow stretch of track suspended three stories above the streets, with commercial buildings rising around them and taller buildings in the distance.

—Where are we? Emmett asked as Ulysses jumped to the ground.

—It's the West Side Elevated. A freight track.

Ulysses raised a hand to help Billy down, leaving Emmett to help himself.

—And the camp you mentioned?

—Not far.

Ulysses began walking in the narrow space between the train and the guardrail at the elevated's edge.

—Watch the ties, he warned without turning back.

For all the celebration of the New York City skyline in poetry and song, as Emmett walked he barely paid it notice. In his youth, he had never dreamed of coming to Manhattan. He hadn't read the books or watched the movies with an envious eye. He had come to New York for one reason and one reason alone—to reclaim his car. Now that they were here, Emmett's attention could turn to finding Duchess by finding his father.

When he'd awoken that morning, the first word on his lips had been *Statler*, as if his mind had continued sorting through the alphabetical combinations in his sleep. That's where Duchess had said the booking agencies were: the Statler Building. As soon as they arrived in the city, Emmett figured, he and Billy would go straight to Times Square to obtain Mr. Hewett's address.

When Emmett had explained his intentions to Ulysses, Ulysses frowned. He pointed out that they wouldn't be arriving in New York until five o'clock, so by the time he made it to Times Square, the agencies would be closed. It made more sense for Emmett to wait until morning. Ulysses said that he would take Emmett and Billy to a camp where they could sleep safely for the night; and on the following day he would watch over Billy while Emmett went uptown.

Ulysses had a way of saying what you should do as if it were a foregone conclusion, a trait that quickly got under Emmett's skin. But Emmett couldn't argue with the reasoning. If they arrived at five o'clock, it would be too late to go in search of the office. And when Emmett went to Times Square in the morning, it would be much more efficient if he could go alone.

On the elevated, Ulysses was walking with a long and purposeful stride, as if he were the one who had urgent business in the city.

While trying to catch up, Emmett checked to see where they were going. Earlier that afternoon, the train had shed two thirds of its freight cars, but there were still seventy cars between theirs and the locomotive. As he looked ahead, all Emmett could see was the same narrow gap between the boxcars and the guardrail receding into the distance.

—How do we get down from here? he asked Ulysses.

—We don't.

—Are you saying the camp is up here on the tracks?

—That's what I'm saying.

—But where?

Ulysses stopped and turned to Emmett.

—Did I say I was going to take you there?

—Yes.

—Then why don't you let me do so.

Ulysses let his gaze linger on Emmett for a second to make sure that his point had been made, then he looked over Emmett's shoulder.

—Where's your brother?

Turning, Emmett was startled to find that Billy wasn't there. So distracted had he been by his own thoughts and by trying to keep up with Ulysses, he had lost his awareness of his brother's whereabouts.

Seeing the expression on Emmett's face, Ulysses's own expression turned to one of consternation. Saying something curt under his breath, Ulysses brushed past Emmett and began walking back the way they'd come as Emmett tried to catch up, the color rising to his cheeks.

They found Billy right where they had left him—beside the boxcar in which they had ridden. Because if Emmett was not enraptured by the sight of New York, the same could not be said of Billy. When they had disembarked, he had taken two steps toward the railing, climbed on top of an old wooden crate, and looked out into the cityscape, mesmerized by its scale and verticality.

—Billy . . . , said Emmett.

Billy looked up at his brother, clearly no more aware of their separation than Emmett had been.

—Isn't it just like you imagined, Emmett?

—Billy, we've got to keep moving.

Billy looked up at Ulysses.

—Which one is the Empire State Building, Ulysses?

—The Empire State Building?

Ulysses said this with an impatience that sprang more from habit than urgency. But upon hearing his own voice, he softened his tone and pointed uptown.

—It's the one with the spire. But your brother's right. We've got to move along. And you need to keep closer. If at any time you can't reach out and touch one of the two of us, then you're not close enough. Understand?

—I understand.

—All right then. Let's go.

As the three resumed walking over the uneven ground, Emmett noticed that for the third time the train rolled forward for a few seconds, then stopped. He was wondering why it would do that, when Billy took his hand and looked up with a smile.

—That was the answer, he said.

—The answer to what, Billy?

—The Empire State Building. It's the tallest building in the world.

After they had walked past half of the boxcars, Emmett saw that some fifty yards ahead the elevated angled to the left. Due to a trick in perspective, just beyond the bend an eight-story building seemed to be rising straight from the tracks. But when they got closer, Emmett could see that it hadn't been a trick of perspective, after all. The building actually rose directly over the tracks—because the rails ran right through the middle of it. On the wall above the opening was a large yellow sign reading:

Private Property
No Admittance

Fifteen feet short, Ulysses signaled for them to stop.

From where they were standing, they could hear the sounds of activity up ahead on the other side of the train: the sliding of freight-car doors, the squeaking of dollies, and the shouting of men.

—That's where we're going, said Ulysses in a lowered voice.

—Through the building? whispered Emmett.

—It's the only way to get where we're headed.

Ulysses explained that at the moment there were five boxcars in the bay. Once the crew finished unloading them, the train would roll forward so that the crew could unload the next five. That's when they would go. And as long as they stayed behind the boxcar and moved at the same pace as the train, no one was going to see them.

This struck Emmett as a bad idea. He wanted to express his concern to Ulysses and explore whether there was an alternative route, but from farther up the tracks came a release of steam and the train began to move.

—Here we go, said Ulysses.

He led them into the building, walking in the narrow space between the boxcar and the wall at the exact same pace as the train. Half of the way through, the train suddenly stopped and they stopped with it. The sounds of the warehouse activity were louder now and Emmett could see the rapid movements of the laborers expressed by the shadows that flitted between the boxcars. Billy looked up as if intending to ask a question, but Emmett held a finger to his lips. Eventually, there was another release of steam and the train began to roll again. Being careful to move at the same speed as the car, the three emerged on the other side of the building unnoticed.

Once outside, Ulysses picked up his pace in order to put some distance between them and the warehouse. As before, they were walking in the narrow gap between the boxcars and the guardrail. But when they finally passed the locomotive, a great vista opened on their right.

Anticipating Billy's sense of wonder, this time Ulysses stopped.

—The Hudson, he said, gesturing toward the river.

After giving Billy a moment to appreciate the ocean liners, tug-boats, and barges, Ulysses made eye contact with Emmett, then continued on. Understanding the point, Emmett took his brother by the hand.

—Look how many ships there are, Billy said.

—Come on, said Emmett. You can look at them while we walk.

As Billy followed along, Emmett could hear him counting the vessels under his breath.

After they had walked a bit, the way forward was blocked by a tall wire fence that transected the elevated from guardrail to guardrail. Stepping into the middle of the tracks, Ulysses took hold of a section of the fence that had been cut and pulled it back so that Emmett and Billy could pass through. On the other side, the rails continued receding southward, but they were overgrown with weeds and grass.

—What happened to this stretch of the line? asked Emmett.

—They don't use it no more.

—Why?

—Things get used and then they don't, said Ulysses in his impatient way.

A few minutes later, Emmett could finally see where they were headed. On a siding that abutted the abandoned tracks was a makeshift encampment with a scattering of tents and lean-tos. As they drew closer, he could see the smoke rising from two separate fires and the rangy silhouettes of men in motion.

Ulysses led them to the closer of the two fires, where two white tramps sat on a railroad tie eating from tin plates and a clean-shaven black man stirred the contents of a cast-iron pot. When the black man saw Ulysses, he smiled.

—Well, look who we have here.

—Hey, Stew, said Ulysses.

But the cook's expression of welcome transitioned to one of surprise when Emmett and Billy emerged from behind.

—They're with me, explained Ulysses.

—*Traveling* with you? asked Stew.

—Didn't I just say so?

—I guess you did. . . .

—There space over by your hut?

—I believe there is.

—I'll go see. In the meantime, why don't you fix us something to eat.

—The boys too?

—The boys too.

It seemed to Emmett that Stew was about to express surprise again, then thought better of it. The tramps who had stopped eating looked on with interest when Ulysses drew open a pouch that had been in his pocket. It took a moment for Emmett to realize that Ulysses intended to pay for his and his brother's meal.

—Wait, Emmett said. Let us pay for you, Ulysses.

Removing the five-dollar bill that Parker had stuffed in his shirt pocket, Emmett took a few steps forward and held it out to Stew. As he did so, he realized it wasn't a five-dollar bill. It was a fifty.

Stew and Ulysses both stared at the bill for a moment, then Stew looked to Ulysses, who in turn looked to Emmett.

—Put that away, he said sternly.

Feeling the color rising to his face again, Emmett returned the money to his pocket. Only once he had done so did Ulysses turn back to Stew and pay for the three meals. Then he addressed Billy and Emmett together in his presumptive fashion.

—I'm going to claim us some ground. You two sit and have something to eat. I'll be back in a minute.

As Emmett watched Ulysses walk off, he was disinclined to sit or
to eat. But Billy already had a plate of chili and cornbread in his lap
and Stew was fixing another.

—It's as good as Sally's, Billy said.

Telling himself it was the polite thing to do, Emmett accepted the
plate.

With the first bite he realized how hungry he was. It had been some
hours since they had eaten the last of the food from the Pullman car.
And Billy was right. The chili was as good as Sally's. Maybe better.
From the smokiness, you could tell that Stew used a good deal of
bacon, and the beef seemed of surprisingly good quality. When Stew
offered to bring a second helping, Emmett didn't object.

As Emmett waited for the return of his plate, he cautiously studied
the two tramps who were sitting on the other side of the fire. Given
their worn clothing and unshaven faces, it was hard to tell how old they
were, though Emmett suspected they were younger than they appeared.

The tall, thin one on the left was not paying Emmett or his brother
any heed, almost purposefully. But the one on the right, who was
smiling in their direction, suddenly waved.

Billy waved back.

—Welcome, weary travelers, he called across the fire. From where
do you hail?

—Nebraska, Billy called back.

—Nebraskee! replied the tramp. Plenty's the time I've been to Nebraskee. What brings you to the Big Apple?

—We've come to get Emmett's car, said Billy. So we can drive to
California.

At the mention of the car, the tall tramp who'd been ignoring them
looked up with sudden interest.

Emmett put a hand on his brother's knee.

—We're just passing through, he said.

—Then you've come to the right spot, said the smiling one. There's no better place in the world for passing through.

—Then why can't you seem to pass through it, said the tall one.

The smiling man turned to his neighbor with a frown, but before he could respond, the tall one looked at Billy.

—You've come for your car, you say?

Emmett was about to interject, but Ulysses was suddenly standing at the edge of the fire, looking down at the tall man's plate.

—Looks like you're done with your supper, he said.

The two tramps both looked up at Ulysses.

—I'm done when I say I'm done, said the tall one.

Then he tossed his plate on the ground.

—Now I'm done.

When the tall one got up, the smiling man winked at Billy and rose as well.

Ulysses watched the two of them walk away, then he sat on the tie where they'd been sitting and stared across the fire at Emmett, pointedly.

—I know, said Emmett. I know.

Woolly

F IT HAD BEEN up to Woolly, they wouldn't have spent the night in Manhattan. They wouldn't even have driven through it. They would have gone straight to his sister's house in Hastings-on-Hudson, and from there to the Adirondacks.

The problem with Manhattan, from Woolly's point of view, the problem with Manhattan was that it was so terribly permanent. What with its towers made of granite and all the miles of pavement stretching as far as the eye can see. Why, every single day, millions of people went pounding along the sidewalks and across the marble-floored lobbies without even putting a dent in them. To make matters worse, Manhattan was absotively filled with expectations. There were so many expectations, they had to build the buildings eighty stories high so they would have enough room to stack them one on top of the other.

But Duchess wanted to see his father, so they took the Lincoln Highway to the Lincoln Tunnel, and the Lincoln Tunnel under the Hudson River, and now here they were.

If they were going to be in Manhattan, thought Woolly as he propped up his pillow, at least this was the way to do it. Because once they emerged from the Lincoln Tunnel, Duchess had not taken a left and headed uptown. Instead, he had taken a right and driven all the way down to the Bowery, a street on which Woolly had never been, to visit his father at a little hotel, of which Woolly had never heard. And then, while Woolly was sitting in the lobby looking out at all the activity in the street, he happened to see a fellow walking by with a stack of newspapers—a fellow in a baggy coat and floppy hat.

—The Birdman! exclaimed Woolly to the window. What an extraordinary coincidence!

Leaping from his chair, he rapped on the glass. Only to discover when the fellow turned about that he wasn't the Birdman, after all. But having been rapped at, the fellow entered the lobby with his stack of papers and made a beeline for Woolly's chair.

If Duchess was, as he liked to say, allergic to books, Woolly had a related affliction. He was allergic to the daily news. In New York City, things were happening all the time. Things that you were expected not only to be knowledgeable about, but on which you were expected to have an opinion that you could articulate at a moment's notice. In fact, so many things were happening at such a rapid pace, they couldn't come close to fitting them all in a single newspaper. New York had the *Times*, of course, the paper of record, but in addition, it had the *Post*, the *Daily News*, the *Herald Tribune*, the *Journal-American*, the *World-Telegram*, and the *Mirror*. And those were just the ones that Woolly could think of off the top of his head.

Each of these enterprises had a battalion of men covering beats, questioning sources, hunting down leads, and writing copy until well after supper. Each ran presses in the middle of the night and rushed off delivery trucks in every conceivable direction so that the news of the day would be on your doorstep when you woke at the crack of dawn in order to catch the 6:42.

The very thought of it sent chills down Woolly's spine. So, as the baggy-coated fellow approached with his stack of newspapers, Woolly was ready to send him on his way.

But as it turned out, the baggy-coated fellow wasn't selling today's newspapers. He was selling yesterday's newspapers. And the day before yesterday's. And the day before that!

—It's three cents for yesterday's *Times*, he explained, two cents for two days ago, a penny for three days ago, or a nickel for all three.

Well, that's a different kettle of fish altogether, thought Woolly. News that was one, two, and three days old didn't arrive with anywhere near the same sense of urgency as the news of the day. In fact, you could hardly call it news. And you didn't have to receive an A in Mr. Kehlenbeck's math class to know that getting three papers for a nickel was a bargain. But, alas, Woolly didn't have any money.

Or did he . . . ?

For the first time since putting on Mr. Watson's pants, Woolly put his hands in Mr. Watson's pockets. And would you believe, would you actually believe that out of the right-hand pocket came some rumpled bills.

—I'll take all three, said Woolly, with enthusiasm.

When the fellow handed Woolly the papers, Woolly handed him a dollar, adding magnanimously that he could keep the change. And though the fellow was pleased as could be, Woolly was fairly certain that he had gotten the better part of the deal.

Suffice it to say, when evening arrived and Duchess was running around Manhattan in search of his father, and Woolly was lying on his bed with his pillow propped and the radio on, having taken two extra drops of medicine from the extra bottle he'd put in Emmett's book bag, he turned his attention to the newspaper of three days past.

And what a difference three days made. Not only did the news seem much less pressing, if you chose your headlines carefully, the stories often had a touch of the fantastic. Like this one from Sunday's front page:

ATOM SUBMARINE
PROTOTYPE SIMULATES
A DIVE TO EUROPE

This story went on to explain how the first atomic submarine had completed the equivalent of a voyage across the Atlantic—while somewhere in the middle of the Idaho desert! The whole premise struck Woolly as incredible as something you'd find in Billy's big red book.

And then there was this one from the front page of two days past.

CIVIL DEFENSE TEST
IS AT 10 A.M. TODAY

Normally, *defense* and *test* were just the sort of words that made Woolly uneasy and generally prompted him to skip an article altogether. But in the two-day-old *Times*, the article went on to explain that in the course of this test, a fleet of imaginary enemy planes would be dropping imaginary atomic bombs on fifty-four cities, causing imaginary devastation all across America. In New York City alone, three different imaginary bombs were to drop, one of which was to land imaginarily at the intersection of Fifty-Seventh Street and Fifth Avenue— right in front of Tiffany's, of all places. As part of the test, when the warning alarm sounded, all normal activities in the fifty-four cities were to be suspended for ten minutes.

—All normal activities suspended for ten minutes, read Woolly out loud. Can you imagine?

Somewhat breathlessly, Woolly turned to yesterday's paper in order to see what had happened. And there on the front page—above the fold, as they say—was a photograph of Times Square with two police officers looking up the length of Broadway and not another living soul in sight. No one gazing in the window of the tobacconist. No one coming out of the Criterion Theatre or going into the Astor Hotel. No one ringing a cash register or dialing a telephone. Not one single person hustling, or bustling, or hailing a cab.

What a strange and beautiful sight, thought Woolly. The city of New York silent, motionless, and virtually uninhabited, sitting perfectly idle, without the hum of a single expectation for the very first time since its founding.

Duchess

AFTER GETTING WOOLLY SETTLED in his room with a few drops of medicine and the radio tuned to a commercial, I made my way to a dive called the Anchor on West Forty-Fifth Street in Hell's Kitchen. With dim lighting and indifferent clientele, it was just the sort of place my old man liked—a spot where a has-been could sit at the bar and rail against life's iniquities without fear of interruption.

According to Bernie, Fitzy and my old man were in the habit of meeting here every night around eight o'clock and drinking for as long as their money held out. Sure enough, at 7:59 the door swung open and in shuffled Fitzy, right on cue.

You could tell he was a regular from the way that everyone ignored him. All things considered, he hadn't aged so badly. His hair was a little thinner and his nose a little redder, but you could still see a bit of the Old Saint Nick hiding under the surface, if you squinted hard enough.

Walking right past me, he squeezed between two stools, spread some nickels on the bar, and ordered a shot of whiskey—in a highball glass.

A shot looks so measly in a highball glass, it struck me as an odd request for Fitzy to make. But when he lifted the drink from the bar, I could see his fingers trembling ever so slightly. No doubt he had learned the hard way that when a shot is served in a shot glass it's a lot easier to spill.

With his whiskey safely in hand, Fitzy retreated to a table in the corner with two seats. It was clearly the spot where he and my father were in the habit of drinking, because once he got comfortable, Fitzy raised his glass to the empty chair. He must be the last living soul on earth, I thought, who would raise a glass to Harry Hewett. As he began to move the whiskey to his lips, I joined him.

—Hello, Fitzy.

Fitzy froze for a moment and stared over the top of the glass. Then for what must have been the first time in his life, he put his glass back on the table without having taken a drink.

—Hey, Duchess, he said. I almost didn't recognize you. You've gotten so much bigger.

—It's all the manual labor. You should try it some time.

Fitzy looked down at his drink, then at the bartender, then at the door to the street. When he had run out of places to look, he looked back at me.

—Well, it's nice to see you, Duchess. What brings you to town?

—Oh, this and that. I need to see a friend up in Harlem tomorrow, but I'm also looking for my old man. He and I have got a little unfinished business, as it were. Unfortunately, he checked out of the Sunshine Hotel in such a hurry, he forgot to leave me word of where he was going. But I figured if anyone in the city of New York would know where Harry was, it would be his old pal Fitzy.

Fitzy was shaking his head before I finished speaking.

—No, he said. I don't know where your father is, Duchess. I haven't seen him in weeks.

Then he looked at his untouched drink with a downcast expression.

—Where are my manners, I said. Let me buy you a drink.

—Oh, that's okay. I still have this one.

—That little thing? It hardly does you justice.

Getting up, I went to the bar and asked the bartender for a bottle of whatever Fitzy was drinking. When I came back, I pulled the cork and filled his glass to the brim.

—That's more like it, I said as he looked down at the whiskey without a smile.

What a cruel irony, I thought to myself. I mean, here was the very thing that Fitzy had been dreaming of for half his life. Prayed for even. A highball glass filled to the top with whiskey—and at someone else's expense, no less. But now that it was sitting there in front of him, he wasn't so sure that he wanted it.

—Go on, I encouraged. There's no need to stand on ceremony.

Almost reluctantly, he raised the glass and tipped it in my direction. The gesture wasn't quite as heartfelt as the one he'd shown my old man's empty chair, but I expressed my gratitude nonetheless.

This time, when the glass made it to his lips he took a healthy swallow, like he was making up for the drink he hadn't taken before. Then, setting the glass down, he looked at me and waited. Because that's what has-beens do: They wait.

When it comes to waiting, has-beens have had plenty of practice. Like when they were waiting for their big break, or for their number to come in. Once it became clear that those things weren't going to happen, they started waiting for other things. Like for the bars to open, or the welfare check to arrive. Before too long, they were waiting to see what it would be like to sleep in a park, or to take the last two puffs from a discarded cigarette. They were waiting to see what new indignity they could become accustomed to while they were waiting to be forgotten by those they once held dear. But most of all, they waited for the end.

—Where is he, Fitzy?

Fitzy shook his head more at himself than at me.

—Like I said, Duchess, I haven't seen him in weeks. I swear to it.

—Normally, I'd be inclined to believe any word that fell from your lips. Particularly when you *swore* to it.

That one made him wince.

—It's just that when I sat down, you didn't seem so surprised to see me. Now, why would that be?

—I don't know, Duchess. Maybe I was surprised on the inside?

I laughed out loud.

—Maybe you were at that. Though, you know what I think? I think you weren't surprised because my old man told you I might be coming around. But in order for him to have done that, he must have spoken to you in the last few days. In fact, it probably happened while you were sitting right here.

I tapped the table with a finger.

—And if he told you he was hightailing it out of town, he must have told you where he was headed. After all, you two are as thick as thieves.

At the word *thieves*, Fitzy winced again. Then he looked even more downcast, if such a thing could be imagined.

—I'm sorry, he said softly.

—What's that?

I leaned a little forward, like I couldn't quite hear him, and he looked up with what appeared to be a genuine pang of regret.

—I'm so sorry, Duchess, he said. I'm sorry I put those things about you in that statement. Sorry that I signed it.

For a guy who didn't want to talk, suddenly you couldn't stop him.

—I had been drinking the night before, you see. And I get real uneasy around police, but especially when they're asking me questions. Questions about what I might have seen or heard, even though my sight and hearing weren't what they used to be. Or my memory either. Then when the officers began to express some frustration, your father took me aside and tried to help refresh my memory. . . .

As Fitzy went on, I picked up the bottle of whiskey and gave it a gander. In the middle of the label was a big green shamrock. It made me smile to see it. I mean, what luck did a glass of whiskey ever bring anyone. And Irish whiskey at that.

As I sat there feeling the weight of the bottle in my hand, it suddenly occurred to me that here was another fine example of something that had been carefully crafted for one purpose, yet was perfectly suited to another. Hundreds of years ago, the whiskey bottle had been designed to have a body that was big enough for holding, and a neck that was narrow enough for pouring. But if you happened to invert the bottle, taking hold of the neck, suddenly it's as if it had been designed to hit a blighter over the head. In a way, the whiskey bottle was sort of like a pencil with an eraser—with one end used for saying things, and the other for taking them back.

Fitzy must have been reading my mind because he was suddenly very quiet. And from the expression on his face, I could see that he had become frightened. His face had grown pale and the tremor in his fingers had gotten noticeably worse.

It may well have been the first time in my life that someone had become frightened of me. In a way, I couldn't believe it. Because I hadn't the slightest intention of hurting Fitzy. What would be the point? When it came to hurting Fitzy, he had the whole concession.

But under the circumstances, I figured his trepidation could be used to my advantage. So when he asked if we could just call it water under the bridge, I made a show of slowly setting the bottle down on the table.

—Would that I could, I mused. Would that I could turn back the clock and allow you to undo what you have done, Patrick FitzWilliams. But alas, my friend, the water isn't under the bridge. It isn't over the dam, for that matter. Rather, it is all around us. In fact, it is right here in this very room.

He gave me such a look of woe that I almost felt sorry for him.

—Whatever the reasons you did what you did, Fitzy, I think we can agree that you owe me one. If you tell me where my old man is, we'll call it even. But if you don't, I'll have to use my imagination to think of some other way for the two of us to settle up.

Sally

I FOUND MY FATHER OUT on the north corner fixing a stretch of fence with Bobby and Miguel, their horses standing idly by and a few hundred head of cattle grazing on the range behind them.

Turning off the road onto the shoulder, I skidded to a stop right where they were working and climbed from the cab as they shielded their eyes from the dust.

Always the comedian, Bobby made an elaborate show of coughing while my father shook his head.

—Sally, he said, you keep driving that truck over rough road like that and it's going to give out on you.

—I imagine I know by now what Betty can handle and what she can't.

—All I can say is that when the transmission falls out, don't expect me to replace it.

—Don't you worry about that. Because if I know what to expect from my truck, I know even better what to expect from you.

He was silent for a moment, and I suspect he was trying to decide if he should send the boys on their way.

—All right, he said, as if he were coming to an understanding with himself. You've barreled out here for a reason. I can see that plain enough. You might as well tell me what it is.

I opened the passenger-side door, took out the FOR SALE sign that was lying on the seat, and held it up so he could get a good long look at it.

—I found this in the trash.

He nodded.

—That's where I put it.

—And where, if you don't mind my asking, did it come from?

—The Watson place.

—Why would you take down the FOR SALE sign from the Watson place?

—Because it's no longer for sale.

—And how would you happen to know that?

—Because I bought it.

He said this in a curt and definitive manner, trying to show that he'd been about as patient as he intended to be, that he didn't have time for this sort of talk, that he and the boys had work to do, and that the moment had come for me to get in my truck and head back to the house, where, surely, I should be in the middle of making supper by now. But he was talking to the wrong person if he thought he knew something about patience that I didn't know.

For a moment, I bided my time. Without taking a step, I looked off in the distance in a thoughtful fashion, then I turned my gaze right back upon him.

—The speed with which you bought the place . . . It makes one wonder just how long you've been lying in wait to do so.

Bobby pushed the dust on the ground with the tip of his boot and Miguel looked back at the cattle while my father scratched the back of his neck.

—Boys, he said after a moment, I suspect you've got some work to do.

—Yes, sir, Mr. Ransom.

They mounted their horses and rode off toward the herd in the unhurried fashion of men at work. My father didn't turn to watch them go, but he waited for the sound of their hooves to recede before he spoke again.

—Sally, he said, using his I'm-going-to-say-this-once-and-only-once voice, there's been no lying and there's been no waiting. Charlie defaulted on his mortgage, the bank foreclosed, they put it up for sale, and I bought it. That's all there is to it. It didn't come as a surprise to anyone at the bank, it won't come as a surprise to anyone in the county, and it shouldn't come as a surprise to you. Because that's what ranchers do. When the opportunity presents itself and the price is right, a rancher will add to his land, contiguously.

—*Contiguously*, I said, impressed.

—Yes, he replied. Contiguously.

We stared at each other.

—So, in all those years that Mr. Watson struggled with the farm, you were too busy to lend a hand. But the moment the opportunity *presented itself*, your appointment book was clear. Is that about it? It sure sounds like lying and waiting to me.

For the first time, he raised his voice.

—Damn it, Sally. What did you expect me to do? Drive over there and take up his plow? Plant his seeds and harvest his crops? You cannot live another man's life for him. If a man has got the least bit of pride, he wouldn't want you to. And Charlie Watson may not have been a very good farmer, but he was a proud man. Prouder than most.

I gave the distance another thoughtful look.

—It is interesting, though, isn't it, how even as the bank was getting ready to put the property on the market, you were sitting on the porch step, telling the son of the owner that maybe it was time for him to pick up stakes and make a fresh start somewhere else.

He studied me for a moment.

—Is that what this is about? You and Emmett?

—Don't try to change the subject.

He shook his head again, like he had when I'd first arrived.

—He was never going to stay, Sally. Any more than his mother was. You watched it yourself. As soon as he could, he took a job in town.

And what did he do with his first bit of savings? He bought himself a car. Not a truck or a tractor, Sally. A car. Though I have no doubt that Emmett grieved deeply for the loss of his father, I suspect he was *relieved* by the loss of the farm.

—Don't talk to me about Emmett Watson like you know him so well. You don't know the first thing that's going through his mind.

—Maybe. But after fifty-five years in Nebraska, I think I can tell a stayer from a goer.

—Is that so, I said. Then tell me, Mr. Ransom: Which am I?

You should have seen his face when I said that. For a moment he went all white. Then, just as quickly, he went red.

—I know it's not easy for a young girl to lose her mother. In some ways it's harder on her than it is on the husband who's lost his wife. Because a father is not equipped to raise a young girl in the manner she should be raised. But that is especially so when the girl in question is contrary by nature.

Here he gave me a good long look, just in case it wasn't perfectly clear that he was talking about me.

—Many has been the night that I have knelt at the side of my bed and prayed to your mother, asking for guidance on how best to respond to your willfulness. And in all these years, your mother—God rest her soul—has not answered me once. So I have had to rely on my memories of how she cared for you. Though you were only twelve when she died, you were plenty contrary already. And when I would express my concern about that, your mother would tell me to be patient. Ed, she would say, our youngest is strong in spirit, and that should stand her in good stead when she becomes a woman. What we need to do is give her a little time and space.

It was his turn to look off in the distance for a moment.

—Well, I trusted your mother's counsel then and I trust it now. And that's why I have indulged you. I have indulged you in your manner and your habits; indulged you in your temper and your tongue.

But Sally, so help me God, I have come to see that I may have done you a terrible disservice. For by giving you full rein, I have allowed you to become a willful young woman, one who is accustomed to nursing her furies and speaking her mind, and who is, in all likelihood, unsuited to matrimony.

Oh, he enjoyed delivering that little speech. Standing there with his legs apart and his feet planted firmly on the ground, he acted as if he could draw his strength straight from the land because he owned it.

Then his expression softened and he gave me a look of sympathy that served only to infuriate.

Tossing the sign at his feet, I turned and climbed in the cab of my truck. Putting her in gear, I revved the engine, then drove down the road at seventy miles an hour, kicking up every piece of gravel, taking every divot, so that the chassis shook and the doors and windows rattled. Swerving into the entrance of the ranch, I aimed her at the front door and skidded to a stop with five feet to spare.

It was only as the dust blew past that I noticed a man with a hat sitting on our porch. And it was only when he rose and stepped into the light that I could see it was the sheriff.

Ulysses

As Ulysses watched the Watson boys retreat from the campfire in order to get ready for bed, Stew came to his side.

—They moving on tomorrow?

—No, said Ulysses. The older boy's got some business to see to uptown. He should be back in the afternoon and they'll be spending the night.

—All right then. I'll keep their bedding in place.

—You can keep mine too.

Stew turned a little sharply in order to look at Ulysses.

—You staying another night?

Ulysses looked back at Stew.

—That's what I just said, didn't I?

—That's what you said.

—There a problem with that?

—Nope, said Stew. No problem by me. Just that I seem to remember someone saying at some point that he never spent two nights in a row in the same place.

—Well then, said Ulysses, come Friday, he will have.

Stew nodded his head.

—I left some coffee on the fire, he said after a moment. I guess I'll go see to it.

—Sounds like a good idea, said Ulysses.

After watching Stew return to the campfire, Ulysses found himself scanning the lights of the city all the way from Battery Park to the George Washington Bridge—lights that held no enticement for him and promised no comfort.

But Billy had told him about the understanding he had with his brother, and it struck Ulysses as a reasonable one. He would stay two nights on the island of Manhattan. Come tomorrow, he and the boy would pass time as acquaintances, so the next day they could part company as friends.

FIVE

Woolly

As they pulled into his sister's driveway, Woolly could see that no one was home.

Woolly could always tell when a house was empty just by looking at the windows. Sometimes when he looked at the windows, he could hear all the activity inside the house, like the sounds of footsteps running up and down the stairs or celery stalks being chopped in the kitchen. Sometimes, he could hear the silence of two people sitting alone in different rooms. And sometimes, like now, from the way the windows looked back, he could tell that no one was home.

When Woolly turned off the engine, Duchess whistled.

—How many people did you say live here?

—Just my sister and her husband, Woolly replied. Although my sister's expecting.

—Expecting what? Quintuplets?

Woolly and Duchess got out of the Studebaker.

—Should we knock? asked Duchess.

—They won't be here.

—Will you be able to get in?

—They like to keep the front door locked, but they often leave the door in the garage open.

Woolly followed Duchess to one of the garage doors and watched as he pulled it up with a rattle.

Inside, the first two bays were empty. The first bay must have been where his sister parked, thought Woolly, because the oil spot on the concrete had the shape of a great big balloon—just like the one in Billy's book. The oil spot in the second bay, on the other hand, looked like one of those little storm clouds that hang over the head of a character in the funny papers when he's in a bad mood.

Duchess whistled again.

—What is that, he said, pointing to the fourth bay.

—A Cadillac convertible.

—Your brother-in-law's?

—No, said Woolly a little apologetically. It's mine.

—Yours!

Duchess spun on Woolly with an expression of such exaggerated surprise it made Woolly smile. Duchess didn't get surprised very often, so it always made Woolly smile when it happened. Woolly followed Duchess as he crossed the garage to have a better look.

—Where'd you get it?

—I inherited it, I guess. From my father.

Duchess gave Woolly a solemn acknowledgment. Then he walked the length of the car, running his hand along the long black hood and admiring the whitewall tires.

Woolly was glad that Duchess hadn't walked all the way around the car, because on the other side were the dents in the door from when Woolly had bumped into a lamppost.

"Dennis" had been very, very upset when Woolly had arrived with the dents one Saturday evening. Woolly knew that "Dennis" had been very, very upset because that's exactly how upset he'd said he was.

Just look at what you've done, he said to Woolly, while glaring at the damage.

Dennis, said his sister, interceding. *It isn't your car. It's Woolly's.*

Which was probably something that Woolly should have said: *It isn't your car, "Dennis." It's mine.* But Woolly hadn't thought to say it. At least, he hadn't thought to say it until after Sarah had said it already. Sarah always knew the right thing to say before Woolly did. When Woolly was in the middle of a conversation at boarding school or at a party in New York, he often thought to himself how much easier the conversation would be going if Sarah were there to say the right things on his behalf.

But the evening he had arrived with the dents in the door and Sarah had said to "Dennis" that the car wasn't his, it was Woolly's, this had only seemed to make "Dennis" more upset.

That it is his car is precisely my point. (Woolly's brother-in-law always made his points precisely. Even when he was very, very upset, he was very, very precise.) *When a young man is fortunate enough to be given something of great value from his own father, he should treat it with respect. And if he doesn't know how to treat it with respect, then he doesn't deserve to have it at all.*

Oh, Dennis, said Sarah. *It's not a Manet, for God's sake. It's a machine.*

Machines are the foundation of everything this family has, said "Dennis."

And everything it hasn't, said Sarah.

There she goes again, thought Woolly with a smile.

—May I? asked Duchess, gesturing to the car.

—What's that? Oh, yes. Of course, of course.

Duchess reached for the handle of the driver's door, hesitated, then took a step to his right and opened the door to the back.

—After you, he said with a flourish.

Woolly slid into the back seat and Duchess slid in after him. After closing the door, Duchess gave a sigh of appreciation.

—Forget the Studebaker, he said. This is how Emmett should arrive in Hollywood.

—Billy and Emmett are going to San Francisco, Woolly pointed out.

—Either way. This is how they should make the trip to California.

—If Billy and Emmett would like to make the trip to California in the Cadillac, they're welcome to do so.

—On the level?

—Nothing would make me happier, assured Woolly. The only problem is that the Cadillac is much older than the Studebaker, so it probably wouldn't get them to California anywhere near as quickly.

—Maybe so, said Duchess. But in a car like this, what's the rush.

As it turned out, the door inside the garage was locked, so Woolly and Duchess went back outside, and Woolly took a seat on the front step beside the flowerpots as Duchess removed the bags from the trunk.

—It could take me a few hours, said Duchess. Are you sure you're going to be all right?

—Most definitely, said Woolly. I'll just wait here until my sister comes back. I'm sure she won't be long.

Woolly watched as Duchess got in the Studebaker and backed out of the driveway with a wave. Once alone, Woolly retrieved the extra bottle of medicine from the book bag, unscrewed the eyedropper, and squeezed a few extra drops onto the tip of his tongue. Then he took a moment to admire the enthusiasm of the sunshine.

—There is nothing more enthusiastic than sunshine, he said to himself. And no one more reliable than grass.

At the word *reliable*, Woolly suddenly thought of his sister Sarah, who was another paragon of reliability. Putting the bottle in his pocket, he stood, lifted, and looked—and, sure enough, waiting patiently under the flowerpot was the key to his sister's house. All keys look alike, of course, but Woolly could tell that this one was the key to his sister's house because it turned in the lock.

Opening the door, Woolly stepped inside and paused.

—Hallo? he called. Hallo, hallo?

Just to be certain, Woolly gave a fourth hallo into the hallway that led to the kitchen, and another up the stairs. Then he waited to see if anyone would answer.

As he waited and listened, he happened to look down at the little table at the bottom of the staircase where a telephone sat. Shiny, smooth, and black, it looked like a younger cousin of the Cadillac. One thing about it that wasn't shiny, smooth, and black was the little rectangle of paper in the middle of the dial on which the phone number of the house had been written in a delicate hand—so that the phone would know exactly who it was, thought Woolly.

When no one answered Woolly's hallo, he stepped into the large, sunlit room on his left.

—This is the living room, he said, as if he were giving himself a tour.

Not much had changed in the room since he had been there last. His grandfather's grandfather clock was still by the window unwound. The piano was still in the corner unplayed. And the books still sat on their shelves unread.

One thing different was that there was now a giant oriental fan in front of the fireplace, as if the fireplace were shy of its appearance. Woolly wondered if it was there all the time, or if his sister removed it in winter so that they could build a fire. But if she did remove it, where did she put it? It seemed so delicate and awkward. Perhaps it could be folded up like a normal fan, thought Woolly, and tucked away in a drawer.

Satisfied with this notion, Woolly took a moment to wind the clock, then exited the living room and continued with his tour.

—This is the dining room, he said, where you will have dinner on birthdays and holidays. . . . Here is the only door in the house that doesn't have a doorknob and that swings back and forth. . . . And this is the kitchen. . . . And this is the back hallway. . . . And here is "Dennis's" office, in which no one is supposed to go.

Working his way through the rooms in this manner, Woolly completed a circuit such that he was right back at the foot of the stairs.

—And this is the staircase, he said as he ascended it. This is the hall. This is my sister and "Dennis's" room. This is the bathroom. And here . . .

Woolly stopped before a door that was slightly ajar. Easing it open, he entered a room that both was and wasn't what he expected.

For while his bed was still there, it had been moved to the center of the room and was covered with a great big piece of canvas. The canvas, which was a dingy white, had been splattered with hundreds of blue and gray driplets—like one of those paintings at the Museum of Modern Art. The closet, where Woolly's dress shirts and jackets had hung, was utterly empty. Not even a hanger had been left behind, or the box of mothballs that used to hide in the shadows of the upper shelf.

Three of the room's four walls were still white, but one of them— the one where the ladder was standing—was now blue. A bright friendly blue, like the blue of Emmett's car.

Woolly couldn't take issue with the fact that his closet was empty or that his bed was under a tarp because the room both was and wasn't his. When his mother had remarried and moved to Palm Beach, Sarah had let him use this room. She had let him use it over the Thanksgiving and Easter vacations, and for those weeks when he had left one boarding school and had yet to go to the next. Even though Sarah had encouraged him to think of the room as his own, he had always known that it wasn't meant to be a forever room, at least not for him. It was meant to be a forever room for somebody else.

From the lumpy shape of the tarp, Woolly could tell that some boxes had been stacked on the bed before it had been covered—giving it the appearance of a very little barge.

Checking first to make sure that none of the driplets on the tarp were wet, Woolly folded it back. On the bed were four cardboard boxes with his name written on them.

Woolly paused for a moment to marvel at the handwriting. For even though his name had been written in letters two inches tall with a big black marker, you could still tell it was his sister's handwriting—the very same handwriting that had been used to write the tiny little numbers on the tiny little rectangle in the telephone dial. Isn't that interesting, thought Woolly, that a person's handwriting is the same no matter how big or small.

Reaching out to open the box that was nearest, Woolly hesitated. He suddenly remembered the troubling theory of Schrödinger's Cat, which had been described by Professor Freely in physics class. In this theory, a physicist named Schrödinger had posited (that was the word that Professor Freely used: *posited*) that there was a cat with some poison in a box in a state of benign uncertainty. But once you opened the box, then the cat would either be purring or poisoned. So it was with a touch of caution that any man should venture to open a box, even if it was one that had his name on it. Or perhaps, especially if it had his name on it.

Steeling his nerves, Woolly opened the lid and breathed a sigh of relief. Inside were all the clothes that had been in the bureau that was and wasn't his. In the box below, Woolly found all of the things that had been on top of the bureau. Like the old cigar box, and the bottle of aftershave that he had been given for Christmas and never used, and the runner-up's trophy from the tennis club with the little golden man who would be serving a tennis ball for all eternity. And at the very bottom of the box was the dark blue dictionary that Woolly's mother had conferred upon him when he was headed off to boarding school for the very first time.

Woolly took the dictionary out and felt its reassuring heft in his hands. How he had loved this dictionary—because its purpose was to tell you exactly what a word meant. Pick a word, turn to the appropriate page, and there was the word's meaning. And if there was a word in the definition you didn't recognize, you could look up that word to find out exactly what *it* meant.

When his mother had given him the dictionary, it had been part of a set—tucked in a slipcase alongside a matching thesaurus. And as much as Woolly had loved the dictionary, he had loathed the thesaurus. Just the thought of it gave him the heebie-jeebies. Because the whole purpose of it seemed to be the opposite of the dictionary's. Instead of telling you exactly what a word meant, it took a word and gave you ten other words that could be used in its place.

How was one to communicate an idea to another person if when one had something to say, one could choose from ten different words for every word in a sentence? The number of potential variations boggled the mind. So much so that shortly after arriving at St. Paul's, Woolly had gone to his math teacher, Mr. Kehlenbeck, and asked him if one had a sentence with ten words and each word could be substituted with ten other words, then how many sentences could there be? And without a moment's hesitation, Mr. Kehlenbeck had gone to the chalkboard, scratched out a formula, and done a few quick calculations to prove incontrovertibly that the answer to Woolly's question was ten billion. Well, when confronted with a revelation like that, how was one to even begin writing an answer to an essay question during end-of-term exams?

Nonetheless, when Woolly left St. Paul's to attend St. Mark's, he had dutifully carried the thesaurus with him and set it down on his desk, where it remained snugly in its case, smirking at him with its tens of thousands of words that could be substituted one for the other. For the next year, it taunted, teased, and goaded him until finally, one evening shortly before Thanksgiving break, Woolly had taken the thesaurus from its case, carried it down to the football field, doused it with some gasoline that he'd discovered in the crew coach's launch, and set the dastardly thing on fire.

In retrospect, it probably would have been peaches and cream if Woolly had thought to set the thesaurus on fire on the fifty-yard line. But for some reason Woolly couldn't quite remember, he had put the book in the end zone, and when he'd thrown the match, the flames had quickly followed a trail of gas that had been sloshed on the grass, engulfed the gas can, and triggered an explosion that set the goalpost on fire.

Backing up to the twenty-yard line, Woolly had watched at first in shock and then amazement as the fire made its way along the crossbar and up the posts until the whole thing was in flames. Suddenly, it didn't look like a goalpost at all. It looked like a fiery spirit raising its arms to the sky in a state of exultation. And it was very, very beautiful.

When they called Woolly before the disciplinary committee, it was Woolly's intention to explain that all he had wanted was to free himself from the tyranny of the thesaurus so that he could do a better job in his exams. But before he was given a chance to speak, the Dean of Students, who was presiding over the hearing, said that Woolly was there to answer for the *fire* he had set on the football field. A moment later, Mr. Harrington, the faculty representative, referred to it as a *blaze*. Then Dunkie Dunkle, the student council president (who also happened to be captain of the football team), referred to it as a *conflagration*. And Woolly knew right then and there that no matter what he had to say, they were all going to take the side of the thesaurus.

As Woolly placed his dictionary back in the box, he heard the tentative creak of a footstep in the hall, and when he turned, he found his sister standing in the doorway—with a baseball bat in her hands.

— · —

—I'm sorry about the room, said Sarah.

Woolly and his sister were sitting in the kitchen at the little table in the nook across from the sink. Sarah had already apologized for greeting Woolly with a baseball bat after finding the front door wide open. Now she was apologizing for taking away the room that was and wasn't his. Sarah was the only one in Woolly's family who said she was sorry and meant it. The only problem, it seemed to Woolly, was that she often said she was sorry when she hadn't the slightest reason to be so. Like now.

—No, no, said Woolly. There's no need to apologize on my account. I think it's wonderful that it's going to be the baby's room.

—We thought we might move your things to the room by the back stairs. You would have much more privacy there, and it would be easier for you to come and go as you please.

—Yes, said Woolly in agreement. By the back stairs would be dandy.

Woolly nodded twice with a smile and then looked down at the table.

After giving Woolly a hug upstairs, Sarah had asked if he was hungry and offered to make him a sandwich. So that's what was in front of him now—a grilled cheese sandwich cut into two triangles, one pointing up and one pointing down. As he looked at the triangles, Woolly could tell that his sister was looking at him.

—Woolly, she said after a moment. What are you doing here?

Woolly looked up.

—Oh, I don't know, he said with a smile. Gadding about, I suppose. Traveling hither and yon. You see, my friend Duchess and I each got a leave of absence from Salina and we decided to take a little trip and see some friends and family.

—Woolly . . .

Sarah gave a sigh that was so delicate, Woolly could hardly hear it.

—I got a call from Mom on Monday—after she got a call from the warden. So I know you don't have a leave of absence.

Woolly looked back down at his sandwich.

—But I phoned the warden so that I could speak to him myself. He told me that you have been an exemplary member of the community. And seeing as you only have five months left on your sentence, he said if you were to come right back of your own accord, he would do his best to limit the repercussions. Can I call him, Woolly? Can I call and tell him that you are on your way back?

Woolly turned his plate around so that the grilled cheese triangle pointing up was now pointing down, and the grilled cheese triangle pointing down was now pointing up. The warden called Mom who called Sarah who called the warden, thought Woolly. Then he broke into a smile.

—Do you remember? he asked. Do you remember when we would play telephone? All of us together in the great room at the camp?

For a moment, Sarah looked at Woolly with an expression that seemed so sorrowfully sad. But it was only for a moment. Then she broke into a smile of her own.

—I remember.

Sitting up in his chair, Woolly began remembering for the both of them, because while he wasn't any good at rememorizing, he was very good at remembering.

—As the youngest, I always got to go first, he said. And I would lean against your ear and hide my mouth behind my hand so that no one else could hear me, and I would whisper: *The captains were playing cribbage on their ketches.* Then you would turn to Kaitlin and whisper to her, and Kaitlin would whisper to Dad, and Dad would whisper to cousin Penelope, and cousin Penelope would whisper to Aunt Ruthie, and so it would go—all the way around the circle until it reached Mother. Then Mother would say: *The Comptons ate their cabbage in the kitchen.*

At the recollection of their mother's inevitable befuddlement, the brother and sister broke into laughter that was almost as loud as the laughter they had laughed all those years ago.

Then they were quiet.

—How is she? Woolly asked, looking down at his sandwich. How is Mom?

—She's well, said Sarah. When she called, she was on her way to Italy.

—With Richard.

—He is her husband, Woolly.

—Yes, yes, Woolly agreed. Of course, of course, of course. For richer or for poorer. In sickness and in health. And till death do them part—but not for one minute longer.

—Woolly . . . It wasn't a minute.

—I know, I know.

—It was four years after father died. And with you at school and Kaitlin and me married, she was all by herself.

—I know, he said again.

—You don't have to like Richard, Woolly, but you can't begrudge your mother the comforts of companionship.

Woolly looked at his sister, thinking: *You can't begrudge your mother the comforts of companionship.* And he wondered, if he had whispered that sentence to Sarah, and she had whispered it to Kaitlin, and Kaitlin had whispered it to his father, and so on all the way around the ring, when it finally reached his mother, what would the sentence have become?

Duchess

WITH THE COWBOY AT the courthouse and Old Testament Ackerly, the balancing of accounts had been pretty straightforward. They were in the manner of one minus one, or five minus five. But when it came to Townhouse, the math was a little more complicated.

There was no question I owed him for the *Hondo* fiasco. I didn't make it rain that night, and I sure as hell didn't intend to bum a ride from a cop, but that didn't change the fact that had I just slogged my way home through the potato fields, Townhouse could have eaten his popcorn, seen the feature, and slipped back into the barracks undetected.

To his credit, Townhouse didn't make a big deal of it, even after Ackerly got out the switch. And when I tried to apologize, he just shrugged it off—like a guy who's come to expect that he's going to get a beating every now and then whether he deserves it or not. Still, I could tell he wasn't thrilled with the turn of events, any more than I would have been were the positions reversed. So in exchange for his taking the beating, I knew I owed him something.

What made the math complicated was the Tommy Ladue business. The son of an Okie who hadn't had enough sense to leave Oklahoma back in the thirties, Tommy Ladue was the sort of guy who looked like he was wearing overalls even when he wasn't.

When Townhouse joined us in Bunkhouse Four as Emmett's bunkmate, Tommy was none too pleased. As an Oklahoman, he said, he was of a mind that the Negroes should be housed in their own barracks and eat at their own tables in the company of their own kind. To look at the picture of Tommy's family in front of their farmhouse, you might wonder what the Ladues of Oklahoma were trying so hard to keep the black folks from, but that didn't seem to occur to Tommy.

That first night, as Townhouse was stowing his newly issued clothes in his footlocker, Tommy came over to set a few things straight. He explained that while Townhouse could come and go to his bed, he was not welcome in the western half of the bunkhouse. In the bathroom, which had four sinks, he was only to use the one that was farthest from the door. And as to eye contact, he'd best keep that to a minimum.

Townhouse looked like someone who could take care of himself, but Emmett had no patience with that sort of talk. He told Tommy that an inmate was an inmate, a sink was a sink, and Townhouse could move as freely through the barracks as the rest of us. If Tommy had been two inches taller, twenty pounds heavier, and twice as courageous, he might have taken a swing at Emmett. Instead, he went back to the western half of the bunkhouse in order to nurse his grievance.

Life on a work farm is designed to dull your wits. They wake you at dawn, work you till dusk, give you half an hour to eat, half an hour to settle down, and then it's out with the lights. Like one of those blindered horses in Central Park, you're not supposed to see anything other than the next two steps in front of you. But if you're a kid who's been raised in the company of traveling entertainers, which is to say small-time grifters and petty thieves, you never let yourself get *that* unobservant.

Case in point: I had noticed how Tommy had been cozying up to Bo Finlay, the like-minded guard from Macon, Georgia; I had overheard them casting aspersions upon the darker races as well as the white men who favored them; one night behind the kitchen, I had seen Bo slipping two narrow blue boxes into Tommy's hands; and at two in the morning, I had watched as Tommy tiptoed across the bunkhouse in order to stow them inside Townhouse's footlocker.

So, I wasn't particularly surprised when during the morning review, Old Testament Ackerly—in the company of Bo and two other guards—announced that someone had been stealing from the pantry; I wasn't surprised when he walked straight up to Townhouse and ordered him to unpack his things onto his freshly made bed; and I certainly wasn't surprised when all that came out of Townhouse's footlocker were his clothes.

The ones who were surprised were Bo and Tommy—so surprised, they didn't have the good sense not to look at each other.

In a hilarious show of poor self-restraint, Bo actually brushed Townhouse aside and flipped his mattress over in order to see what was hiding underneath.

—Enough of that, said the warden, looking none too happy.

That's when I piped up.

—Warden Ackerly? I says, says I. If the pantry has been pilfered, and some scoundrel has impugned our honor by claiming that the culprit resides in Bunkhouse Four, I am of the opinion that you should search every one of our footlockers. For that is the only way to restore our good name.

—We'll decide what to do, said Bo.

—I'll decide what to do, said Ackerly. Open 'em up.

At Ackerly's command, the guards began moving from bunk to bunk, emptying each and every footlocker. And lo and behold, what did they find at the bottom of Tommy Ladue's but a brand-new box of Oreos.

—What can you tell us about this, said Ackerly to Tommy, while holding up the damning dessert.

A wise young man might have stood his ground and declared that he had never seen that light-blue box. A wily one might even have asserted with the confidence of the technically honest: *I did not put those cookies in my locker.* Because, after all, he hadn't. But without skipping a beat, Tommy looked from the warden to Bo and sputtered:

—If I was the one who took the Oreos, then where's the *other* box!

God bless him.

Later that night, while Tommy was sweating it out in the penalty shed and Bo was muttering into his mirror, all the boys in Bunkhouse Four gathered around to ask me what the hell had happened. And I told them. I told them how I'd seen Tommy cozying up to Bo, and the suspicious exchange behind the kitchen, and the late-night planting of evidence.

—But how did the cookies get from Townhouse's locker into Tommy's? asked some helpful half-wit, right on cue.

By way of response, I took a look at my fingernails.

—Let's just say they didn't walk there themselves.

The boys all had a good laugh over that one.

Then the never-to-be-underestimated Woolly Martin asked the pertinent question.

—If Bo gave Tommy two boxes of cookies and one of the boxes ended up in Tommy's locker, then what happened to the other box?

On the wall in the middle of the barracks was a big green board painted with all the rules and regulations we were meant to abide by. Reaching behind it, I retrieved the narrow blue box and produced it with a flourish.

—Voilà!

Then we all had a gay old time, passing around the cookies and laughing about Tommy's sputtering and the flipping of the mattress by Bo.

But once the laughter subsided, Townhouse shook his head and observed that I had taken quite a chance. At that, all of them looked at me with a touch of curiosity. Why did I do it, they were suddenly wondering. Why did I take the risk of pissing off Tommy and Bo for a barrackmate I hardly knew? And a black one at that.

In the silence that followed, I rested a hand on the hilt of my sword and looked from visage to visage.

—Took a chance? I said. No chance was taken here today, my friends. The chance was *given*. Each one of us has come from disparate parts to serve our disparate sentences for the commission of disparate crimes. But faced with a shared tribulation, we are given an opportunity—a rare and precious opportunity—to be men of one accord. Let us not shirk before what Fortune has laid at our feet. Let us take it up like a banner and march into the breach, such that many years from now, when we look back, we will be able to say that though we were condemned to days of drudgery, we faced them undaunted and shoulder to shoulder. We few, we happy few, we band of brothers.

Oh, you should have seen them!

They were rapt, I tell you, hanging on every syllable. And when I hit them with the old *band of brothers*, they let out a rousing cheer. If my father had been there, he would have been proud, if he weren't so inclined to be jealous.

After all the backs had been slapped and the boys had returned to their bunks with smiles on their faces and cookies in their stomachs, Townhouse approached.

—I owe you, he said.

And he was right. He did.

Even if we were a band of brothers.

But all these months later, the question remained: How *much* did he owe me? If Ackerly had found those cookies in Townhouse's footlocker, Townhouse would have been the one sweating in the penalty shed instead of Tommy, and for four nights instead of two. It was a credit to my account all right, but as credits go, I knew it wasn't enough to offset the eight strokes of the switch that Townhouse had received on his back.

That's what I was mulling over when I left Woolly at his sister's house in Hastings-on-Hudson, and what I kept mulling over all the way to Harlem.

—·—

At some point, Townhouse had told me that he lived on 126th Street, which seemed straightforward enough. But I had to drive the length of it six times before I found him.

He was sitting at the top of a brownstone's stoop, his boys assembled around him. Pulling over to the curb across the street, I watched through the windshield. On the step below Townhouse sat a big fat fella with a smile on his face, then a fair-skinned black with freckles, and on the bottom step, two kids in their early teens. I guess it was arranged like a little platoon, with the captain at the top, then his first lieutenant, his second lieutenant, and two foot soldiers. But the order could have been reversed, with Townhouse on the bottom step, and he still would have towered over the rest of them. It made you wonder what they had done with themselves while he was in Kansas. They'd probably bitten their nails and counted the days until his release. Now with Townhouse back in charge, they could exhibit a studied indifference, advertising to any who passed that they cared as little about their futures as they did about the weather.

When I crossed the street and approached, the young teens rose and took a step toward me, as if they were going to ask me for the password.

Looking over their heads, I addressed Townhouse with a smile.

—So, is this one of those dangerous street gangs I keep hearing about?

When Townhouse realized it was me, he looked almost as surprised as Emmett had.

—Jesus Christ, he said.

—You know this cracker? asked the freckle-faced one.

Townhouse and I both ignored him.

—What are you doing here, Duchess?

—I came to see you.

—About what?

—Come on down and I'll explain.

—Townhouse don't come off the stoop for no one, said freckles.

—Shut up, Maurice, said Townhouse.

I looked at Maurice with a feeling of sympathy. All he had wanted was to be a dutiful soldier. What he didn't understand was that when he says something like *Townhouse don't come off the stoop for no one*, a man like Townhouse has no choice but to do exactly that. Because while he may not take instructions from the likes of me, he doesn't take instructions from his second lieutenant either.

Townhouse rose to his feet and the boys made way for him like the Red Sea making way for Moses. When he got to the sidewalk, I told him how good it was to see him, but he just shook his head.

—You AWOL?

—In a manner of speaking. Woolly and I are passing through on our way to his family's place upstate.

—Woolly's with you?

—He is. And I know he'd love to see you. We're going to the Circus tomorrow night for the six o'clock show. Why don't you come along?

—The Circus isn't my sort of thing, Duchess, but give Woolly my regards just the same.

—I'll do so.

—All right then, Townhouse said after a moment. What's so important that you had to come to Harlem just to see me.

I gave him the shrug of the penitent.

—It's the *Hondo* fiasco.

Townhouse looked at me like he had no idea what I was talking about.

—You know. The John Wayne picture that we went to see on that rainy night back in Salina. I feel bad because of the beating you took.

At the word *beating*, Townhouse's boys dropped any semblance of indifference. It was like a jolt of electricity had gone right up the stoop. The big fella must have been too insulated to feel the full force of the charge because he just shifted in place, but Maurice came to his feet.

—A beating? asked the big fella with a smile.

I could see that Townhouse wanted to tell the big fella to shut up too, but he kept his eyes on me.

—Maybe I took a beating and maybe I didn't, Duchess. Either way, I don't see as it would be any cause of concern for you.

—You're your own man, Townhouse. I'd be the first to say so. But let's face it: You wouldn't have had to take this beating that you did or didn't take, if I hadn't hitched the ride from the cop.

This sent another jolt of electricity up the stoop.

Townhouse took a deep breath and gazed down the street almost wistfully, like he was looking back on simpler times. But he didn't contradict me. Because there was nothing to contradict. I was the one who baked the lasagna and he was the one who cleaned up the kitchen. It was as simple as that.

—What now? he asked after a moment. Don't tell me you came all this way to apologize.

I laughed.

—No, I don't put much stake in apologies. They always seem a day late and a dollar short. What I had in mind is something more concrete. Like a settling of accounts.

—A settling of accounts.

—Exactly.

—And how is that supposed to work?

—If it were only a matter of the movie, it could have been a switch for a switch. Eight minus eight and we'd be done. The problem is that you still owe me for the Oreo incident.

—The Oreo incident? said the big fella with an even bigger smile.

—It may not be worth the same as a switching, I continued, but it should count for something. Rather than an eight minus eight sort of situation, what we have here is more of an eight minus five. So I figure if you take three swings at me, that should make us even.

All the boys on the stoop were looking at me with varying degrees of disbelief. An act of honor has a way of doing that to the common man.

—You want to have a fight, said Townhouse.

—No, I said with a wave of the hand. Not a *fight*. A fight would imply that I'd try to hit you back. What I'm going to do is stand here and let you hit me, uncontested.

—You're going to *let* me hit you.

—Three times, I emphasized.

—What the fuck? said Maurice, his disbelief having transitioned into some form of hostility.

But the big fella, he was trembling with soundless laughter. After a moment, Townhouse turned to him.

—What do you make of this, Otis?

Wiping the tears from his eyes, Otis shook his head.

—I don't know, T. On the one hand, it seems pretty crazy. But on the other, if a white boy comes all the way from Kansas to ask you for a beating, I think you gotta give it to him.

As Otis began laughing again in his silent way, Townhouse just shook his head. He was disinclined to do it. I could tell. And if it were just the two of us, he probably would have sent me on my way, unsatisfied. But Maurice was staring at me now with a look of borrowed indignation.

—If you won't hit him, I will, he said.

There he goes again, I thought. Maurice just didn't seem to understand the chain of command. To make matters worse, when he volunteered to hit me, he did so with just enough bravado to imply that maybe the reason Townhouse was stalling was because he wasn't up to the task.

Townhouse turned to Maurice very slowly.

—Maurice, he said, just because you're my cousin doesn't mean I'm not willing to shut you the fuck up.

That put so much color into Maurice's face that his freckles almost disappeared. Then he was the one gazing down the street wishing it was simpler times.

It made me feel a little sorry for him, watching him get humiliated like that in front of the rest of us. But I also could tell that through his injudiciousness, he had raised Townhouse's temperature, which was just as well.

Sticking my chin out toward Townhouse, I pointed to it.

—Just give me a pop, T. What've you got to lose?

When I called him T, Townhouse grimaced like I knew he would.

Showing disrespect toward Townhouse was the last thing I wanted to do, but the challenge before me was to get him to take that first swing. Once he took the first one, I knew the rest would come easy. Because even if he didn't gripe about the switching, I'm sure he still carried a bit of a grudge.

—Come on, I said, intending to call him T one more time.

Before I got the chance, he delivered. The punch landed right where it was supposed to, but it only knocked me a few steps back, like he hadn't put everything into it.

—There you go, I said encouragingly. That's a pretty good one. But this time, why don't you give it some of the old Joe Louis.

And that's what he did. I mean, I didn't even see it coming. One second I'm standing there egging him on, and the next second I'm lying on the sidewalk aware of that strange aroma that you only smell when your skull has been rattled.

Planting both hands on the concrete, I pushed myself off the ground, rose to my feet, and went back to the hitting spot—just like Emmett.

The young teens were practically jumping up and down.

—Give it to him, Townhouse, they shouted.

—He asked for it, muttered Maurice.

—Mother Mary, said Otis in sustained disbelief.

Though all four spoke at once, I could hear each of them as clearly as if they'd spoken alone. But Townhouse couldn't. He couldn't hear any of them at all because he wasn't on 126th Street. He was back at Salina. Back in that moment that he'd sworn he'd never think about again: taking Ackerly's beating as the rest of us watched. It was the fire of justice that was burning through Townhouse now. The fire of justice that appeases the injured spirit and sets the record straight.

The third blow was an uppercut that put me flat on the pavement. It was a thing of beauty, I tell you.

Townhouse took two steps back, heaving a little from the exertion, the sweat running down his forehead. Then he took another step back like he needed to, like he was worried that if he were any closer, he would hit me again and again, and might not be able to stop.

I gave him the friendly wave of one crying uncle. Then being careful to take my time so the blood wouldn't rush from my head, I got back on my feet.

—That's the stuff, I said with a smile, after spitting some blood on the sidewalk.

—Now we're square, said Townhouse.

—Now we're square, I agreed, and I stuck out my hand.

Townhouse stared at it for a moment. Then he took it in a firm grip and looked me eye to eye—like we were the presidents of two nations who had just signed an armistice after generations of discord.

At that moment, we were both towering over the boys, and they knew it. You could tell from the expressions of respect on the faces of Otis and the teens, and the expression of dejection on the face of Maurice.

I felt bad for him. Not man enough to be a man, or child enough to be a child, not black enough to be black, or white enough to be white, Maurice just couldn't seem to find his place in the world. It made me want to tousle his hair and assure him that one day everything was going to be all right. But it was time to move along.

Letting go of Townhouse's hand, I gave him a tip of the hat.

—See you round, pardner, I said.

—Sure, said Townhouse.

I'd felt pretty good when I settled the scores with the cowboy and Ackerly, knowing that I was playing some small role in balancing the scales of justice. But those feelings were nothing compared to the satisfaction I felt after letting Townhouse settle his score with me.

Sister Agnes had always said that good deeds can be habit forming. And I guess she was right, because having given Sally's jam to the kids at St. Nick's, as I was about to leave Townhouse's stoop I found myself turning back.

—Hey, Maurice, I called.

He looked up with the same expression of dejection, but with a touch of uncertainty too.

—See that baby-blue Studebaker over there?

—Yeah?

—She's all yours.

Then I tossed him the keys.

I would have loved to see the look on his face when he caught them. But I had already turned away and was striding down the middle of 126th Street with the sun at my back, thinking: *Harrison Hewett, here I come.*

Emmett

A T QUARTER TO EIGHT in the evening, Emmett was sitting in a run-down saloon at the edge of Manhattan with a glass of beer and a photograph of Harrison Hewett on the bar in front of him.

Taking a drink, Emmett studied the picture with interest. It showed the profile of a handsome forty-year-old man looking off in the distance. Duchess had never said exactly how old his father was, but from his stories one got the sense that Mr. Hewett's career dated back to the early 1920s. And hadn't Sister Agnes guessed that he was about fifty when he'd brought Duchess to the orphanage in 1944? That would make Mr. Hewett about sixty now—and this photograph about twenty years out of date. It also meant the photograph might well have been taken before Duchess was born.

Because the photograph was so old and the actor so young, Emmett had no problem seeing the family resemblance. In Duchess's words, his father had the nose, chin, and appetites of John Barrymore. If Duchess hadn't quite inherited his father's appetites, he had definitely inherited the nose and chin. Duchess's coloring was lighter, but perhaps that came from his mother, whoever she was.

However good-looking Mr. Hewett had been, Emmett couldn't help picture him with a certain distaste as the man of fifty who drove off in a convertible with a lovely young girl in the passenger seat, having just abandoned his eight-year-old son.

Sister Agnes had been right when she observed that Emmett was angry at Duchess for taking his car. And Emmett knew that she was also right when she observed that what Duchess needed more than anything else was a friend who, upon occasion, could save him from his own misguided intentions. Whether Emmett was up to the task remained to be seen. Either way, he would have to find Duchess first.

—·—

When Emmett had woken at seven that morning, Stew was already up and about.

Seeing Emmett, he pointed to an overturned crate where there was a bowl, a pot of hot water, soap, a razor, and towel. Stripping to the waist, Emmett bathed his upper body and shaved. Then having eaten a breakfast of ham and eggs—at his own expense—and received assurances from Ulysses that Billy would be watched over, he followed Stew's directions through a gap in some fencing and down a caged metal staircase, which led from the tracks down to Thirteenth Street. Shortly after eight, he was standing on the corner of Tenth Avenue looking eastward, feeling like he had a jump on the day.

But Emmett underestimated every aspect of what was to follow. He underestimated how long it would take to walk to Seventh Avenue. He underestimated how difficult it would be to find the entrance to the subway, passing it twice. He underestimated how disorienting the station would be once he got inside—with its network of gangways and staircases, and its bustling, purposeful crowd.

After being spun around by the current of commuters, Emmett found the token booth, he found a map of the subway system, he identified the Seventh Avenue line and determined there were five stops to Forty-Second Street, each step in the process posing its own challenges, its own frustrations, its own causes for humility.

As Emmett came down the steps to the platform, a train was beginning to board. Quickly, he joined the crowd that was pressing its way into the car. When the doors closed and Emmett found himself tucked shoulder-to-shoulder with some and face-to-face with others, he had the disorienting feeling of being at once self-conscious and ignored. Everyone on board seemed to have chosen some fixed point at which to stare with precision and disinterest. Following suit, Emmett trained his gaze on an advertisement for Lucky Strike cigarettes and began counting stops.

At the first two, it seemed to Emmett that people were getting off and on in equal number. But at the third stop, people mostly got off. And at the fourth, so many people got off that Emmett found himself in a nearly empty car. Leaning over to look through the narrow window onto the platform, he saw with a touch of unease that the station was Wall Street. When he had studied the map at Fourteenth Street, he hadn't paid much attention to the names of the intervening stops, seeing no need to do so, but he was fairly certain that Wall Street wasn't among them.

And wasn't Wall Street in lower Manhattan . . . ?

Stepping quickly to a map that was posted on the subway car's wall, Emmett ran a finger down the length of the Seventh Avenue line. Finding the Wall Street stop revealed that in his haste he had boarded an express train headed south rather than a local headed north. By the time he realized this, the doors had already closed. A second look at the map told Emmett that in another minute, the train would be somewhere under the East River on its way to Brooklyn.

Taking one of the now-empty seats, Emmett closed his eyes. Once again, he was headed in the wrong direction by a factor of a hundred and eighty degrees, but this time he had no one to blame but himself. At every step, there had been someone he could have asked for assistance, someone who could have eased his way by directing him to the right staircase, the right platform, the right train. Yet he had refused to ask a soul. With a grim self-awareness, Emmett remembered how critical he had been of his father's reluctance to ask the more experienced farmers around him for advice—as if to do so would somehow leave him unmanned. Self-reliance as folly, Emmett had thought.

As he rode from Brooklyn back to Manhattan, Emmett was determined not to make the same mistake twice. When he arrived at the station at Times Square, he asked the man in the token booth which exit would lead him downtown; on the corner of Forty-Second Street, he asked the man in the newsstand where he could find the Statler Building; and when he reached the Statler Building, he asked the uniformed man at the front desk which of the agencies in the building were the biggest.

By the time Emmett arrived at the Tristar Talent Agency on the thirteenth floor, there were already eight people gathered in the small waiting room—four men with dogs, two with cats, a woman with a monkey on a leash, and a man in a three-piece suit and bowler hat who had an exotic bird on his shoulder. He was talking to the middle-aged receptionist. When he finished, Emmett approached the desk.

—Yes? the receptionist asked, as if she were already bored with whatever Emmett had to say.

—I'm here to see Mr. Lehmberg.

She took a pencil from a holder and held it over a pad.

—Name?

—Emmett Watson.

The pencil scratched.

—Animal?

—I'm sorry?

She looked up from the pad and spoke with exaggerated patience.

—What sort of animal have you got?

—I don't have an animal.

—If there's no animal in your act, then you're in the wrong place.

—I don't have an act, explained Emmett. I need to speak to Mr. Lehmberg on a different matter.

—It's one thing at a time in this office, sonny. You want to talk to Mr. Lehmberg on a different matter, you'll have to come back on a different day.

—It shouldn't take more than a minute . . .

—Why don't you take a seat, Mac, said a man with a bulldog at his feet.

—I may not need to see Mr. Lehmberg at all, persisted Emmett. You might be able to help me.

The receptionist looked up at Emmett with an expression of serious doubt.

—I'm looking for someone who might have been one of Mr. Lehmberg's clients. A performer. I'm just trying to track down his address.

As Emmett completed his explanation, the receptionist's face darkened.

—Do I look like a phone book?

—No, ma'am.

As several of the performers behind Emmett laughed, he felt the color rising to his cheeks.

Stabbing her pencil back into its holder, the receptionist picked up the phone and dialed a number.

Imagining she might be calling Mr. Lehmberg, after all, Emmett remained at the desk. But when the call went through, the receptionist began talking to a woman named Gladys about what had happened on a television show the night before. Avoiding eye contact with the waiting performers, Emmett turned and headed back into the hallway— just in time to see the doors to the elevator closing.

But before they shut completely, the tip of an umbrella jutted through the gap. A moment later, the doors reopened to reveal the man with the bowler hat and the bird on his shoulder.

—Thank you, said Emmett.

—Not at all, said the man.

It hadn't looked like rain that morning, so Emmett guessed the umbrella was somehow part of the act. Looking up from the umbrella, Emmett realized the gentleman was staring at him expectantly.

—Lobby? he asked.

—Oh, I'm sorry. No.

Fumbling a little, Emmett removed from his pocket the list that the deskman downstairs had given him.

—Fifth floor, please.

—Ah.

The gentleman pressed the corresponding button. Then reaching into his pocket he produced a peanut, which he handed to the bird on his shoulder. Standing on one claw, the bird took the peanut with the other.

—Thank you, Mr. Morton, it squawked.

—My pleasure, Mr. Winslow.

As Emmett watched the bird shell the peanut with a startling facility, Mr. Morton noted his interest.

—An African grey, he said with a smile. One of the most intelligent of all our feathered friends. Mr. Winslow here, for example, has a vocabulary of one hundred and sixty-two words.

—One hundred and sixty-three, squawked the bird.

—Is that so, Mr. Winslow. And what was the hundred and sixty-third word?

—ASPCA.

The gentleman coughed in embarrassment.

—That is not a word, Mr. Winslow. It is an acronym.

—Acronym, squawked the bird. One hundred and sixty-four!

Only when the gentleman smiled at Emmett a little sadly did Emmett realize this little exchange was part of the act too.

Having reached the fifth floor, the elevator came to a stop and its doors opened. With a word of thanks, Emmett stepped off and the doors began to close. But once again, Mr. Morton stuck the tip of his umbrella in the gap. This time when the doors reopened, he got off the elevator, joining Emmett in the hall.

—I don't wish to intrude, young man, but I couldn't help hearing your inquiry back in Mr. Lehmberg's office. By any chance, are you now headed to McGinley & Co.?

—I am, said Emmett in surprise.

—May I offer you a piece of friendly advice?

—His advice is nice and worth the price.

When Mr. Morton gave the bird a hangdog expression, Emmett laughed out loud. It was the first time that he had laughed out loud in a good long while.

—I'd appreciate any advice you're willing to give, Mr. Morton.

The gentleman smiled and pointed his umbrella down the hallway, which was lined with identical doors.

—When you go into Mr. McGinley's office, you will not find his receptionist, Miss Cravitts, any more helpful than you found Mrs. Burk. The ladies who manage the desks in this building are naturally reticent, disinclined you might even say, to be helpful. This may seem ungenerous, but you have to understand that they are besieged from morning to night by artists of all persuasions who are trying to talk their way into a meeting. In the Statler Building, the Cravittses and Burks are all that stand between a semblance of order and the Colosseum. But if these ladies must be reasonably stern with performers, they have to be all the more so with those who come seeking names and addresses. . . .

Mr. Morton set the point of his umbrella down on the floor and leaned on the handle.

—In this building, for every performer an agent represents, there are at least five creditors in hot pursuit. There are outraged audience members, ex-wives, and cheated restaurateurs. There is only one person for whom the gatekeepers show the slightest courtesy, and that is the man who holds the purse strings—whether he be hiring for a Broadway show or bar mitzvah. So, if you're going into Mr. McGinley's office, may I suggest you introduce yourself as a producer.

As Emmett considered this advice, the gentleman studied him discreetly.

—I can see from your expression that the notion of misrepresenting yourself goes against the grain. But you should take heart, young man, that within the walls of the Statler Building, he who misrepresents himself well, represents himself best.

—Thank you, said Emmett.

Mr. Morton nodded. But then he raised a finger with an additional thought.

—This performer you're looking for. . . . Do you know his specialty?

—He's an actor.

—Hmm.

—Is something wrong?

Mr. Morton gestured vaguely.

—It's your appearance. Your age and attire. Let us just say that your image clashes with what one might expect from a theatrical producer.

Mr. Morton studied Emmett a little more brazenly, then smiled.

—May I suggest that you present yourself as the son of a rodeo owner.

—The man I'm looking for is a Shakespearean actor . . .

Mr. Morton laughed.

—Even better, he said.

And when he began to laugh again, his parrot laughed with him.

When Emmett paid his visit to the offices of McGinley & Co., he took care to do exactly as Mr. Morton had advised at every step, and he was not disappointed. When he entered the waiting room, which was crowded with young mothers and redheaded boys, the receptionist met him with the same expression of impatience that he'd been given at Tristar Talent. But as soon as he explained that he was the son of a touring rodeo operator looking to hire a performer, her expression brightened.

Standing and straightening her skirt, she ushered Emmett into a second waiting room, one that was smaller but with better chairs, a water cooler, and no other people. Ten minutes later, Emmett was shown into Mr. McGinley's office, where he was greeted with the warmth of an old acquaintance and offered a drink.

—So, said Mr. McGinley, resuming his seat behind his desk, Alice tells me you're looking for a man for your rodeo!

Emmett had been skeptical when Mr. Morton observed that the hunt for a Shakespearean actor to cast in a rodeo was *even better.* When he explained himself to Mr. McGinley, he did so with some hesitation. But as soon as he was finished speaking, Mr. McGinley slapped his hands together in satisfaction.

—A nice twist, if I do say so myself! There's no shortage of performers complaining that they've been pigeonholed into this, or pigeonholed into that. But time and again, the mistake that producers actually make is not pigeonholing their actors; it's pigeonholing their *audiences.* This group only wants this, they'll tell you, while that group only wants that. When, in all likelihood, what your theatrical devotee is hungry for is a little more horseplay, while what your fan of the rodeo craves is a little more *savoir faire!*

Mr. McGinley broke into a wide grin. Then suddenly serious, he put a hand on a pile of files that were stacked on his desk.

—Rest assured, Mr. Watson, that your troubles are behind you. For not only do I have an army of fine Shakespearean actors at my disposal, four of them can ride horses and two of them can shoot!

—Thank you, Mr. McGinley. But I am looking for a *particular* Shakespearean.

Mr. McGinley leaned forward with enthusiasm.

—Particular in what way? British? Classically trained? A tragedian?

—I'm looking for a monologist whom my father saw perform some years ago and has never forgotten. A monologist by the name of Harrison Hewett.

Mr. McGinley patted his desk three times, quietly.

—Hewett?

—That's right.

Patting the desk one last time, Mr. McGinley pressed the button on his intercom.

—Alice? Bring me the file on . . . Harrison Hewett.

A few moments later Alice entered and handed a folder to Mr. McGinley that could not have held more than a single sheet of paper. After taking a quick look inside, Mr. McGinley laid it on his desk.

—Harrison Hewett is an excellent choice, Mr. Watson. I can see why your father has never forgotten him. And he's a man who thrives on artistic challenges, so I am certain he would leap at the chance to perform in your revue. But by way of clarification, I should note that we represent Mr. Hewett on a cooperative basis. . . .

By Mr. Morton's estimation, the chances were better than fifty percent that Mr. McGinley would say exactly this.

—If an agent states that he represents a performer on a cooperative basis, explained Mr. Morton, this means that he does not represent the performer at all. But not to worry. The agents in the Statler Building are in universal agreement that to get a bird in the hand, they would happily pay ten percent to the bush. As a result, they all maintain active lists of the performers who work with their competitors, so that, for the appropriate commission, they can send an interested party up or down the stairs.

In Emmett's case, it was a trip up to a Mr. Cohen on the eleventh floor. As Mr. McGinley had called in advance, Emmett was greeted at the door and whisked straight into another interior waiting room. Ten minutes later, he was shown into Mr. Cohen's office, where he was greeted warmly and offered another drink. Again, the idea of introducing a Shakespearean actor into a rodeo was celebrated for its ingenuity. But this time, when the button on the intercom was pressed and a folder brought in, it was almost two inches thick—stuffed with yellowed news clippings and playbills and a stack of outdated headshots, one of which was given to Emmett.

Once Mr. Cohen had assured Emmett that Mr. Hewett (who was a close personal friend of Will Rogers) would be thrilled by this opportunity, he asked how Emmett might be reached.

Following Mr. Morton's instructions, Emmett explained that since he was leaving the city on the following morning, he needed to hammer out any details right then and there. This sent the office into a flurry of activity as terms were agreed to and contracts written up.

—If they actually prepare contracts, Emmett had asked Mr. Morton, should I agree to sign them?

—Sign anything they put in front of you, my boy! Make sure the agent signs them too. Then insist upon receiving two executed copies for your files. For once an agent has your signature, he would give you the keys to his own mother's house.

The address that Mr. Cohen gave Emmett for Harrison Hewett led him to a dingy hotel on a dingy street in downtown Manhattan. From the well-mannered man who answered the door of room 42, Emmett learned to his disappointment that Mr. Hewett was no longer a resident, but he also learned that Mr. Hewett's son had been there the previous morning and had apparently checked into the hotel for the night.

—Perhaps he's still here, said the gentleman.

In the lobby, the clerk with the pencil-thin moustache said sure, sure, he knew who Emmett was talking about. Harry Hewett's kid. He showed up asking about his old man's whereabouts, then booked two rooms for the night. But he wasn't there no more. He and his daydreaming pal had left around noon.

—With my fucking radio, added the clerk.

—Did he happen to say where he was going?

—He might have.

—Might have? asked Emmett.

The clerk leaned back in his chair.

—When I helped your friend find his father, he gave me ten bucks . . .

According to the clerk, Emmett would be able to find Duchess's father by speaking to a friend of his who drank at a West Side saloon every night after eight. With time to spare, Emmett walked up Broadway until he found a coffee shop that was busy, clean, and well lit. Sitting at the counter, he ordered the special and a piece of pie. He finished his meal with three cups of coffee, and a cigarette that he bummed from his waitress—an Irish woman named Maureen, who, despite being ten times busier than Mrs. Burk, had ten times her grace.

The information from the hotel clerk sent Emmett back to Times Square, which in the hour before dusk was already incandescent with brightly lit signs announcing cigarettes, cars, appliances, hotels, and theaters. The sheer scale and garishness of it all made Emmett disinclined to buy a single thing that was being advertised.

Emmett returned to the newsstand on the corner of Forty-Second Street, where he found the same newsman from earlier in the day. This time the newsman pointed to the northern end of the square, where a giant sign for Canadian Club whiskey was shining ten stories above the street.

—See that sign? Just beyond it, take a left onto Forty-Fifth and keep walking till you've run out of Manhattan.

Over the course of the day, Emmett had grown accustomed to being ignored. He'd been ignored by the commuters on the subway train, by the pedestrians on the sidewalks and the performers in the waiting rooms, chalking it up to the inimicality of city life. So he was a little surprised to discover that once he was beyond Eighth Avenue, he wasn't ignored anymore.

On the corner of Ninth Avenue, he was eyed by a beat cop in the middle of his rounds. On Tenth Avenue he was approached by one young man offering to sell him drugs and another offering to sell him his company. As he approached Eleventh, he was beckoned by an old black beggar, whom he avoided by quickening his pace, only to run right into an old white beggar a few steps later.

Having found the anonymity of the morning somewhat off-putting, Emmett would have welcomed it now. He felt he understood why the people of New York walked with that purposeful urgency. It was a dissuasive signal to the vagrants and drifters and the rest of the fallen.

Just before the river, he found the Anchor—the bar the clerk had told him about. Given its name and location, Emmett had imagined it would be a spot that catered to sailors or members of the merchant marine. If it ever had, the association had lapsed long ago. For inside there wasn't a man you might call seaworthy. To Emmett's eye, they all looked one step above the old beggars he'd dodged in the street.

Having learned from Mr. Morton how reluctant the agents were to share whereabouts, Emmett was worried that the bartender might be equally tight-lipped; or perhaps like the clerk at the Sunshine Hotel, he would expect to be handsomely reimbursed. But when Emmett explained that he was looking for a man named FitzWilliams, the bartender said that he'd come to the right place. So Emmett had taken a seat at the bar and ordered the beer.

—·—

When the door of the Anchor opened shortly after eight and a man in his sixties entered, the bartender gave Emmett the nod. From his stool, Emmett watched as the old man made his way slowly to the bar, picked up a glass and half-empty bottle of whiskey, and retreated to a table in the corner.

As FitzWilliams poured himself a drink, Emmett recalled the stories that Duchess had told of his rise and fall. It wasn't easy to imagine
that this thin, shuffling, forlorn-looking man had once been paid handsomely to play the part of Santa Claus. Leaving some money on the
bar, Emmett approached the old performer's table.

—Excuse me. Are you Mr. FitzWilliams?

When Emmett said the word *mister*, FitzWilliams looked up with
a touch of surprise.

—Yes, he admitted after a moment. I am Mr. FitzWilliams.

Taking the empty chair, Emmett explained that he was a friend of
Duchess's.

—I gather he may have come here last night to speak with you.

The old performer nodded, as if now he understood, as if he should
have known.

—Yes, he said in a tone that verged on an admission. He was here.
He was trying to find his father because of a little unfinished business
between them. But Harry had left town, and Duchess didn't know
where he'd gone, so he came to see Fitzy.

FitzWilliams offered Emmett a half-hearted smile.

—I'm an old friend of the family's, you see.

Returning the smile, Emmett asked FitzWilliams if he had told
Duchess where Mr. Hewett had gone.

—I did, the old performer said, nodding his head at first, then
shaking it. I told him where Harry went. To the Olympic Hotel in
Syracuse. And that's where Duchess will go, I suppose. After he sees
his friend.

—Which friend is that?

—Oh, Duchess didn't say. But it was . . . It was in Harlem.

—Harlem?

—Yes. Isn't that funny?

—No, it makes perfect sense. Thank you, Mr. FitzWilliams. You've
been very helpful.

When Emmett pushed back his chair, FitzWilliams looked up in surprise.

—You're not going, are you? Surely, as two old friends of the Hewetts, we should have a drink in their honor?

Having learned what he had come to learn, and certain that Billy would be wondering where he was by now, Emmett had no desire to remain at the Anchor.

But having initially looked like he didn't want to be disturbed, the old performer suddenly looked like he didn't want to be alone. So Emmett got another glass from the bartender and returned to the table.

After FitzWilliams had poured their whiskeys, he raised his glass.

—To Harry and Duchess.

—To Harry and Duchess, echoed Emmett.

When they both had taken a drink and set down their glasses, FitzWilliams smiled a little sadly, as if moved by a bittersweet memory.

—Do you know why they call him that? Duchess, I mean.

—I think he told me it was because he was born in Dutchess County.

—No, said FitzWilliams, with a shake of the head and his half-hearted smile. That wasn't it. He was born here in Manhattan. I remember the night.

Before continuing, FitzWilliams took another drink, almost as if he needed to.

—His mother, Delphine, was a beautiful young Parisienne and a singer of love songs in the manner of Piaf. In the years before Duchess was born, she performed at all the great supper clubs. At El Morocco and the Stork Club and the Rainbow Room. I'm sure she would have become quite famous, at least in New York, if it weren't for becoming so sick. It was tuberculosis, I think. But I really can't remember. Isn't that terrible? A beautiful woman like that, a friend, dies in the prime of her life, and I can't even remember from what.

Shaking his head in self-condemnation, FitzWilliams raised his glass, but set it back down without taking a drink, as if he sensed that to have done so would have been an insult to her memory.

The story of Mrs. Hewett's death caught Emmett a little off guard. For in the few times that Duchess had mentioned his mother, he had always spoken as if she had abandoned them.

—At any rate, FitzWilliams continued, Delphine doted on her little boy. When there was money, she would quietly hide some from Harry so that she could buy him new clothes. Cute little outfits like those, what do you call them . . . lederhosen! She would dress him up in his finery, letting his hair grow down to his shoulders. But when she became bedridden and she would send him downstairs into the taverns to bring Harry home, Harry would . . .

FitzWilliams shook his head.

—Well, you know Harry. After a few drinks, it's hard to tell where Shakespeare ends and Harry begins. So when the boy would come through the door, Harry would stand up from his stool, make an elaborate flourish, and say, *Ladies and Gentlemen, I present to you, the Duchess of Alba*. And the next time it would be *the Duchess of Kent*, or *the Duchess of Tripoli*. Pretty soon some of the others began calling the boy Duchess. Then we all called him Duchess. Every last one of us. To the point where no one could even remember his given name.

FitzWilliams raised his glass again, this time taking a good, long drink. When he set the glass down, Emmett was startled to see that the old performer had begun to cry—letting the tears roll down his cheeks without bothering to wipe them away.

FitzWilliams gestured to the bottle.

—He gave me that, you know. Duchess, I mean. Despite everything. Despite all of it, last night he came here and bought me a brand-new bottle of my favorite whiskey. Just like that.

FitzWilliams took a deep breath.

—He was sent away to a work camp in Kansas, you know. At the age of sixteen.

—Yes, said Emmett. That's where we met.

—Ah. I see. But in all your time together, did he ever tell you . . . did he ever tell you how he came to be there?

—No, said Emmett. He never did.

Then after taking the liberty of pouring a little more of the old man's whiskey into both of their glasses, Emmett waited.

Ulysses

THOUGH THE BOY HAD already read the story once from beginning to end, Ulysses asked him to read it again.

Shortly after ten—with the sun having set, the moon yet to rise, and the others retreating to their tents—Billy had taken out his book and asked if Ulysses would like to hear the story of Ishmael, a young sailor who joined a one-legged captain on his hunt for a great white whale. Though Ulysses had never heard the story of Ishmael, he had no doubt it would be a good one. Each of the boy's stories had been good. But when Billy had offered to read this new adventure, with a touch of embarrassment Ulysses had asked if he would read the story of his namesake instead.

The boy hadn't hesitated. By the waning light of Stew's fire, he had turned to the back of his book and illuminated the page with his flashlight beam—a circle of light within a circle of light within a sea of darkness.

As Billy began, Ulysses felt a moment of worry that having read the story once before, the boy might paraphrase or skip over passages, but Billy seemed to understand that if the story was worth reading again, it was worth reading word for word.

Yes, the boy read the story exactly as he had in the boxcar, but Ulysses didn't hear it the same way. For this time, he knew what was to come. He knew now to look forward to some parts and dread others—to look forward to how Ulysses bested the Cyclops by hiding his men under the pelts of sheep, and to dread the moment when the covetous crew unleashed the winds of Aeolus, setting their captain's ship off course at the very moment that his homeland had come into view.

When the story was over, and Billy had closed his book and switched off his light, and Ulysses had taken up Stew's shovel to cover the embers, Billy asked if he would tell a story.

Ulysses looked down with a smile.

—I don't have any storybooks, Billy.

—You don't have to tell a story from a book, Billy replied. You could tell a story from yourself. Like one from the war overseas. Do you have any of those?

Ulysses turned the shovel in his hand.

Did he have any stories from the war? Of course, he did. More than he cared to remember. For his stories had not been softened by the mists of time or brightened by the tropes of a poet. They remained vivid and severe. So vivid and severe that whenever one happened to surface in his mind, Ulysses would bury it—just as he had been about to bury the embers of this fire. If Ulysses couldn't stomach the sharing of the memories with himself, he certainly wasn't going to share them with an eight-year-old boy.

But Billy's request was a fair one. Generously, he had opened the pages of his book and told the stories of Sinbad and Jason and Achilles, and of Ulysses's namesake twice. He had certainly earned a telling in return. So setting the shovel aside, Ulysses threw another log on the fire and resumed his seat on the railroad tie.

—I have a story for you, he said. A story about my own encounter with the king of the winds.

—When you were sailing across the wine-dark sea?

—No, said Ulysses. When I was walking across the dry and dusty land.

The story began on a rural road in Iowa in the summer of 1952.

A few days before, Ulysses had boarded a train in Utah, intending to travel over the Rockies and across the plains to Chicago. But halfway through Iowa, the boxcar in which he was traveling was shunted onto a siding in order to wait for a different locomotive, which was scheduled to arrive who knew when. Forty miles away was the junction in Des Moines, where he could easily catch another train headed east, or one headed north toward the Lakes, or south to New Orleans. With that in mind, Ulysses had disembarked and begun working his way across the countryside on foot.

He had walked about ten miles down an old dirt road when he began to sense that something was amiss.

The first sign was the birds. Or rather, the absence of them. When you're traveling back and forth across the country, Ulysses explained, the one great constant is the companionship of birds. On your way from Miami to Seattle or Boston to San Diego, the landscape is always changing. But wherever you go, the birds are there. The pigeons or buzzards, condors or cardinals, blue jays or blackbirds. Living on the road, you wake to the sound of their singing at dawn, and you lay yourself down to their chatter at dusk.

And yet . . .

As Ulysses walked along this rural road, there wasn't a bird to be seen, not circling over the fields or perched upon the telephone wires.

The second sign was the caravan of cars. While throughout the morning Ulysses had been passed by the occasional pickup or sedan moving along at forty miles an hour, suddenly he saw an assortment of fifteen cars, including a black limousine, speeding in his direction. The vehicles were driving so fast, he had to step off the shoulder in order to shield himself from the gravel that was kicked up by their tires.

After watching them race past, Ulysses turned back to look in the direction from which they'd come. That's when he saw that the sky in the east was turning from blue to green. Which in that part of the country, as Billy well knew, could only mean one thing.

Behind Ulysses was nothing but knee-high corn for as far as the eye could see, but half a mile ahead was a farmhouse. With the sky growing darker by the minute, Ulysses began to run.

As he drew closer, Ulysses could see that the farmhouse had already been battened down, its doors and shutters closed. He could see the owner securing the barn, then dashing to the hatch of his shelter, where his wife and children waited. And when the farmer reached his family, Ulysses could see the young boy pointing in his direction.

As the four looked his way, Ulysses slowed from a run to a walk with his hands at his side.

The farmer instructed his wife and children to go into the shelter— first the wife so that she could help the children, then the daughter, and then the little boy, who continued to look at Ulysses right up until the moment he disappeared from sight.

Ulysses expected the father to follow his family down the ladder, but leaning over to say one last thing, he closed the hatch, turned toward Ulysses, and waited for his approach. Maybe there was no lock on the shelter's hatch, thought Ulysses, and the farmer figured if there was going to be a confrontation then better to have it now, while still aboveground. Or maybe he felt if one man intends to refuse harbor to another, he should do so face-to-face.

As a sign of respect, Ulysses came to a stop six paces away, close enough to be heard, but far enough to pose no threat.

The two men studied each other as the wind began to lift the dust around their feet.

—I'm not from around these parts, Ulysses said after a moment. I'm just a Christian working my way to Des Moines so I can catch a train.

The farmer nodded. He nodded in a manner that said he believed Ulysses was a Christian and that he was on his way to catch a train, but that under the circumstances neither of those things mattered.

—I don't know you, he said simply.

—No, you don't, agreed Ulysses.

For a moment, Ulysses considered helping the man come to know him—by telling him his name, telling him that he'd been raised in Tennessee and that he was a veteran, that he'd once had a wife and child of his own. But even as these thoughts passed through Ulysses's mind, he knew that the telling of them wouldn't matter either. And he knew it without resentment.

For were the positions reversed, were Ulysses about to climb down into a shelter, a windowless space beneath the ground that he had dug with his own hands for the safety of his family, and were a six-foot-tall white man suddenly to appear, he wouldn't have welcomed him either. He would have sent him on his way.

After all, what was a man in the prime of his life doing crossing the country on foot with nothing but a canvas bag slung over his shoulder? A man like that must have made certain choices. He had chosen to abandon his family, his township, his church, in pursuit of something different. In pursuit of a life unhindered, unanswered, and alone. Well, if that's what he had worked so hard to become, then why in a moment like this should he expect to be treated as anything different?

—I understand, said Ulysses, though the man had not explained himself.

The farmer looked at Ulysses for a moment, then turning to his right, he pointed to a thin white spire rising from a grove of trees.

—The Unitarian church is a little less than a mile. It's got a basement. And you've got a good chance of making it, if you run.

—Thank you, said Ulysses.

As they stood facing each other, Ulysses knew that the farmer had been right. Any chance he had of making it to the church in time was predicated on his going as quickly as he could. But Ulysses had no intention of breaking into a run in front of another man, however good his advice. It was a matter of dignity.

After waiting, the farmer seemed to understand this, and with a shake of the head that laid no blame on anyone, including himself, he opened his hatch and joined his family.

With a glance at the steeple, Ulysses could tell that the shortest route to the church was directly across the fields rather than by way of the road, so that's the way he went, running as the crow would fly. It didn't take long for him to realize that this was a mistake. Though the corn was only a foot and a half high and the farmer's rows were wide and well kept, the ground itself was soft and uneven, making for cumbersome work. Given all the fields he'd slogged across in Italy, he should have known better. But it seemed too late to switch back to the road now, so with his eye on the steeple he pressed ahead as best he could.

When he was halfway to the church, the twister appeared in the distance at two o'clock, a dark black finger reaching down from the sky—the inversion of the steeple both in color and intent.

With every step now, Ulysses's progress was slowing. There was so much debris kicking up from the ground that he had to advance with a hand in front of his face to protect his eyes. Then he was holding up both hands with his gaze partly averted, as he stumbled onward toward the upward and downward spires.

Through the gaps in his fingers and the veil of the unsettled dust, Ulysses became aware of rectangular shadows rising from the ground around him, shadows that looked at once orderly and in disarray. Dropping his hands for a second, he realized he had entered a graveyard and he could hear the bell in the steeple beginning to toll, as if rung by an invisible hand. He couldn't have been more than fifty yards from the church.

But in all likelihood, it was fifty yards too far.

For the twister was turning counterclockwise and its winds were pushing Ulysses away from his goal rather than toward it. As hail began raining down upon him, he prepared for one final push. *I can make it*, he told himself. Then running with all his might, he began closing the distance between himself and the sanctuary—only to stumble over a low-lying gravestone and come crashing to the ground with the bitter resignation of the abandoned.

—Abandoned by who? asked Billy, with his book gripped in his lap and his eyes open wide.

Ulysses smiled.

—I don't know, Billy. By fortune, by fate, by my own good sense. But mostly by God.

The boy began shaking his head.

—You don't mean that, Ulysses. You don't mean that you were abandoned by God.

—But that's exactly what I mean, Billy. If I learned anything in the war, it's that the point of utter abandonment—that moment at which you realize no one will be coming to your aid, not even your Maker— is the very moment in which you may discover the strength required to carry on. The Good Lord does not call you to your feet with hymns from the cherubim and Gabriel blowing his horn. He calls you to your feet by making you feel alone and forgotten. For only when you have seen that you are *truly* forsaken will you embrace the fact that what happens next rests in your hands, and your hands alone.

Lying on the ground of that graveyard, feeling the old abandonment and knowing it for what it was, Ulysses reached up and took hold of the top of the nearest gravestone. As he hoisted himself upward, he realized the stone he was pushing on was not weathered or worn. Even through the maelstrom of dust and debris he could see it had the dark gray luminescence of a stone that had just been planted. Rising to his full height, Ulysses found himself looking over the shoulders of the marker down into a freshly dug grave, at the bottom of which was the shiny black top of a casket.

This is where the caravan of cars had been coming from, realized Ulysses. They must have been right in the middle of the interment when they received warning of the tornado's approach. The reverend must have hurried through whatever verses would suffice to commit the soul of the deceased to Heaven, and then everyone had dashed for their cars.

From the look of the coffin, it must have been for a man of some wealth. For this was no pine box. It was polished mahogany with handles of solid brass. On the lid of the coffin was a matching brass plaque with the dead man's name: Noah Benjamin Elias.

Sliding down into the narrow gap between the coffin and the wall of the grave, Ulysses bent over to unscrew the clasps and open the coffin's lid. Inside was Mr. Elias lying in state, dressed in a three-piece suit with his hands crossed neatly on his chest. His shoes were as black and shiny as his coffin, and curving across his vest was the thin gold chain of a watch. Though only about five foot six, Mr. Elias must have weighed over two hundred pounds—having dined in a manner suited to his station.

What was the nature of Mr. Elias's earthly success? Was he the owner of a bank or lumberyard? Was he a man of grit and determination, or of greed and deceit? Whichever he was, he was no longer. And all that mattered to Ulysses was that this man who was only five foot six had had a big enough sense of himself to be buried in a coffin that was six feet long.

Reaching down, Ulysses took hold of Elias by the lapels, just as you would when you intended to shake some sense into someone. Pulling him up out of the coffin, Ulysses hoisted him into a standing position so that they were almost face-to-face. Ulysses could see now that the mortician had applied rouge on the dead man's cheeks and scented him with gardenia, giving him the unsettling semblance of a harlot. Bending his knees in order to get under the weight of the cadaver, Ulysses raised him up out of his resting place and dumped him at the side of the grave.

Taking one last look at the great black finger that was swaying left and right as it bore down upon him, Ulysses lay back in the pleated white silk that lined the empty coffin, reached up a hand, and—

Pastor John

W HEN THE VENGEANCE OF the Lord is visited upon us, it does not rain down from the heavens like a shower of meteors trailing fire. It does not strike like a bolt of lightning accompanied by claps of thunder. It does not gather like a tidal wave far out at sea and come crashing down upon the shores. No. When the vengeance of the Lord is visited upon us, it begins as a breath in the desert.

Gentle and undaunting, this little expiration turns three times above the hardened ground, quietly stirring the dust and the scent of the sagebrush. But as it turns three times more, and three times again, this little whirlwind grows to the size of a man and begins to move. Spiraling across the land it gains in velocity and volume, growing to the size of a colossus, swaying and sweeping up into its vortex all that lays within its path—first the sand and stones, the shrubs and varmints, and then the works of men. Until at long last, towering a hundred feet tall and moving at a hundred miles an hour, swirling and spinning, turning and twisting, it comes inexorably for the sinner.

Thus concluded the thoughts of Pastor John as he stepped from the darkness and swung his oaken staff in order to smite the Negro called Ulysses on the crown of his head.

—·—

Left for dead. That's what Pastor John had been. With the tendons of his right knee torn, the skin of his cheeks abraded, his right eye swollen shut, he lay among the bushes and brambles preparing to deliver his own absolution. But at the very moment of his demise, the Lord had found him by the side of the tracks and breathed new life into his limbs. Lifting him up from the gravel and scrub, He had carried him to the edge of a cool running stream, where his thirst was slaked, his wounds washed, and into his hands delivered the branch of an ancient oak to be used as a staff.

In the hours that followed, not once did Pastor John wonder where he was going, how he would get there, or to what end—for he could feel the Spirit of the Lord working through him, making of him Its instrument. From the riverbank, It led him back through the woods to a siding where ten empty boxcars had been left unattended. Once he was safely inside, It brought forth a locomotive that hitched the cars and carried him eastward to the city of New York.

When Pastor John disembarked in the great railyard situated between Pennsylvania Station and the Hudson River, the Spirit shielded him from the eyes of the railway guards and led him not into the crowded streets but up onto the tracks of an elevated line. With his weight on his staff in order to spare his knee, Pastor John moved along the elevated, casting his shadow down upon the avenues. Once the sun had set, the Spirit led him onward—through an empty warehouse, through a gap in a fence, through the high and scraggly grass, through the darkness itself, until in the distance he could see a campfire shining like a star.

Drawing closer, Pastor John saw that in His infinite wisdom the Good Lord had lit the fire not only to guide him, but to illuminate the faces of the Negro and the boy—even as it made Pastor John's presence invisible to them. In the shadows outside the circle of the fire, Pastor John stopped and listened as the boy finished a story and asked if the Negro would tell one of his own.

Oh, how John had laughed to hear Ulysses rattle on about his frightful tornado. For that little twister was nothing compared to the widening gyre which is the vengeance of the Lord. Did he seriously think that he could throw a pastor from a moving train without fear of retribution? That his actions would somehow escape the eyes of the Divine and the hand of judgment?

The Lord God is all-seeing and all-knowing, Pastor John said without speaking. *He has paid witness to your misdeeds, Ulysses. He has paid witness to your arrogance and trespass. And He has brought me here to deliver His reprisal!*

With such fury did the Spirit of the Lord breathe into the limbs of Pastor John, when he brought his oaken staff down upon the Negro's head, the force of the blow snapped the staff in two.

When Ulysses slumped to the ground and Pastor John stepped into the light, the boy, complicit with the Negro at every step, stretched out his hands in the silent horror of the damned.

—May I join you by your fire? asked the pastor with a loud and hearty laugh.

His staff truncated, Pastor John was forced to limp toward the boy, but this didn't worry him. For he knew the boy would go nowhere and say nothing. Rather, he would withdraw into himself like a snail into its shell. Sure enough, when Pastor John pulled him up by the collar of his shirt, he could see that the boy had clenched his eyes closed and begun his incantation.

—There is no Emmett here, said the pastor. No one is coming to your aid, William Watson.

Then with the boy's collar fast in his grip, Pastor John raised the broken staff and prepared to deliver that lesson which Ulysses had interrupted two days before. To deliver it with interest!

But just when the staff was poised to fall, the boy opened his eyes.

—I am truly forsaken, he said with a mysterious gusto.

Then he kicked the pastor in his injured knee.

With an animal howl, Pastor John let loose the boy's shirt and dropped his staff. Hopping in place with tears of pain falling from his one good eye, Pastor John became more committed in his intent to teach the boy a lesson he wouldn't soon forget. But even as he thrust his hands outward, he could see through his tears that the boy was gone.

Eager to pursue, Pastor John looked frantically about for something to replace his broken staff.

—Aha! he shouted.

For there on the ground was a shovel. Picking it up, Pastor John stuck the blade into the dirt, leaned on the handle, and began moving slowly toward the darkness into which the boy had disappeared.

After a few steps, he could just make out the silhouettes of an encampment: a small pile of firewood covered with a tarp, a makeshift washstand, a line of three empty bedrolls, and a tent.

—William, he called softly. Where are you, William?

—What's going on out there, came a voice from inside the tent.

Holding his breath, Pastor John took a step to the side and waited as a stocky Negro emerged. Not seeing the pastor, he walked a few feet forward and stopped.

—Ulysses? he asked.

When Pastor John hit him with the flat of the shovel, he fell to the ground with a groan.

Off to his left Pastor John could hear other voices now. The voices of two men who may have heard the commotion.

—Forget the boy, he said to himself.

Using the shovel as his crutch, he hobbled as quickly as he could back to the campfire and made his way to where the boy had been sitting. There on the ground were the book and flashlight. But where was that damnable rucksack?

Pastor John looked back in the direction from which he had just come. Could it have been by the bedrolls? No. Where the book and the flashlight were, the rucksack was sure to be. Leaning over carefully, Pastor John dropped the shovel, picked up the flashlight, and switched it on. With a hop, he trained the beam onto the back side of the railroad ties and began moving from right to left.

There it is!

Sitting down on a tie with his injured leg stretched before him, Pastor John retrieved the rucksack and set it in his lap. Even as he did so, he could hear the music within.

With growing excitement, he undid the straps and began withdrawing items and tossing them aside. Two shirts. A pair of pants. A washcloth. At the very bottom he found the tin. Liberating it from the bag, he gave it a celebratory shake.

Tomorrow morning, he would pay a visit to the Jews on Forty-Seventh Street. In the afternoon, he would go to a department store for a new set of clothes. And tomorrow night, he would check into a fine hotel, where he would take a long, hot bath and send out for oysters, a bottle of wine, perhaps even some female companionship. But now, it was time to leave. Returning the flashlight and tin to the rucksack, he cinched its straps and hooked it over his shoulder. Ready at last to be on his way, Pastor John leaned to his left in order to pick up the shovel, only to find that it was no longer where he had—

Ulysses

FIRST THERE WAS DARKNESS without recognition. Then slowly, an awareness of it. An awareness that it wasn't the darkness of space—cold, vast, and remote. It was a darkness that was close and warm, a darkness that was covering him, embracing him in the manner of a velvet shroud.

Creeping from the corners of his memory came the realization that he was still in the fat man's coffin. He could feel along his shoulders the smooth, pleated silk of the lining and, behind that, the sturdiness of the mahogany frame.

He wanted to raise the lid, but how much time had passed? Was the tornado gone? Holding his breath, he listened. He listened through the pleated silk and polished mahogany and heard nothing. Not the sound of the wind whistling, or of hail falling on the coffin lid, or of the church bell swinging on its hook unattended. In order to be certain, he decided to open the coffin a crack. Turning his palms upward, he pressed at the lid, but the lid wouldn't budge.

Was it possible that he had become weakened with hunger and fatigue? Surely, not that much time had passed. Or had it? Suddenly, it occurred to him with a touch of horror that in the aftermath of the storm, while he was unconscious, someone might have happened upon the open grave and shoveled the mound of topsoil onto the coffin, finishing the job.

He would have to try again. After rolling his shoulders and flexing his fingers in order to restore the circulation to his limbs, he drew a breath, put his palms again against the inner surface of the lid, and pushed with all his might as the sweat that formed on his brow ran in droplets into his eyes. Slowly, the lid began to open, and cooler air rushed into the coffin. With a sense of relief, Ulysses gathered his strength and pushed the lid all the way back, expecting to be gazing up into the afternoon sky.

But it wasn't the afternoon.

It looked to be the middle of the night.

Raising a hand gently in the air, he saw that his skin reflected a flickering light. Listening, he heard the long, hollow horn of a ship and the laughter of a gull, as if he were somewhere at sea. But then, coming from a short distance, he heard a voice. The voice of a boy declaring his forsakenness. The voice of Billy Watson.

And suddenly, Ulysses knew where he was.

An instant later, he heard a grown man howling in anger or in pain. And though Ulysses didn't yet understand what had happened to himself, he knew what he must do.

Having rolled onto his side, with a great sluggish effort he raised himself onto his knees. Wiping the sweat from his eyes, he discovered by the light of the fire that it was blood, not sweat. Someone had hit him on the head.

Rising to his feet, Ulysses looked around the fire for Billy and for the man who had howled, but no one was there. He wanted to call out for Billy, but understood that to do so would signal to an unknown enemy that he had regained consciousness.

He needed to get away from the fire, outside of the circle of light. Under the veil of darkness, he would be able to gather his wits and strength, find Billy, and then begin the process of hunting his adversary down.

Stepping over one of the railroad ties, he walked five paces into the darkness and took his bearings. There was the river, he thought, turning on his feet; there was the Empire State Building; and there was their encampment. As he looked in the direction of Stew's tent he thought he saw movement. Quietly, almost too softly to hear, came the voice of a man calling Billy, calling him by his given name. The man's voice may have been almost too soft to hear, but it wasn't too soft to recognize.

While remaining in the darkness, Ulysses began circumventing the fire moving carefully, quietly, inevitably toward the preacher.

Ulysses stopped short when he heard Stew call his name. A moment later he heard the clang of metal and the thud of a body falling to the ground. Feeling a flash of anger with himself for being too cautious, Ulysses prepared to charge into the encampment when he saw a silhouette emerge from the darkness, moving unevenly.

It was the preacher using Stew's shovel as a crutch. Dropping the shovel on the ground, he picked up the boy's flashlight, switched it on, and began searching for something.

Keeping an eye on the preacher, Ulysses crept to the edge of the fire, reached over a railroad tie, and retrieved the shovel. When the preacher gave an exclamation of discovery, Ulysses stepped back into the darkness and watched as he picked up Billy's knapsack and sat with it in his lap.

In an excited voice, the preacher began talking to himself about hotels and oysters and female companionship while withdrawing Billy's belongings and tossing them on the ground—until he found the tin of dollars. At the same time, Ulysses began moving forward until he was directly behind the preacher. And when the preacher, having slung the knapsack over his shoulder, leaned to his left, Ulysses brought the shovel down.

With the preacher now lying in a heap at his feet, Ulysses felt himself heaving. Given his own injury, the effort to subdue the preacher had taken all his immediate strength. Worried that he might even faint, Ulysses stabbed the shovel into the ground and leaned on its hilt as he looked down to make certain the preacher was unmoving.

—Is he dead?

It was Billy, standing at his side looking down at the preacher too.

—No, said Ulysses.

Astoundingly, the boy seemed relieved.

—Are you all right? asked Billy.

—Yes, said Ulysses. Are you?

Billy nodded.

—I did like you said, Ulysses. When Pastor John told me that I was alone, I imagined that I had been forsaken by everyone, including my Maker. Then I kicked him and hid beneath the firewood tarp.

Ulysses smiled.

—You did well, Billy.

—What the hell is going on?

Billy and Ulysses looked up to find Stew standing behind them with a butcher knife in hand.

—You're bleeding too, Billy said with concern.

Stew had been hit on the side of the head so the blood had run down from his ear onto the shoulder of his undershirt.

Ulysses was suddenly feeling better now, more clearheaded and sure of foot.

—Billy, he said, why don't you go over there and fetch us the basin of water and some towels.

Sticking his knife through his belt, Stew came alongside Ulysses and looked at the ground.

—Who is it?

—A man of ill intent, said Ulysses.

Stew shifted his gaze to Ulysses's head.

—You better let me take a look at that.

—I've had worse.

—We've all had worse.

—I'll be all right.

—I know, I know, said Stew with a shake of the head. You're a big, big man.

Billy arrived with the basin and towels. The two men cleaned their faces and then gingerly dabbed at their wounds. When they were done, Ulysses sat Billy down beside him on one of the railroad ties.

—Billy, he began, we've had quite a bit of excitement tonight.

Billy nodded in agreement.

—Yes, we have, Ulysses. Emmett will hardly believe it.

—Well, that's just what I wanted to talk to you about. What with your brother trying to find his car and having to get you to California before the Fourth of July, he's got a lot on his mind. Maybe it's for the best if we keep what happened here tonight between us. At least for now.

Billy was nodding.

—It's probably for the best, he said. Emmett has a lot on his mind.

Ulysses patted Billy on the knee.

—One day, he said, you will tell him. You will tell him and your children too, about how you bested the preacher, just like one of the heroes in your book.

When Ulysses saw that Billy understood, he got up in order to speak with Stew.

—Can you take the boy back to your tent? Maybe give him something to eat?

—All right. But what are you going to do?

—I'm going to see to the preacher.

Billy, who had been listening behind Ulysses's back, stepped around him with a look of concern.

—What does that mean, Ulysses? What does that mean that you're going to see to the preacher?

Ulysses and Stew looked from the boy to each other and back again.

—We can't leave him here, explained Ulysses. He's going to come to just like I did. And whatever villainy had been on his mind before I crowned him is going to be there still. Only more so.

Billy was looking up at Ulysses with a furrowed brow.

—So, continued Ulysses, I'm going to take him down the stairs and drop him—

—At the police station?

—That's right, Billy. I'm going to drop him at the police station.

Billy nodded to indicate that this was the right thing to do. Then Stew turned to Ulysses.

—You know the stairs that go down to Gansevoort?

—I do.

—Someone's bent back the fencing there. It'll be an easier route, given what you'll be carrying.

Thanking Stew, Ulysses waited for Billy to gather his things, for Stew to put out the fire, and for the two to go back to Stew's tent before he turned his attention to the preacher.

Taking him under the armpits, Ulysses raised him up and draped him over his shoulders. The preacher wasn't heavier than Ulysses had expected, but he was gangly, making him an awkward burden. Shifting the body back and forth by increments, Ulysses tried to center it before he began walking in short, steady strides.

When he reached the staircase, if Ulysses had stopped to think, he might have rolled the preacher down the steps to preserve his own strength. But he was moving now, and he had the preacher's weight evenly distributed across his shoulders, and he was worried that if he stopped he might lose his balance or his momentum. And he would need them both. Because from the bottom of the stairs, it was a good two hundred yards to the river.

Duchess

WOOLLY'S SISTER CAME INTO the kitchen like a ghost. Appearing in the doorway in her long white robe and crossing the unlit room without a sound, it was like her feet didn't touch the floor. But if she was a ghost, she wasn't the harrowing sort—one of those that howl and moan and send shivers down your spine. She was the forlorn sort. The kind of ghost who wanders the halls of an empty house for generations, in search of something or someone that no one else can even remember. A visitation, I think they call it.

Yeah, that's it.

A visitation.

Without switching on the light, she filled the kettle and turned on the burner. From the cabinet she took out a mug and a tea bag and set them on the counter. From the pocket of her robe, she took out a little brown bottle and set it beside the mug. Then she went back to the sink and stood there looking out the window.

You got the sense that she was good at looking out the window—like maybe she'd gotten a lot of practice. She didn't fidget or tap her feet. In fact, she was so good at it, so good at getting lost in her thoughts, that when the kettle whistled it seemed to catch her by surprise, as if she couldn't remember having turned it on in the first place. Slowly, almost reluctantly, she left her spot at the window, poured the water, picked up the mug in one hand and the little brown bottle in the other, and turned toward the table.

—Trouble sleeping? I asked.

Caught off guard, she didn't cry out or drop her tea. She just gave the same little expression of surprise that she had given when the kettle whistled.

—I didn't see you there, she said, slipping the little brown bottle back in the pocket of her robe.

She hadn't answered my question about whether she had trouble sleeping, but she didn't need to. Every aspect of the way she moved in the dark—crossing the room, filling the pot, lighting the stove—suggested this was something of a routine. It wouldn't have surprised me in the least to learn that every other night she came down to the kitchen at two in the morning while her husband slept soundly, none the wiser.

Gesturing back toward the stove, she asked if I'd like some tea. I pointed to the glass in front of me.

—I found a little whiskey in the living room. I hope you don't mind.

She smiled softly.

—Of course not.

After taking the seat opposite mine, she trained her gaze on my left eye.

—How does it feel?

—Much better, thanks.

I had left Harlem in such high spirits that when I got back to Woolly's sister's house, I'd completely forgotten the beating I'd taken. When she answered the door and gasped, I practically gasped back.

But once Woolly had made the introductions and I had explained the spill I'd taken in the train station, she got a cute little first aid kit out of her medicine cabinet, sat me here at the kitchen table, cleaned the blood off my lip, and gave me a bag of frozen peas to hold over my eye. I would have preferred using a raw steak like a heavyweight champ, but beggars can't be choosers.

—Would you like another aspirin? she asked.

—No, I'll be all right.

We were both quiet for a moment as I took a sip of her husband's whiskey and she took a sip of her tea.

—You're Woolly's bunkmate . . . ?

—That's right.

—So, was it your father who was on the stage?

—He was under it as often as he was on it, I said with a smile. But yeah, that's my old man. He started out as a Shakespearean and ended up doing vaudeville.

She smiled at the word *vaudeville*.

—Woolly has written to me about some of the performers your father worked with. The escape artists and magicians . . . He was quite taken with them.

—Your brother loves a good bedtime story.

—Yes, he does, doesn't he.

She looked across the table as if she wanted to ask me something, but then shifted her gaze to her tea.

—What? I prompted.

—It was a personal question.

—Those are the best kind.

She studied me for a moment, trying to gauge whether or not I was being sincere. She must have decided I was.

—How did you end up at Salina, Duchess?

—Oh, that's a long one.

—I've barely started my tea. . . .

So, having poured myself another finger of whiskey, I recounted my little comedy, thinking: Maybe everyone in Woolly's family liked a good bedtime tale.

It was in the spring of 1952, just a few weeks after my sixteenth birthday, and we were living in room 42 at the Sunshine Hotel, with pops on the bedsprings and me on the floor.

At the time, my old man was what he liked to call *betwixt and between*, which just meant that having gotten fired from one job, he had yet to find the next job to get fired from. He was spending his days with his old pal, Fitzy, who was living across the hall. In the early afternoons, they would shuffle off to scour around the park benches, fruit carts, newsstands, and any other spots where someone was likely to drop a nickel and not bother to pick it back up. Then they would head down into the subways and sing sentimental songs with their hats in their hands. Men who knew their audience, they would perform "Danny Boy" for the Irish on the Third Avenue line and "Ave Maria" for the Italians at Spring Street station, crying their eyes out like they meant every word. They even had a Yiddish number about the days in the shtetl that they'd roll out when they were on the platform of the Canal Street stop. Then in the evenings—after giving me two bits and sending me off to a double feature—they would take their hard-earned pay to a dive on Elizabeth Street and drink every last penny of it.

Since the two of them didn't get up until noon, when I woke in the morning I would wander the hotel looking for something to eat or someone to talk to. At that hour, it was pretty slim pickings, but there were a handful of early risers, and the best of them, without a doubt, was Marceline Maupassant.

Back in the twenties, Marceline had been one of the most famous clowns in Europe, performing for sold-out runs in Paris and Berlin, complete with standing ovations and lines of women waiting at the backstage door. To be sure, Marceline was no ordinary clown. He wasn't a guy who painted his face and tromped around in oversize shoes honking a horn. He was the real McCoy. A poet and a dancer. A man who observed the world closely and felt things deeply—like Chaplin and Keaton.

One of his greatest bits was as a panhandler on a bustling city street. When the curtain came up, there he would be, navigating a crowd of metropolitans. With a little bow, he would try to get the attention of two men arguing over headlines by the newsstand; with a doff of his crooked hat, he would try to address a nanny whose mind was on the colicky baby in her care. Whether with a doff or a bow, everyone he tried to engage would go on about their business as if he weren't even there. Then when Marceline was about to approach a shy young woman with a downcast expression, a nearsighted scholar would bump into him, knocking his hat from his head.

Off in pursuit of the hat Marceline would go. But each time he was about to grab it, a distracted pedestrian would send it skidding in the other direction. After making several attempts at retrieval, to his utter dismay Marceline would realize that a rotund police officer was about to step on the hat unawares. With no other choice, Marceline would raise a hand in the air, snap his fingers—and everyone would be frozen in place. Everyone, that is, except Marceline.

Now the magic would happen.

For a few minutes, Marceline would glide about the stage, skating in between the immobile pedestrians with a delicate smile, as if he hadn't a care in the world. Then taking a long-stemmed rose from the flower vendor, he would present it shyly to the downcast young woman. He would interject a point or two to the men who were arguing by the newsstand. He would make faces for the baby in the pram. He would laugh and comment and counsel, all without making a sound.

But as Marceline was about to make another circuit through the crowd, he would hear a delicate chiming. Stopping at center stage, he would reach into his shabby vest and remove a solid gold pocket watch, clearly a vestige from another time in his life. Popping the lid, he would regard the hour and realize with a doleful look that his little game had gone on long enough. Putting the watch away, he would carefully take his crooked hat from under the fat policeman's foot—which had been hovering in the air for all this time, a feat of gymnastics in itself. Brushing it off, he would place it on his head, face the audience, snap his fingers, and all the activities of his fellow men would resume.

It was an act worth seeing more than once. Because the first time you saw the show, when Marceline snapped his fingers at the end, it would seem like the world had gone right back to the way it was. But the second or third time you saw it, you might begin to realize that the world wasn't *exactly* the way it was. As the shy young woman is walking away, she smiles to discover the long-stemmed rose in her hands. The two men debating by the newsstand pause in their arguments, suddenly less sure of their positions. The nanny who was trying so diligently to appease her crying charge is startled to find him giggling. If you went to see Marceline's performance more than once, all of this you might notice in the seconds before the curtain came down.

In the fall of 1929, at the height of his fame in Europe, Marceline was lured to New York by the promise of a six-figure contract for a six-month residency at the Hippodrome. With all the enthusiasm of an artist, he packed his bags for an extended stay in the Land of the Free. But as it so happened, the very moment that he was boarding his steamship in Bremen, the stock market on Wall Street had begun its precipitous plunge.

By the time he disembarked on the West Side piers, his American producers had been ruined, the Hippodrome was closed, and his contract was canceled. A telegram waiting for him at his hotel from his bankers in Paris informed him that he too had lost everything in the crash, leaving not even enough for a safe passage home. And when he knocked on the doors of other producers, he discovered that despite his fame in Europe, virtually no one in America knew who he was.

Now what had been knocked from Marceline's head was his self-esteem. And every time he leaned over to pick it back up, a passing pedestrian would kick it out of reach. Off in pursuit of it he went, from one sorry spot to the next, until at long last he found himself performing pantomimes on street corners and living in the Sunshine Hotel—right down the hall, in room 49.

Naturally enough, Marceline became a drinker. But not in the fashion of Fitzy and my old man. He wouldn't go to some dive where he could relive old glories and air old complaints. In the evenings, he'd buy a bottle of cheap red wine and drink it alone in his room with the door closed, refilling his glass in a smooth, elaborate motion, as if it were part of the act.

But in the mornings, he would leave his door ajar. And when I gave it a tap, he would welcome me with a doff of the hat that he no longer owned. Sometimes, if he had a little money on hand, he would send me out for milk, flour, and eggs and cook us tiny little crepes on the bottom of an electric iron. And as we ate our breakfast sitting on his floor, rather than talk about his past he would ask about my future— about all the places I would go, and all the things I would do. It was a grand old way to start the day.

Then one morning when I went down the hall, his door wasn't ajar. And when I tapped, there wasn't an answer. Placing an ear against the wood, I heard the slightest creaking, like someone turning on the bedsprings. Worried he might be sick, I opened the door a crack.

—Mr. Marceline? I said.

When he didn't reply, I opened the door the rest of the way, only to find that the bed hadn't been slept in, the desk chair was toppled over in the middle of the room, and Marceline was hanging from the ceiling fan.

The creaking, you see, hadn't come from the bedsprings. It had come from the weight of his body turning slowly back and forth.

When I woke my father and brought him to the room, he simply nodded his head as if it were what he had expected all along. Then he sent me down to the front desk to have them call the authorities.

Half an hour later there were three policemen in the room—two patrolmen and a detective taking statements from me and my father and the neighboring tenants who'd come poking their heads through the door.

—Was he robbed? one of the tenants asked.

By way of response, a patrolman gestured to Marceline's desk, where the contents of his pockets had been laid out, including a five-dollar bill and some change.

—Then where's the watch?

—What watch? asked the detective.

Everyone began talking at once—explaining about the solid gold pocket watch that had been so central to the old clown's act that he had never been willing to part with it, not even when he was broke.

After looking at the patrolmen, who shook their heads, the detective looked at my father. Then my father looked at me.

—Now, Duchess, he said, placing an arm over my shoulder, this is very important. I'm going to ask you a question, and I want you to tell me the truth. When you found Marceline, did you see his watch?

Silently, I shook my head.

—Maybe you found it on the floor, he suggested helpfully. And you picked it up, so it wouldn't get broken.

—No, I said with another shake of the head. I never saw his watch.

Patting me on the shoulder almost sympathetically, my father turned to the detective and gave the shrug of one who's tried his best.

—Search them, said the detective.

Imagine my surprise when the patrolman asked me to turn out my pockets and there, among the gum wrappers, was a golden watch on a long, golden chain.

Imagine my surprise, I say, because I was surprised. Stunned. Astounded even. For all of two seconds.

After that, it was plain as day what had happened. My old man had sent me downstairs to the front desk so that he could frisk the body. And when the watch was mentioned by the meddlesome neighbor, my father had draped his arm over my shoulder and given his little speech so that he could slip it into my pocket before he was patted down.

—Oh, Duchess, he said with such disappointment.

Within the hour, I was at the police station. As a minor committing his first offense, I was a good candidate for being released into my father's care. But given the value of the old clown's watch, the crime wasn't petty theft. It was grand larceny. To make matters worse, there had been reports of a few other thefts at the Sunshine Hotel, and Fitzy claimed in a sworn statement that he had seen me coming out of one or two rooms in which I didn't belong. As if that weren't enough, the people from child services discovered—to my father's utter shock—that I hadn't been to school in five years. When I appeared before the juvenile judge, my father was forced to admit that as a hardworking widower he was not in a position to protect me from the malevolent influences of the Bowery. For my own good, all agreed, I should be placed in a juvenile reform program until the age of eighteen.

When the judge delivered his decision, my father asked if he could offer a few words of advice to his wayward son before I was carted away. The judge acquiesced, probably assuming that my father would take me aside and be quick about it. Instead, my old man stuck his thumbs under his suspenders, puffed out his chest, and addressed the judge, the bailiff, the peanut gallery, and the stenographer. Especially the stenographer!

—As we part, my son, he said to one and all, my blessing goes with thee. But in my absence carry with you these few precepts: Be thou familiar, but by no means vulgar. Give every man thy ear, but few thy voice. Take each man's censure, but reserve thy judgment. And this above all: to thine own self be true. For then it must follow, as night follows day, that thou cannot be false to any man. Farewell, my son, he concluded. Farewell.

And as they led me from the room, he actually shed a tear, the old fox.

—How terrible, said Sarah.

And I could see from her face that she meant it. Her expression had suggestions of sympathy, indignation, and protectiveness. You could just tell that whether or not she became happy in her own life, she was bound to be a wonderful mother.

—It's okay, I said, trying to ease her distress. Salina wasn't all that bad. I got three meals a day and a mattress. And if I hadn't gone there, I never would have met your brother.

When I followed Sarah to the sink to clean my empty glass, she thanked me and smiled in her generous way. Then she wished me good night and turned to go.

—Sister Sarah, I said.

When she turned back, she raised her eyebrows in inquiry. Then she watched with that same muted surprise as I reached into the pocket of her robe and removed the little brown bottle.

—Trust me, I said. These won't do you any good.

And when she walked out of the kitchen, I stuck the bottle in the bottom of the spice rack, feeling like I'd done my second good deed of the day.

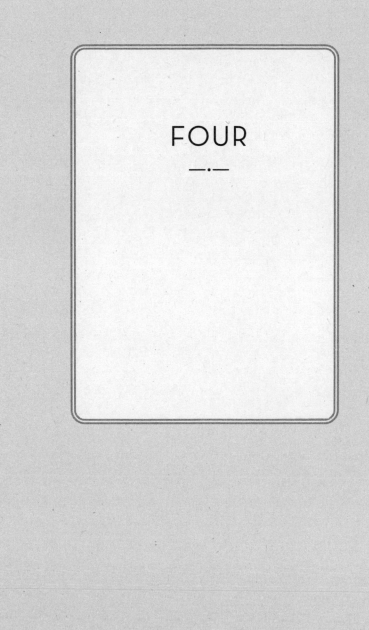

FOUR

Woolly

On Friday at half past one, Woolly was standing in his absolute favorite spot in the store. And that was really saying something! Because at FAO Schwarz, there were so many wonderful spots to stand in. Why, to get to this spot, he had to pass through the collection of giant stuffed animals—including the tiger with the hypnotizing eyes, and the life-size giraffe whose head nearly hit the ceiling. He had to pass through motorsports, where two boys were racing little Ferraris around a figure-eight track. And at the top of the escalator, he had to pass through the magic set area where a magician was making the jack of diamonds disappear. But even with all of that to see, there was nowhere in the store that made Woolly quite as happy as the big glass case with the dollhouse furniture.

Twenty feet long with eight glass shelves, it was even bigger than the trophy case in the gym at St. George's, and it was filled from bottom to top and side to side with perfect little replicas. On the left side of the case was a whole section dedicated to Chippendale furniture—with Chippendale highboys and Chippendale desks and a dining-room set with twelve Chippendale chairs neatly arranged around a Chippendale table. The table was just like the one that his family used to have in the dining room of their brownstone on Eighty-Sixth Street. Naturally, they didn't eat at the Chippendale every day. It was reserved for special occasions like birthdays and holidays, when they would set the table with the best china and light all the candles in the candelabra. At least, that is, until Woolly's father died; and his mother remarried, moved to Palm Beach, and donated the table to the Women's Exchange.

Boy, had his sister Kaitlin gotten mad about that!

How could you, she had said to their mother (or sort of shouted) when the moving men appeared to pick up the set. *That was Great-grandma's!*

Oh, Kaitlin, replied his mother. *What could you possibly want with a table like that? Some fusty old thing that seats a dozen people. No one even gives dinner parties anymore. Isn't that right, Woolly.*

At the time, Woolly hadn't known whether people gave dinner parties or not. He still didn't know. So he hadn't said anything. But his sister had said something. She had said it to him as the moving men carried the Chippendale out the door.

Take a good hard look, Woolly, she said. *Because you'll never see a table like that again.*

So he had taken a good hard look.

But as it turned out, Kaitlin had been wrong. For Woolly had seen a table like that again. He had seen it right here in the display case at FAO Schwarz.

The furniture in the display case was arranged chronologically. So as you moved from left to right you could travel all the way from the Court of Versailles to a living room in a modern-day apartment, with a phonograph, and a cocktail table, and a pair of Mies van der Rohe chairs.

Woolly understood that Mr. Chippendale and Mr. van der Rohe were held in the highest esteem for the designs of their chairs. But it seemed to him that the men who made these perfect little replicas deserved at least as much esteem, if not more. For to make a Chippendale or van der Rohe chair in such tiny dimensions surely had to be harder than to make one you could sit on.

But Woolly's favorite part of the case was all the way over to the right, where there was a series of kitchens. At the top there was what was called the Prairie Kitchen, with a simple wooden table and a butter churn and a cast-iron frying pan on a cast-iron stove. Next came the Victorian Kitchen. You could tell this was the sort of kitchen in which a cook did the cooking because there was no table or chairs at which to sit and eat your supper. Instead, there was a long, wooden island over which hung six copper pots in descending order of size. And finally, there was the Kitchen of Today, with all the wonders of the modern era. In addition to a bright white stove and a bright white refrigerator, there was a table for four with a red Formica top and four chrome chairs with red vinyl seats. There was a KitchenAid mixer, and a toaster with a little black lever and two little pieces of toast. And in the cabinet over the counter, you could see all the little boxes of cereal and the tiny cans of soup.

—I knew I'd find you here.

Woolly turned to discover his sister standing at his side.

—How did you know? he asked in surprise.

—How did I know! repeated Sarah with a laugh.

And Woolly laughed too. Because, of course, of course, he knew exactly how she knew.

When they were younger, every December Grandma Wolcott would take them to FAO Schwarz so that they could each pick out their own Christmas present. One year, as the family was getting ready to leave with all of their coats buttoned and all of the big red bags filled to the limit, they realized that in the midst of the holiday bustle, young Woolly had somehow gone missing. Members of the family were dispatched to every floor, calling out his name, until Sarah finally found him here.

—How old were we then?

She shook her head.

—I don't know. It was a few years before Grandma died, so I suppose I was fourteen and you were seven.

Woolly shook his head.

—That was so hard. Wasn't it?

—What was so hard?

—Choosing a Christmas present—from here of all places!

Woolly waved his arms about in order to encompass all of the giraffes, Ferraris, and magic sets in the building.

—Yes, she said. It was very hard to choose. But especially for you.

Woolly nodded.

—And then after, he said, after we had picked out our presents and Grandma had sent the bags home with the driver, she would take us to the Plaza for tea. Do you remember?

—I remember.

—We would sit in that big room with the palm trees. And they would bring those towers with the little watercress and cucumber and salmon sandwiches on the lower levels, and the little lemon tarts and chocolate eclairs on top. And Grandma would make us eat our sandwiches before we ate the cakes.

—*You have to climb your way to heaven.*

Woolly laughed.

—Yes, that was it. That's what Grandma used to say.

As Woolly and Sarah came off the escalator onto the ground floor, Woolly was explaining his brand-new notion that the dollhouse-chair makers deserved just as much regard, if not more, than Mr. Chippendale and Mr. van der Rohe. But as they were approaching the front door, someone was shouting urgently behind them.

—Excuse me! Excuse me, sir!

When Woolly and his sister looked back to see the source of the commotion, they discovered that a man with a very managerial appearance was chasing after them with a hand in the air.

—Just a moment, sir, the man called as he worked his way definitively in Woolly's direction.

Intending to wear an expression of comic surprise, Woolly turned to his sister. But she was still watching the man approach with a slight hint of dread. A slight but heartbreaking hint.

Reaching them, the man paused to catch his breath, then addressed Woolly.

—I apologize most sincerely for the shouting. But you've forgotten your bear.

Woolly's eyes opened wide.

—The bear!

He turned to his sister, who looked at once mystified and relieved.

—I'd forgotten the bear, he said with a smile.

A young woman who had been trailing after the manager now appeared, holding a panda that was almost as big as she was.

—Thank you both, said Woolly, taking the bear in his arms. Thank you ten times over.

As the two employees returned to their stations, Sarah turned to Woolly.

—You bought a giant panda?

—It's for the baby!

—Woolly, she said with a smile and a shake of the head.

—I considered the grizzly and polar bears, Woolly explained, but they both seemed a little too fierce.

By way of illustration, Woolly would have liked to raise his claws and bare his teeth, but his arms were too full of the panda.

His arms were so full of the panda that he couldn't get through the revolving door. So the man in the bright red uniform, who always stands guard at the entrance of FAO Schwarz, leapt into action.

—Allow me, he said gallantly.

Then he opened the unrevolving door to let the brother, sister, and bear onto Fifth Avenue, which they promptly crossed.

It was a beautiful day, with the sun shining down on all the horse carriages and hot-dog carts lined along the edge of Central Park.

—Come sit with me a moment, said Sarah, in a manner that suggested a serious conversation was coming.

A little reluctantly, Woolly followed his sister to a bench and sat down, placing the panda between them. But Sarah lifted the panda and put it to her side so that there was nothing between them.

—Woolly, she said, there's something I want to ask you.

As she looked at him, Woolly could see in her face an expression of concern, but also an expression of uncertainty, as if suddenly she wasn't sure that she wanted to ask him whatever it was that she had wanted to ask, after all.

Reaching out, Woolly laid his hand on her forearm.

—You don't have to ask me something, Sarah. You don't have to ask me anything.

Looking at her, Woolly could see the feeling of concern continuing to struggle with the feeling of uncertainty. So he did his best to reassure.

—Questions can be so tricky, he said, like forks in the road. You can be having such a nice conversation and someone will raise a question, and the next thing you know you're headed off in a whole new direction. In all probability, this new road will lead you to places that are perfectly agreeable, but sometimes you just want to go in the direction you were already headed.

They were both silent for a second. Then Woolly squeezed his sister's arm from the excitement of an additional thought.

—Have you ever noticed, he said, have you ever noticed how so many questions begin with the letter *W*?

He counted them off on his fingers.

—Who. What. Why. When. Where. Which.

He could see his sister's concern and uncertainty lifting for a moment as she smiled at this fascinating little fact.

—Isn't that interesting? he continued. I mean, how do you think that happened? All those centuries ago when words were first being coined, what was it about the sound of the *W* that made the word coiners use it for all of the questions? As opposed to, say, the *T* or the *P*? It makes you feel sort of sorry for *W*, doesn't it? I mean, it's a pretty big burden to carry. Especially since half the time when someone asks you a question with a *W*, they aren't really asking you a question. They're making a statement in disguise. Like, like . . .

Woolly adopted the posture and tone of their mother.

—*When are you going to grow up!* And *Why would you do such a thing!* And *What in God's name were you thinking!*

Sarah laughed, and it was good to see her do so. Because she was a great laugher. She was the absotively best laugher Woolly had ever known.

—All right, Woolly. I'm not going to ask you a question.

Now she was the one who reached out a hand to take a forearm.

—Instead, I want you to make me a promise. I want you to promise me that after your visit, you'll go back.

Woolly wanted to look down at his feet, but he could feel her fingers on his forearm. And he could see in her face that though her concern remained, the expression of uncertainty was gone.

—I promise, he said. I promise . . . that I'll go back.

Then she squeezed his forearm just as he had squeezed hers, and looking like a great weight had been lifted from her shoulders, she leaned back on the bench, so he did the same. And as they sat there beside the panda, they found themselves looking over Pulitzer Fountain— right at the Plaza Hotel.

With a big smile, Woolly stood and turned to his sister.

—We should go have tea, he said. For old times' sake.

—Woolly, Sarah said with a slump of the shoulders. It's after two o'clock. I still need to pick up my dress at Bergdorf's, have my hair done, and get back to the apartment so I can change in time to meet Dennis at Le Pavillon.

—Oh, blah, blah, blah, said Woolly.

Sarah opened her mouth to make another point, but Woolly picked up the panda and waggled it back and forth in front of his sister.

—Oh blah, blah, blah, he said in a panda's voice.

—All right, said Sarah with a laugh. For old times' sake, let's have tea at the Plaza.

Duchess

ON FRIDAY AT HALF PAST ONE, I was standing in front of the hutch in Woolly's sister's dining room admiring the orderly arrangement of her china. Like the Watsons, she had place settings that were worthy of being handed down, and perhaps already had been. But here were no teetering towers of coffee cups, no thin layer of dust. Sister Sarah's china was arranged in perfectly aligned vertical stacks, and each plate had a little circle of felt to protect its surface from the plate above it. On a shelf under the china was a long black case that contained an equally orderly arrangement of the family silver.

Locking the hutch's lower cabinet, I put the key back where I'd found it: in the tureen that was on display in the middle of the middle shelf. The lady of the house clearly had a nice sense of symmetry, which was no less laudable for being easy to decipher.

Wandering down the hall from the dining room, I satisfied myself that I had visited every room on the ground floor, then headed up the back stairs.

—·—

Over breakfast, Sarah had explained that she and Dennis would be spending the weekend at their apartment in the city because they had dinner engagements on both nights. When she added that she needed to head in before noon in order to run a few errands, and Woolly suggested that he come along to keep her company, Sarah looked at me.

—Would that be all right? she asked. If Woolly joined me in the city for a few hours?

—I don't see why not.

So it was settled. Woolly would drive in with Sarah, and I would come later in the Caddy to pick him up on our way to the Circus. When I asked Woolly where we should meet, naturally he suggested the statue of Abraham Lincoln in Union Square. Shortly after eleven, they pulled out of the driveway and headed for the city, leaving me with the run of the house.

For starters, I went into the living room. Pouring myself a finger of scotch, I put Sinatra on the hi-fi and kicked up my feet. The record was one I'd never heard before, but Ol' Blue Eyes was in fine form, singing an assortment of lightly swinging love songs with full orchestration including "I Get a Kick Out of You" and "They Can't Take That Away from Me."

On the cover of the album, two pairs of sweethearts were out for a stroll, while Sinatra leaned against a lamppost by himself. Dressed in a dark gray suit with a tilted fedora on his head, Sinatra was holding a cigarette so loosely between two fingers it looked like he might drop it. Just seeing the picture made you want to smoke, and wear a hat, and lean on lampposts all by your lonesome.

For a moment, I wondered whether Woolly's brother-in-law had bought the record. But only for a moment. Because, of course, it must have been Sarah.

Cuing up the record for a second time, I poured myself a second whiskey and meandered down the hall. According to Woolly, his brother-in-law was something of a Wall Street wunderkind, though you wouldn't have known it from his office. There was no ticker tape, or whatever they used nowadays to tell them what to buy and sell. There were no ledgers or adding machines or slide rules. In their place was ample evidence of the sporting life.

On a shelf right across from the desk—where Dennis could easily see it—was a stuffed fish mounted on a post, forever turning its mouth toward the hook. On the shelf above the fish was a recent photo of four men having just finished a round of golf. Luckily it was in color, so you could take note of all the clothes you would never want to wear. Scanning the faces of the golfers, I picked out the one who seemed particularly smug and figured that was Dennis. To the left of the shelves was another photograph hanging above two empty J hooks that jutted from the wall. This photo was of a college baseball team with a two-foot trophy on the grass.

What there wasn't was a picture of Woolly's sister. Not on the wall, not on a shelf, not on the wunderkind's desk.

After rinsing out my whiskey glass in the kitchen, I found what I guess you'd call a pantry. But it wasn't like the one at St. Nick's, stacked from floor to ceiling with bags of flour and cans of tomatoes. This one had a little copper sink with a copper counter, and vases in every imaginable color and size, so that Sarah could perfectly display every bouquet of flowers that Dennis would never bring her. On the brighter side, Dennis had made sure that the pantry had a specially designed cabinet in which to store a few hundred bottles of wine.

From the kitchen I proceeded to the dining room, where I surveyed the china and silver, as previously reported; I stopped in the living room to recork the whiskey and switch off the phonograph, then headed upstairs.

Skipping over the room where Woolly and I had spent the night, I poked my head into another guest room, then what looked like a sewing room, before coming upon a bedroom that was being painted.

In the middle of the room, someone had pulled the protective tarp off the boxes that were stacked on the bed, exposing them to the hazards of the light blue paint. This didn't seem the sort of thing that Woolly's sister would do, so I took the initiative of putting the tarp back in place. And what did I discover leaning against the bedframe but a Louisville Slugger.

That must have been what was resting on those J hooks in Dennis's office, I thought to myself. He had probably hit a home run fifteen years ago, and he had hung the bat on the wall so he could be reminded of the fact whenever he wasn't looking at his fish. But for some strange reason, someone had brought it here.

Picking it up and weighing it in my hands, I shook my head in disbelief. Why hadn't I thought of it before?

In shape and principle, a Louisville Slugger couldn't be that different from the clubs our ancestors used to subdue wildcats and wolves. And yet, somehow it seems as sleek and modern as a Maserati. The gentle tapering of the shaft that ensures a perfect distribution of weight. . . . The lip at the base that catches the heel of the hand to maximize the strength of the swing without allowing the bat to slip from your grasp. . . . Carved, sanded, and polished with the same devotion that's brought to the crafting of violins and ships, a Louisville Slugger is simultaneously a thing of beauty and a thing of purpose.

In fact, I challenge you to name a more perfect example of form following function than when Joltin' Joe, having rested the barrel of a bat on his shoulder, suddenly sets his body in motion in order to greet the projectile that's headed toward him at ninety miles an hour and send it hurtling back in the opposite direction with a satisfying crack.

Yep, I thought to myself. You can forget your two-by-fours, your frying pans, and your whiskey bottles. When it comes to dispensing justice, all you need is a good old American baseball bat.

Walking down the hall with a whistle on my lips, I used the tip of the bat to push open the door of the master suite.

It was a lovely, light-filled room in which there was not only a bed, but a chaise longue, a high-back chair with a footstool, and a matching pair of his and her bureaus. There was also a matching pair of his and her closets. In the one on the left was a long line of dresses. Most of them were as bright and elegant as their owner, although tucked in the corner were a few skimpy numbers that I was almost too shy to look at, and she was certainly too shy to wear.

In the second closet were shelves with neatly folded oxford shirts and a hanging pole with a collection of three-piece suits progressing from tan to gray to blue to black. On a shelf above the suits was a row of fedoras arranged in a similar progression.

The clothes make the man, or so the saying goes. But all you have to do is look at a row of fedoras to know what a bunch of baloney that is. Gather together a group of men of every gradation—from the powerhouse to the putz—have them toss their fedoras in a pile, and you'll spend a lifetime trying to figure out whose was whose. Because it's the man who makes the fedora, not versa vice. I mean, wouldn't you rather wear the hat worn by Frank Sinatra than the one worn by Sergeant Joe Friday? I should hope so.

In all, I figured that Dennis had about ten fedoras, twenty-five suits, and forty shirts, for mixing and matching. I didn't bother calculating all the potential combinations of outfits. It was plain enough to the naked eye that were one to go missing, no one would even notice.

Emmett

On Friday at half past one, Emmett was approaching a brownstone on 126th Street.

—Here we go again, said the fair-skinned black youth who was leaning on the railing at the top of the stoop.

When the fair-skinned one spoke, the big one who was sitting on the bottom step looked up at Emmett with an expression of welcome surprise.

—You here for a beating too? he asked.

As he began to shake with a noiseless laughter, the door to the building opened and out came Townhouse.

—Well, well, he said with a smile. If it isn't Mr. Emmett Watson.

—Hey, Townhouse.

Townhouse paused for a moment to stare at the fair-skinned one, who was partially blocking his way. When he begrudgingly stepped aside, Townhouse came down the stoop and took Emmett's hand.

—It's good to see you.

—It's good to see you too.

—I gather they let you out a few months early.

—Because of my father.

Townhouse nodded in an expression of sympathy.

The fair-skinned one was watching the interaction with a sour expression.

—Who's this then? he asked.

—A friend, Townhouse replied without looking back.

—That Salina must have been one friendly place.

This time Townhouse did look back.

—Shut up, Maurice.

For a moment, Maurice returned Townhouse's stare, then he looked up the street in his sour way while the jovial one shook his head.

—Come on, Townhouse said to Emmett. Let's take a walk.

As the two went down the street together, Townhouse didn't say anything. Emmett could tell that he was waiting to gain some distance from the others. So Emmett didn't say anything either until they had turned the corner.

—You don't seem that surprised to see me.

—I'm not. Duchess was here yesterday.

Emmett nodded.

—When I heard he'd gone to Harlem, I figured he was coming to see you. What did he want?

—He wanted me to hit him.

Emmett stopped and turned to Townhouse, so Townhouse stopped and turned too. For a moment, they stood eye to eye without speaking— two young men of different race and upbringing, but of similar casts of mind.

—He wanted you to hit him?

Townhouse responded in a lowered voice, as if he were speaking in confidence, though no one was within earshot.

—That's what he wanted, Emmett. He'd gotten some idea in his head that he owed me something—because of the switching I took from Ackerly—and if I gave him a few pops we'd be even.

—What'd you do?

—I hit him.

Emmett looked at his friend with a touch of surprise.

—He didn't give me much of a choice. He said he'd come all the way uptown to settle the score, and he made it clear he wasn't leaving until it was settled. Then when I hit him, he insisted I hit him again. Twice. He took all three in the face without even raising his fists, at the foot of the stoop where we were standing a minute ago, right in front of the boys.

Emmett looked away from Townhouse, considering. It wasn't lost on him that five days before he had taken a similar beating to settle a score of his own. Emmett wasn't prone to superstitions. He didn't favor four-leaf clovers or fear black cats. But the notion of Duchess taking three punches in front of a gathering of witnesses gave him a strange sense of foreboding. But that didn't alter what needed to be done.

Emmett looked back at Townhouse.

—Did he say where he was staying?

—No.

—Did he say where he was going?

Townhouse paused for a moment, then shook his head.

—He didn't. But listen, Emmett, if you're set on finding Duchess, you should know that you're not the only one looking for him.

—What do you mean?

—Two cops were here last night.

—Because he and Woolly skipped?

—Maybe. They didn't say. But they were definitely more interested in Duchess than Woolly. And I got the sense there might be more to it than hunting down a couple of kids who've gone over the fence.

—Thanks for letting me know.

—Sure. But before you go, I've got something you're going to want to see.

Townhouse led Emmett eight blocks away to a street that seemed more Hispanic than black—with a bodega and three men playing dominoes out on the sidewalk as a Latin dance number played on a radio. At the end of the block, Townhouse came to a stop across the street from a body shop.

Emmett turned to him.

—Is that *the* body shop?

—That's it.

The shop in question was owned by a man named Gonzalez, who had moved to New York from southern California after the war, with his wife and two sons—twins who were known in the neighborhood as Paco and Pico. From the time the boys were fourteen, Gonzalez had them working in the shop after school—cleaning tools, sweeping floors, and taking out the trash—so they would gain some understanding of what it took to earn an honest dollar. Paco and Pico got the understanding all right. And when at the age of seventeen they were given the responsibility of closing up on weekends, they got into a little business of their own.

Most of the cars in the shop were there because of a loose fender or a dent in a door, but otherwise in good working order. So on Saturday nights, the brothers began renting out the cars in the shop to the boys in the neighborhood for a few bucks an hour. When Townhouse was sixteen, he asked out a girl by the name of Clarise, who happened to be the best-looking girl in the eleventh grade. When she said yes, Townhouse borrowed five bucks from his brother and rented a car from the twins.

His plan was to pack a little picnic and drive Clarise over to Grant's Tomb, where they could park under the elm trees and gaze out on the Hudson. But as luck would have it, the only car the twins had available that night was a Buick Skylark convertible with chrome finishes. The car looked so good, it would have been a crime to get a girl like Clarise in the front seat and spend the evening watching barges being pushed up the river. Instead, Townhouse lowered the top, turned up the radio, and drove his date up and down 125th Street.

—You should have seen us, Townhouse had said one night at Salina as they lay on their bunks in the dark. I was wearing my Easter Sunday suit, which was almost as blue as the car, and she was in a bright yellow dress that was cut so low in the back you could see half her spine. That Skylark could have gone from zero to sixty in four seconds, but I was driving at twenty miles an hour so we could wave at everyone we recognized, and half the people we didn't. Down 125th we'd go, cruising past all the finely dressed folk out in front of the Hotel Theresa and the Apollo and Showman's Jazz Club; and when we got to Broadway, I'd turn her around and drive all the way back. Every time we made the circuit, Clarise would slide a little closer, until there was no more closer to slide.

In the end it was Clarise who suggested they go to Grant's Tomb to park under the elms, and that's where they were, making the most of the shadows, when the flashlights of two patrolmen shone into the car.

It turned out that the owner of the Skylark was one of those finely dressed folk in front of the Apollo Theater. Given all the waving that Townhouse and Clarise had been doing, it didn't take long for the cops to find them in the park. After untangling the young couple, one of the cops drove Clarise home in the Skylark while the other drove Townhouse to the station in the back of the black-and-white.

As a minor who had never been in trouble, Townhouse might have gotten off with a stern talking-to had he given up the twins. But Townhouse was no squealer. When the officers asked him how he happened to be behind the wheel of a car he didn't own, Townhouse said that he'd snuck into Mr. Gonzalez's office, slipped the key off the hook, and driven the car off the lot when no one was looking. So instead of the stern talking-to, Townhouse got twelve months in Salina.

—Come on, he said.

Crossing the street, the two passed the office where Mr. Gonzalez was talking on the phone and entered the repair area. In the first bay was a Chevy with its rear caved in, while in the second was a Road-master with a buckled hood, as if the two cars had been on opposite ends of the same collision. Somewhere out of sight, a radio was playing a dance number that to Emmett's ear could have been the same one he'd heard when they had passed the domino players, though he knew it probably wasn't.

—Paco! Pico! Townhouse called above the music.

The brothers emerged from behind the Chevy, dressed in dirty jumpsuits, cleaning their hands on rags.

If Paco and Pico were twins, you wouldn't have guessed so from a glance—the former being tall, thin, and shaggy, the latter stocky and close-cropped. It was only when they broke out into big white-toothed smiles that you could see the family resemblance.

—This is the friend I was telling you about, said Townhouse.

Turning to Emmett, the brothers offered him the same toothy grin. Then Paco gestured with his head toward the far end of the garage.

—It's over here.

Emmett and Townhouse followed the brothers past the Roadmaster to the last bay, where a car was under a tarp. Together, the brothers pulled back the cover to reveal a powder-blue Studebaker.

—That's my car, said Emmett in surprise.

—No kidding, said Townhouse.

—How'd it end up here?

—Duchess left it.

—Is it running all right?

—More or less, said Paco.

Emmett shook his head. There was just no making sense of what, when, or where Duchess chose to do what he did. But as long as the car was back in Emmett's possession and in good working order, he didn't need to make sense of Duchess's choices.

Doing a quick circuit, Emmett was pleased to find that there were no more dents in the car than when he had bought it. But when he opened the trunk, the kit bag wasn't there. More importantly, when he pulled back the piece of felt that covered the spare, he discovered that the envelope wasn't there either.

—Everything all right? asked Townhouse.

—Yeah, said Emmett, closing the trunk with a quiet click.

Walking toward the front of the car, Emmett glanced through the driver's window, then turned to Paco.

—Have you got the keys?

But Paco turned to Townhouse.

—We've got them, said Townhouse. But there's something else you need to know.

Before Townhouse could explain, an angry shout came from the other side of the garage.

—What the fuck is this!

Emmett assumed it must be Mr. Gonzalez, annoyed that his sons weren't at work, but when he turned he saw the one called Maurice marching toward them.

—What the fuck is this, Maurice repeated, though more slowly, punching every other word.

After muttering to Emmett that this was his cousin, Townhouse waited for Maurice to reach them before he deigned to reply.

—What the fuck is what, Maurice?

—Otis said you were going to hand over the keys, and I couldn't believe it.

—Well, now you can.

—But it's *my* car.

—There's nothing yours about it.

Maurice looked at Townhouse with an expression of amazement.

—You were right there when that nutjob gave me the keys.

—Maurice, said Townhouse, you've been climbing my tree all week and I've had just about enough of it. So, why don't you mind your own business before I mind it for you.

Clamping his teeth shut, Maurice stared at Townhouse for a moment, then he turned and marched away.

Townhouse shook his head. As a final slight to his cousin, he adopted the expression of one who was trying to remember the important shit he'd been saying before he was so needlessly interrupted.

—You were gonna tell him about the car, Paco prompted.

With a nod of remembrance, Townhouse turned back to Emmett.

—When I told the cops last night that I hadn't seen Duchess, they must not have believed me. Because this morning they were back, asking questions up and down the block. Like whether anyone had seen a couple of white boys hanging out on my stoop, or driving around the neighborhood—in a light-blue Studebaker . . .

Emmett closed his eyes.

—That's right, said Townhouse. Whatever trouble Duchess has gotten himself into, it looks like he was in your car when he got into it. And if your car was involved, the cops will eventually get around to thinking that you're involved too. That's one of the reasons I stashed it here instead of leaving it on the street. But the other reason is that when it comes to paint jobs, the Gonzalez brothers are artistes. Ain't that right, boys?

—*Los Picassos*, replied Pico, speaking for the first time.

—After *we're* through with her, said Paco, even her own mother wouldn't recognize her.

The two brothers began laughing, but stopped when they saw that neither Emmett nor Townhouse had joined in.

—How long would it take? asked Emmett.

The brothers looked at each other, then Paco shrugged.

—If we get started tomorrow and make good headway, we could have her ready by . . . Monday morning?

—*Sí*, said Pico nodding in agreement. *El lunes.*

Another delay, thought Emmett. But since the envelope was missing, he couldn't leave New York until he found Duchess anyway. And

Townhouse was right about the car. If the police were actively looking for a light-blue Studebaker, there was no point in driving one.

—Monday morning it is, said Emmett. And thanks to you both.

Outside the garage, Townhouse offered to walk Emmett back to the subway, but Emmett wanted to know something first.

—When we were at your stoop and I asked where Duchess was going, you hesitated—like someone who knows something that he doesn't want to admit to knowing. If Duchess told you where he was headed, I need you to tell me.

Townhouse blew some air.

—Look, he said, I know you like Duchess, Emmett. So do I. He's a loyal friend in his own crazy way, and he's one of the most entertaining shit slingers whom I've ever had the pleasure to meet. But he is also like one of those guys who are born with no peripheral vision. He can see everything that's right in front of him, see it more clearly than most, but the second that something is pushed an inch to the left or right, he doesn't even know it's there. And that can lead to all kinds of trouble. For him, and for anyone within spitting distance. All I'm saying, Emmett, is now that you've got your car, maybe you should let Duchess be.

—Nothing would make me happier than to let Duchess be, said Emmett, but it's not so simple. Four days ago, just as Billy and I were about to head to California, he took off with Woolly in the Studebaker, which was problem enough. But before my father died, he put an envelope with three thousand dollars in the trunk of the car. It was there when Duchess drove off, and now it's gone.

—Shit, said Townhouse.

Emmett nodded.

—Don't get me wrong: I am glad to have the car back. But I *need* that money.

—All right, Townhouse said, nodding his head in concession. I don't know where Duchess is staying. But before he left yesterday, he was trying to convince me to join him and Woolly at the Circus.

—The circus?

—That's right. In Red Hook. On Conover Street right near the river. Duchess said he was going to be there tonight for the six o'clock show.

As the two walked from the body shop to the subway station, Townhouse went the long way around in order to point out landmarks. Not the landmarks of Harlem, but the landmarks of their conversations. Places that had come up in the course of their time together, mentioned as they worked side by side in the fields or lay on their bunks at night. Like the apartment building on Lenox Avenue where his grandfather had kept pigeons on the roof, the same roof where he and his brother had been allowed to sleep on hot summer nights. And the high school where Townhouse had been a star shortstop. And on 125th Street, Emmett got a glimpse of that lively stretch of road on which Townhouse and Clarise had driven back and forth on their ill-fated Saturday night.

In leaving Nebraska, Emmett had little to regret. He didn't regret leaving behind their home or their possessions. He didn't regret leaving behind his father's dreams or his father's grave. And when he had driven those first few miles of the Lincoln Highway, he had savored the sensation of putting distance between himself and his hometown, even if he was headed in the wrong direction.

But as they walked through Harlem and Townhouse pointed out the landmarks of his youth, Emmett wished that he could return to Morgen, if only for a day, in the company of his friend, so that he could point out the landmarks of his life, the landmarks of the stories that he had told to pass the time. Like the airplanes that he had so painstakingly assembled and that still hung over Billy's bed; and the two-story house on Madison, the first that he'd helped build in Mr. Schulte's employ; and the wide, unforgiving land that may have bested his father, but which never lost its beauty in his eyes. And yes, he would show Townhouse the fairgrounds too, just as Townhouse without shame or hesitation had shown him the lively stretch of road that had led to his undoing.

When they reached the subway station, Townhouse followed Emmett inside and stayed with him right up until the turnstiles. Before they parted, almost as an afterthought, he asked if Emmett wanted him to come along that night—when he went looking for Duchess.

—That's all right, replied Emmett. I don't imagine he'll give me any trouble.

—No, he won't, agreed Townhouse. At least, not as intended.

After a moment, Townhouse shook his head and smiled.

—Duchess gets some crazy ideas into his head, but he was right about one thing.

—What's that? asked Emmett.

—I did feel much better after hitting him.

Sally

ALF THE TIME WHEN you could use the help of a man, he's nowhere to be found. He's off seeing to one thing or another that could just as easily be seen to tomorrow as seen to today and that just happens to be five steps out of earshot. But as soon as you need him to be somewhere else, you can't push him out the door.

Like my father at this very minute.

Here it is Friday at half past twelve, and he's cutting his chicken fried steak like he was some kind of surgeon and the life of his patient depended upon every placement of the knife. And when he has finally cleaned his plate and had two cups of coffee, for once in a blue moon he asks for a third.

—I'll have to brew another pot, I warn.

—I've got time, he says.

So I dump the spent grinds in the trash, rinse out the percolator, fill it back up, set it on the stove, and wait for it to simmer, thinking how nice it must be in this relentless world to have so much time at your bidding.

—·—

For as long as I can remember, my father has gone into town on Friday afternoon to run his errands. As soon as he's through with lunch, he'll climb in his truck with a purposeful look and head off to the hardware

store, the feedstore, and the pharmacy. Then around seven o'clock—
just in time for supper—he'll pull into the driveway with a tube of
toothpaste, ten bushels of oats, and a brand-new pair of pliers.

How on God's green earth, you may rightly wonder, does a man
turn twenty minutes of errands into a five-hour excursion? Well, that's
an easy one: by yakking. Certainly, he's yakking with Mr. Wurtele at
the hardware store, Mr. Horchow at the feedstore, and Mr. Danziger
at the pharmacy. But the yakking isn't limited to the proprietors. For
on Friday afternoons, in each of these establishments an assembly of
seasoned errand runners convenes to forecast the weather, the harvest,
and the national elections.

By my estimation, a solid hour is spent prognosticating at each one
of the stores, but apparently three hours isn't enough. Because after
predicting the outcomes of all the day's unknowables, the assembly of
elders will retire to McCafferty's Tavern, where they can opine for two
hours more in the company of bottles of beer.

My father is nothing if not a creature of habit so, as I say, this has
been going on for as long as I remember. Then suddenly about six
months ago, when my father finished his lunch and pushed back his
chair, rather than heading straight out the door to his truck, he went
upstairs to change into a clean white shirt.

It didn't take long for me to figure that a woman had somehow
worked her way into my father's routine. Especially since she was partial to perfume, and I'm the one who has to wash his clothes. But the
questions remained: Who was this woman? And where on earth did
he meet her?

She wasn't someone in the congregation, I was pretty sure of that.
Because on Sunday mornings when we filed out of the service onto
the little patch of grass in front of the chapel, there wasn't a woman—
married or unmarried—who gave him a measured greeting or an awkward glance. And it wasn't Esther who keeps the books at the feedstore,

because she wouldn't've recognized a bottle of perfume if it fell from the heavens and hit her on the head. I might have thought it was one of the women who are known, upon occasion, to stop in at McCafferty's, but once my father started changing his shirt, he stopped coming home with the smell of beer on his breath.

Well, if he didn't meet her at church, the stores, or the bar, I just couldn't figure it. So I had no choice but to follow him.

On the first Friday in March, I made a pot of chili so I wouldn't have to worry about cooking dinner. After serving my father lunch, I watched out of the corner of my eye as he went out the door in his clean white shirt, climbed in his truck, and pulled out of the drive. Once he was half a mile down the road, I grabbed a wide-brimmed hat from the closet, hopped into Betty, and set off on my own.

Just like always, he made his first stop at the hardware store, where he did a bit of business and whiled away an hour in the company of like-minded men. Next it was off to the feedstore and then the pharmacy, where there was a little more business and a lot more whiling. At each of these stops a few women made an appearance in order to do a little business of their own, but if he exchanged more than a word with them, it wasn't so's you'd notice.

But then at five o'clock, when he came out of the pharmacy and climbed in his truck, he didn't head down Jefferson on his way to McCafferty's. Instead, after passing the library, he took a right on Cypress, a left on Adams, and pulled over across from the little white house with blue shutters. After sitting for a minute, he got out of his truck, crossed the street, and rapped on the screen door.

He didn't have to wait more than a minute for his rap to be answered. And standing there in the doorframe was Alice Thompson.

By my reckoning, Alice couldn't have been more than twenty-eight years old. She was three grades ahead of my sister in school and a Methodist, so I didn't have cause to know her very well. But I knew what everyone else knew: that she had graduated from Kansas State and then married a fellow from Topeka who got himself killed in Korea. A widow without children, Alice had returned to Morgen in the fall of '53 and taken a job as a teller at the Savings and Loan.

That's where it must have happened. While going to the bank was not a part of my father's Friday routine, he did stop in every other Thursday in order to pick up the payroll for the boys. One week he must have ended up at her window and been taken by her mournful look. The following week I could just imagine him carefully picking his place in line so that he'd end up at her window instead of Ed Fowler's, and then doing his damnedest to make a little conversation while she was trying to count the cash.

As I was sitting in Betty staring at the house, maybe you'd imagine that I was unsettled, or angry, or indignant that my father should be casting off memories of my mother in order to romance a woman who was half his age. Well, imagine all you like. It won't cost you nothing, and it'll cost me less. But later that night, after I'd served the chili, cleaned the kitchen, and switched off the lights, I knelt at the side of my bed, clasped my hands together, and prayed. *Dear Lord*, I said, *please give my father the wisdom to be gracious, the heart to be generous, and the courage to ask for this woman's hand in holy matrimony—so that someone else can do his cooking and cleaning for a change.*

Every night for the next four weeks, I made a similar prayer.

But then on the first Friday in April, my father didn't come home at seven in time for supper. He didn't come home while I was cleaning up the kitchen or climbing into bed. It was nearly midnight when I heard him pull into the drive. Parting the curtains, I saw his truck parked at a forty-five-degree angle with the headlights still on as he weaved his way to the door. I heard him walk past the supper I'd left out for him and stumble up the stairs.

They say the Lord answers all prayers, it's just that sometimes he

answers no. And I guess he answered no to mine. Because the following morning, when I took his shirt from the hamper, what it smelled
of was whiskey instead of perfume.

—·—

Finally, at quarter till two my father found the bottom of his coffee
cup and pushed back his chair.

—Well, I guess I'd best get going, he said, and I didn't argue.

Once he'd climbed in his truck and pulled out of the drive, I looked
at the clock and saw that I had just over forty-five minutes to spare.
So I did the dishes, straightened up the kitchen, and set the table. By
then it was two twenty. Taking off my apron, I mopped my brow and
sat on the bottom step of the stairs, where there was always a nice
little breeze in the afternoon, and from where I'd have no trouble
hearing the phone when it rang in my father's office.

And that's where I sat for the next half an hour.

Standing up, I straightened out my skirt and returned to the kitchen.
With my hands on my hips, I looked it over. It was neat as a pin: the
chairs tucked in; the counter wiped; the dishes neatly stacked in their
cabinets. So I set about making a chicken pot pie. When that was done,
I cleaned the kitchen again. Then, even though it wasn't Saturday, I
took the vacuum from the closet and vacuumed the rugs in the living
room and den. I was about to carry the vacuum upstairs to see to the
bedrooms when it occurred to me that with all the racket a vacuum
makes, I might not be able to hear the phone from upstairs. So I put
the vacuum back in the closet.

For a moment I stood there just staring at it, all curled up on the
closet floor, wondering to myself which of the two of us was designed
to serve the other. Then slamming the door shut, I went in my father's
office, sat in his chair, took out his phone book, and looked up the
number for Father Colmore.

Emmett

WHEN THEY EMERGED FROM the station at Carroll Street, Emmett knew he had made a mistake in bringing his brother.

His instincts had told him that he shouldn't do it. Townhouse hadn't been able to remember the exact address of the circus, so it was probably going to take some legwork to find it. Once Emmett was inside, he was going to have to find Duchess in the crowd. And once he found Duchess, there was the possibility, however remote, that Duchess wouldn't hand over the envelope without raising some sort of nonsense. All in all, it would have been smarter to leave Billy in the care of Ulysses, where he'd be safe. But how do you tell an eight-year-old boy who has wanted to go to the circus all his life that you intend to go to one without him? So at five o'clock, they descended the steel staircase from the tracks and headed for the subway together.

Initially, Emmett took some comfort from the fact that he knew the right station to go to, knew the right platform, knew the right train, having already made the journey to Brooklyn once, albeit in error. But the day before, when he had switched from the Brooklyn-bound train to the Manhattan-bound train, he had never left the station. So it was only when they came out of the Carroll Street stop that Emmett got a sense of how rough this part of Brooklyn was. And as they worked their way through Gowanus into Red Hook, it only seemed to get worse. The landscape soon became dominated by long, windowless warehouses abutted by the occasional flophouse or bar. It hardly seemed the neighborhood for a circus, unless they had raised a tent on the wharf. But as the river came into view, there was no sign of a tent, no flags, no marquees.

Emmett was about to turn back when Billy pointed across the street to a nondescript building with a small, brightly lit window.

It turned out to be a ticket booth occupied by a man in his seventies.

—Is this the circus? Emmett asked.

—The early show's started, the old man said, but it's two bucks a head just the same.

When Emmett paid, the old man slid the tickets across the counter with the indifference of one who's been sliding tickets across a counter all his life.

Emmett was relieved to find the lobby more in keeping with his expectations. The floor was covered in a dark, red carpet and the walls painted with figures of acrobats and elephants and an open-jawed lion. There was also a concession stand selling popcorn and beer, and a large easel advertising the main event: THE ASTOUNDING SUTTER SISTERS OF SAN ANTONIO, TEXXXAS!

As Emmett gave their tickets to the usherette in the blue uniform, he asked where they should sit.

—Anywhere you like.

Then after giving Billy a wink, she opened the door and told them to enjoy the show.

Inside it was like a small, indoor rodeo with a dirt floor surrounded by an oval bulwark and twenty rows of stadium seating. By Emmett's estimate, the hall was only a quarter full, but with the lighting trained on the oval, the faces of the audience members weren't easy to make out.

As the brothers sat on one of the benches, the lights dimmed and a spotlight illuminated the ringmaster. In keeping with tradition, he was dressed like a master of the hunt, with leather riding boots, a bright red jacket, and top hat. Only when he began to speak did Emmett realize he was actually a woman wearing a false moustache.

—And now, she announced through a red megaphone, returning from the East where she mesmerized the Raja of India and danced for the King of Siam, the Circus is proud to present the one, the only, Delilah!

With an extension of the ringmaster's hand, the spotlight shot across the oval to a gate in the bulwark through which an enormous woman in a pink tutu came riding the tricycle of a child.

As the audience erupted into laughter and bawdy cheers, two seals with old-fashioned police helmets strapped to their heads appeared and began to bark. Off Delilah went, pedaling frantically around the oval as the seals gave chase and the crowd egged them on. Once the seals had successfully corralled Delilah back through the gate, they turned and acknowledged the audience's appreciation by bobbing their heads and clapping their fins.

Next, two cowgirls rode into the ring—one dressed in white leather with a white hat on the back of a white horse, the other all in black.

—The Astounding Sutter Sisters, called the ringmaster through her megaphone as they trotted around the arena waving their hats to the cheers of the crowd.

After circling the arena once, the sisters began performing a series of stunts. Riding at a reasonable speed, they swung themselves from one side of their saddles to the other in perfect synchronicity. Then, while riding at a faster clip, the Sutter in black leapt from her horse to her sister's and back again.

Pointing at the arena, Billy looked up at his brother with an expression of amazement.

—Did you see that?

—I did, said Emmett with a smile.

But when Billy turned his attention back to the action, Emmett turned his to the audience. For the sisters' act, the lights in the arena had been raised, making it easier for Emmett to search the faces of the crowd. Having completed a first pass to no avail, Emmett looked to his immediate left and began working his way around the oval more systematically, looking from row to row and aisle to aisle. Emmett still couldn't find Duchess, but he noted with a touch of surprise that most of the audience members were men.

—Look! Billy exclaimed, pointing at the sisters, who were now standing on the backs of their horses as they rode side by side.

—Yes, said Emmett. They're very good.

—No, said Billy. Not the riders. Over there in the audience. It's Woolly.

Following the direction of Billy's finger, Emmett looked across the arena, and there in the eighth row was Woolly, sitting by himself. Emmett had been so focused on finding Duchess, it hadn't occurred to him to look for Woolly.

—Good job, Billy. Come on.

Following the wide center aisle, Emmett and Billy circumnavigated the arena to where Woolly sat with a bag of popcorn in his lap and a smile on his face.

—Woolly! called Billy as he ran the final steps.

At the sound of his name, Woolly looked up.

—*Mirabile dictu!* Out of nowhere, here come Emmett and Billy Watson. What serendipity! What a turn of events! Have a seat, have a seat.

Though there was plenty of space for the brothers to sit, Woolly slid along the bench to make more room.

—Isn't it a great show? asked Billy while removing his backpack.

—It is, agreed Woolly. It most certainly definitely is.

—Look, said Billy, pointing to the middle of the arena, where four clowns had driven four small cars.

Moving behind his brother, Emmett took the empty seat on Woolly's right.

—Where's Duchess?

—What's that? asked Woolly, without taking his eyes off the sisters, who were now jumping over the cars and scattering the clowns.

Emmett leaned closer.

—Where's Duchess, Woolly?

Woolly looked up as if he hadn't the faintest idea. Then he remembered.

—He's in the living room! He went to see some friends in the living room.

—Where's that?

Woolly pointed to the end of the oval.

—Up the steps and through the blue door.

—I'm going to get him. In the meantime, can you keep an eye on Billy?

—Of course, said Woolly.

Emmett held Woolly's gaze for a moment to stress the importance of what he'd just asked. Woolly turned to Billy.

—Emmett's going to go get Duchess, Billy. So you and I have to keep an eye on each other. Okay?

—Okay, Woolly.

Woolly turned back to Emmett.

—See?

—All right, said Emmett with a smile. Just don't go anywhere.

Woolly gestured to the arena.

—Why would we?

Climbing behind Woolly, Emmett made his way around the center aisle to the steps at the top of the oval.

Emmett wasn't one for circuses. He wasn't one for magic shows or rodeos. He hadn't even liked going to the football games at his high school, which were attended by nearly everyone in town. He'd simply never taken to the idea of sitting in a crowd to watch someone do something more interesting than what you were doing yourself. So when he began climbing the steps and he heard the double crack of toy pistols and a cheer from the crowd, he didn't bother looking back. And when he opened the blue door at the top of the steps and two more cracks of the pistol were followed by even louder cheers, he didn't look back then either.

If he had looked back, what Emmett would have seen was the Sutter sisters riding in opposite directions with their six-shooters drawn. As the two passed each other, he would have seen them take aim and shoot the hats from each other's heads. As the two passed a second time, he would have seen them shoot the shirts off their backs—revealing bare midriffs and lacy bras, one black, one white. And if he had waited just a few minutes more before stepping through the door, he would have seen the Sutter sisters firing their pistols in rapid succession until both of them were galloping on the backs of their horses as naked as Lady Godiva.

When the door at the top of the steps swung shut behind him, Emmett found himself at the end of a long, narrow hallway on either side of which were six doors, all of them closed. As Emmett walked its length, the muffled cheers of the crowd began to recede and he could hear a piece of classical music being played on a piano. It was coming from behind the door at the end of the hallway—a door that was illustrated with the large insignia of a bell like the one that was used by the phone company. When he put his hand on the knob, the classical piece slowed and then seamlessly transitioned into a saloon-style rag.

Opening the door, Emmett stood on the threshold of a large, luxurious lounge. Composed of at least four separate sitting areas, the room had couches and chairs upholstered in rich, dark fabrics. On the side tables were lamps with tasseled shades, and on the walls were oil paintings of ships. Stretched out on two facing couches, wearing nothing but delicate shifts, were a redhead and brunette, both smoking pungent cigarettes. While at the back of the room, near an elaborately carved bar, a blonde in a silk wrap leaned against the piano, tapping her fingers in time to the music.

Almost every element of the scene took Emmett by surprise: the plush furniture, the oil paintings, the scantily clad women. But nothing took him by more surprise than the fact that the person playing the piano was Duchess—wearing a crisp white shirt and a fedora tilted back on his head.

When the blonde at the piano looked to see who had come through the door, Duchess followed her gaze. Seeing Emmett, he ran his fingers once down the length of the keyboard, pounded a final chord, and leapt to his feet with a generous grin.

—Emmett!

The three women looked at Duchess.

—Do you know him? asked the blonde in an almost childlike voice.

—This is the guy I was telling you about!

The three women all turned their gazes back on Emmett.

—You mean the one from North Dakota?

—Nebraska, corrected the brunette.

The redhead lazily pointed her cigarette at Emmett with an expression of sudden understanding.

—The one who loaned you the car.

—Exactly, said Duchess.

The women all smiled at Emmett in recognition of his generosity. Striding across the room, Duchess took Emmett by the arms.

—I can't believe you're here. Just this morning, Woolly and I were lamenting your absence and counting the days until we'd see you again. But wait! Where are my manners?

Slipping an arm over Emmett's shoulder, Duchess led him toward the women.

—Let me introduce you to my three fairy godmothers. Here on my left, we have Helen. The second one in history to launch a thousand ships.

—Charmed, the redhead said to Emmett, extending her hand.

As Emmett reached to take it, he realized that her shift was so diaphanous, the dark circles around her nipples were visible through the fabric. Feeling the color rising to his cheeks, he averted his gaze.

—By the piano we have Charity. I don't think I have to tell you how she got her name. And here on my right is Bernadette.

Emmett was relieved when Bernadette, who was dressed exactly like Helen, didn't bother to extend her hand.

—That's quite a belt buckle, she said with a smile.

—It's nice to meet you, Emmett said to the women a little awkwardly.

Duchess turned to face him with a grin.

—This is so great, he said.

—Yeah, said Emmett, without much enthusiasm. Listen, Duchess, if I could have a word. Alone . . .

—Sure thing.

Duchess led Emmett away from the women, but rather than take him back into the hallway, where they would have privacy, he took him to a corner of the lounge about fifteen feet away.

Duchess studied Emmett's face for a moment.

—You're mad, he said. I can tell.

Emmett barely knew where to begin.

—Duchess, he found himself saying, I did not *lend* you my car.

—You're right, replied Duchess, holding up both hands in surrender. You're absolutely right. It would have been much more accurate for me to say I borrowed it. But like I told Billy back at St. Nick's, we were only using it to run that errand upstate. We would have had it back in Morgen before you knew it.

—Whether you took it for a year or a day doesn't change the fact that it's *my* car—with my money in it.

Duchess looked at Emmett like he didn't understand him for a second.

—Oh, you mean the envelope that was in the trunk. You don't have to worry about that, Emmett.

—Then you have it?

—Sure. But not on me. This is the big city, after all. I left it at Woolly's sister's place, along with your kit bag, where they'd be safe and sound.

—Then let's go get them. And on the way, you can tell me all about the cops.

—What cops?

—I saw Townhouse, and he says the cops came around this morning, asking about my car.

—I can't imagine why they would be, said Duchess, looking genuinely stupefied. That is, unless . . .

—Unless what?

Duchess was nodding his head now.

—On the way here, when I wasn't looking, Woolly parked in front of a fire hydrant. Next thing I knew, there was a patrolman asking him for the driver's license he didn't have. What with Woolly being Woolly, I convinced the cop not to write him a ticket. But he might have put a description of the car in the system.

—Great, said Emmett.

Duchess nodded soberly, but then suddenly snapped his fingers.

—You know what, Emmett? It doesn't matter.

—And why is that?

—Yesterday, I made the trade of the century. Maybe not as good as Manhattan for a string of beads, but pretty damn close. In exchange for one scuffed-up Studebaker hardtop, I landed you a 1941 Cadillac convertible in mint condition. There couldn't be more than a thousand miles on her, and the provenance is impeccable.

—I don't need your Cadillac, Duchess, wherever it came from. Townhouse gave me back the Studebaker. It's getting a new coat of paint and I'm picking it up on Monday.

—You know what, said Duchess, with a finger in the air. That's even better. Now we'll have the Studebaker *and* the Caddy. After we go to the Adirondacks, we can caravan to California.

—Oooh, said Charity from across the room. A caravan!

Before Emmett could dispel anybody's ideas about a caravan to California, a door behind the piano opened and in lumbered the woman who had ridden the tricycle, though now in a giant terrycloth robe.

—Well, well, she said in a raspy voice. Who do we have here?

—It's Emmett, said Duchess. The one I told you about.

She looked at Emmett with narrowed eyes.

—The one with the trust?

—No. The one I borrowed the car from.

—You're right, she said with a touch of disappointment. He does look like Gary Cooper.

—I wouldn't mind being cooped up with him, said Charity.

Everyone but Emmett laughed, and no one louder than the big woman.

As Emmett felt the color rising to his cheeks again, Duchess put a hand on his shoulder.

—Emmett Watson, let me introduce you to the sprightliest lifter of spirits in the city of New York: Ma Belle.

Ma Belle laughed again.

—You're even worse than your father.

When everyone was quiet for a moment, Emmett took hold of Duchess by the elbow.

—It's been nice to meet you all, he said, but Duchess and I need to be going.

—Not so soon, said Charity with a frown.

—I'm afraid we have some people waiting, explained Emmett.

Then he pressed his fingers into the soft spots of Duchess's joint.

—Ow, said Duchess freeing his elbow. If you were in such a hurry, why didn't you say so? Just give me a minute to talk with Ma Belle and Charity. Then we can go.

Patting Emmett on the back, Duchess went over to confer with the two women.

—So, said the redhead, you're off to Tinseltown.

—What's that? asked Emmett.

—Duchess tells us you're all going to Hollywood.

Before Emmett could process this news, Duchess turned and slapped his hands.

—Well, ladies, it's been divine. But the time has come for me and Emmett to hit the road.

—If you must, said Ma Belle. But you can't leave without having a drink.

Duchess looked from Emmett to Ma Belle.

—I don't think we have time, Ma.

—Poppycock, she said. Everyone's got time for a drink. And besides, you can't head off to California without letting us toast to your good fortune. It's just not done. Isn't that right, ladies?

—Yes, a toast! the ladies agreed.

Giving Emmett a shrug of resignation, Duchess went to the bar, popped the cork from a bottle of champagne that was waiting on ice, filled six glasses, and handed them around.

—I don't want any champagne, Emmett said quietly when Duchess reached him.

—It's rude not to join in a toast on your behalf, Emmett. And bad luck to boot.

Emmett closed his eyes for a moment, then took the glass.

—First, Ma Belle said, I'd like to thank our friend Duchess for bringing us these lovely bottles of bubbly.

—Hear, hear! cheered the ladies, as Duchess took a bow at every point of the compass.

—It is always bittersweet to lose the company of good friends, continued Ma Belle. But we take heart from the fact that our loss is Hollywood's gain. In closing, I would like to offer you a few lines from that great Irish poet William Butler Yeats: Through the teeth and over the gums, look out stomach here she comes.

Then Ma Belle emptied her glass at a throw.

The ladies all laughed and emptied theirs. Having little choice, Emmett did the same.

—There, said Duchess with a smile. Was that so bad?

As Charity excused herself from the room, Duchess began going from one woman to the next in order to express a farewell in a predictably wordy fashion.

Given the spirit of the moment, Emmett was trying his best to maintain his composure, but he had nearly run out of patience. To make matters worse, what with all the bodies and cushions and tassels, the room had grown overly warm, and the sweet smell of the women's cigarettes off-putting.

—Duchess, he said.

—All right, Emmett. I'm just saying my last goodbyes. Why don't you wait in the hallway, and I'll be right with you.

Setting down his glass, Emmett gladly retreated into the hallway to wait.

While the cooler air did provide Emmett some relief, the hallway suddenly seemed like it was longer and narrower than it had been before. And that there were more doors too. More doors on his left and more on his right. And though he was looking straight ahead, the arrangement of the doors began to give him a sense of vertigo, as if the axis of the building was being tipped and he might fall the length of the hallway and break through the door at the opposite end.

It must be the champagne, thought Emmett.

Shaking his head, he turned and looked back into the living room, only to see that Duchess was now sitting on the edge of the redhead's couch, refilling her glass.

—Christ, he said under his breath.

Emmett began walking back toward the living room, prepared, if necessary, to grab Duchess by the scruff of the neck. But before he had taken two steps, Ma Belle appeared on the threshold and began walking in his direction. Given her girth, there was barely enough room for her to fit in the hallway, and certainly not enough room for her to get past Emmett.

—Come on, she said with an impatient wave of the hand. Clear the way.

As she barreled toward him, Emmett, who was backing up, realized that the door to one of the rooms was open, so he stepped inside to let her pass.

But when she came in line with Emmett, rather than continuing down the hall, she paused and shoved him with a fleshy hand. As he stumbled back into the room, she pulled the door shut and Emmett heard the unmistakable sound of a key turning in a lock. Bounding forward, Emmett grabbed the knob and tried the door. When it wouldn't open, he began banging on it.

—Open the door! he shouted.

As he was repeating his demand, he was struck by the memory of a woman shouting the same thing at him through a closed door somewhere else. Then from behind Emmett came the voice of a different woman. A voice that was softer and more inviting.

—What's the rush, Nebraska?

Turning, Emmett discovered the one called Charity lying on her side on a luxurious bed, patting the covers with a delicate hand. Looking around, Emmett saw that there were no windows in the room, only more paintings of ships, including a large one over a bureau that depicted a schooner in full sail leaning into a high wind. The silk wrap that Charity had been wearing was now draped across the back of an arm chair, and she was in a peach-colored negligee with ivory trim.

—Duchess thought you might be a little nervous, she said in a voice that didn't sound so childlike anymore. But you don't need to be nervous. Not in this room. Not with me.

Emmett began to turn toward the door, but she said *not that way, this way*, so he turned back.

—Come over here, she said, and lie down beside me. Because I want to ask you some things. Or I can tell you some things. Or we don't have to talk at all.

Emmett felt himself taking a step in her direction, a difficult step, his foot landing on the floorboards with a slow and heavy tread. Then he was standing at the edge of the bed with its dark red covers, and she had taken his hand in hers. Looking down, he could see that she was holding it with the palm turned up, as a gypsy would. Emmett wondered, for a second, with a touch of fascination, if she was about to tell his fortune. Instead, she laid his hand against her breast.

Slowly, he drew it away from the smooth, cool silk.

—I've got to get out of here, he said. You need to help me get out of here.

She gave him a little pout, as if he had hurt her feelings. And he felt bad that he had hurt her feelings. He felt so bad that he was inclined to reach out and assure her. Instead, he turned once more toward the door. But this time when he turned, he turned and turned and turned.

Duchess

WAS IN HIGH SPIRITS. That's my excuse.

All day, I had been hopscotching from one pleasant surprise to the next. First, I'd been given the run of Woolly's sister's house and ended up with a fine set of threads; I'd had a nice visit with Ma Belle and the girls; against all odds, Emmett had shown up, giving me the chance (with Charity's help) to perform my third good deed in as many days; and now, here I was sitting behind the wheel of a 1941 Cadillac heading into Manhattan with the top down. The only wrench in the works was that Woolly and I had ended up with Billy in tow.

When Emmett had shown up at Ma Belle's, it hadn't occurred to me for one second that he had brought along his brother, so I was a little surprised to find him at Woolly's side. Don't get me wrong. Billy was a sweet kid as far as kids go. But he was also something of a know-it-all. And if know-it-alls are prone to get under your skin, no know-it-all gets under your skin like a young know-it-all.

We hadn't even been together for an hour and he had already corrected me three times. First, it was to point out that the Sutter sisters hadn't been shooting each other with real guns—like I was the one who needed an introduction to the elements of stagecraft! Next, it was to point out that a seal is a mammal, not some kind of fish, because it has warm blood and a backbone and yatata, yatata, yatata. Then as we were driving onto the Brooklyn Bridge with the skyline stretching before us in all its glory, and I happened to ask in my elevated state whether anyone could think of a single example in the history of mankind of a river crossing that felt more transformative, rather than quietly appreciating the poetry of the moment and the spirit of the remark, the kid—who's sitting in the back seat like a little millionaire—felt the necessity of chiming in.

—I can think of an example, says he.

—The question was rhetorical, says I.

But now he's got Woolly intrigued.

—What's your example, Billy?

—The crossing of the Delaware by George Washington. On Christmas night in 1776, General Washington crossed the river's icy waters to sneak up on the Hessians. Catching them unawares, Washington's troops routed the enemy and captured one thousand prisoners. The event was memorialized in a famous painting by Emanuel Leutze.

—I think I've seen that painting! exclaimed Woolly. Isn't Washington standing in the bow of a rowboat?

—Nobody stands in the bow of a rowboat, I pointed out.

—In Emanuel Leutze's painting, Washington is standing in the bow of a rowboat, said Billy. I can show you a picture, if you'd like. It's in Professor Abernathe's book.

—Of course, it is.

—That's a good one, said Woolly, who was always up for a bit of history.

As it was Friday evening, there was some traffic and we ended up coming to a stop at the top of the bridge—which provided us with the perfect opportunity to appreciate the view in silence.

—I know another one, said Billy.

Woolly turned toward the back seat with a smile.

—Which one, Billy?

—When Caesar crossed the Rubicon.

—What happened that time?

You could almost hear the kid sitting up in his seat.

—In 49 B.C. when Caesar was the governor of Gaul, the Senate, which had become wary of his ambitions, recalled him to the capital, instructing him to leave his troops at the banks of the Rubicon. Instead, Caesar marched his soldiers across the river into Italy and led them straight to Rome, where he soon seized power and launched the Imperial Era. That's where the expression *crossing the Rubicon* comes from. It means passing a point of no return.

—Another good one, said Woolly.

—Then there was Ulysses, who crossed the river Styx. . . .

—I think we get the idea, I said.

But Woolly wasn't finished.

—What about Moses? he asked. Didn't he cross a river?

—That was the Red Sea, said Billy. It was when he was—

No doubt the kid had intended to give us chapter and verse on Moses, but for once, he interrupted himself.

—Look! he said, pointing in the distance. The Empire State Building!

All three of us turned our attention to the skyscraper in question, and that's when the idea hit me. Like a little bolt of lightning, it zapped me on the top of the head and sent a tingling sensation up and down my spine.

—Isn't that where his office is? I asked, peeking at Billy in the rearview mirror.

—Whose office? asked Woolly.

—Professor Abercrombie's.

—You mean Professor Abernathe's?

—Exactly. How does it go, Billy? *I write to you from the junction of Thirty-Fourth Street and Fifth Avenue on the isle of Manhattan.* . . .

—Yes, said Billy, his eyes opening wide. That's how it goes.

—Then why don't we pay him a visit.

Out of the corner of my eye, I could see that Woolly was disconcerted by my suggestion. But Billy wasn't.

—We can pay him a visit? he asked.

—I don't see why not.

—Duchess . . . , said Woolly.

I ignored him.

—What's that he calls you in the introduction, Billy? *Dear Reader?* What author wouldn't want to receive a visit from one of his dear readers? I mean, writers must work twice as hard as actors, right? But they don't get any standing ovations, or curtain calls, or people waiting outside the backstage door. Besides, if Professor *Abernathe* didn't want to receive visits from his readers, why would he have put his address on the first page of his book?

—He probably wouldn't be there at this hour, countered Woolly.

—Maybe he's working late, I countered right back.

As the traffic began to move again, I pulled into the right lane in order to take the uptown exit, thinking to myself that if the lobby wasn't open, we were going to climb that building like King Kong.

Having headed west on Thirty-Fifth Street, I took the left onto Fifth Avenue and pulled over right in front of the building's entrance. A second later, one of the doormen was on me.

—You can't park there, buddy.

—We're just going to be a minute, I said, slipping him a five. In the meantime, maybe you and President Lincoln can get to know each other.

Now, instead of telling me where I couldn't park, he was opening Woolly's door and ushering us into the building with a tip of the hat. Capitalism, they call it.

As we entered the lobby, Billy had a look of anxious excitement. He just couldn't believe where we were and what we were about to do. In his wildest dreams, he hadn't imagined it. Woolly, on the other hand, looked at me with a frown that was decidedly out of character.

—What? I said.

Before he could answer, Billy was tugging at my sleeve.

—How will we find him, Duchess?

—You know where to find him, Billy.

—I do?

—You read it to me yourself.

Billy's eyes opened wide.

—On the fifty-fifth floor.

—Exactly.

With a smile I gestured to the elevator bank.

—Are we taking the elevator?

—We're certainly not taking the stairs.

We boarded one of the express cars.

—I've never been in an elevator, Billy said to the operator.

—Enjoy the ride, the operator replied.

Then he pulled the lever and sent us shooting up into the building.

Normally, Woolly would have been humming a ditty on a ride like this, but I was the one who was doing the humming tonight. And Billy, he was quietly counting the floors as we passed them. You could tell by the movement of his lips.

—Fifty-one, he mouthed. Fifty-two, fifty-three, fifty-four.

At the fifty-fifth floor, the operator opened the doors and we disembarked. When we proceeded from the elevator bank into the hallway, we found rows of doors stretching to our left and right.

—What do we do now? asked Billy.

I pointed to the nearest door.

—We'll start there and work our way around the floor until we find him.

—Clockwise? Billy asked.

—Anywise you like.

So we set about going from door to door—clockwise—and Billy would read out the names that were etched on the little brass plaques, just like he'd called out the floors on the elevator, only this time out loud. It was quite a parade of paper pushers. In addition to attorneys and accountants, there were brokers of real estate, insurance, and stocks. Not from the big firms, you understand. These were the shops operated by the guys who couldn't make it in the big firms. The guys who resoled their shoes, and read the funny pages while waiting for the phone to ring.

The first twenty shingles Billy read in a punchy, upbeat manner, like each one was a pleasant little surprise. The next twenty he read with a little less enthusiasm. After those, his delivery began to flag. You could almost hear the thumb of reality beginning to press down on that spot in the soul from which youthful enthusiasm springs. Reality was almost certainly going to leave its mark on Billy Watson tonight. And that mark was likely to stay with him for the rest of his life as a helpful reminder that while the heroes in storybooks are usually figments of the imagination, most of the men who write about them are figments of the imagination too.

When we turned the fourth corner, we could see the last stretch of doors leading up to the spot where we'd begun. Slower and slower Billy moved, softer and softer he spoke, until finally, in front of the second-to-last door, he came to a stop and said nothing at all. He must have read out fifty little plaques by then, and though I was standing behind him, I could tell from his posture that he'd simply had enough.

After a moment, he looked up at Woolly with what must have been an expression of disappointment on his face, because Woolly suddenly had an expression of sympathy on his. Then Billy turned to look at me. Only his expression wasn't of disappointment. It was of wide-eyed amazement.

Turning back to the little brass plaque, he extended a finger and read the inscription out loud.

—Office of Professor Abacus Abernathe, MLA, PhD.

Turning to Woolly with my own expression of amazement, I

realized that the sympathy on his face hadn't been meant for Billy; it had been meant for me. Because once again, the feet I had pulled the rug out from under were my own. After spending a few days with this kid, you'd think I might have known better. But like I said: I blame the high spirits.

Well, when circumstances conspire to spoil your carefully laid plans with an unexpected reversal, the best thing you can do is take credit as quickly as possible.

—What'd I tell you, kid.

Billy gave me a smile, but then he looked at the doorknob with a touch of apprehension, as if he weren't sure he had the gumption to turn it.

—Allow me! exclaimed Woolly.

Stepping forward, Woolly turned the knob and opened the door. Inside, we found ourselves in a small reception area with a desk, coffee table, and a few chairs. The room would have been dark but for a faint light that shone through the open transom over an interior door.

—I guess you were right, Woolly, I said with an audible sigh. Looks like nobody's home.

But Woolly raised a finger to his lips.

—Shhh. Did you hear that?

We all looked up when Woolly pointed at the transom.

—There it is again, he whispered.

—There's what? I whispered back.

—The scratching of a pen, said Billy.

—The scratching of a pen, said Woolly with a smile.

Billy and I followed Woolly as he tiptoed across the reception area and gently turned the second knob. Behind this door was a much bigger room. It was a long rectangle lined from floor to ceiling with books and furnished with a standing globe, a couch, two high-back chairs, and a large wooden desk, behind which sat a little old man writing in a little old ledger by the light of a green-shaded lamp.

Wearing a wrinkled seersucker suit, he had thinning white hair and a pair of reading glasses perched on the tip of his nose. In other words, he looked so much the part of a professor, you had to figure that all the books on the shelves were for show.

At the sound of our entry, the old man looked up from his work without a hint of surprise or dismay.

—May I help you?

After the three of us had taken a few steps, Woolly nudged Billy one step more.

—Ask him, he encouraged.

Billy cleared his throat.

—Are you Professor Abacus Abernathe?

After moving his reading glasses to the top of his head, the old man tilted the shade of his lamp so that he could get a better look at the three of us. Though mostly, he trained his gaze on Billy, having understood in the instant that the boy was the reason we were there.

—I am Abacus Abernathe, he replied. What can I do for you?

Although there seemed to be no end to the things that Billy knew, apparently what he did not know was what Abacus Abernathe could do for him. Because rather than give an answer, Billy looked back at Woolly with an unsure expression. So Woolly spoke on his behalf.

—We're sorry to interrupt you, Professor, but this is Billy Watson from Morgen, Nebraska, who's just arrived in New York City for the very first time. He is only eight years old but he has read your *Compendium* of adventurers twenty-four times.

Having listened to Woolly with interest, the professor shifted his gaze back to Billy.

—Is that so, young man?

—It is so, said Billy. Except that I have read it twenty-five times.

—Well, said the professor, if you have read my book twenty-five times and have come all the way from Nebraska to New York City to tell me so, then the least I can do is offer you a chair.

With an open hand, he invited Billy to take one of the high-back chairs in front of his desk. For Woolly and me, he gestured to the couch by the bookcase.

Let me say right now that it was a very nice couch. It was upholstered with dark brown leather, pinpointed with shiny brass rivets, and almost as big as a car. But if three people who come into a room accept a fourth person's offer of a seat, then no one's going anywhere anytime soon. It's human nature. Having taken all the trouble of making themselves comfortable, people are going to feel the need to chew the fat for at least half an hour. In fact, if they run out of things to say after twenty minutes, they'll start making them up just to be polite. So when the professor offered us the seats, I opened my mouth with every intention of observing that it was getting quite late and our car was at the curb. But before I could get a word out, Billy was climbing onto the high-back chair and Woolly was settling into the couch.

—Now tell me, Billy, said the professor—once we were all irreparably ensconced—what brings you to New York?

As conversations go, it was a classic opener. It was the sort of question that any New Yorker would ask a visitor with a reasonable expectation of a one- or two-sentence reply. Like *I'm here to see my aunt,* or *We have tickets for a show.* But this was Billy Watson, so instead of one or two sentences, what the professor got was the whole megillah.

Billy started back in 1946, on the summer night that his mother walked out on them. He explained about Emmett's doing the hitch at Salina and his father dying of cancer and the brothers' plan to follow the trail of a bunch of postcards so that they could find their mother at a fireworks display in San Francisco on the Fourth of July. He even explained about the escapade and how since Woolly and I had borrowed the Studebaker, he and Emmett had to hitch a ride to New York on the Sunset East.

—Well, well, well, said the professor, who hadn't missed a word. And you say that you traveled to the city by freight train?

—That's where I began your book for the twenty-fifth time, said Billy.

—In the boxcar?

—There wasn't a window, but I had my army surplus flashlight.

—How fortuitous.

—When we decided to go to California and make a fresh start, Emmett agreed with you that we should only carry what we could fit in a kit bag. So I put everything I need in my backpack.

Having leaned back in his chair with a smile, the professor suddenly leaned forward again.

—You wouldn't happen to have the *Compendium* in your backpack now?

—Yes, said Billy. That's just where I have it.

—Then, perhaps I could inscribe it for you?

—That would be terrific! exclaimed Woolly.

At the professor's encouragement, Billy slid off the high-back chair, took off his backpack, undid the straps, and removed the big red book.

—Bring it here, said the professor with a wave of the hand. Bring it over here.

When Billy came around the desk, the professor took the book and held it under his light in order to appreciate the wear and tear.

—There are few things more beautiful to an author's eye, he confessed to Billy, than a well-read copy of one of his books.

Setting the book down, the professor took up his pen and opened to the title page.

—It was a gift, I see.

—From Miss Matthiessen, said Billy. She's the librarian at the Morgen Public Library.

—A gift from a librarian, no less, the professor said with added satisfaction.

Having written in Billy's book at some length, the professor applied his signature with a great big theatrical flourish—since when it comes to New York City, even the old guys who write compendiums perform for the back row. Before returning the book, the professor flitted once through the pages as if to make sure they were all there. Then letting out a little expression of surprise, he looked at Billy.

—I see that you haven't filled in any of the *You* chapter. Now, why is that?

—Because I want to start *in medias res*, explained Billy. And I'm not sure yet where the middle is.

It sounded like a kooky answer to me, but it left the professor beaming.

—Billy Watson, he said, as a seasoned historian and professional teller of tales, I think I can say with confidence that you have already been through enough adventures to warrant the beginning of your chapter! However . . .

Here, the professor opened one of his desk drawers and took out a black ledger just like the one that he'd been working in when we arrived.

—Should the eight pages in your *Compendium* prove insufficient for recording your story in its entirety—as I am almost certain they will—you can continue in the pages of this journal. And should you run out of pages in it, drop me a line, and I shall happily send you another.

Then, after handing over the two books, the professor shook Billy's hand and said what an honor it had been to meet him. And that, as they say, should have been that.

But after Billy had carefully put away his books, cinched the straps on his backpack, and taken the first few steps toward the exit, he suddenly stopped, turned, and faced the professor with a furrowed brow—which with Billy Watson could only mean one thing: more questions.

—I think we've taken up enough of the professor's time, I said, laying a hand on Billy's shoulder.

—That's all right, said Abernathe. What is it, Billy?

Billy looked at the floor for a second, then up at the professor.

—Do you think heroes return?

—You mean like Napoleon returning to Paris, and Marco Polo returning to Venice . . . ?

—No, said Billy shaking his head. I don't mean returning to a place. I mean returning in time.

The professor was quiet for a moment.

—Why do you ask that, Billy?

This go-round, the old scrivener definitely got more than he bargained for. Because without taking a seat, Billy launched into a story that was longer and wilder than the first one. While he was on the Sunset East, he explained, and Emmett had gone looking for food, a pastor who'd invited himself into Billy's boxcar tried to take Billy's collection of silver dollars with the intention of tossing Billy from the train. In the nick of time, a big black guy dropped through the hatch, and it ended up being the pastor who got the old heave-ho.

But apparently, the pastor, the silver dollars, and the last-minute rescue weren't even the point of the story. The point was that the black guy, whose name was Ulysses, had left behind a wife and son when he crossed the Atlantic to fight in the war and had been wandering the country on freight trains ever since.

Now, when an eight-year-old boy is spinning a yarn like this one— with black men dropping through ceilings and pastors being thrown from trains—you might think it would test the limits of someone's willingness to suspend his disbelief. Especially a professor's. But it didn't test Abernathe's in the least.

As Billy told his story, the good professor resumed his seat in slow motion, carefully lowering himself into his chair, then gently leaning back, as if he didn't want a sudden sound or movement to interrupt the boy's story, or his own attention to it.

—He thought he was named Ulysses for Ulysses S. Grant, said Billy, but I explained to him that he must be named for the Great Ulysses. And that having already wandered for over eight years without his wife and son, he was sure to be reunited with them once his ten years of wandering were complete. But if heroes don't return in time, Billy concluded with a touch of concern, then maybe I shouldn't have said that to him.

When Billy stopped speaking, the professor closed his eyes for a moment. Not like Emmett does when he's trying to hold in his exasperation, but like a lover of music who has just heard the ending of his favorite concerto. When he opened his eyes again, he looked from Billy to the books along his walls and back again.

—I have no doubt that heroes return in time, he said to Billy. And I think you were perfectly right to tell him what you did. But I . . .

Now it was the professor who looked at Billy with hesitation, and Billy who encouraged the professor to continue.

—I was just wondering, if this man called Ulysses is still here in New York?

—Yes, said Billy. He is here in New York.

The professor sat for a moment, as if working up the courage to ask a second question of this eight-year-old.

—I know it is late, he said at last, and you and your friends have other places to be, and I have no grounds on which to ask for this favor, but is there any chance that you might be willing to bring me to him?

Woolly

I T WAS ON A TRIP TO GREECE with his mother in 1946, while standing at the foot of the Parthenon, that Woolly first gained an inkling of the List—that itemization of all the places that one was supposed to see. *There it is,* she had said, while fanning herself with her map when they had reached the dusty summit overlooking Athens. *The Parthenon in all its glory.* In addition to the Parthenon, as Woolly was soon to learn, there were the Piazza San Marco in Venice and the Louvre in Paris and the Uffizi in Florence. There were the Sistine Chapel and Notre Dame and Westminster Abbey.

It was something of a mystery to Woolly where the List came from. It seemed to have been compiled by various scholars and eminent historians long before he was born. No one had ever quite explained to Woolly *why* one needed to see all the places on the List, but there was no mistaking the importance of doing so. For his elders would inevitably praise him if he had seen one, frown at him if he expressed disinterest in one, and chastise him in no uncertain terms if he happened to be in the vicinity of one and failed to pay it a visit.

Suffice it to say, when it came to seeing the items on the List, Woolly Wolcott Martin was Johnny-on-the-spot! Whenever he traveled, he took special care to obtain the appropriate guidebooks and secure the services of the appropriate drivers to get him to the appropriate sights at the appropriate times. *To the Colosseum, signore, and step on it!* he would say, and off they would zip through the crooked streets of Rome with all the urgency of policemen in pursuit of a gang of thieves.

Whenever Woolly arrived at one of the places on the List, he always had the same threefold response. First was a sense of awe. For these were not your run-of-the-mill stopping spots. They were big and elaborate and fashioned from all sorts of impressive materials like marble and mahogany and lapis lazuli. Second was a sense of gratitude toward his forebears since they had gone to all the trouble of handing down this itemization from one generation to the next. But third and most important was a sense of relief—a relief that having dropped his bags at his hotel and dashed across the city in the back of a taxi, Woolly could check one more item off the List.

But having considered himself a diligent checker-offer since the age of twelve, earlier that evening when they were driving to the circus, Woolly had something of an epiphany. While the List had been handed down with consistency and care by five generations of Wolcotts— which is to say, Manhattanites—for some strange reason it did not include a single sight in the city of New York. And though Woolly had dutifully visited Buckingham Palace, La Scala, and the Eiffel Tower, he had never, ever, not even once driven across the Brooklyn Bridge.

Growing up on the Upper East Side, Woolly had had no need to cross it. To get to the Adirondacks, or Long Island, or any of those good old boarding schools up in New England, you would travel by way of the Queensborough or Triborough bridges. So after Duchess had driven them down Broadway and circled round City Hall, it was with a palpable sense of excitement that Woolly realized they were suddenly approaching the Brooklyn Bridge with every intention of driving across it.

How truly majestic was its architecture, thought Woolly. How inspiring the cathedral-like buttresses and the cables that soared through the air. What a feat of engineering, especially since it had been built back in eighteen something-something, and ever since had supported the movement of multitudes from one side of the river to the other and back again, every single day. Surely, the Brooklyn Bridge deserved to be on the List. It certainly had as much business being there as the Eiffel Tower, which was made from similar materials at a similar time but which didn't take anybody anywhere.

It must have been an undersight, decided Woolly.

Like his sister Kaitlin and the oil paintings.

When his family had visited the Louvre and the Uffizi, Kaitlin had expressed the highest admiration for all those paintings lined along the walls in their gilded frames. As they walked from gallery to gallery, she was always giving Woolly the shush and pointing with insistence at some portrait or landscape that he was supposed to be quietly admiring. But the funny thing of it was that their townhouse on Eighty-Sixth Street had been chock-full of portraits and landscapes in gilded frames. As had been their grandmother's. And yet, in all those years of growing up, not once had he seen his sister stop in front of one of them in order to contemplate its majesty. That's why Woolly called it an undersight. Because Kaitlin didn't notice those oil paintings even though they were right under her nose. That must have been why the Manhattanites who'd handed down the List had failed to include any of the sights of New York. Which, come to think of it, made Woolly wonder what else they had forgotten.

And then.

And then!

Just two hours later, when they were driving over the Brooklyn Bridge for a second time in one night, Billy stopped speaking midsentence in order to point in the distance.

—Look! he exclaimed. The Empire State Building!

Well, that definitely belongs on the List, thought Woolly. It was the tallest building in the world. It was so tall, in fact, a plane had actually crashed into the top of it once. And yet, even though it was located right there in the middle of Manhattan, Woolly had never, ever, not even once set foot inside.

As such, when Duchess suggested they go there in order to pay a visit to Professor Abernathe, you might have expected Woolly to feel the same excitement that he'd felt when he realized they'd be driving over the Brooklyn Bridge. But what he felt was a pang of anxiety—a pang that stemmed not from the thought of riding a teeny little elevator up into the stratosphere, but from the tone of Duchess's voice. Because Woolly had heard that tone before. He had heard it from three headmasters and two Episcopal ministers and a brother-in-law named "Dennis." It was the tone that people used when they were about to set you straight.

Now and then, it seemed to Woolly, in the course of your everyday life, you are likely to be blessed with a notion. Say, for instance, it's the middle of August and you're drifting in your rowboat in the middle of the lake with the dragonflies skimming the water, when suddenly the thought occurs to you: Why doesn't summer vacation last until the twenty-first of September? After all, the *season* doesn't come to its conclusion on Labor Day weekend. The season of summer lasts until the autumnal equinox—just as surely as the season of spring lasts until the summer solstice. And look at how carefree everyone feels in the middle of summer vacation. Not only the children, but the grownups too, who take such pleasure in having a tennis game at ten, a swim at noon, and a gin and tonic at six o'clock on the dot. It stands to reason that if we all agreed to let summer vacation last until the equinox, the world would be a much happier place.

Well, when you have a notion like this, you have to be *very* careful in choosing whom you share it with. Because if certain people get wind of your notion—people like your headmaster or your minister or your brother-in-law "Dennis"—they are likely to feel it's their moral responsibility to sit you down and set you straight. Having gestured for you to take the big chair in front of their desk, they will explain not only how misguided your notion is, but how much better a person you're bound to be once you recognize this fact for yourself. And that was the tone that Duchess was using on Billy—the one that preceded the dispelling of an illusion.

You can just imagine the satisfaction that Woolly felt, the jubilation even, when after elevating all the way up to the fifty-fifth floor, trudging down all the corridors, and squinting at every little plaque, with only two more plaques to go, they came upon the one that read: Professor Abacus Abernathe, ABC, PHD, LMNOP.

Poor Duchess, thought Woolly with a smile of sympathy. Maybe he's the one who will be learning a lesson tonight.

As soon as they entered the professor's inner sanctum, Woolly could see that he was a sensitive man, a genial man. And even though he had a high-back chair in front of a big oak desk, Woolly could tell that he was not the sort who would want to sit you down and set you straight. What's more, he was not the sort to hurry you along because time was money, or of the essence, or a stitch in nine, or what have you.

When you are asked a question—even a question that on the surface seems relatively simple and straightforward—you may have to go quite a ways back in order to provide all the little details that will be necessary for someone to make sense of your answer. Despite this, there are many inquisitors who, as soon as you start providing these essential details, will start to make a face. They'll fidget in their seat. Then they'll do their best to hurry you along by pressing you to leap from point A to point Z while skipping all the letters in between. But not Professor Abernathe. When he asked Billy a deceptively simple question and Billy went all the way back to the cradle in order to give a comprehensive reply, the professor leaned back in his chair and listened with the attentiveness of Solomon.

So when Woolly and Billy and Duchess finally rose to take their leave, having visited two of the city's world-famous sites in a single night (Check! Check!), and proven the irrefutable existence of Professor Abacus Abernathe, you might have thought that the night could not get any better.

And you'd be wrong.

Thirty minutes later, they were all in the Cadillac—the professor included—driving down Ninth Avenue to the West Side Elevated, another place of which Woolly had never heard.

—You take that next right, said Billy.

As instructed, Duchess took the right onto a cobblestone street lined with trucks and meatpacking facilities. Woolly could tell they were meatpacking facilities because on one loading dock, two men in long white coats were carrying sides of beef off a truck while over another was a large neon sign in the shape of a steer.

A moment later, Billy told Duchess to take another right and then a left and then he pointed to some wire caging rising from the street.

—There, he said.

When Duchess pulled over, he didn't turn off the engine. On this little stretch, there were no more meatpackers and no more neon signs. Instead, there was an empty lot in which was parked a car without its wheels. At the end of the block, a lone silhouette, stocky and short, passed under a streetlamp, then disappeared into the shadows.

—Are you sure this is it? Duchess asked.

—I'm sure this is it, said Billy while slipping on his backpack.

Then just like that, he was out of the car and walking toward the caging.

Woolly turned to Professor Abernathe in order to raise his eyebrows in surprise, but Professor Abernathe was already on his way to catch up with Billy. So Woolly leapt from the car in order to catch up with the professor, leaving Duchess to catch up with him.

Inside the caging was a staircase of steel that disappeared overhead.

Now it was the professor who looked to Woolly with his eyebrows raised, though more in excitement than surprise.

Reaching out, Billy took hold of a patch of the fencing and began pulling it back.

—Here, said Woolly. Allow me, allow me.

Extending his fingers through the mesh, Woolly pulled so that everyone could slip through. Then up the stairs they went, going round and round, their eight feet clanging on the old metal treads. When they reached the top, Woolly pulled back another bit of fencing so that everyone could slip out.

Oh, what amazement did Woolly feel when he emerged from the caging into the open air. To the south, you could see the towers of Wall Street, while to the north, the towers of Midtown. And if you looked very carefully to the south-southwest, you could just make out the Statue of Liberty—another New York City landmark that surely belonged on the List and to which Woolly had never been.

—Never been, yet! Woolly pronounced in defiance to no one but himself.

But what was amazing about the elevated tracks wasn't the view of Wall Street or Midtown or even the great big summer sun that was setting over the Hudson. What was amazing was the flora.

While they had been in Professor Abernathe's office, Billy had explained that they would be going to a segment of elevated railroad that had stopped being used three years before. But to Woolly's eye, it looked like it had been abandoned for decades. Everywhere you turned there were wildflowers and shrubs, and the grass between the railroad ties had grown almost as high as their knees.

In just three years, thought Woolly. Why, that's less time than it takes to go to boarding school, or to get a college degree. It's less time than a presidential term, or the span between Olympics.

Only two days before, Woolly had remarked to himself how terribly permanent Manhattan remained, despite being marched upon by millions of people every day. But apparently, it wasn't the marching of the millions that was going to bring the city to its end. It was their absence. For here was a glimpse of a New York left to itself. Here was a patch of the city upon which people had turned their backs for just a moment and up through the gravel had come the shrubs and ivy and grass. And if this is what it was like after just a few years of disuse, thought Woolly, imagine what it will be like after a few decades.

As Woolly looked up from the flora in order to share his observation with his friends, he realized that they had pressed ahead without him, working their way toward a campfire in the distance.

—Wait up, he called. Wait up!

As Woolly rejoined his party, Billy was introducing the professor to a tall black man, the one named Ulysses. Though the two men had never met, both had learned something of the other from Billy, and when they shook hands, it struck Woolly that they did so with solemnity, a great and enviable solemnity.

—Please, said Ulysses, as he gestured to the railroad ties around the fire much as the professor had gestured to the couch and chair in his office.

When they had taken their seats, everyone was silent for a moment as the fire crackled and sparked, and it seemed to Woolly that he and Billy and Duchess were young warriors who had been given the privilege of witnessing the meeting between two tribal chiefs. But in the end, it was Billy who spoke first, encouraging Ulysses to tell his tale.

After nodding at Billy, Ulysses turned his eyes to the professor and began. First, he explained how he and a woman named Macie, both alone in the world, had met in a dance hall in St. Louis, fallen in love, and been joined in holy matrimony. He explained how, when the war began, Macie had kept him close to her side as his able-bodied neighbors joined the fray, and how she had tightened her grip once she was radiant with child. He explained how despite her warnings, he had enlisted, fought in Europe, and returned some years later to find that—good as her word—she and the boy had disappeared without a trace. Finally, he described how he had returned to Union Station that day, boarded the first train to anywhere, and been riding the rails ever since. And it was one of the saddest stories that Woolly had ever heard.

For a moment no one spoke. Even Duchess, who was always eager to follow someone else's story with a story of his own, kept his silence, sensing, perhaps, as Woolly did, that something of great consequence was unfolding right before their eyes.

After a few minutes, as if he had needed the moment of silence in order to gather himself, Ulysses continued.

—I am of the opinion, Professor, that everything of value in this life must be earned. That it *should* be earned. Because those who are given something of value without having to earn it are bound to squander it. I believe that one should earn respect. One should earn trust. One should earn the love of a woman, and the right to call oneself a man. And one should also earn the right to hope. At one time I had a wellspring of hope—a wellspring that I had not earned. And not knowing what it was worth, on the day I left my wife and child, I squandered it. So over these last eight and a half years, I have learned to live without hope, just as surely as Cain lived without it once he entered the land of Nod.

To live without hope, said Woolly to himself as he nodded his head and wiped the tears from his eyes. To live without hope in the land of Nod.

—That is, said Ulysses, until I met this boy.

Without taking his gaze from the professor, Ulysses put a hand on Billy's shoulder.

—When Billy said that as one named Ulysses, I might be destined to see my wife and child again, I felt a stirring within me. And when he read to me from your book, I felt it even more strongly. So much more strongly, that I dared to wonder if, after all these years of traveling the country alone, I might finally have earned the right to hope again.

As Ulysses said this, Woolly sat up straighter. Earlier that day, he had tried to give his sister Sarah some sense of how a statement disguised as a question could be an ugly sort of thing. But beside the campfire, when Ulysses said to Professor Abernathe, *I might finally have earned the right to hope again*, Woolly understood that here was a question disguised as a statement. And Woolly found it to be beautiful.

Professor Abernathe seemed to understand this as well. For after a moment of silence, he offered an answer. And as the professor spoke, Ulysses listened with the same deference that the professor had shown to him.

—My life, such as it is, Mr. Ulysses, has been the opposite of yours in many respects. I have never been to war. I have not traveled this country. In fact, for most of the last thirty years, I have remained on the island of Manhattan. And for most of the last ten, I have remained in that.

Turning, the professor pointed to the Empire State Building.

—There I have sat in a room surrounded by books, as insulated from the sounds of crickets and seagulls as from the reach of violence and compassion. If you are right, as I suspect you are—that what is valuable must be earned or it's bound to be squandered—then surely, I am among the squanderers. One who has lived his life in the third person and the past tense. So let me start by acknowledging that anything I say to you, I say with the utmost humility.

Ceremoniously, the professor bowed his head to Ulysses.

—But having confessed that I have lived my life through books, I can at least report that I have done so with conviction. Which is to say, Mr. Ulysses, that I have read a great deal. I have read thousands of books, many of them more than once. I have read histories and novels, scientific tracts and volumes of poetry. And from all of these pages upon pages, one thing I have learned is that there is just enough variety in human experience for every single person in a city the size of New York to feel with assurance that their experience is unique. And this is a wonderful thing. Because to aspire, to fall in love, to stumble as we do and yet soldier on, at some level we must believe that what we are going through has never been experienced quite as *we* have experienced it.

The professor turned his gaze from Ulysses so that he could make eye contact with everyone in the circle, including Woolly. But returning his gaze to Ulysses, the professor raised a finger in the air.

—However, he continued, having observed that there is enough variety in human experience to sustain our sense of individuality in a locus as vast as New York, I strongly suspect that there is only *just* enough variety to do so. For were it in our power to gather up all the personal stories that have been experienced in different cities and townships around the world and across time, I haven't the slightest doubt that doppelgängers would abound. Men whose lives—despite the variation here and there—were just as our own in every material respect. Men who have loved when we loved, wept when we wept, accomplished what we have accomplished and failed as we have failed, men who have argued and reasoned and laughed exactly as we.

The professor looked around again.

—Impossible, you say?

Though no one had said a word.

—It is one of the most basic principles of infinity that it must, by definition, encompass not only one of everything, but everything's duplicate, as well as its triplicate. In fact, to imagine that there are additional versions of ourselves scattered across human history is substantially less outlandish than to imagine that there are none.

The professor turned his gaze back to Ulysses.

—So, do I think it is possible that your life could be an echo of the life of the Great Ulysses, and that after ten years you could be reunited with your wife and son? I am certain of it.

Ulysses had taken in what the professor had said with the greatest gravity. Now he stood, and the professor stood, and the two clasped hands, each seeming to have found an unexpected solace from the other. But when the two men let their hands drop and Ulysses turned, the professor took him by the arm and drew him back.

—But there is something you need to know, Mr. Ulysses. Something that I didn't put in Billy's book. In the midst of his travels, when the Great Ulysses visited the underworld and met the ghost of Tiresias, the old soothsayer told him that he was destined to wander the seas until he had appeased the gods through an act of tribute.

Had Woolly been in Ulysses's position, upon hearing this additional piece of news, he would have felt a great sense of defeat. But Ulysses didn't seem to. Instead, he nodded his head at the professor, as if this was just as it should be.

—What act of tribute?

—What Tiresias tells Ulysses is that he must take up an oar and carry it into the countryside until he has reached a land so unfamiliar with the ways of the sea that a man in the road will stop to ask: *What is that you carry upon your shoulder?* At that spot, the Great Ulysses was to plant the oar in the ground in Poseidon's honor, and thenceforth he would be free.

—An oar . . . , said Ulysses.

—Yes, said the professor excitedly, in the case of the Great Ulysses, an oar. But in your case, it would be something different. Something pertinent to *your* story, to your years of wandering. Something . . .

The professor began looking about.

—Something like that!

Bending over, Ulysses picked up the heavy piece of iron the professor had pointed to.

—A spike, he said.

—Yes, said the professor, a spike. You must carry that to the place where someone is so unfamiliar with the railways that they ask you what it is, and on that spot, you should hammer it into the ground.

—·—

When Woolly and Billy and Duchess were ready to leave, Professor Abernathe decided to stay behind in order to speak with Ulysses further. Then, just a few minutes after the three of them had gotten in the Cadillac, both Billy and Duchess had fallen asleep. So, as Woolly drove up the West Side Highway toward his sister's house, he had a moment to himself.

If Woolly were perfectly honest, most of the time he'd rather not have a moment to himself. Moments with other people, he found, were much more likely to be filled with laughter and surprises than moments with oneself. And moments with oneself were more likely to circle inward toward some thought that one didn't want to be having in the first place. But on this occasion, on this occasion that he found himself with a moment to himself, Woolly welcomed it.

Because it provided him with the opportunity to revisit the day. He began at FAO Schwarz, when he was standing in his favorite spot and his sister had suddenly appeared. Then it was across the street to the Plaza for old times' sake where they had tea with the panda and retold some of the grand old stories. Upon parting with his sister, finding it to be a lovely day, Woolly had walked all the way to Union Square so he could pay his respects to Abraham Lincoln. Then it was off to the circus, and over the Brooklyn Bridge, and up the Empire State Building where Professor Abernathe had bestowed upon Billy a book filled with blank pages in which to set down his adventures. Then Billy had taken them all to the overgrown elevated, where they had sat around the campfire and listened to the extraordinary exchange between Ulysses and the professor.

But after that, after all of the all of that, when it was finally time to go, and Ulysses had shaken Billy's hand and thanked him for his friendship, and Billy had wished Ulysses well on his quest to find his family, Billy had taken a pendant from around his neck.

—This, he said to Ulysses, is the medal of St. Christopher, the patron saint of travelers. It was given to me by Sister Agnes before our journey to New York, but I think that you should have it now.

And then, so that the medal could be hung around his neck, Ulysses knelt before Billy, just as the members of the Round Table had knelt before King Arthur in order to be knighted.

—When you put it, said Woolly to no one but himself, while wiping a tear from the corner of his eye, when you put it all together just like that, with the beginning at the beginning, the middle in the middle, and the end at the end, there is no denying that today was a one-of-a-kind kind of day.

THREE

—.—

Woolly

CORIANDER! SAID WOOLLY TO himself with enthusiasm.

For while Duchess was showing Billy how to *properly* stir a sauce, Woolly had set about alphabetizing the spice rack. And it didn't take long for him to discover just how many spices began with the letter C. In the entire rack there was only one that started with the letter *A*: Allspice, whatever that was. And Allspice was followed by just two spices that began with the letter *B*: Basil and Bay Leaves. But once Woolly moved on to spices that began with the letter *C*, well, it seemed there was no end to them! So far, there had been Cardamom, Cayenne, Chili Powder, Chives, Cinnamon, Cloves, Cumin, and now, Coriander.

It certainly made one wonder.

Perhaps, thought Woolly, perhaps it was like the matter of the *W*s at the beginning of questions. At some point in ancient times, the letter *C* must have seemed particularly suitable to the naming of spices.

Or maybe it was at some *place* in ancient times. Some place where the letter *C* had more sway over the alphabet. All of a sudden Woolly seemed to remember from one of his history classes that many moons ago there had been something called the Spice Route—a long and arduous trail along which tradesmen traveled in order to bring the spices of the East to the kitchens of the West. He even remembered a map with an arrow that arced across the Gobi Desert and over the Himalayas until it touched down safely in Venice, or some such spot.

That the C spices originated on the other side of the globe struck Woolly as a clear possibility, since he didn't even know what half of them tasted like. He knew Cinnamon, of course. In fact, it was one of his favorite flavors. Not only was it used in the making of apple and pumpkin pie, it was the *sine qua non* of the cinnamon bun. But Cardamom, Cumin, and Coriander? These mysterious words struck Woolly as having a distinctly oriental ring.

—Aha! said Woolly, when he discovered the bottle of Curry hiding behind the Rosemary in the second-to-last row of the rack.

For Curry was most certainly definitely a flavor from the East.

Making some space, Woolly tucked the Curry beside the Cumin. Then he turned his attention to the very last row, running his fingers along the labels of the Oregano and the Sage and the—

—What in the world are *you* doing there? Woolly wondered to himself.

But before he could answer his own question, Duchess was asking another.

—Where did he go?

Looking up from the spice rack, Woolly discovered Duchess in the doorway with his hands on his hips and Billy nowhere to be seen.

—I turn my back for one minute and he abandons his post.

It was true, thought Woolly. Billy had left the kitchen despite having been put in charge of stirring the sauce.

—He hasn't gone back to that goddamn clock, has he? asked Duchess.

—Let me investigate.

Quietly, Woolly headed down the hallway and peeked into the living room, where, in fact, Billy had returned to the grandfather clock.

Earlier that morning, when Billy had asked when Emmett would arrive, Duchess had replied with a great deal of confidence that he would be there in time for supper—which was to be served at eight o'clock on the dot. Normally, this would have prompted Billy to take an occasional glance at his army surplus watch, but the watch had been broken by Emmett on the freight train. So he really had no choice but to pay an occasional visit to the living room instead, where the hands on the grandfather clock now indicated, rather unambiguously, that it was 7:42.

Woolly was tiptoeing back toward the kitchen in order to explain this to Duchess when the telephone rang.

—The phone! Woolly exclaimed to himself. Maybe it's Emmett.

Making a quick detour into his brother-in-law's office, Woolly zipped around the desk and picked up the receiver on the very third ring.

—Hello, hello! he said with a smile.

For a moment Woolly's friendly greeting was met with silence. Then a question was posed in what could only be described as a sharply pointed voice.

—Who is this? the woman on the other end of the line wanted to know. Is that you, Wallace?

Woolly hung up.

For a moment he stared at the phone. Then plucking the receiver out of its cradle, he dropped it on the desk.

What Woolly loved about the game of telephone was that a phrase coming out at the end of the line could be so very different from the phrase that had first gone in. It could be more mysterious. Or surprising. Or amusing. But when someone like his sister Kaitlin spoke into an *actual* telephone, it did not come out even slightly more mysterious or surprising or amusing. It came out just as sharply pointed as it was at the start.

On the desktop the receiver began buzzing like a mosquito in a bedroom in the middle of the night. Woolly swept the phone into one of the drawers and closed it as best he could, what with the cord sticking out.

—Who was that? asked Duchess, when Woolly returned to the kitchen.

—A wrong number.

Billy, who also must have been hoping it had been Emmett, turned to Duchess with a worried look.

—It is almost eight o'clock, he said.

—Is it? said Duchess, in a manner suggesting that one hour was much like the next.

—How's the sauce coming? Woolly asked, in hopes of changing the subject.

Duchess held the stirring spoon out to Billy.

—Why don't you give it a try.

After a moment, Billy took the spoon and dipped it in the pot.

—It looks pretty hot, Woolly cautioned.

Billy nodded and blew carefully. When he put the spoon in his mouth, Woolly and Duchess leaned forward in unison, eager to hear the verdict. What they heard instead was the ding-dong of the doorbell.

The three looked at one another. Then Duchess and Billy were off like a shot, the former down the hallway and the latter through the dining-room door.

Woolly smiled for a moment at the sight of it. But then he had a worrisome thought: What if this was another instance of Schrödinger's Cat? What if the ringing of the bell initiated two different potential realities such that if the door were opened by Billy, it would be Emmett who was standing on the stoop, while were it opened by Duchess, it would be a door-to-door salesman? In a state of scientific uncertainty and heightened anxiety, Woolly hurried down the hall.

Duchess

W HEN THE NEW BOYS would arrive at St. Nick's, Sister Agnes would put them to work.

If we are asked to apply ourselves to that which is before us, she would say, *we are less likely to fret over that which is not.* So when they showed up on the doorstep looking a little shell-shocked, a little shy, and generally on the verge of tears, she would send them to the dining room to put out the silverware for lunch. Once the tables were set, she'd send them to the chapel to lay out the hymnals in the pews. Once the hymnals were in place, there were towels to be collected, sheets to be folded, and leaves to be raked—until the new boys weren't the new boys anymore.

And that's what I did with the kid.

Why? Because breakfast wasn't even over before he was asking when his brother would arrive.

Personally, I didn't expect Emmett to show up before noon. Knowing Charity, I figured he would've had his hands full until two in the morning. Assuming he slept until eleven and lingered under the covers, he might make it to Hastings-on-Hudson by two in the afternoon. At the earliest. To be on the safe side, I told Billy he'd be here for dinner.

—What time is dinner?

—Eight o'clock.

—Eight o'clock on the dot? asked Woolly.

—On the dot, I confirmed.

Nodding, Billy excused himself politely, paid a visit to the clock in the living room, and returned with the news that it was 10:02.

The implication was plain enough. There were 598 minutes between now and his brother's promised arrival, and Billy intended to count every one of them. So as soon as Woolly started clearing the breakfast dishes, I asked Billy if he'd give me a hand.

First, I brought him to the linen closet, where we picked out a fine tablecloth and spread it across the dining-room table, taking care to ensure that it draped over the ends in equal measure. At the four places, we laid out linen napkins, each with a different flower embroidered on it. When we turned our attention to the hutch and Billy observed it was locked, I observed that keys were rarely far from their escutcheons, and reached my hand into the tureen.

—Voilà.

With the hutch's doors open, out came the fine china plates for the appetizer, main course, and dessert. Out came the crystal for the water and wine. Out came the two candelabra and the flat black case that held the family silver.

Having instructed Billy how to lay out the cutlery, I figured I'd have to tighten up his work once he was finished. But when it came to setting places, it turned out Billy was a natural. It looked like he had positioned each fork, knife, and spoon with his ruler and compass.

As we stood back to admire our work, he asked if tonight was going to be a special dinner.

—Exactly.

—Why is it a special dinner, Duchess?

—Because it's a reunion, Billy. A reunion of the Four Musketeers.

The kid broke out in a big smile over that one, but then his brow furrowed. With Billy Watson there was never more than a minute between the smile and the furrow.

—If it's a special dinner, what are we going to eat?

THE LINCOLN HIGHWAY | 435

—An excellent question. At the request of one Woolly Martin, we are going to have a little something known as *Fettuccine Mio Amore*. And that, my friend, is as special as it gets.

After getting Billy to write out a shopping list of all the ingredients we would need, we were off to Arthur Avenue, driving at a speed of three hundred questions an hour.

—What's Arthur Avenue, Duchess?

—It's the main drag in the Italian section of the Bronx, Billy.

—What's an Italian section?

—It's where all the Italians live.

—Why do all the Italians live in one place?

—So they can mind each other's business.

What's a trattoria, Duchess?

What's a paisano?

What's an artichoke and pancetta and cannoli?

When we returned a few hours later, it was too early to start cooking, so having confirmed that Billy's mathematics were up to snuff, I took him into Woolly's brother-in-law's office to do a little accounting.

Seating him at the desk with a pad and pencil, I lay down on the rug and rattled off all the expenses that Woolly and I had racked up since leaving St. Nick's. The six tanks of gas; the room and board at two Howard Johnson's; the beds and towels at the Sunshine Hotel; and the two meals at the diner on Second Avenue. To be on the safe side, I had him add an extra twenty for future outlays, then tally the whole list under the heading of Operational Expenses. Once we recovered Woolly's trust from the Adirondacks, these costs were to be reimbursed to Emmett before a single dollar was divvied.

In a separate column under the heading of Personal Expenses, I had Billy include the long-distance call to Salina; the ten bucks for Bernie at the Sunshine Hotel; the bottle of whiskey for Fitzy; the champagne and companionship at Ma Belle's; and the tip for the doorman at the Empire State Building. Since none of these outlays were essential to our shared endeavor, I figured they should come out of my end.

At the last second, I remembered the expenditures on Arthur Avenue. You could argue that they belonged under the Operational Expenses since we'd all be eating them together. But with an ah-what-the-hell, I told Billy to put them in my column. Tonight, dinner was on me.

Once Billy had all the numbers down and he'd double-checked his sums, I encouraged him to take out a fresh sheet of paper and transcribe the two tallies. At a suggestion like that, most kids would have wanted to know why after doing the job once, they had to do it all over again. But not Billy. With his instinctive preference for the neat and tidy, he took out a new piece of paper and began duplicating his work with the same precision that he had laid out the forks and knives.

When he was finished, Billy nodded his head three times, giving the tally his patented seal of approval. But then his brow furrowed.

—Shouldn't it have a title, Duchess?

—What did you have in mind?

Billy thought about it for a second while biting the end of his pencil. Then after writing it out in big capital letters, he read:

—The Escapade.

Now, how do you like that?

When the expense report was finished, it was after six o'clock—time to start cooking. After laying out the ingredients, I taught Billy everything that Lou, the chef at Leonello's, had taught to me. First, how to make a basic tomato sauce from canned tomatoes and a soffritto (*What's a soffritto, Duchess?*). Once that was on the stove, I showed him how to properly dice the bacon and properly slice the onion. Taking out a saucepan, I showed him how to properly sauté them together with the bay leaves. How to simmer them in white wine with oregano and pepper flakes. And finally, how to stir in one cup of the tomato sauce, and not a teaspoon more.

—The important thing now, I explained, is to keep an eye on it, Billy. I've got to go to the washroom, so I want you to stand right where you are and occasionally give it a stir. All right?

—All right, Duchess.

Handing Billy the spoon, I excused myself and headed for Dennis's office.

Having said that I didn't think Emmett would be here by two, I'd thought for sure that he'd be here by six. After quietly closing the door, I dialed Ma Belle. It took her twenty rings to answer, but after giving me an earful about the etiquette of calling someone while they're in the middle of their bath, she brought me up to speed.

—Uh oh, I said as I hung up the phone.

Having done one accounting with Billy, I found myself doing another on my own: With Emmett already a little peeved about the Studebaker, I had hoped to make it up to him by giving him the night with Charity; but clearly that hadn't gone as planned. How was I supposed to know that Woolly's medicine was so strong? Then to top it all off, I'd forgotten to leave an address. Yep, I thought to myself, there is a distinct possibility that when Emmett arrives, he'll be in a bad mood. Assuming, that is, that he can find us . . .

Returning to the kitchen, I discovered Woolly staring at the spice rack and no one tending the sauce. That's when things began to accelerate.

First, Woolly went off on reconnaissance.

Then the telephone rang and Billy reappeared.

Then Woolly returned with word of a wrong number, Billy announced it was nearly eight, and the doorbell rang.

Please, oh please, oh please, I said to myself as I dashed down the hall. With my heart in my mouth and Billy hot on my heels, I swung the door open—and there was Emmett in a clean set of clothes, looking only a little worse for wear.

Before anyone had a chance to speak, the clock in the living room began to chime the hour of eight.

Turning to Billy, I stuck out my arms and said:

—What'd I tell you, kid?

Emmett

AT THE START OF Emmett's junior year, the new math teacher, Mr. Nickerson, had presented Zeno's paradox. In ancient Greece, he'd said, a philosopher named Zeno argued that to get from point A to point B, one had to go halfway there first. But to get from the halfway mark to point B, one would have to cross half of that distance, then halfway again, and so on. And when you piled up all the halves of halves that would have to be crossed to get from one point to another, the only conclusion to be drawn was that it couldn't be done.

Mr. Nickerson had said this was a perfect example of paradoxical reasoning. Emmett had thought it a perfect example of why going to school could be a waste of time.

Just imagine, thought Emmett, all the mental energy that had been expended not only to formulate this paradox, but to pass it down through the ages, translating it from language to language so that it could be scratched on a chalkboard in the United States of America in 1952—five years after Chuck Yeager broke the sound barrier over the Mojave Desert.

Mr. Nickerson must have noticed Emmett's expression at the back of the classroom, because when the bell rang, he asked Emmett to stay.

—I just want to make sure you followed the argument this morning.

—I followed it, said Emmett.

—And what did you think?

Emmett looked out the window for a moment, unsure of whether he should share his point of view.

—Go ahead, encouraged Mr. Nickerson. I want to hear your take.

All right then, thought Emmett.

—It seemed to me a long and complicated way of proving something that my six-year-old brother could disprove in a matter of seconds with his own two feet.

But as Emmett said this, Mr. Nickerson didn't seem the least put out. Rather, he nodded his head with enthusiasm, as if Emmett was on the verge of making a discovery as important as Zeno's.

—What you're saying, Emmett, if I understand you, is that Zeno appears to have pursued his proof for argument's sake rather than for its practical value. And you're not alone in making that observation. In fact, we have a word for the practice, which is almost as old as Zeno: *Sophistry*. From the Greek *sophistes*—those teachers of philosophy and rhetoric who gave their students the skills to make arguments that could be clever or persuasive but which weren't necessarily grounded in reality.

Mr. Nickerson even wrote the word out on the chalkboard right below his diagram of the infinitely bisected journey from A to B.

Isn't that just perfect, thought Emmett. In addition to handing down the lessons of Zeno, scholars have handed down a specialized word, the sole purpose of which is to identify the practice of teaching nonsense as sense.

At least that's what Emmett had thought while standing in Mr. Nickerson's classroom. What he was thinking as he walked along a winding, tree-lined street in the town of Hastings-on-Hudson was maybe Zeno hadn't been so crazy after all.

—·—

That morning, Emmett had come to consciousness with a sensation of floating—like one who's being carried down a wide river on a warm summer day. Opening his eyes, he found himself under the covers of an unfamiliar bed. On the side table was a lamp with a red shade that cast the room in a rosy hue. But neither the bed nor the lamplight was soft enough to mollify the ache in his head.

Emitting a groan, Emmett made an effort to raise himself, but from across the room came the patter of bare feet, then a hand that gently pressed against his chest.

—You just lie there and be quiet.

Though she was now wearing a simple white blouse and her hair was pulled back, Emmett recognized his nurse as the young woman in the negligee who, the night before, had been lying where he was lying now.

Turning toward the hallway, Charity called out, *he's awake*, and a moment later Ma Belle, dressed in a giant floral housedress, was standing in the doorway.

—So he is, she said.

Emmett hoisted himself up again, this time with more success. But as he did so, the covers fell from his chest and he realized with a start that he was naked.

—My clothes, he said.

—You think I'd let them put you in one of my beds while dressed in those filthy things, said Ma Belle.

—Where are they . . . ?

—Waiting for you right there on the bureau. Now, why don't you get yourself out of bed and come have something to eat.

Ma Belle turned to Charity.

—Come on, honey. Your vigil here has ended.

When the two women closed the door, Emmett threw back the covers and rose carefully, feeling a little uneasy on his feet. Crossing to the bureau he was surprised to find his clothes freshly laundered and neatly folded in a pile, his belt coiled on top. As Emmett buttoned his shirt, he found himself staring at the painting he had noticed the night before. Only now he could see that the mast was at an angle not because the ship was leaning into a high wind, but because it was foundering against the rocks with some sailors hanging from the rigging, others scrambling into a dory, and the head of one bobbing in the high white wake on the verge of being either dashed upon the rocks or swept out to sea.

As Duchess never tired of saying: *Exactly*.

When Emmett exited the bedroom, he made a point of turning to his left without looking down the vertiginous succession of doors. In the lounge, he found Ma Belle in a high-back chair with Charity standing at her side. On the coffee table were a breakfast cake and coffee.

Dropping onto the couch, Emmett ran a hand over his eyes.

Ma Belle pointed to a pink rubber bag on a plate beside the coffee pot.

—There's an ice pack, if you're partial to them.

—No thanks.

Ma Belle nodded.

—I never understood the attraction myself. After a big night, I wouldn't want a bag of ice anywhere near me.

A big night, thought Emmett with a shake of the head.

—What happened?

—They gave you a mickey, said Charity with a mischievous smile.

Ma Belle scowled.

—It wasn't a mickey, Charity. And there was no *they*. It was just Duchess being Duchess.

—Duchess? said Emmett.

Ma Belle gestured at Charity.

—He wanted to give you a little present. In honor of finishing your time at that work farm. But he was worried you might get a case of the jitters—what with your being a Christian and a virgin.

—There's nothing wrong with being a Christian or a virgin, Charity said supportively.

—Well, I'm not so sure about that, said Ma Belle. Anyway, in order to set the mood, I was supposed to suggest a toast and Duchess was going to put a little something in your drink to help you relax. But the little something must have been stronger than he thought it was, because once we got you into Charity's room, you spun around twice and out went the lights. Isn't that right, honey?

—It's a good thing you landed in my lap, she said with a wink.

Both of them seemed to find this an amusing turn of events. It just made Emmett grind his teeth.

—Oh, don't get all angry on us now, said Ma Belle.

—If I'm angry, it's not with you.

—Well, don't get angry with Duchess either.

—He didn't mean no harm, said Charity. He just wanted you to have a good time.

—That's a fact, said Ma Belle. And at his own expense.

Emmett didn't bother pointing out that the intended good time, like the champagne the night before, had been paid for with his money.

—Even as a boy, said Charity, Duchess was always making sure that everybody else was having a good time.

—Anyway, continued Ma Belle, we're supposed to tell you that Duchess, your brother, and that other friend . . .

—Woolly, said Charity.

—Right, said Ma Belle. Woolly. They'll all be waiting for you at his sister's house. But first, you should have something to eat.

Emmett ran a hand over his eyes again.

—I'm not sure I'm hungry, he said.

Ma Belle frowned.

Leaning forward, Charity spoke a little under her breath.

—Ma Belle doesn't generally serve breakfast.

—You're damn right, I don't.

After accepting a cup of the coffee and a slice of the coffee cake in order to be polite, Emmett was reminded that half the time, manners are there for your own good. For as it turned out, the coffee and cake were just what he needed. So much so that he readily accepted the offer of seconds.

As he ate, Emmett asked how the ladies had come to know Duchess when he was a boy.

—His father worked here, said Charity.

—I thought he was an actor.

—He was an actor all right, said Ma Belle. And when he couldn't get any work onstage, he acted like a waiter or a maître d'. But for a few months after the war, he acted like our ringmaster. Harry could act like just about anything, I suppose. But most of the time, he acted like his own worst enemy.

—In what way?

—Harry's a charmer with a soft spot for the sauce. So while he could talk his way into a job in a matter of minutes, he could drink his way back out of it almost as quickly.

—But when he was working at the Circus, chipped in Charity, he would leave Duchess with us.

—He'd bring Duchess here? asked Emmett, a little shocked.

—That's right, said Ma Belle. At the time, he was probably about eleven years old. And while his father was downstairs, he'd work up here in the lounge. Taking hats and pouring drinks for the customers. He made good money too. Not that his father let him keep it.

Emmett looked around the room, trying to imagine Duchess at the age of eleven taking hats and pouring drinks in a house of ill repute.

—It wasn't like it is now, Ma Belle said, following his gaze. Back then on a Saturday night, the Circus was standing-room-only and we had ten girls working up here. And it wasn't just the boys from the Navy Yard. We had *society* people.

—Even the mayor came, Charity said.

—What happened?

Ma Belle shrugged.

—Times changed. The neighborhood changed. Tastes changed.

Then she looked around the room a little nostalgically.

—I thought it was the war that was going to put us out of business; but in the end, it was the suburbs.

Shortly before noon, Emmett was ready to take his leave. Receiving a peck on the cheek from Charity and a shake of the hand from Ma Belle, he thanked them for the clean clothes, for the breakfast, for their kindness.

—If you could just give me the address, I'll be on my way.

Ma Belle looked at Emmett.

—What address?

—The one for Woolly's sister.

—Why would I have that?

—Didn't Duchess leave it with you?

—He didn't leave it with me. How 'bout you, honey?

When Charity shook her head, Emmett closed his eyes.

—Why don't we check the phone directory, Charity suggested brightly.

Charity and Ma Belle both looked to Emmett.

—I don't know her married name.

—Well, I guess you're shit-out-of-luck.

—Ma, chided Charity.

—All right, all right. Let me think.

Ma Belle looked off for a moment.

—This friend of yours—Woolly. What's his story?

—He's from New York. . . .

—So we gathered. But what borough?

Emmett looked back without understanding.

—What *neighborhood*. Brooklyn? Queens? Manhattan?

—Manhattan.

—That's a start. Do you know where he went to school?

—He went to boarding school. St. George's . . . St. Paul's . . . St. Mark's . . .

—He's Catholic! said Charity.

Ma Belle rolled her eyes.

—Those aren't Catholic schools, honey. Those are WASP schools. Fancy ones at that. And having known more than my share of their alumni, I'd bet you a blue blazer that your friend Woolly is from the Upper East Side. But which one did he go to: St. George's, St. Paul's, or St. Mark's?

—All of them.

—All of them?

When Emmett explained that Woolly had been kicked out of two, Ma Belle shook with laughter.

—Ho, boy, she said at last. If you get thrown out of one of those schools, to get into another you need to come from a pretty old family. But to get thrown out of two and go to a third? You need to have arrived on the *Mayflower*! So what's this Woolly character's *real* name?

—Wallace Wolcott Martin.

—Of course, it is. Charity, why don't you go in my office and bring me the black book that's in my desk drawer.

When Charity returned from the room behind the piano, Emmett was expecting her to have a little address book. Instead, she was carrying a large black volume with a dark red title.

—The *Social Register*, explained Ma Belle. This is where everybody's listed.

—Everybody? asked Emmett.

—Not my everybody. When it comes to the *Social Register*, I've been on it, under it, behind and in front of it, but I've never been in it.

Because it was designed to list the *other* everybody. Here. Make room, Gary Cooper.

When Ma Belle dropped onto the couch at Emmett's side, he could feel the cushions sink a few inches closer to the floor. Glancing at the cover of the book, Emmett couldn't help but notice it was the 1951 edition.

—It's out of date, he said.

Ma Belle gave him a frown.

—You think it's easy to get ahold of one of these?

—He doesn't know, said Charity.

—No, I suppose not. Listen, if you were looking for some Polish or Italian friend whose grandparents landed on Ellis Island, then, first of all, there wouldn't be no book in which to look. But even if there was a book, the problem would be that those sort change their names and addresses like they change their clothes. That's why they came to America in the first place. To get out of the rut their ancestors put them in.

With a show of reverence, Ma Belle laid her hand on the book in her lap.

—But with this crowd, nothing ever changes. Not the names. Not the addresses. Not a single damn thing. And that's the whole point of who *they* are.

It took Ma Belle five minutes to find what she was looking for. As a young man, Woolly didn't have his own entry in the registry, but he was listed as one of the three children of Mrs. Richard Cobb, née Wolcott; widow of Thomas Martin; member of the Colony Club and the DAR; formerly of Manhattan, currently of Palm Beach. Her two daughters, Kaitlin and Sarah, were both married and listed with their husbands: Mr. & Mrs. Lewis Wilcox of Morristown, New Jersey, and Mr. & Mrs. Dennis Whitney of Hastings-on-Hudson, New York.

Duchess hadn't said which sister they were staying with.

—Either way, said Ma Belle, you've got to go back to Manhattan to catch the train. If I were you, I'd start with Sarah, since Hastings-on-Hudson is the shorter ride.

—.—

When Emmett left Ma Belle's, it was already half past twelve. In the interest of saving time, he hailed a cab, but when he instructed the driver to take him to the train station in Manhattan, the driver asked which one.

—There's more than one train station in Manhattan?

—There's two, pal: Penn Station and Grand Central. Which do you want?

—Which one is bigger?

—Both is bigger than the other.

Emmett had never heard of Grand Central, but he remembered the panhandler in Lewis saying that the Pennsylvania Railroad was the largest in the nation.

—Penn Station, he said.

When Emmett arrived, he figured he had chosen well because the façade of the station had marble columns that towered four stories over the avenue, and the interior was a vast expanse under a soaring glass ceiling with legions of travelers. But when he found the information booth, Emmett learned that there were no trains to Hastings-on-Hudson leaving from Penn. Those were on the Hudson River Line out of Grand Central. So instead of going to Sarah's house, Emmett boarded the 1:55 for Morristown, New Jersey.

When he arrived at the address that Ma Belle had given him, he asked the cabbie to wait while he went to knock on the door. The woman who answered said that yes, she was Kaitlin Wilcox, in a reasonably friendly manner. But as soon as Emmett asked whether her brother, Woolly, happened to be there, she grew almost angry.

—Suddenly, everyone wants to know if my brother is here. But why would he be? What's this all about? Are you in league with that girl? What are you two up to? Who are you?

As he made his way quickly toward the cab, Emmett could hear her shouting from the front door, demanding once more to know who he was.

So it was back to the Morristown depot, where Emmett took the 4:20 to Penn Station, then a cab to Grand Central, which, as it turned out, had its own marble columns, its own soaring ceiling, its own legions of travelers. There, he waited half an hour to board the 6:14 for Hastings-on-Hudson.

When Emmett arrived shortly after 7:00, he climbed into his fourth taxi of the day. But ten minutes into the ride, he saw the meter advance a nickel to $1.95, and it occurred to him that he might not have enough money for the fare. Opening his wallet, he confirmed that the various trains and taxis had left him with only two dollars.

—Can you pull over? he asked.

With a quizzical glance in the mirror, the cabbie pulled onto the shoulder of a tree-lined road. Holding up his wallet, Emmett explained that all he had left was what the meter was showing.

—If you're out of money, then you're out of the cab.

Nodding in understanding, Emmett handed the cabbie the two dollars, thanked him for the ride, and got out. Fortunately, before pulling away, the cabbie had the graciousness to roll down the passenger window and give Emmett directions: *About two miles up take a right onto Forest; another mile after that take a left onto Steeplechase Road.* When the cab pulled away, Emmett began to walk, his mind taken up with the scourge of infinitely bisected journeys.

America is three thousand miles wide, he thought to himself. Five days before, he and Billy had set out with the intention of driving fifteen hundred miles west to California. Instead, they had traveled fifteen hundred miles east to New York. Having arrived, Emmett had crisscrossed the city from Times Square to lower Manhattan and back. To Brooklyn and Harlem. And when, at long last, it seemed his destination was within reach, Emmett had taken three trains, four taxis, and now was on foot.

He could just imagine how Mr. Nickerson would have diagrammed it: with San Francisco on the left side of the chalkboard, Emmett's zigzagging progression on the right, and every leg of his journey growing shorter than the last. Only, the paradox that Emmett had to contend with wasn't Zeno's. It was the fast-talking, liberty-taking, plan-upending paradox known as Duchess.

But as exasperating as this was, Emmett understood that having to spend his afternoon shuttling back and forth was probably for the best. Because when he had walked out of Ma Belle's earlier that day burning with frustration, had Duchess been standing in the street, Emmett would have pounded him into the ground.

Instead, the train rides and taxi rides and this three-mile walk had given him the time not only to revisit all the causes for fury—the Studebaker, the envelope, the mickey—but the causes for temperance too. Like the promises he had made to Billy and Sister Agnes. And the advocacy of Ma Belle and Charity. But most of all, what gave Emmett pause, and called for some sense of measure, was the story that Fitzy FitzWilliams had told him over glasses of whiskey in that dead-end bar.

For almost a decade, Emmett had quietly nursed a sense of condemnation toward his father's follies—the single-minded commitment to an agrarian dream, the unwillingness to ask for help, and the starry-eyed idealism that sustained him, even as it cost him his farm and his wife. But for all his shortcomings, Charlie Watson had never come close to betraying Emmett in the manner that Harry Hewett had betrayed Duchess.

And for what?

A trinket.

A bauble stripped from the body of a clown.

The irony hidden in the old performer's story wasn't lost on Emmett for a second. It announced itself loud and clear—as a rebuke. For of all the boys whom Emmett had known at Salina, he would have ranked Duchess as one of the most likely to bend the rules or the truth in the service of his own convenience. But in the end, Duchess was the one who had been innocent. He was the one who had been sent to Salina having done nothing at all. While Townhouse and Woolly had stolen cars. And he, Emmett Watson, had ended another man's life.

What right did he have to demand of Duchess that he atone for his sins? What right did he have to demand it of anyone?

Within seconds of ringing the Whitneys' bell, Emmett could hear the sound of running inside. Then the door swung open.

At some level, Emmett must have been expecting Duchess to appear contrite, because he felt a sharp stab of annoyance to find him standing there smiling, looking almost victorious as he turned to Billy and extended his arms—just as he had in the doorway of the Watsons' barn—in order to say:

—What'd I tell you, kid?

With a big smile, Billy stepped around Duchess in order to give Emmett a hug. Then he began to gush.

—You're not going to believe what happened, Emmett! After we left the circus—while you were with your friends—Duchess drove us to the Empire State Building so that we could find Professor Abernathe's office. We rode the express elevator all the way to the fifty-fifth floor and not only did we find his office, we found Professor Abernathe! And he gave me one of his notebooks in case I ran out of blank pages. And when I told him about Ulysses—

—Hold on, said Emmett, smiling in spite of himself. I want to hear all about it, Billy. I really do. But first, I need to talk to Duchess alone for just a minute. Okay?

—Okay, Emmett, said Billy, sounding a little unsure of the idea.

—Why don't you come with me, said Woolly to Billy. I wanted to show you something anyway!

Emmett watched as Billy and Woolly climbed the stairs. Only when they had disappeared down the hall did he turn to face Duchess.

Emmett could see that Duchess had something to say. He had all the telltale signs: his weight on the balls of his feet, his hands ready to gesture, his expression eager and earnest. But he wasn't simply getting ready to speak. He was going to launch himself heart and soul into another explanation.

So before he could say a word, Emmett grabbed him by the collar and drew back his fist.

Woolly

IT WAS QUITE TRUE that in Woolly's experience, when somebody said they wanted to speak to someone else in private, it could be difficult to know what to do with yourself. But when Emmett asked to speak to Duchess, Woolly knew exactly what to do. In fact, he had been thinking about it ever since 7:42.

—Why don't you come with me, he said to Billy. I wanted to show you something anyway!

Leading Billy upstairs, Woolly took him to the bedroom that was and wasn't his.

—Come in, come in, he said.

When Billy stepped inside, Woolly closed the door—leaving it a few inches ajar so that they wouldn't be able to hear what Emmett had to say to Duchess, but they would be able to hear when Emmett was ready to call them back.

—Whose room is this?

—Once upon a time it was mine, said Woolly with a smile. But I gave it up so that the baby can be closer to my sister.

—And now you have the room by the back staircase.

—Which is much more sensible, said Woolly, what with all my comings and goings.

—I like the blue, Billy said. It's like the color of Emmett's car.

—That's just what I thought!

Once they had appreciated the hue of the blue, Woolly turned his attention to the covered pile in the middle of the room. Throwing back the tarp, he located the box he was looking for, opened the top, set aside the tennis trophy, and took out the cigar box.

—Here we go, he said.

Then since the bed was covered with Woolly's belongings, he and Billy sat on the floor.

—Is that a collection? Billy asked.

—It is, said Woolly. Though not like your silver dollars, or your bottle caps back in Nebraska. Because it's not a collection of different versions of the same thing. It's a collection of the same version of different things.

Opening the lid, Woolly tilted the box toward Billy.

—See? These are the sorts of things that one rarely uses, but that one should set safely aside so that one knows exactly where to find them when they're suddenly in need. For instance, this is where I keep my father's shirt studs and cuff links should I suddenly have to wear a tuxedo. And those are some French francs, should I happen to go to France. And that's the biggest piece of sea glass that I have ever found. But here . . .

Gently pushing aside his father's old wallet, Woolly removed a wristwatch from the bottom of the box and handed it to Billy.

—The dial is black, said Billy in surprise.

Woolly nodded.

—And the numbers are white. The very opposite of what you'd expect. It's called an officer's watch. They made them this way so that when an officer needed to look at the time on the field of battle, enemy snipers wouldn't be able to aim for the white of his dial.

—Was it your father's?

—No, said Woolly with a shake of the head. It was my grandfather's. He wore it in France during the First World War. But then he gave it to my mother's brother, Wallace. And then Uncle Wallace gave it to me as a Christmas present when I was younger than you. He's the Wallace that I was named after.

—Your name is Wallace, Woolly?

—Oh yes. Very much so.

—Is that why they call you Woolly? So that people won't get you and your uncle confused when you're together?

—No, said Woolly. Uncle Wallace died years ago. In a war, just like my father. Only, it wasn't in one of the world wars. It was in the Spanish Civil War.

—Why did your uncle fight in the Spanish Civil War?

Quickly wiping away a tear, Woolly shook his head.

—I'm not sure, Billy. My sister says that he had done so many things that were expected of him, he wanted to do one thing that no one expected at all.

They both looked at the watch, which Billy was holding gently in his hand.

—You see, said Woolly, it has a second hand too. Only, instead of it being a big second hand going around the big dial like the one on your watch, it's a tiny little second hand going around its own little dial. Seconds are very important to keep track of in wars, I should think.

—Yes, said Billy, I should think so too.

Then Billy held the watch out in order to return it.

—No, no, said Woolly. It's for you. I took it out of the box because I want you to have it.

Shaking his head, Billy said that such a watch was far too precious to be given away.

—But that's not so, countered Woolly excitedly. It's not a watch that's too precious to be given away. It's a watch that's too precious for keeping. It was handed down from my grandfather to my uncle, who handed it down to me. Now I am handing it down to you. And one day—many years from now—you can hand it down to someone else.

Perhaps Woolly hadn't put his point to perfection, but Billy seemed to understand. So Woolly told him to wind it up! But first, he explained the watch's only quirk—that once a day it should be wound *exactly* fourteen times.

—If you wind it only twelve times, said Woolly, by the end of the day, it will be running five minutes slow. Whereas, if you wind it sixteen times, it will be running five minutes fast. But if you wind it exactly fourteen times, then it will keep the time exactly.

After taking this in, Billy wound the watch exactly fourteen times while quietly counting to himself.

What Woolly did not tell Billy was that sometimes—like when he first arrived at St. Paul's—he would wind the watch sixteen times for six days in a row on porpoise so that he could be half an hour ahead of everybody else. While other times, he would wind it twelve times for six days in a row so that he could be half an hour behind. Either way—whether he wound it sixteen times or wound it twelve—it was a little like when Alice stepped through the looking glass, or the Pevensies through the wardrobe, only to find themselves in a world that was and wasn't theirs.

—Go ahead and put it on, said Woolly.

—You mean I can wear it now?

—Of course, said Woolly. Of course, of course, of course. That's the whole point!

So, without any help, Billy strapped it on his wrist.

—Doesn't that look fine, said Woolly.

And having said so, Woolly would have repeated himself for emphasis, but for the fact that from somewhere downstairs suddenly came a sound that was very much like a gunshot. Exchanging wide-eyed glances, Woolly and Billy leapt to their feet and dashed out the door.

Duchess

MMETT WAS IN A bad mood all right. He was trying to hide it because that's the kind of guy he is. But I could tell just the same. Especially when he cut Billy off in the middle of his story, saying he wanted to speak to me alone.

Hell, if I were him, I'd want to speak to me alone too.

Another one of Sister Agnes's favorite sayings was *the wise man tattles on himself.* Her point, of course, was that if you did something wrong—whether it was behind the maintenance shed or in the dead of night—she was going to find out. After assembling the clues, she was going to puzzle it out from the comfort of her armchair like Sherlock Holmes. Or she'd discern it from your manner. Or hear it straight from the mouth of God. Whatever the source, she would come to know of your transgressions, of that there was no doubt. So in the interests of saving time, it was best to tattle on yourself. To admit you've overstepped, express contrition, and promise to make amends—ideally, before anyone else could get a word in edgewise. So the second Emmett and I were alone, I was ready.

As it turned out, Emmett had a different idea. An even better one. Because before I could get a word out of my mouth, he had grabbed me by the collar in order to lay one on me. I closed my eyes and waited for redemption.

But nothing happened.

Peeking out of my right eye, I saw that he was grinding his teeth, struggling with his own instincts.

—Go ahead, I told him. You'll feel better. I'll feel better!

But even as I tried to give him encouragement, I could feel the slackening in his grip. Then he shoved me back a foot or two. So I ended up getting to give my apology, after all.

—I am so sorry, I said.

Then, without taking a breath, I began ticking my missteps off on my fingers.

—I borrowed the Studebaker without asking; I stranded you in Lewis; I misjudged your interest in the Caddy; and on top of all that, I screwed up your night at Ma Belle's. What can I say? I showed poor judgment. But I'm going to make it up to you.

Emmett raised both hands in the air.

—I don't want you to make anything up to me, Duchess. I accept your apology. I just don't want to talk about it anymore.

—All right, I said. I appreciate your willingness to put this chapter behind us. But first things first . . .

Producing his envelope from my back pocket, I returned it with a touch of ceremony. He was visibly relieved to have it in hand. He may even have let out a sigh. But at the same time, I could tell he was weighing the contents.

—It's not all there, I admitted. But I've got something else for you.

From another pocket, I produced the accounting.

Emmett seemed a little perplexed when he took the paper in hand, but even more so once he'd had a look.

—Is this Billy's handwriting?

—It sure is. I'm telling you, Emmett, that kid's got a head for figures.

I stepped to Emmett's side and gestured loosely at the columns.

—It's all there. The necessary expenses like the gas and hotels, which will be reimbursed to you off the top. Then there's the more discretionary expenses, which will come out of my end—just as soon as we get to the Adirondacks.

Emmett looked up from the sheet with a hint of disbelief.

—Duchess, how many times do I have to tell you that I am not going to the Adirondacks. As soon as the Studebaker's ready, Billy and I are heading for California.

—I get it, I said. Since Billy wants to be there by the Fourth of July, it makes sense to get a move on. But you said your car won't be ready until Monday, right? And you must be starving. So tonight, let's have a nice meal, just the four of us. Then tomorrow, Woolly and I will take the Caddy to the camp and pick up the dough. We've got to make a quick stop in Syracuse to see my old man, but then we'll hit the highway. We shouldn't be more than a few days behind you.

—Duchess . . . , said Emmett, with a woeful shake of the head.

He even looked a little defeated, which was out of character for such a can-do guy. Obviously, something about the plan didn't sit right with him. Or maybe there was some new complication I didn't know about. Before I got the chance to ask, we heard a small explosion coming from the street. Turning slowly, Emmett stared at the front door for a moment. Then he closed his eyes.

Sally

I F I WERE BLESSED one day to have a child, I would no sooner raise her to be an Episcopalian than I would to be a Catholic. The Episcopalians may be Protestant by designation, but you wouldn't know it from their services—what with all the vestments and English hymns. I guess they like to call it high church. I call it high and mighty.

But one thing you can count on from the Episcopal Church is that they'll keep their records straight. They're almost as insistent upon it as the Mormons. So, when Emmett didn't call as promised on Friday at 2:30, he left me little choice but to contact Father Colmore over at St. Luke's.

Once I got him on the line, I explained that I was trying to track down a member of the congregation of an Episcopal church in Manhattan, and did he have any ideas on how I might go about doing so. Without a second thought, he told me I should contact Reverend Hamilton Speers, the Rector of St. Bartholomew's. He even gave me the number.

This St. Bartholomew's must be some kind of church, I'll tell you that. Because when I called, instead of getting Reverend Speers, I reached a receptionist who asked me to hold (despite the fact it was a long-distance call); then she patched me through to an assistant rector, who, in turn, wanted to know why I needed to speak to the reverend. I explained that I was distantly related to a family in his congregation, that my father had died in the night, and while I needed to alert my

New York cousins to his passing, for the life of me I could not find my father's address book.

Now, in the strictest sense, this was not an honest claim. But while the Christian religion generally frowns upon the drinking of spirits, a sip of red wine is not only countenanced, it plays an essential role in the sacrament. And I figure that while the church generally frowns upon prevarication, a little white lying can be as Christian as the sip of Sunday wine, if performed in the service of the Lord.

What was the name of the family? The assistant wanted to know.

When I replied it was the family of Woolly Martin, he asked me to hold again. A few nickels later, Reverend Speers was on the line. First, he wanted to express his deepest sympathies for my loss, and his wishes that my father rest in peace. He went on to explain that Woolly's family, the Wolcotts, had been members of the St. Bartholomew's congregation since its founding in 1854, and that he had personally married four of them and baptized ten. No doubt he had buried a good deal more.

In a matter of minutes, I had the phone numbers and addresses of Woolly's mother, who was in Florida, and the two sisters, who were both married and living in the New York area. I tried the one called Kaitlin first.

The Wolcotts may have been members of St. Bartholomew's since its founding in 1854, but Kaitlin Wolcott Wilcox must not have paid much attention to the lessons. For when I said that I was trying to find her brother, she became wary. And when I said I'd heard he might be staying with her, she became outright unfriendly.

—My brother is in Kansas, she said. Why would he be here? Who told you that he would be here? Who is this?

And so forth.

Next I dialed Sarah. This time the phone rang and rang and rang.

When I finally hung up, I sat there for a moment, drumming my fingers on my father's desk.

In my father's office.

Under my father's roof.

Going into the kitchen, I retrieved my purse, counted out five dollars, and left them by the phone in order to cover the cost of the long-distance calls. Then I went to my room, took my suitcase from the back of my closet, and started to pack.

—.—

The journey from Morgen to New York took twenty hours spread over the course of a day and a half.

To some that may seem like an onerous bit of driving. But I don't believe that I'd had twenty hours of uninterrupted time to think in my entire life. And what I found myself thinking on, naturally enough I suppose, was the mystery of our will to move.

Every bit of evidence would suggest that the will to be moving is as old as mankind. Take the people in the Old Testament. They were always on the move. First, it's Adam and Eve moving out of Eden. Then it's Cain condemned to be a restless wanderer, Noah drifting on the waters of the Flood, and Moses leading the Israelites out of Egypt toward the Promised Land. Some of these figures were out of the Lord's favor and some of them were in it, but all of them were on the move. And as far as the New Testament goes, Our Lord Jesus Christ was what they call a peripatetic—someone who's *always* going from place to place—whether on foot, on the back of a donkey, or on the wings of angels.

But the proof of the will to move is hardly limited to the pages of the Good Book. Any child of ten can tell you that getting-up-and-going is topic number one in the record of man's endeavors. Take that big red book that Billy is always lugging around. It's got twenty-six stories in it that have come down through the ages and almost every one of them is about some man going somewhere. Napoleon heading off on his conquests, or King Arthur in search of the Holy Grail. Some of the men in the book are figures from history and some from fancy, but whether real or imagined, almost every one of them is on his way to someplace different from where he started.

So, if the will to move is as old as mankind and every child can tell you so, what happens to a man like my father? What switch is flicked in the hallway of his mind that takes the God-given will for motion and transforms it into the will for staying put?

It isn't due to a loss of vigor. For the transformation doesn't come when men like my father are growing old and infirm. It comes when they are hale, hearty, and at the peak of their vitality. If you asked them what brought about the change, they will cloak it in the language of virtue. They will tell you that the American Dream is to settle down, raise a family, and make an honest living. They'll speak with pride of their ties to the community through the church and the Rotary and the chamber of commerce, and all other manner of stay-puttery.

But maybe, I was thinking as I was driving over the Hudson River, just maybe the will to stay put stems not from a man's virtues but from his vices. After all, aren't gluttony, sloth, and greed all about staying put? Don't they amount to sitting deep in a chair where you can eat more, idle more, and want more? In a way, pride and envy are about staying put too. For just as pride is founded on what you've built up around you, envy is founded on what your neighbor has built across the street. A man's home may be his castle, but the moat, it seems to me, is just as good at keeping people in as it is at keeping people out.

I do believe that the Good Lord has a mission for each and every one of us—a mission that is forgiving of our weaknesses, tailored to our strengths, and designed with only us in mind. But maybe He doesn't come knocking on our door and present it to us all frosted like a cake. Maybe, just maybe what He requires of us, what He expects of us, what He hopes for us is that—like His only begotten Son—we will go out into the world and find it for ourselves.

As I climbed out of Betty, Emmett, Woolly, and Billy all came spilling out of the house. Billy and Woolly both had big smiles on their faces, while Emmett, per usual, was acting like smiles were a precious resource.

Woolly, who had obviously been raised right, wanted to know if I had any bags.

—How nice of you to ask, I replied without looking at Emmett. My suitcase is in the back of the truck. And Billy, there's a basket in the passenger seat, if you'd be so kind. But no peeking.

—We'll get everything, said Billy.

As Billy and Woolly carried my things inside, Emmett shook his head.

—Sally, he said with more than a hint of exasperation.

—Yes, Mr. Watson.

—*What* are you doing here?

—What am I doing here? Well, let me see. I didn't have much on the calendar that was particularly pressing. And I have always wanted to see the big city. And then there was that small matter of sitting around yesterday afternoon and waiting for the phone to ring.

That took him down a notch.

—I'm sorry, he said. The truth is I completely forgot about calling you. Since leaving Morgen, it's been one problem after another.

—We all do have our trials, I said.

—Fair enough. I won't bother with excuses. I should have called. But when I failed to, was it really necessary for you to drive all the way here?

—Maybe not. I suppose I could have crossed my fingers and hoped that you and Billy were all right. But I figured you'd want to know why the sheriff came to see me.

—The sheriff?

Before I could explain, Billy had his arm around my waist and was looking up at Emmett.

—Sally brought more cookies and preserves.

—I thought I told you no peeking, I said.

Then I tussled his hair, which clearly had not been washed since I'd seen him last.

—I know you said that, Sally. But you didn't mean it. Did you?

—No, I didn't mean it.

—Did you bring *strawberry* preserves? asked Woolly.

—I did. And raspberry too. Speaking of preserves, where's Duchess?

Everybody looked up a little surprised, as if they'd only just noticed that Duchess was missing. But at that very moment, he emerged from the front door wearing a shirt and tie under a clean white apron, saying:

—Dinner is served!

Woolly

O H, WHAT A NIGHT they were having!
To start things off, at the stroke of eight Duchess opened the front door to reveal Emmett on the doorstep, a cause for celebration in itself. Not fifteen minutes later—just after Woolly had presented his uncle's watch to Billy—there was a small explosion and who to their wondering eyes should appear, but Sally Ransom, having driven all the way from Nebraska. And before they had a chance to celebrate *that*, Duchess was standing in the doorway announcing that dinner was served.

—Right this way, he said, as they all went back inside.

But instead of heading to the kitchen, Duchess led them into the dining room, where the table had been set with china and crystal and the two candelabra, even though it wasn't a birthday or holiday.

—My, oh my, said Sally when she came through the door.

—Miss Ransom, why don't you sit here, said Duchess, pulling out her chair.

Then Duchess seated Billy next to Sally, Woolly across the table, and Emmett at the head. Duchess reserved the other end of the table for himself, the one that was closest to the kitchen door, through which he promptly disappeared. But even before the door had stopped swinging, he was back with a napkin over his arm and a bottle of wine in hand.

—You can't appreciate a good Italian dinner, he said, without a little *vino rosso*.

Circling the table, Duchess poured a glass for everyone, including Billy. Then having set the bottle down, he was through the kitchen door and back again, this time carrying four plates at the same time with one in each hand, and another balanced on the crook of each arm—the exact set of circumstances, thought Woolly, for which the swinging door had been designed!

After zipping once around the table in order to serve a plate to everyone else, Duchess disappeared and reappeared in order to serve one to himself. Only this time when he came through the door, his apron was gone and he was wearing a vest with all the buttons buttoned.

When Duchess resumed his seat, Sally and Emmett were staring at their plates.

—What in tarnation, said Sally.

—Stuffed artichokes, said Billy.

—I didn't make them, Duchess confessed. Billy and I picked them up earlier today on Arthur Avenue.

—That's the main drag in the Italian section of the Bronx, said Billy.

Emmett and Sally both looked from Duchess to Billy and back to their plates, no less perplexed.

—You scrape the meat off the leaves with your bottom teeth, explained Woolly.

—You what? said Sally.

—Like this!

In order to demonstrate, Woolly plucked one of the leaves, scraped it with his teeth, and dropped it on his plate.

Within a matter of minutes, everyone was having a grand old time plucking leaves, and sipping wine, and discussing with due admiration the very first person in the history of mankind who'd had the audacity to eat an artichoke.

When everyone had finished their appetizer, Sally straightened the napkin in her lap and asked what they were having next.

—*Fettuccine Mio Amore*, said Billy.

Emmett and Sally looked to Duchess for an elaboration, but since he was clearing plates, he asked Woolly to do the honors.

468 | AMOR TOWLES

So Woolly told them the whole story. He told them of Leonello's—that restaurant at which no reservations were taken and no menus given. He told them of the jukebox and the mobsters and Marilyn Monroe. He told them of Leonello himself, who went from table to table greeting his customers and sending them drinks. And finally, he told them how when the waiter came to your table, he didn't even mention *Fettuccine Mio Amore*, because if you didn't know enough to ask for it, then you didn't deserve to eat it.

—I helped make it, said Billy. Duchess showed me how to properly slice an onion.

Sally was staring at Billy in a mild state of shock.

—Properly?!

—Yes, said Billy. Properly.

—And how, pray tell, is that?

Before Billy could explain, the door swung open and Duchess appeared with all five plates.

As he had been describing Leonello's, Woolly could see that Emmett and Sally were a little skeptical, and he couldn't blame them. For when it came to telling stories, Duchess was a bit of a Paul Bunyan, for whom the snow was always ten feet deep, and the river as wide as the sea. But after the very first bite, everyone at the table could set their doubts aside.

—Isn't this delicious, said Sally.

—I've got to hand it to you both, said Emmett. Then raising his glass, he added: To the chefs.

To which Woolly responded: Hear, hear!

And hear, hear said they all.

The dinner was so delicious that everyone asked for a second helping, and Duchess poured some more wine, and Emmett's eyes began to glitter as Sally's cheeks grew red, and the candle wax dribbled delightfully down the arms of the candelabra.

Then everyone was asking somebody else to tell something. First, it was Emmett asking Billy to tell about the visit to the Empire State Building. Then it was Sally asking Emmett to tell about the ride on the freight train. Then Woolly asking Duchess to tell about the magic tricks that he had seen on the stage. And finally, it was Billy asking Duchess if *he* knew any magic tricks.

—Over the years, I suppose I've learned a few.

—Will you do one for us?

Taking a sip of wine, Duchess thought for a moment, then said: Why not.

After pushing back his plate, Duchess took the corkscrew from the pocket of his vest, removed the cork, and set it on the table. Then picking up the wine bottle, he poured out the dregs, and forced the cork back inside—not simply into the neck where it usually resides, but all the way *through* the neck so that it dropped down to where the dregs had been.

—As you can see, he said, I have placed the cork in the bottle.

Then he passed the bottle around so that everyone in turn could confirm the bottle was made of solid glass and the cork was truly inside. Woolly even turned the bottle upside down and gave it a shake in order to prove what everyone knew in principle: that if it was hard to push a cork all the way into a bottle, it was impossible to shake it back out.

When the bottle had completed its circuit, Duchess rolled up his sleeves, held up his hands to show that they were empty, then asked Billy if he would be so kind as to give us a countdown.

To Woolly's great satisfaction, not only did Billy accept the task, he used the tiny little second hand in the dial of his new watch in order to execute it precisely.

Ten, he said as Duchess picked up the bottle and lowered it into his lap out of sight. *Nine . . . Eight . . . ,* he said, as Duchess breathed and exhaled. *Seven . . . Six . . . Five . . . ,* as Duchess began rolling his shoulders back and forth. *Four . . . Three . . . Two*, as his eyelids fell so low it looked like he had closed them altogether.

How long is ten seconds? thought Woolly as Billy's countdown took place. It is long enough to confirm that a heavyweight boxer has lost his bout. Long enough to announce the arrival of another new year. But it didn't seem anywhere near long enough to remove a cork from the bottom of a bottle. And yet, and yet, at the very moment that Billy said *One*, with one hand Duchess thumped the empty bottle on the table, and with the other set the cork upright at its side.

With a gasp, Sally looked at Billy and Emmett and Woolly. And Billy looked at Woolly and Sally and Emmett. And Emmett looked at Billy and Woolly and Sally. Which is to say that everybody looked at everybody. Except for Duchess, who stared straight ahead with the inscrutable smile of a sphinx.

Then everyone was talking all at once. Billy was pronouncing it magic. And Sally was saying, *I never!* And Woolly was saying, *Wonderful, wonderful, wonderful.* And Emmett, he wanted to see the bottle.

So Duchess passed the bottle around and everyone got to see that it was empty. Then Emmett suggested, rather skeptically, that there must have been two bottles and two corks, and Duchess had made the switch in his lap. So everyone looked under the table and Duchess turned around with his arms extended, but there was no second bottle to be found.

Now everyone was talking again, asking Duchess to show them how he did it. Duchess replied that a magician never reveals his secrets. But after a *proper* amount of pleading and prodding, he agreed to do so, nonetheless.

—What you do, he explained after returning the cork to the bottom of the bottle, is take your napkin, slide the folded corner into the bottle's neck like so, toss the cork until it lands in the trough of the fold, then gently withdraw.

Sure enough, as Duchess gently pulled, the folded napkin corner wrapped around the cork, drew it through the neck, and liberated it from the bottle with a satisfying pop.

—Let me try, said Billy and Sally at once.

—Let's all try! suggested Woolly.

Bounding from his chair, Woolly dashed through the kitchen into the pantry where "Dennis" stored his wine. Grabbing three bottles of *vino rosso*, he brought them into the kitchen, where Duchess pulled the corks so that Woolly could pour the contents down the drain.

Back in the dining room, Billy, Emmett, Sally, and Woolly each forced their own corks down into their own bottles and folded their own napkins as Duchess circled the table giving helpful instructions.

—Fold it a little more at the corner like this. . . . Toss the cork up a little more like that. . . . Get it to rest a little deeper in the trough. Now pull, but gently.

Pop, pop, pop went Sally's, and Emmett's, and Billy's corks.

Then everyone looked to Woolly, a circumstance which generally made Woolly want to get up and leave the room. But not after dining on artichokes and *Fettuccine Mio Amore* with four of his closest friends. Not tonight!

—Hold on, hold on, he said. I've got it, I've got it.

Biting the tip of his tongue, Woolly jostled and coaxed, then ever so, ever so gently he began to tug. And as he tugged, everyone around the table, even Duchess, held their breath until the moment that Woolly's cork went *pop* and they all erupted into a great round of hurrahs!

And that's when the swinging door swung and in walked "Dennis."

—My, oh my, said Woolly.

—What in God's name is going on here? "Dennis" demanded, using one of those *W* questions for which he expected no answer.

Then the swinging door swung again and there was Sarah with an expression of anticipatory concern.

Stepping abruptly forward, "Dennis" picked up the bottle that was in front of Woolly and looked around the table.

—Château Margaux '28! You drank four bottles of Château Margaux '28?!

—We only drank one bottle, said Billy.

—That's true, said Woolly. We poured the other three bottles down
the drain.

But as soon as Woolly had said this, he realized he shouldn't have.
Because "Dennis" was suddenly as red as his Château Margaux.

—You poured them out!

Sarah, who had been standing quietly behind her husband holding
open the door, now stepped into the room. This is where she would
say what needed to be said, thought Woolly, the very thing that he
would later wish he'd had the presence of mind to say himself. But
when she stepped around "Dennis" and had the chance to take in the
scene in its entirety, she picked up the napkin from beside Woolly's
plate, which, like all the others on the table, was stained with big red
splotches of wine.

—Oh, Woolly, she said, ever so softly.

Ever so heartbreakingly softly.

Everyone was silent now. And for a moment, no one seemed to
know where to look. Because they didn't quite want to look at each
other, or the bottles, or the napkins. But when "Dennis" put the empty
bottle of Château Margaux on the table, it was as if a spell had been
broken, and they all looked directly at Woolly, especially "Dennis."

—Wallace Martin, he said, can I speak to you in private.

When Woolly followed his brother-in-law into the office, he could tell
that a bad situation had just gotten worse. Because despite "Dennis"
having made it perfectly clear that he did not like people going into
his office when he wasn't there, here was his telephone stuffed in the
desk drawer with the cord hanging out.

—Sit down, "Dennis" said as he returned the phone to its proper
spot with a bang.

Then he looked at Woolly for a good long minute, which was something that the people sitting behind desks often seemed to do. Having insisted upon speaking to you without further delay, they sit there for a good long minute without saying a word. But even a good long minute comes to an end.

—I suppose you're wondering why your sister and I are here?

In fact, Woolly hadn't thought to wonder that at all. But now that "Dennis" mentioned it, it did seem worthy of wondering, since the two of them were supposed to be spending the night in the city.

Well, it turned out that on Friday afternoon, Kaitlin had received a phone call from a young woman asking if Woolly was at her house. Then earlier today, a young man had appeared on Kaitlin's doorstep with the very same question. Kaitlin couldn't understand why people would be asking if Woolly was there, when he was supposed to be completing his sentence in Salina. Naturally enough, she became concerned, so she decided to call her sister. But when she dialed Sarah's house and Woolly answered, not only had he hung up on her, he apparently had left the phone off the hook, because when Kaitlin kept calling back, all she got was a busy signal. This turn of events left Kaitlin little choice but to track Sarah and "Dennis" down—even though they were dining at the Wilsons.

When Woolly was a boy, punctuation had always struck him as something of an adversary—a hostile force that was committed to his defeat, whether through espionage, or by storming his beaches with overwhelming force. In seventh grade, when he had admitted this to the kind and patient Miss Penny, she explained that Woolly had it upside down. Punctuation, she said, was his ally, not his enemy. All those little marks—the period, the comma, the colon—were there to help him make sure that other people understood what he was trying to say. But apparently "Dennis" was so certain that what he had to say would be understood, he didn't need any punctuation at all.

—After giving our apologies to our hosts and driving all the way home to Hastings what do we find but a pickup truck blocking the driveway a mess in the kitchen strangers in the dining room drinking our wine and the table linens my God the table linens that your grandmother gave your sister now soiled beyond repair because you have treated them like you treat everything else like you treat everyone else which is to say without the slightest respect

"Dennis" studied Woolly for a moment, as if he were genuinely trying to understand him, trying to take the full measure of the man.

—At the age of fifteen your family sends you to one of the finest schools in the country and you get yourself thrown out for a reason I cant even remember then its off to St Marks where you get kicked out again for burning down a goalpost of all things and when no reputable school is willing to give you a second look your mother convinces St Georges to take you in by invoking the memory of your uncle Wallace who not only excelled there as a student but eventually served on its board of trustees and when you get thrown out of there and find yourself not in front of a disciplinary committee but in front of a judge what does your family do but lie about your age so that you wont be tried as an adult and hire a lawyer from Sullivan and Cromwell no less who convinces the judge to send you to some special reformatory in Kansas where you can grow vegetables for a year but apparently you dont even have the backbone to see that inconvenience through to its conclusion

"Dennis" stopped for the weighty pause.

As Woolly well knew, the weighty pause was an essential part of speaking to someone in private. It was the signal for both the speaker and the listener that what was coming next was of the utmost importance.

—I gather from Sarah that if you return to Salina they will let you complete your sentence in a matter of months so that you can apply to college and go on with your life but the one thing that has become abundantly clear Wallace is that you do not yet value an education and the best way for someone to learn the value of an education is to spend a few years doing a job which doesnt require one so with that in mind tomorrow I will be reaching out to a friend of mine at the stock exchange who is always looking for a few young men to serve as runners and maybe he will have a little more success than the rest of us in teaching you what it means to earn your keep

And right then Woolly knew for certain what he should have known the night before—as he stood in such high spirits among the wildflowers and the knee-high grass—that he was never going to visit the Statue of Liberty.

Emmett

WHEN MR. WHITNEY FINISHED speaking to Woolly, he had gone upstairs to his bedroom, followed a few minutes later by his wife. Saying he wanted to check on the progress of the stars, Woolly had gone out the front door, followed a few minutes later by Duchess, who wanted to make sure that he was all right. And Sally, she had gone upstairs in order to get Billy settled. Which left Emmett alone in the kitchen with the mess.

And Emmett was glad of it.

When Mr. Whitney had come through the dining-room door, Emmett's emotions had switched in the instant from merriment to shame. What had they been thinking, the five of them? Carousing in another man's house, drinking his wine and staining his wife's linens in pursuit of a childish game. Adding to the sting of embarrassment was the sudden memory of Parker and Packer in their Pullman car with their food thrown about and the half-empty bottle of gin on its side. How quickly Emmett had judged those two; condemned them for the spoiled and callous manner in which they treated their surroundings.

So Emmett did not begrudge Mr. Whitney his anger. He had every right to be angry. To be insulted. To be outraged. The surprise for Emmett had been in Mrs. Whitney's response, in how gracious she had been, telling them in her gentle way when Woolly and Mr. Whitney had left the room, that it was all right, that it was just some napkins and a few bottles of wine, insisting—without a suggestion of resentment—that they leave everything for the housekeeper, then telling them in which rooms they could sleep and in which closets they could find extra blankets and pillows and towels. Gracious was the only word for it. A graciousness that compounded the sense of Emmett's shame.

That's why he was glad to find himself alone, glad to have the chance to clear the dining-room table and set about cleaning the dishes as some small act of penance.

Emmett had just finished washing the plates and was moving on to the glasses when Sally returned.

—He's asleep, she said.

—Thanks.

Without saying another word, Sally took up a dish towel and began drying the plates as he washed the crystal; then she dried the crystal as he washed the pots. And it was a comfort to be doing this work, to be doing this work in Sally's company without either of them feeling the need to speak.

Emmett could tell that Sally was as ashamed as he was, and there was comfort in that too. Not the comfort of knowing that someone else was feeling a similar sting of rebuke. Rather, the comfort of knowing one's sense of right and wrong was shared by another, and thus was somehow more true.

TWO

—.—

Duchess

WHEN IT CAME TO vaudeville, it was all about the setup. That was as true for the comedians as it was for the jugglers and magicians. The members of the audience entered the theater with their own preferences, their own prejudices, their own sets of expectations. So, without the audience members realizing it, the performer needed to remove those and replace them with a new set of expectations—a set of expectations that he was in a better position to anticipate, manipulate, and ultimately satisfy.

Take Mandrake the Magnificent. Manny wasn't what you'd call a great magician. In the first half of his act, he'd produce a bouquet of flowers out of his sleeve, or colored ribbons out of his ears, or a nickel out of thin air—basically the stuff you'd see at a ten-year-old's birthday party. But like Kazantikis, what Manny lacked in the front of his act, he made up for in the finale.

One difference between Mandrake and most of his peers was that rather than having some leggy blonde at his side, he had a large white cockatoo named Lucinda. Many years before while traveling in the Amazon—Manny would explain to the audience—he had discovered a baby bird that had fallen from her nest to the forest floor. After nursing the chick back to health, he had raised her to adulthood and they had been together ever since. Over the course of the act,

Lucinda would perch on her gilded stand and assist by holding a set of keys in her claws or rapping three times on a deck of cards with her beak.

But when the act was winding up, Manny would announce that he was going to attempt a trick he had never performed before. A stage-hand would wheel out a pedestal on which sat a black enamel chest illustrated with a big red dragon. On a recent trip to the Orient, Manny would say, he had discovered the object in a flea market. The moment he saw it, he recognized it for what it was: a Mandarin's Box. Manny knew only a bit of Chinese, but the old man who was selling the curiosity not only confirmed Manny's suspicions, he went on to teach Manny the magic words that made it work.

Tonight, Manny would announce, *for the first time anywhere in the Americas, I will use the Mandarin's Box to make my trusted cockatoo vanish and reappear right before your eyes.*

Gently, Manny would place Lucinda in the chest and shut the doors. Closing his eyes, he would utter an incantation in a Chinese of his own invention, while tapping the chest with his wand. When he reopened the doors, the bird was gone.

After bowing for a round of applause, Manny would ask for silence, explaining that the spell to make the bird reappear was far more complicated than the one that made it vanish. Taking a deep breath, he would double up on his oriental mumbo jumbo, working it to a suitable pitch. Then opening his eyes, he would point his wand. Seemingly from nowhere, a ball of fire would explode and engulf the chest, prompting the audience to gasp and Manny to take two steps back. But once the smoke had cleared, there was the Mandarin's Box without so much as a scratch. Stepping forward, tentatively, Manny would open the doors of the chest . . . reach his hands inside . . . and withdraw a platter on which sat a perfectly roasted bird surrounded by all the fixings.

For a moment, the magician and audience would share the silence of the stunned. Then raising his gaze from the platter, Manny would look out into the theater and say: *Oops*.

How that would bring down the house.

So. Here's what happened on Sunday, the twentieth of June. . . .

Having woken at the crack of dawn, at Woolly's insistence we packed our bags, tiptoed down the back stairs, and slipped out the door without making a sound.

After putting the Caddy in neutral and rolling her out of the drive, we fired her up, put her in gear, and half an hour later were sailing up the Taconic State Parkway like Ali Baba on his magic carpet.

What cars were on the road all seemed to be headed in the opposite direction, so we were making good time, passing through Lagrangeville by seven o'clock and Albany by eight.

After being given the business by his brother-in-law, Woolly had tossed and turned for most of the night and woken up looking as low as I'd ever seen him, so when I saw a blue steeple on the horizon, I put on the blinker.

Being back in the bright orange booth seemed to lift his spirits. Though he didn't seem as interested in his place mat, he ate almost half of his pancakes and all of my bacon.

Not long after we passed Lake George, Woolly had me turn off the highway and we began winding our way through the great bucolic wilderness that makes up ninety percent of New York's landmass and none of its reputation. With the townships getting farther apart and the trees getting closer to the road, Woolly almost seemed himself, humming along with the commercials even though the radio wasn't on. It must have been about eleven when he sat up on the edge of his seat and pointed to a break in the woods.

—You take that next right.

Turning onto a dirt road, we began winding our way through a forest of the tallest trees that I had ever seen.

To be perfectly honest, when Woolly had first told me about the hundred and fifty grand that was stashed in a safe at the family's camp, I had my doubts. I just couldn't seem to picture all that money sitting in some log cabin in the woods. But when we emerged from the trees, rising before us was a house that looked like a hunting lodge owned by the Rockefellers.

When Woolly saw it, he breathed an even bigger sigh of relief than I did, as if he'd had his own doubts. Like maybe the whole place had been a figment of his imagination.

—Welcome home, I said.

And he gave me his first smile of the day.

When we got out of the car, I followed Woolly around to the front of the house and across the lawn to where a giant body of water shimmered in the sun.

—The lake, Woolly said.

With the trees coming right down to the shoreline, there wasn't another residence in sight.

—How many houses are on this lake? I asked.

—One . . . ? he asked back.

—Right, I said.

Then he began giving me the lay of the land.

—The dock, he said pointing to the dock.

And the boathouse, he said pointing to the boathouse. And the flagpole, he said pointing to the flagpole.

—The caretaker hasn't been here yet, he observed with another sigh of relief.

—How can you tell?

—Because the raft isn't on the lake and the rowboats aren't at the dock.

Turning, we took a moment to appreciate the house, which looked down over the water like it had been there since the beginning of America. And maybe it had.

—Perhaps we should get our things . . . ? Woolly suggested.

—Allow *me*!

Hopping to it like a bellboy at the Ritz, I skipped over to the car and opened the trunk. Setting aside the Louisville Slugger, I took out our book bags, then followed Woolly to the narrow end of the house, where two lines of white-painted stones led to a door.

On the top of the stoop were four overturned flowerpots. No doubt when the raft was on the lake and the rowboats at the dock, they would be planted with whatever sort of flower that WASPs found to be ornamental without being showy.

After peeking under three of the pots, Woolly retrieved a key and unlocked the door. Then showing a decidedly un-Woolly presence of mind, he put the key back where he'd found it before letting us inside.

First, we entered a little room in which cubbyholes, hooks, and baskets held an orderly arrangement of everything you'd need for the great outdoors: coats and hats, rods and reels, bows and arrows. In front of a glass cabinet showcasing four rifles were several large white chairs stacked one on top of the other, having been hauled in from their picturesque spots on the lawn.

—The mudroom, Woolly said.

As if mud had ever found its way onto the shoe of a Wolcott!

Over the gun cabinet there was a big green sign like the one in the barracks at Salina, painted with its own rules and regulations. Most everywhere else on the wall—hanging right up to the ceiling—were dark-red boards in the shape of chevrons with lists painted in white.

—The winners, Woolly explained.

—Of what?

—The tournaments we used to have on the Fourth of July.

Woolly pointed from one to another.

—Riflery, archery, the swim race, the canoe race, the twenty-yard dash.

As I gazed over the boards, Woolly must have thought I was looking for his name because he volunteered that it wasn't there.

—I'm not very good at winning, he confessed.

—It's overrated, I assured.

Exiting the mudroom, he led me down the hall, naming rooms as we went.

—The tearoom . . . the billiard room . . . the game closet . . .

Where the hallway ended, it opened into a large living area.

—We call this the great room, said Woolly.

And they weren't kidding. Like the lobby of a grand hotel, it had six different seating areas with couches and wing-back chairs and standing lamps. There was also a card table topped with baize, and a fireplace that looked like it belonged in a castle. Everything was in its proper place, except for the dark-green rocking chairs huddled by the outside doors.

Seeing them, Woolly seemed disappointed.

—What is it?

—Those really belong on the porch.

—No time like the present.

Setting our bags down and tossing my fedora on a chair, I helped Woolly shuttle the rockers onto the porch, being careful to arrange them, per his instructions, at equal intervals. Once they were all in place, Woolly asked if I wanted to see the rest of the house.

—Absotively, I said, which brought an even bigger smile. I want to see all of it, Woolly. But we can't forget the reason we're here. . . .

After looking at me with curiosity for a moment, Woolly put a finger of recognition in the air. Then he led me down the hallway on the other side of the great room and opened a door.

—My great-grandfather's study, he said.

As we had walked through the house, it seemed laughable I had ever doubted that money could be stashed here. Given the scale of the rooms and the quality of the furnishings, there could have been fifty grand stuffed under a mattress in the maid's room and another fifty lost among the cushions of the couches. But if the majesty of the house boosted my confidence, that was nothing compared to Great-grandpa's study. Here was a room of a man who knew not only how to make money, but how to keep it. Which, after all, are two different things entirely.

In some ways, it was like a small version of the great room, with the same wooden chairs, and red rugs, and another fireplace. But there was also a great big desk, bookcases, and one of those little sets of steps that the bookish use to reach the volumes on upper shelves. On one wall was a painting of a bunch of colonial fellows in tight pants and white wigs gathered around a desk. But over the fireplace was a portrait of a man in his late fifties with fair coloring and a handsome, decisive-looking face.

—Your great-grandfather? I asked.

—No, said Woolly. My grandfather.

In a way, I was relieved to hear it. Hanging a portrait of oneself over the fireplace in one's study didn't seem a very Wolcotty thing to do.

—It was painted at the time my grandfather took over for my great-grandfather at the paper company. When he died shortly thereafter, my great-grandfather had it moved here.

Looking from Woolly to the portrait I could see the family resemblance. Except for the decisive part, of course.

—What happened to the paper company? I asked.

—Uncle Wallace took over when Grandpa died. He was only twenty-five at the time and he ran it until he was about thirty, but then he died too.

I didn't bother observing that the head of the Wolcott paper company was a job to be avoided. I suspect Woolly knew that already.

488 | AMOR TOWLES

Turning, Woolly walked over to the painting of the colonials and held out a hand.

—The presentation of the Declaration of Independence.

—No kidding.

—Oh yes, said Woolly. There's John Adams and Thomas Jefferson and Ben Franklin and John Hancock. They're all there.

—Which one's the Wolcott, I asked with a Puckish grin.

But taking another step forward, Woolly pointed to a small head at the back of the crowd.

—Oliver, he said. He also signed the Articles of Confederation and was the governor of Connecticut. Though that was seven generations ago.

We both nodded for a few seconds, in order to give old Ollie his due. Then reaching up, Woolly opened the painting like it was a cabinet door and, lo and behold, there was Great-grandpa's safe, looking like it had been fashioned from the metal of a battleship. With a nickel-plated handle and four little dials, it must have been a foot and a half square. If it was also a foot and a half deep, it would be big enough to hold the life savings of seventy generations of Hewetts. But for the solemnity of the moment, I would have whistled.

From Great-grandpa's perspective, the contents of the safe were probably an expression of the past. In this grand old house, behind this venerable old painting, were documents that had been signed decades before, jewelry that had been handed down from generation to generation, and cash that had been accumulated over several lifetimes. But in just a few moments, some of the safe's contents would have been transformed into a representation of the future.

Emmett's future. Woolly's future. My future.

—There it is, said Woolly.

—There it is, I agreed.

Then we both let out a sigh.

—Would you like to . . . ? I asked, gesturing at the dials.

—What's that? Oh, no. You go right ahead.

—All right, I said, trying to resist the temptation of rubbing my hands together. Just give me the combination, and I'll do the honors.

After a moment of silence, Woolly looked at me with an expression of genuine surprise.

—Combination? he asked.

Then I laughed. I laughed until my kidneys hurt and the tears poured out of my eyes.

Like I said: When it comes to vaudeville, it's all about the setup.

Emmett

THAT'S A FINE JOB, said Mrs. Whitney. I really can't thank you
enough.

—It was my pleasure, said Emmett.

They were standing at the threshold of the baby's room looking at
the walls, which Emmett had just finished painting.

—You must be hungry after all that work. Why don't you come
down and I'll fix you a sandwich.

—I'd appreciate that, Mrs. Whitney. Just let me clean up.

—Of course, she said. But please. Call me Sarah.

That morning, Emmett had come downstairs to find that Duchess and
Woolly were gone. Having woken in the early hours, they had driven
off in the Cadillac, leaving only a note behind. Mr. Whitney was gone
too, having headed back to their apartment in the city without taking
time for breakfast. And Mrs. Whitney, she was standing in the kitchen
dressed in dungarees, her hair pulled back in a kerchief.

—I promised I'd finally finish painting the baby's room, she explained with a look of embarrassment.

It didn't take much convincing for her to let Emmett take over
the job.

With Mrs. Whitney's approval, Emmett moved the boxes of Woolly's belongings to the garage, stacking them in the spot where the

Cadillac had been. With some tools he found in the basement, he took apart the bed and stowed the pieces beside the boxes. When the room was empty, he finished taping the trim, laid the tarp across the floor, stirred the paint, and went to work.

When you had the job set up right—with the room clear and the trim taped and the floor protected—painting was peaceful work. It had a rhythm about it that allowed your thoughts to quiet down, or fall silent altogether. Eventually, all that you were aware of was the movement of the brush sweeping back and forth, turning the primed white wall to its new shade of blue.

When Sally saw what Emmett was doing, she nodded her head in approval.

—You want a hand?

—I've got it.

—You spilled some paint on the tarp over there by the window.

—Yep.

—All right, she said. Just so's you know.

Then Sally looked up and down the hallway with a bit of a frown, as if she were disappointed there wasn't another room that needed painting. She wasn't used to being idle, certainly not as an uninvited guest in another woman's home.

—Maybe I'll take Billy into town, she said. Find a soda fountain where we can have lunch.

—Sounds like a good idea, agreed Emmett, placing the brush on the rim of the can. Let me get you some money.

—I think I can afford to buy your brother a hamburger. Besides, the last thing Mrs. Whitney needs now is you tracking paint all through her house.

—·—

When Mrs. Whitney went downstairs to make the sandwiches, Emmett brought all the work materials down the back staircase (having checked his shoes twice to make sure there was no paint on the soles). In the garage, he cleaned the brushes, the paint tray, and his hands with turpentine. Then he joined Mrs. Whitney in the kitchen where a ham sandwich and glass of milk were waiting on the table.

When Emmett sat down, Mrs. Whitney took the chair opposite him with a cup of tea, but nothing to eat.

—I need to go into the city to join my husband, she said, but I gather from your brother that your car's in the shop and won't be ready until tomorrow.

—That's right, said Emmett.

—In that case, why don't you three stay the night. You can help yourself to what's in the refrigerator for dinner, and in the morning you can lock the door behind you when you go.

—That's very generous of you.

Emmett doubted that Mr. Whitney would have welcomed such an arrangement. If anything, he had probably communicated to his wife that he wanted them out of the house as soon as they awoke. Emmett felt his suspicion confirmed when Mrs. Whitney added, almost as an afterthought, that if the phone were to ring, they should leave it unanswered.

As Emmett ate, he noticed that in the middle of the table was a folded piece of paper standing upright between the salt and pepper shakers. Following his gaze, Mrs. Whitney acknowledged that it was Woolly's note.

When Emmett had first come down in the morning and Mrs. Whitney had told him that Woolly had gone, she had seemed almost relieved by his departure, but a little worried too. As she looked at the note, the same emotions returned to her face.

—Would you like to read it? she asked.

—I wouldn't presume.

—That's all right. I'm sure Woolly wouldn't mind.

Emmett's normal instinct would have been to demur a second time, but he sensed that Mrs. Whitney wanted him to read the note. Putting down his sandwich, he took it from its slot between the shakers.

Written in Woolly's hand and addressed to *Sis*, the note said that Woolly was sorry for muddling things up. Sorry about the napkins and the wine. Sorry about the phone in the drawer. Sorry to be leaving so early in the morning without having the chance to say a proper good-bye. But she shouldn't worry. Not for a minute. Not for a moment. Not for the blink of an eye. All would be well.

Cryptically, he concluded the note with the postscript: *The Comptons ate their cabbage in the kitchen!*

—Will it? Mrs. Whitney asked when Emmett set the note down on the table.

—I'm sorry?

—Will all be well?

—Yes, replied Emmett. I'm sure it will.

Mrs. Whitney nodded, but Emmett could see that this was less an expression of agreement with his reply than of gratitude for his reassurance. For a moment, she looked down into her tea, which must have been tepid by now.

—My brother wasn't always in trouble, she said. He was Woolly, of course, but things changed for him during the war. Somehow, when Father accepted his commission in the navy, it was Woolly who ended up at sea.

She smiled a little sadly at her own witticism. Then she asked if Emmett knew why her brother had been sent to Salina.

—He told us once that he had taken someone's car.

—Yes, she said with a bit of a laugh. That was it, more or less.

It happened when Woolly was at St. George's, his third boarding school in as many years.

—One spring day in the middle of classes, she explained, he decided to walk into town in search of an ice cream cone, of all things. When he arrived at the little shopping center a few miles from campus, he noticed there was a firetruck parked at the curb. Having looked around and found no signs of any firemen, he became convinced—in a way that only my brother can become convinced—that it must have been forgotten. Forgotten like—oh, I don't even know—like an umbrella on the back of a chair, or a book on the seat of a bus.

With a smile of affection, she shook her head, then continued.

—Eager to return the firetruck to its rightful owners, Woolly climbed behind the wheel and went looking for the station house. Around the town he drove with a fireman's hat on his head—as it was later reported—tooting the horn for any children he passed. After circling for God knows how long, he found a station house, parked the engine, and walked all the way back to campus.

The affectionate smile that Mrs. Whitney had been wearing began to fade now as her mind leapt forward to all that followed.

—As it turned out, the firetruck had been in the parking lot of the shopping center because several of the firemen were in the grocery store. And while Woolly was driving around, a call came in for a stable that was on fire. By the time the engine from a neighboring town arrived, the stable had burned to the ground. Thankfully, there were no people hurt. But the young stable hand who was on duty alone couldn't get all of the horses out of the building, and four of them died in the fire. The police tracked Woolly back to the school and that was that.

After a moment, Mrs. Whitney pointed to Emmett's plate in order to ask if he was finished. When he said that he was, she cleared it along with her cup to the sink.

She was trying not to imagine it, thought Emmett. Trying not to imagine those four horses trapped in their stalls, whinnying and rising on their hind legs as the flames grew closer. Trying not to imagine the unimaginable.

Though her back was now to Emmett, he could tell from the movement of her arm that she was wiping away tears. Deciding that he should leave her in peace, Emmett tucked Woolly's note back in its spot and quietly pushed back his chair.

—Do you know what I find so strange? Mrs. Whitney asked, still standing at the sink with her back to Emmett.

When he didn't respond, she turned, wearing a mournful smile.

—When we're young, so much time is spent teaching us the importance of keeping our vices in check. Our anger, our envy, our pride. But when I look around, it seems to me that so many of our lives end up being hampered by a virtue instead. If you take a trait that by all appearances is a merit—a trait that is praised by pastors and poets, a trait that we have come to admire in our friends and hope to foster in our children—and you give it to some poor soul in abundance, it will almost certainly prove an obstacle to their happiness. Just as someone can be too smart for their own good, there are those who are too patient for their own good, or too hardworking.

After shaking her head, Mrs. Whitney looked at the ceiling. When she looked down again, Emmett could see that another tear was making its way down her cheek.

—Those who are too confident . . . or too cautious . . . or too kind . . .

Emmett understood that what Mrs. Whitney was sharing with him was her effort to understand, to explain, to make some sense of the undoing of her bighearted brother. At the same time, Emmett suspected that tucked in Mrs. Whitney's list was an apology for her husband, who was either too smart, too confident, or too hardworking for his own good. Perhaps all three. But what Emmett found himself wondering was what virtue did Mrs. Whitney have too much of? The answer, his instincts told him, though he was almost reluctant to admit it, was probably forgiveness.

Woolly

AND THIS WAS MY favorite rocking chair, said Woolly to no one.

He was standing on the porch, a little while after Duchess had gone to the general store. Giving the chair a push, he listened to the thwapping of its rockers as it rocked back and forth, noting how each individual thwap came closer and closer together as the back and forths became smaller and smaller, until they stopped altogether.

Setting the chair in motion again, Woolly looked out at the lake. For the time being, it was so still you could see every cloud in the sky reflected on its surface. But in another hour or so, right around five o'clock, the afternoon breeze would begin to pick up and the surface would ripple and all the reflections would be swept away. Then the curtains in the windows would start to stir.

Sometimes, thought Woolly, sometimes at the end of summer when the hurricanes roamed the Atlantic, the afternoon breeze would grow so strong that the bedroom doors would all slam shut and the rocking chairs would rock themselves.

After giving one last push to his favorite chair, Woolly went back through the double doors into the great room.

—And this is the great room, he said, where we would play Parcheesi and complete jigsaw puzzles on rainy afternoons . . . And this is the hallway . . . And this is the kitchen, where Dorothy made fried chicken and her famous blueberry muffins. And that's the table where we ate when we were too young to dine in the dining room.

Removing from his pocket the note that he had written while sitting at his great-grandfather's desk, Woolly tucked it neatly between the salt and pepper shakers. Then he left the kitchen by means of the only door in the house that swung back and forth.

—And here is the dining room, he said, gesturing to the long table around which his cousins and aunts and uncles would gather. Once you were old enough to eat in here, he explained, you could sit in any seat you wanted as long as it wasn't the seat at the end of the table, because that's where Great-grandpa would sit. And there is the head of the moose.

Exiting the other dining-room door, Woolly reentered the great room, where, after admiring it from corner to corner, he picked up Emmett's book bag and began climbing the stairs, counting as he went.

—Two, four, six, eight, who do we appreciate.

At the top of the stairs, the hallway shot off in both directions, east and west, with bedroom doors on either side.

While there was nothing hanging on the wall to the south, on the wall to the north were photographs everywhere you looked. According to family legend, Woolly's grandmother had been the first person to hang a photograph in the upstairs hallway—a picture of her four young children, which she put right above the side table opposite the stairs. Soon after, a second and third photograph were hung to the left and right of the first photograph. Then a fourth and fifth were hung above and below. Over the years, photographs had been added leftward and rightward, upward and downward, until they radiated in every direction.

Setting down the book bag, Woolly approached the first photograph, then began looking at all the others in the order that they had been hung. There was the picture of Uncle Wallace as a little boy in his little sailor suit. And there the picture of his grandfather out on the dock with the tattoo of the schooner on his arm, getting ready to take his twelve o'clock swim. And there the picture of his father holding up his blue ribbon after winning the riflery contest on the Fourth of July in 1941.

—He always won the riflery contest, said Woolly, while brushing a tear from his cheek with the flat of his hand.

And there, one step farther from the side table, was the one of Woolly with his mother and father in the canoe.

This picture was taken—oh, Woolly didn't know for sure—but around the time that he was seven. Certainly before Pearl Harbor and the aircraft carrier. Before Richard and "Dennis." Before St. Paul's and St. Mark's and St. George's.

Before, before, before.

The funny thing about a picture, thought Woolly, the funny thing about a picture is that while it knows everything that's happened up until the moment it's been taken, it knows absotively nothing about what will happen next. And yet, once the picture has been framed and hung on a wall, what you see when you look at it closely are all the things that were *about* to happen. All the un-things. The things that were unanticipated. And unintended. And unreversible.

Wiping another tear from his cheek, Woolly removed the photograph from the wall and picked up the book bag.

As with the chairs around the dining-room table, there was one bedroom on the hallway that you weren't allowed to sleep in because it was Great-grandpa's. Everyone other than Great-grandpa would sleep in different bedrooms at different times depending on how old they were, or whether they were married, or how early or late in the summer they happened to arrive. Over the years, Woolly had slept in a number of these rooms. But for the longest time, or what seemed like the longest time, he and his cousin Freddy had slept in the second to last room on the left. So that's where Woolly went.

Stepping inside, Woolly set down the book bag and leaned the photograph of him and his parents on the bureau behind the pitcher and glasses. After looking at the pitcher for a moment, he carried it down the hall to the bathroom, filled it with water, and brought it back. Pouring water into one of the glasses, he picked it up and moved it to the bedside table. Then after opening a window, so that the breeze could find its way into the room after five, he began to unpack.

First, he took out the radio and placed it on the bureau beside the pitcher. Then he took out his dictionary and placed it beside the radio. Then he took out the cigar box, in which he kept his collection of the same version of different things, and placed it beside the dictionary. Then he took out his extra bottle of medicine and the little brown bottle that he'd found waiting for him in the spice rack and placed them on the bedside table beside the glass of water.

As he was taking off his shoes, Woolly heard the sound of a car pulling into the driveway—Duchess returning from the general store. Moving to the doorway, Woolly listened to the screen door in the mudroom open and close. Then footsteps passing through the great room. Then furniture being moved in the study. And finally, the sound of clanging.

It wasn't a dainty sort of clanging, like that of a cable car in San Francisco, thought Woolly. It was an emphatic clanging like that of a blacksmith who's beating a red-hot horseshoe on an anvil.

Or perhaps not a horseshoe . . . , thought Woolly with a pang.

Better that it was a blacksmith beating something else. Something like, something like, something like a sword. Yes, that was it. The clanging sounded like an ancient blacksmith hammering on the blade of Excalibur.

With that happier image in mind, Woolly closed the door, switched on the radio, and went to lie down on the bed on the left.

In the story of Goldilocks and the Three Bears, Goldilocks has to climb into three different beds before she finds the one that's just right for her. But Woolly didn't need to climb into three different beds, because he already knew that the one on the left would be just right for him. For as in his youth, it was neither too hard nor too soft, too long nor too short.

Propping up the pillows, Woolly polished off the extra bottle of his medicine and made himself comfortable. As he looked up at the ceiling, his thoughts returned to the jigsaw puzzles that they would complete on rainy days.

Wouldn't it have been wonderful, thought Woolly, if everybody's life was like a piece in a jigsaw puzzle. Then no one person's life would ever be an inconvenience to anyone else's. It would just fit snugly in its very own, specially designed spot, and in so doing, would enable the whole intricate picture to become complete.

As Woolly was having this wonderful notion, a commercial came to its end and the broadcast of a mystery show began. Climbing back out of bed, Woolly turned the volume on the radio down to two and a half.

The important thing to understand about listening to a mystery show on the radio, Woolly well knew, is that all the parts designed to make you anxious—like the whispering of assassins, or the rustling of leaves, or the creaking of steps on a staircase—were relatively quiet. While the parts designed to set your mind at ease—like the sudden epiphany of the hero, or the peeling of his tires, or the crack of his pistol—were relatively loud. So if you turned the volume down to two and a half, you could barely hear the parts designed to make you anxious, while still getting to hear all the parts designed to set your mind at ease.

Returning to his bed, Woolly poured all the little pink pills from the little brown bottle onto the table. With the tip of his finger, he pushed them into the palm of his hand, saying, *One potato, two potato, three potato, four. Five potato, six potato, seven potato, more.* Then washing them down with a big drink of water, he made himself comfortable again.

With the pillows properly propped, the volume properly lowered, and the little pink pills properly swallowed, you might think that Woolly wouldn't know what to think about, what with Woolly being Woolly and prone to all the old Woolly ways.

But Woolly knew exactly what to think about. He had known that he would think about it almost as soon as it had happened.

—I'll start in front of the cabinet at FAO Schwarz, he said to himself with a smile. And my sister will come, and we'll have tea at the Plaza with the panda. And after Duchess meets me at the statue of Abraham Lincoln, he and I will attend the circus, where Billy and Emmett will suddenly reappear. Then we'll go over the Brooklyn Bridge and up the Empire State Building, where we'll meet Professor Abernathe. Then it's off to the grassy train tracks where, sitting by the fire, we'll hear the story of the two Ulysses and the ancient seer who explained how they could find their ways home again—how they could find their ways home, after ten long years.

But one mustn't rush, thought Woolly, as the window curtains stirred, and the grass began to sprout through the seams between the floorboards, and the ivy climbed the legs of the bureau. For a one-of-a-kind kind of day deserves to be relived at the slowest possible pace, with every moment, every twist, every turn of events remembered to the tiniest detail.

Abacus

M ANY YEARS BEFORE, Abacus had come to the conclusion that the greatest of heroic stories have the shape of a diamond on its side. Beginning at a fine point, the life of the hero expands outward through youth as he begins to establish his strengths and fallibilities, his friendships and enmities. Proceeding into the world, he pursues exploits in grand company, accumulating honors and accolades. But at some untold moment, the two rays that define the outer limits of this widening world of hale companions and worthy adventures simultaneously turn a corner and begin to converge. The terrain our hero travels, the cast of characters he meets, the sense of purpose that has long propelled him forward all begin to narrow—to narrow toward that fixed and inexorable point that defines his fate.

Take the tale of Achilles.

In hopes of making her son invincible, the Nereid Thetis holds her newborn boy by the ankle and dips him into the river Styx. From that finite moment in time and pinch of the fingers, the story of Achilles begins. As a strapping young lad, he is educated in history, literature, and philosophy by the centaur Chiron. On the fields of sport, he gains in strength and agility. And with his comrade Patroclus, he forms the closest of bonds.

As a young man, Achilles ventures forth into the world, where he proceeds from one exploit to the next, vanquishing all manner of opponents until his reputation precedes him far and wide. Then, at the very height of his fame and the peak of his physical prowess, Achilles sets sail for Troy to join the likes of Agamemnon, Menelaus, Ulysses, and Ajax in the greatest battle ever fought by men.

But somewhere on this crossing, somewhere in the middle of the Aegean Sea, unbeknownst to Achilles, the widening rays of his life turn their corners and begin their relentless trajectory inward.

Ten long years, Achilles will remain on the fields of Troy. Over the course of that decade, the area of conflict will grow smaller as the battle lines draw ever closer to the walls of the besieged city. The once countless legions of Greek and Trojan soldiers will grow smaller, diminishing with every additional death. And in the tenth year, when Hector, prince of Troy, slays the beloved Patroclus, Achilles's world will grow smaller still.

From that moment, the enemy with all its battalions is reduced in Achilles's mind to the one person responsible for the death of his friend. The sprawling fields of battle are reduced to the few square feet between where he and Hector will stand. And the sense of purpose that at one time encompassed duty, honor, and glory is now reduced to the single burning desire for revenge.

So perhaps it is not surprising that just a matter of days after Achilles succeeds in killing Hector, a poison arrow lofting through the air pierces the one unprotected spot on Achilles's body—the ankle by which his mother had held him when she dipped him in the Styx. And in that very instant, all of his memories and dreams, all of his sensations and sentiments, all of his virtues and vices are extinguished like the flame of a candle that has been snuffed between a finger and a thumb.

Yes, for the longest time, Abacus had understood that the great heroic stories were like a diamond on its side. But of late, what had taken up his thoughts was the realization that it wasn't simply the lives of the renowned that conform to this geometry. For the lives of miners and stevedores conform to it too. The lives of waitresses and nursemaids conform to it. The lives of the ancillary and the anonymous, of the frivolous and the forgotten.

All lives.

His life.

His life too began at a point—on the fifth of May in 1890, when a boy named Sam was born in the bedroom of a small painted cottage on the island of Martha's Vineyard, the only offspring of an insurance adjuster and a seamstress.

Like any child, Sam's first years were spent in the warm circumference of his family. But one day at the age of seven, in the aftermath of a hurricane, Sam accompanied his father to a shipwreck that needed to be assessed on behalf of the insurers. Having journeyed all the way from Port-au-Prince, this vessel had run aground on a shoal off West Chop, and there it remained, its hull breached, its sails in tatters, its cargo of rum washing ashore with the waves.

From that moment, the walls of Sam's life began to branch outward. After every storm, he would insist upon going with his father to see the wrecks: the schooners, the frigates, the yachts. Whether blown upon the rocks or swamped by a turbulent tide, Sam did not simply see a ship in distress. He saw the world the ship embodied. He saw the ports of Amsterdam, Buenos Aires, and Singapore. He saw the spices and textiles and ceramics. He saw the sailors who hailed from every seafaring nation around the globe.

Sam's fascination with shipwrecks led him to fantastical stories of the sea, like those of Sinbad and Jason. The fantastical stories led him to histories of the great explorers, his worldview widening with the reading of each additional page. Eventually, Sam's ever-growing love of history and myth brought him to the ivy-covered halls of Harvard, and then to New York, where—having rechristened himself Abacus and declared himself a writer—he met musicians, architects, painters, financiers, as well as criminals and derelicts too. And finally, he met Polly, that wonder of wonders who brought him joy, companionship, a daughter, and a son.

What an extraordinary passage were those first years in Manhattan! When Abacus experienced firsthand the omnivalent, omnipresent, omnifarious widening that is life.

Or rather, that is the first half of life.

When did the change come? When did the outer limits of his world turn their corner and begin moving inexorably toward their terminal convergence?

Abacus had no idea.

Not long after his children had grown and moved on, perhaps. Certainly, before Polly died. Yes, it was likely at some point during those years when, without their knowing it, her time had begun to run out while he, in the so-called prime of life, went blithely on about his business.

The manner in which the convergence takes you by surprise, that is the cruelest part. And yet it's almost unavoidable. For at the moment when the turning begins, the two opposing rays of your life are so far from each other you could never discern the change in their trajectory. And in those first years, as the rays begin to angle inward, the world still seems so open, you have no reason to suspect its diminishment.

But one day, one day years after the convergence has begun, you cannot only sense the inward trajectory of the walls, you can begin to see the terminal point in the offing even as the terrain that remains before you begins to shrink at an accelerating pace.

In those golden years of his late twenties, shortly after arriving in New York, Abacus had made three great friends. Two men and a woman, they were the hardiest of companions, fellow adventurers of the mind and spirit. Side by side, they had navigated the waters of life

506 | AMOR TOWLES

with a reasonable diligence and their fair share of aplomb. But in just these last five years, the first had been stricken with blindness, the second with emphysema, and the third with dementia. How varied their lot, you might be tempted to observe: the loss of sight, of lung capacity, of cognition. When in reality, the three infirmities amount to the same sentence: the narrowing of life at the far tip of the diamond. Step by step, the stomping grounds of these friends had shrunk from the world itself, to their country, to their county, to their home, and finally to a single room where, blinded, breathless, forgetful, they are destined to end their days.

Though Abacus had no infirmities to speak of yet, his world too was shrinking. He too had watched as the outer limits of his life had narrowed from the world at large, to the island of Manhattan, to that book-lined office in which he awaited with a philosophical resignation the closing of the finger and thumb. And then this . . .

This!

This extraordinary turn of events.

A little boy from Nebraska appears at his doorstep with a gentle demeanor and a fantastical tale. A tale not from a leather-bound tome, mind you. Not from an epic poem written in an unspoken language. Not from an archive or athenaeum. But from life itself.

How easily we forget—we in the business of storytelling—that life was the point all along. A mother who has vanished, a father who has failed, a brother who is determined. A journey from the prairies into the city by means of a boxcar with a vagabond named Ulysses. Thence to a railroad track suspended over the city as surely as Valhalla is suspended in the clouds. And there, the boy, Ulysses, and he, having sat down by a campfire as ancient as the ways of man, began—

—It's time, said Ulysses.

—What's that? said Abacus. Time?

—If you're still coming.

—I'm coming! he said. Here I come!

Rising to his feet in a copse of woods twenty miles west of Kansas City, Abacus scrambled through the underbrush in the dark, tearing the pocket from his seersucker jacket. Breathlessly, he followed Ulysses through the break in the trees, up the embankment, and into the boxcar that was destined to take them who knows where.

Billy

EMMETT WAS ASLEEP. Billy could tell that Emmett was asleep because he was snoring. Emmett didn't snore as loudly as their father used to snore, but he snored loudly enough that you could tell when he was sleeping.

Quietly, Billy slipped out from under the covers and climbed down onto the rug. Reaching under the bed, he found his backpack, opened the upper flap, and removed his army surplus flashlight. Being careful to point the beam at the rug—so he wouldn't wake his brother—Billy switched the flashlight on. Then removing Professor Abernathe's *Compendium of Heroes, Adventurers, and Other Intrepid Travelers*, he turned to chapter twenty-five and took up his pencil.

If Billy were going to start at the very beginning, he would go back to the twelfth of December 1935, the day that Emmett was born. That was two years after their father and mother had married in Boston and moved to Nebraska. It was during the Depression, and Franklin Roosevelt was president, and Sally was almost one year old.

But Billy wasn't going to start at the very beginning. He was going to start *in medias res*. The hard part, as Billy had explained to Emmett in the train station in Lewis, was knowing where the middle was.

One idea that Billy had was to start on the Fourth of July 1946, when he and Emmett and their mother and father went to Seward to watch the fireworks display.

Billy was just a baby at the time, so he couldn't remember what the trip to Seward had been like. But one afternoon, Emmett had told him all about it. He had told Billy about their mother's love of fireworks, and the picnic basket in the attic, and the checkered cloth that they would spread on the lawn in the middle of Plum Creek Park. So Billy could use what Emmett had told him in order to describe the day exactly as it was.

But he also had the photograph.

Reaching into his backpack, Billy removed the envelope that was in the innermost pocket. Opening the flap, he slipped out the photograph and held it near the flashlight's beam. It was a picture of Emmett, Billy in a bassinet, their mother, and the picnic basket all in a row on the checkered cloth. Their father must have been the one who took the picture because he wasn't in it. Everyone in the picture was smiling, and though Billy's father wasn't in the picture, Billy could tell that he must have been smiling too.

Billy had found the photograph together with the postcards from the Lincoln Highway in the metal box that was in the bottom drawer of their father's bureau.

But when Billy had put the postcards in the manila envelope so that he could show them to Emmett when Emmett returned home from Salina, he had put the photograph from Seward in a different envelope. He had put it in a different envelope because he knew that memories of the trip to Seward made his brother angry. Billy knew this because his brother had become angry when he had told Billy about the trip to Seward. And he had never told Billy about it again.

Billy had saved the picture because he knew that Emmett wouldn't always be angry with their mother. Once they had found her in San Francisco, and she had had the chance to tell them all the things that she had been thinking in the years that they had been apart, Emmett wouldn't be angry anymore. Then Billy would give him the picture, and he would be glad that Billy had kept it for him.

But it didn't make sense to start the story there, thought Billy, as he returned the picture to its envelope. Because on the Fourth of July 1946, their mother hadn't even left yet. So that night was closer to the beginning of the story than it was to the middle.

Another idea that Billy had was to start on the night that Emmett hit Jimmy Snyder.

Billy didn't need a photograph to remember that night because he had been there with Emmett and had been old enough to remember it himself.

It was on Saturday, October 4, 1952, the last night of the fair. Their father, who had gone with them to the fair the night before, decided to stay home on Saturday. So Emmett and Billy had driven there together in the Studebaker.

Some years, the temperature at the fair can feel like the beginning of fall, but that year, it felt like the end of summer. Billy remembered because as they drove to the fair they had their windows rolled down, and when they arrived, they decided to leave their jackets in the car.

They had left for the fair at five o'clock so that they could get something to eat, and go on some rides, and still have time to find seats near the front of the fiddling contest. Emmett and Billy both loved the fiddling contest, especially when they had seats near the front. But on that particular night, even though they had plenty of time to spare, they never did get to see the fiddlers.

It was while they were walking from the carousel to the stage that Jimmy Snyder began to say his mean things. At first, Emmett didn't seem to care what Jimmy was saying. Then he began to get angry, and Billy tried to pull him away, but Emmett wouldn't go. And when Jimmy tried to say one last mean thing about their father, Emmett punched him in the nose.

After Jimmy fell back and hit his head, Billy must have closed his eyes, because he didn't remember what the following minutes looked like. He only remembered how they sounded: with Jimmy's friends gasping, then calling for help, then shouting at Emmett as other people jostled around them. And then Emmett, who never once let go of Billy's hand, trying to explain what had happened to one person after another, until the ambulance arrived. And all the while, the calliope at the carousel playing its music and the rifles at the rifle range going *pop, pop, pop.*

But it didn't make sense to start the story there either, thought Billy. Because the night at the fair was before Emmett had been sent to Salina and learned his lesson. So it too belonged in the beginning.

To be *in medias res*, thought Billy, there should be just as many important things that have happened as important things that haven't happened yet. For Emmett, that meant that he should already have been to Seward to watch the fireworks; and their mother should already have followed the Lincoln Highway to San Francisco; and Emmett should already have stopped working on the farm in order to become a carpenter; and he should already have purchased the Studebaker with his savings; and he should already have grown angry at the fair and punched Jimmy Snyder in the nose and been sent to Salina and learned his lesson.

But the arrival of Duchess and Woolly in Nebraska, and the train ride to New York, and the search for the Studebaker, and the reunion with Sally, and the journey they were about to take from Times Square to the Palace of the Legion of Honor in order to find their mother on the Fourth of July, all of these things shouldn't have happened yet.

That's why Billy decided, as he leaned over chapter twenty-five with his pencil in hand, that the perfect place to start the story of Emmett's adventures was when he was driving home from Salina in the front seat of the warden's car.

ONE

Emmett

A T NINE IN THE MORNING, Emmett was walking alone from the train station at 125th Street into west Harlem.

Two hours earlier, Sally had come downstairs into the Whitneys' kitchen with the report that Billy was sound asleep.

—He's probably exhausted, said Emmett.

—I should think so, said Sally.

For a moment, Emmett thought Sally's remark was directed at him—a jab for exposing Billy to so many trials over the preceding days. But after looking at her expression, he could see that she was simply echoing his own sentiments: Billy was worn out.

So the two decided to let him sleep.

—Besides, said Sally. I'll need some time to wash the sheets and make the other beds.

In the meantime, Emmett would take the train to Harlem in order to pick up the Studebaker. Since Billy was set on beginning their journey in Times Square, Emmett suggested the three of them meet there at 10:30.

—All right, said Sally. But how will we find each other?

—Whoever gets there first can wait under the Canadian Club sign.

—And where might that be?

—Trust me, said Emmett. You won't have any trouble finding it.

. . .

When Emmett arrived at the body shop, Townhouse was waiting on the street.

—Your car's ready, he said after they'd shaken hands. You get your envelope back?

—I did.

—Good. Now you and Billy can head out to California. And not a moment too soon. . . .

Emmett looked at his friend.

—The cops came back last night, Townhouse continued. Only, it wasn't the patrolmen, it was two detectives. They asked me the same questions about Duchess, but this time they also asked about you. And they made it clear were I to hear from you or Duchess and not let them know, I'd be buying myself a heap of trouble. Because a car matching the description of your Studebaker was seen near the home of Old Testament Ackerly—on the same afternoon that someone put him in the hospital.

—The hospital?

Townhouse nodded.

—It seems a person or persons unknown went into Ackerly's house in Indiana and hit him on the head with a blunt object. They think he's going to be all right, but he hasn't come to yet. In the meantime, the boys in blue paid a visit to Duchess's old man at some flophouse downtown. He wasn't there, but Duchess had been. With another white youth and a light-blue car.

Emmett passed a hand over his mouth.

—Jesus.

—You said it. Look, as far as I'm concerned, whatever that mother-fucker Ackerly got, he deserved. But for the time being, you should probably gain some distance from the city of New York. And while you're at it, gain some distance from Duchess too. Come on. The twins are inside.

Leading the way, Townhouse took Emmett through the repair bays to where the Gonzalez brothers and the one called Otis were waiting. With the Studebaker back under its tarp, Paco and Pico were wearing their big white smiles—two craftsmen eager to reveal their handiwork.

—All set? Townhouse asked.

—All set, said Paco.

—Then let's to it.

When the brothers pulled back the tarp, Townhouse, Emmett, and Otis were silent for a moment. Then Otis began shaking with laughter.

—Yellow? asked Emmett in disbelief.

The brothers looked from Emmett to each other, then back again.

—What's wrong with yellow? asked Paco, defensively.

—It is the color of a coward, said Otis with another laugh.

Pico began speaking rapidly to his brother in Spanish. When he finished, Paco turned to the others.

—He says it's not the yellow of a coward. It's the yellow of a hornet. But she don't only look like a hornet, she *sting* like one too.

Paco began gesturing to the car, a salesman highlighting a new model's features.

—In addition to the paint job, we took out your dents, polished your chrome, and flushed your transmission. But we also put some extra horsepower under the hood.

—Well, said Otis, at least the cops won't be able to recognize you now.

—And if they do, said Paco, they won't be able to catch you.

The Gonzalez brothers laughed with shared satisfaction.

Regretting his initial response, Emmett expressed his gratitude at some length, especially given the speed at which the brothers had done their work. But when he took the envelope of cash from his back pocket, they both shook their heads.

—This one's for Townhouse, said Paco. We owed him one.

. . .

As Emmett gave Townhouse a ride back to 126th Street, the two laughed about the Gonzalez brothers, about Emmett's car and its brand-new sting. By the time they pulled in front of the brownstone, they were quiet, but neither reached for a door handle.

—Why California? Townhouse asked after a moment.

For the first time aloud, Emmett described his plan for his father's money—the plan to buy a run-down house, repair it, and sell it in order to buy two houses more; and thus, the necessity of being in a state with a large and growing population.

—That's an Emmett Watson plan if ever I heard one, said Townhouse with a smile.

—What about you? asked Emmett. What are you going to do now?

—I don't know.

Townhouse looked out the passenger-side window at his stoop.

—My mother wants me to go back to school. She's got some pipe dream of me getting a scholarship and playing college ball, neither of which is going to happen. And pops, he wants to get me a job at the post office.

—He likes his, right?

—Oh, he doesn't like it, Emmett. He loves it.

Townhouse shook his head with a tempered smile.

—When you're a letter carrier, they give you a route, you know? The blocks that you have to lug your bag up and down every day—like some pack mule on a trail. But for my old man, it doesn't seem to feel like work. Because he knows everybody on his route and everybody knows him. The old ladies, the kids, the barbers, the grocers.

Townhouse shook his head again.

—One night about six years ago, he came home looking real low. Like we'd never seen him before. When Mom asked what was wrong, he burst into tears. We thought someone had died, or something. It turned out that after fifteen years, the powers that be had changed his route. They moved him six blocks south and four blocks east, and it nearly broke his heart.

—What happened? asked Emmett.

—He got up in the morning, trudged out the door, and by the end of the year, he'd fallen in love with that route too.

The two friends laughed together. Then Townhouse put a finger in the air.

—But he never forgot the first route. Every year on Memorial Day, when he's got the day off, he walks the old one. Saying hi to everybody who recognizes him, and half the people who don't. In his words, if you've got a job as a mailman, then the US government is paying you to make friends.

—When you put it that way, it doesn't sound so bad.

—Maybe so, agreed Townhouse. Maybe so. But as much as I love my father, I can't imagine living like that. Covering the same ground day after day, week after week, year after year.

—All right. If not college or the post office, then what?

—I've been thinking about the army.

—The army? asked Emmett in surprise.

—Yeah, the army, said Townhouse, almost as if he were trying out the sound of it on himself. Why not? There's no war right now. The pay's pretty good and it's all for keeps. And if you're lucky, maybe you get stationed overseas and see something of the world.

—You'd be back in a barracks, Emmett pointed out.

—I didn't mind that so much, said Townhouse.

—Falling in . . . following orders . . . wearing a uniform . . .

—That's just it, Emmett. As a black man, whether you end up carrying a mailbag, operating an elevator, pumping gas, or doing time, you're going to be wearing a uniform. So you might as well choose the one that suits you. I figure if I keep my head down, pay my dues, maybe I can climb the ranks. Become an officer. Get myself on the right end of a salute.

—I can see it, said Emmett.

—You know something? said Townhouse. So can I.

When Townhouse finally got out of the car, Emmett did too. Coming around the hood, Emmett met him on the sidewalk, where they shook hands with the silent affection of the kindred.

The week before, when Billy had laid out his postcards and explained to Emmett how they were going to find their mother by attending one of the largest Fourth of July celebrations in the state of California, Emmett had counted his brother's notion as fanciful at best. And yet, despite the fact that Emmett and Townhouse were two young men on the verge of heading out in different directions with no real assurance of where they would land, when Townhouse said at their parting, *I'll see you,* Emmett hadn't the slightest doubt that this was true.

—·—

—What in the Lord's name, said Sally.

—It's my car, said Emmett.

—That looks about as much like a car as one of these signs.

They were standing at the northern end of Times Square, where Emmett had parked the Studebaker right behind Betty.

Sally had good cause to compare his car to the signs around them because it was just as eye catching. So much so, it had begun to attract a small crowd of passersby. Reluctant to make eye contact with them, Emmett had no idea if they were pausing to snicker or admire.

—It's yellow! exclaimed Billy, as he returned from a nearby newsstand. Just like the yellow of corn.

—Actually, said Emmett, it's the yellow of a hornet.

—If you say so, said Sally.

Eager to change the subject, Emmett pointed at the bag in Billy's hand.

—What have you got there?

As Sally returned to her truck, Billy carefully slid what he had purchased out of the bag and handed it to Emmett. It was a postcard of Times Square. At the top of the picture, peeking out from behind the buildings, was a small patch of sky; and just like in the other cards in Billy's collection, it was an unblemished blue.

Standing at Emmett's side, Billy pointed from the postcard to the landmarks.

—You see? There's the Criterion Theatre. And Bond Clothiers. And the Camel cigarette sign. And the Canadian Club sign too.

Billy looked around in appreciation.

—The man at the newsstand says that at night the signs are lit up. Every last one of them. Can you imagine?

—It's quite something.

Billy's eyes opened wide.

—Have you been here when the signs are lit up?

—Briefly, Emmett admitted.

—Hey buddy, said a sailor with his arm over the shoulder of a brunette. How 'bout taking us for a ride?

Ignoring him, Emmett got down on his haunches to speak with his brother more closely.

—I know it's exciting to be here in Times Square, Billy. But we've got a long way to go.

—And we're just getting started.

—That's right. So why don't you take one last look around, we'll say our goodbyes to Sally, and then we'll hit the road.

—Okay, Emmett. I think that's a good idea. I'll take one last look around and then we'll hit the road. But we don't have to say goodbye to Sally.

—Why is that?

—Because of Betty.

—What's wrong with Betty?

—She's a goner, said Sally.

Emmett looked up to find Sally standing by the passenger-side door of his car with her suitcase in one hand and her basket in the other.

—She overheated twice on Sally's trip from Morgen, explained Billy. And there was a big cloud of steam and clanking noises when we arrived in Times Square. Then she conked out.

—I guess I asked a little more of her than she had to give, said Sally. But she got us as far as we needed to go, God bless her.

When Emmett stood back up, Sally looked from him to the Studebaker. After a moment, he stepped forward in order to open the back door on her behalf.

—We should all sit in front, said Billy.

—It might be a little crowded, said Emmett.

—It might be at that, said Sally.

Then putting her suitcase and basket onto the back seat, she closed the back door and opened the front.

—Why don't you slide in first, Billy, she said.

After Billy climbed in with his backpack, Sally climbed in after him. Then she looked straight ahead through the windshield with her hands in her lap.

—Thank you kindly, she said when Emmett closed the door.

By the time Emmett was in the driver's seat, Billy had unfolded his map. Looking up from it, he pointed through the window.

—Officer Williams—the second policeman I spoke to—said the official start of the Lincoln Highway is on the corner of Forty-Second Street and Broadway. From there, you take a right and head toward the river. He said that when the Lincoln Highway was first opened you had to ride a ferry across the Hudson, but now you can take the Lincoln Tunnel.

Gesturing to the map, Emmett explained to Sally that the Lincoln Highway was the first transcontinental road in America.

—You don't have to tell me, she said. I know all about it.

—That's right, said Billy. Sally knows all about it.

Emmett put the car in gear.

As they entered the Lincoln Tunnel, Billy explained to Sally's apparent dismay that they were going under the Hudson River—a river so deep that he had seen a flotilla of battleships sailing up it just a few nights before. Then for her benefit, he launched into a description of the elevated and Stew and the campfires, leaving Emmett to his own thoughts.

Now that they were in motion, what Emmett had imagined he would be thinking about, what he had looked forward to thinking about, was the road ahead. When the Gonzalez brothers had said that they put some extra horsepower under the hood, they weren't kidding. Emmett could feel it—and hear it—every time he put his foot to the accelerator. So if the highway between Philadelphia and Nebraska was reasonably empty, he figured they could average fifty miles an hour, maybe sixty. They could drop Sally in Morgen late the following afternoon, and be on their way, finally heading west, with the landscapes of Wyoming and Utah and Nevada stretching out before them. And at their terminus, the state of California with a population on its way to sixteen million.

But as they emerged from the Lincoln Tunnel, having put the city of New York behind them, what Emmett found himself thinking about rather than the road ahead was what Townhouse had said earlier that morning: that he should gain some distance from Duchess.

It was a sound piece of advice and one consistent with Emmett's own instincts. The only problem was that as long as the assault on Ackerly was an open matter, the police would be looking for Duchess *and* for him. And that was assuming that Ackerly recovered. Should Ackerly die without regaining consciousness, the authorities wouldn't rest until they had one of the two of them in custody.

Glancing to his right, Emmett saw that Billy had gone back to looking at his map while Sally was watching the road.

—Sally . . .

—Yes, Emmett?

—Why did Sheriff Petersen come to see you?

Billy looked up from his map.

—The sheriff came to see you, Sally?

—It was nothing, she assured the two of them. I would feel silly even discussing it.

—Two days ago, it struck you as important enough to drive halfway across the country, pointed out Emmett.

—That was two days ago.

—Sally.

—All right, all right. It was something to do with that bit of trouble you had with Jake Snyder.

—You mean when Jake hit him in town? asked Billy.

—He and I were just working something out, said Emmett.

—So I gather, said Sally. Anyhow. It seems that when you and Jake were working your somethings out, there was another fellow there, a friend of Jake's, and shortly afterward, he was hit on the head in the alley behind the Bijou. This fellow was hit so hard, he had to be taken to the hospital in an ambulance. Sheriff Petersen knows it wasn't you who did it because you were with him at the time. But then he heard talk of a young stranger being in town that day. And that's why he came to see me. To ask if you'd had some visitors.

Emmett looked at Sally.

—Naturally, I said no.

—You said no, Sally?

—Yes, Billy, I did. And that was a lie. But it was a *white* lie. Besides, the idea that one of your brother's friends was involved with that business behind the Bijou is nonsense. Woolly would walk a mile out of his way to avoid stepping on a caterpillar. And Duchess? Well, no one who can cook a dish like Fettuccine Whatsits and then serve it on a perfectly set table would ever hit another man in the head with a two-by-four.

And thus endeth the lesson, thought Emmett.

But he wasn't so sure. . . .

—Billy, on the morning when I went into town, were Duchess and Woolly with you?

—Yes, Emmett.

—The whole time?

Billy thought for a moment.

—Woolly was with me the whole whole time. And Duchess was with us for most of the whole time.

—When wasn't Duchess with you?

—When he went on his walk.

—How long did that last?

Billy thought again.

—As long as *The Count of Monte Cristo*, *Robin Hood*, *Theseus*, and *Zorro*. It's the next left, Emmett.

Seeing the Lincoln Highway marker, Emmett shifted to the other lane and took the turn.

As he drove toward Newark, Emmett could see in his mind's eye what must have happened back in Nebraska. Having been asked by Emmett to lie low, Duchess had gone into town anyway. (Of course, he had.) Once in town, he must have stumbled on Emmett's confrontation with Jake, and witnessed the whole sordid business. But if so, why would he have bothered to hit Jake's friend?

Thinking back on the tall stranger in the cowboy hat leaning against the Studebaker, Emmett remembered his lazy posture and smug expression; he remembered how he had egged Jake on during the fight; and finally, he remembered the first words that the stranger had said: *Seems like Jake's got some unfinished business with you, Watson.*

That's how he had put it, thought Emmett: *unfinished business*. And according to the old performer FitzWilliams, *unfinished business* is exactly what Duchess said he had with his father. . . .

Emmett pulled over and sat with his hands on the wheel.

Sally and Billy looked at him with curiosity.

—What is it, Emmett? asked Billy.

—I think we need to go find Duchess and Woolly.

Sally expressed surprise.

—But Mrs. Whitney said they were on their way to Salina.

—They're not on their way to Salina, said Emmett. They're on their way to the Wolcotts' house in the Adirondacks. The only problem is that I don't know where it is.

—I know where it is, said Billy.

—You do?

Looking down, Billy slid his fingertip slowly away from Newark, New Jersey, away from the Lincoln Highway, and up into the middle of northern New York, where someone had drawn a big red star.

Sally

WHEN WE WERE DRIVING through Why-would-anyone-on-God's-green-earth-live-here, New Jersey, and Emmett pulled over to announce that we needed to go to upstate New York in order to find Duchess and Woolly, I didn't say a word. Four hours later, when he pulled into a roadside motel that looked more like a place to drop off donations than to spend the night, I didn't say a word. And when in the motel's run-down little office, Emmett signed the register with Mr. Schulte's name, I didn't say a word then either.

However . . .

Once we'd found our accommodations and I'd sent Billy into the bathroom to take a bath, Emmett directed his attention right at me. Adopting a measure of gravity, he said he wasn't sure how long it would take for him to find Duchess and Woolly. It could take a few hours, maybe more. But once he returned, the three of us could have something to eat and get a good night's sleep, and if we were back on the road by seven in the morning, he guessed they could drop me off in Morgen on Wednesday night without going much out of their way.

And that's when my allotment of not saying a word was all used up.

—Don't you worry about going out of your way, I said.

—It's no problem, he assured.

—Well, whether it is or it isn't, doesn't make much difference. Because I have no intention of being dropped off in Morgen.

—All right, he said a little hesitantly. Then where do you want to be dropped off?

—San Francisco would do just fine.

For a moment Emmett looked at me. Then he closed his eyes.

—Just because you close your eyes, I said, doesn't mean that I'm not here, Emmett. Not by a long shot. As a matter of fact, when you close your eyes, not only am I here, Billy's here, this lovely motel's here, the whole wide world is here—right where you left it.

Emmett opened his eyes again.

—Sally, he said, I don't know what expectations I may have given you, or what expectations you may have come to on your own. . . .

What's this? I wondered. Expectations he may have given me? Expectations I may have come to on my own? I leaned a little closer to make sure I didn't miss a word.

— . . . But Billy and I have been through a good deal this year. What with losing dad and the farm . . .

—Keep going, I said. You've got my attention.

Emmett cleared his throat.

—It's just that . . . Given all we've been through . . . I think what Billy and I need right now . . . is to make a fresh start together. Just the two of us.

I stared at him a moment. Then I let out a little gasp.

—So that's it, I said. You think I'm inviting myself on the ride to San Francisco with the intention of becoming a part of your household.

He looked a little uncomfortable.

—I'm just saying, Sally. . . .

—Oh, I know what you're saying—because you just said it. It came through loud and clear, despite all the hemming and hawing. So let me be loud and clear right back. For the foreseeable future, Mr. Emmett Watson, the only household I intend to be a part of is mine. A household where all the cooking and cleaning that I'll be doing is for me. Cooking *my* breakfast, *my* lunch, *my* dinner. Cleaning *my* dishes.

Washing *my* clothes. Sweeping *my* floor. So don't you worry about me putting a damper on your fresh start. Last time I checked, there were plenty of fresh starts to go around.

As Emmett walked out the door and climbed into his bright yellow car, I thought to myself that there are surely a lot of big things in America. The Empire State Building and the Statue of Liberty are big. The Mississippi River and the Grand Canyon are big. The skies over the prairie are big. But there is nothing bigger than a man's opinion of himself.

With a shake of the head, I swung the door shut, then I knocked on the bathroom door to see how Billy was coming along.

—·—

Excepting his brother, I guess I know Billy Watson better than just about anybody. I know how he eats his chicken, peas, and mashed potatoes (starting with the chicken, moving on to the peas, and saving the potatoes for last). I know how he does his homework (sitting up straight at the kitchen table and using that little rubber eraser at the end of his pencil to remove any trace of a mistake). I know how he says his prayers (always remembering to include his father, his mother, his brother, and me). But I also know how he gets himself in trouble.

It was on the first Thursday in May.

I remember because I was in the middle of making lemon meringue pies for the church social when I received the call asking me to come on down to the schoolhouse.

I admit that when I walked into the principal's office, I was already a little miffed. I had just finished whipping the egg whites for the meringue when I received the call, so I had to turn off the oven and dump the egg whites in the sink. But when I opened the door and saw Billy sitting on a chair in front of Principal Huxley's desk staring at his shoes, I went red. I know for a fact that Billy Watson has never once in his life had cause to stare at his shoes. So if he's staring at his shoes, it's because someone has made him feel the need to do so, unjustly.

—All right, I said to Principal Huxley. You've got us here in front of you. What seems to be the trouble?

It turned out that shortly after lunch, the school had what they call a duck-and-cover drill. In the middle of class, while the children were receiving regular instruction, the school bell rang five times in a row, at which point the children were supposed to climb under their desks and put their hands over their heads. But apparently, when the bell had rung and Mrs. Cooper had reminded the children what to do, Billy had refused.

Billy does not refuse very often. But when he chooses to refuse, he does so with a capital *R*. And no matter how much cajoling, insisting, or reprimanding Mrs. Cooper resorted to, Billy simply would not join his classmates under their desks.

—I have tried to explain to William, explained Principal Huxley to me, that the purpose of the drill is to ensure his own safety; and that by refusing to participate, he not only puts himself at risk, he gives cause for disruption at the very moment when disruption could do its greatest harm to others.

The years had not been kind to Principal Huxley. His hair had grown scarce on the top of his head, and there was talk in town that Mrs. Huxley had a *friend* in Kansas City. So I suppose there was some call for sympathy. But I hadn't particularly liked Principal Huxley when I was a student at Morgen Elementary, and I saw little reason for liking him now.

I turned to Billy.

—Is this true?

Without looking up from his shoes, Billy nodded his head.

—Perhaps you could tell us why you refused to follow Miss Cooper's instructions, suggested the principal.

For the first time, Billy looked up at me.

—In the introduction to his *Compendium*, Professor Abernathe says that a hero never turns his back on danger. He says a hero always meets it face-to-face. But how is someone supposed to meet danger face-to-face, if he is under his desk with his hands over his head?

Plain speaking and common sense. In my book, there's just no substitute.

—Billy, I said, why don't you wait outside.

—Okay, Sally.

The principal and I both watched as Billy walked out of the office, still staring at his shoes. When the door closed, I turned to the principal so he could see me face-to-face.

—Principal Huxley, I said, while doing my best to maintain my good nature, are you telling me that just nine years after the United States of America defeated the forces of Fascism around the world, you are chastising an eight-year-old boy for his refusal to stick his head under his desk like an ostrich in the sand?

—Miss Ransom . . .

—I have never claimed to be a scientist, I continued. In fact, when I was at the high school, I received a C in physics and a B- in biology. But what little I learned in these subjects suggests to me that the top of a desk is as likely to protect a child from a nuclear explosion as the hairs combed over your head are to protect your scalp from the sun.

I know. It was not a Christian thing to say. But my feathers were up. And I only had another two hours in which to reheat my oven, finish making my pies, and deliver them to the church. So this was no time for serving soft-boiled eggs.

And wouldn't you know it: When I left the office five minutes later, Principal Huxley had agreed that to ensure the safety of the student body, one courageous soul by the name of Billy Watson would be appointed as the Duck-and-Cover Monitor. Henceforth, when the school bell rang five times in a row, rather than hide under his desk, Billy would go from room to room with a clipboard in hand in order to confirm the compliance of everybody else.

As I said, I know Billy better than just about anybody, including how he gets himself in trouble.

So I had no excuse to be surprised when after knocking on the bathroom door three times, I finally opened it to find the water in the bathtub running, the window open, and Billy gone.

Emmett

AFTER DRIVING A MILE down the winding dirt road, Emmett began to suspect he had taken a wrong turn. The man at the filling station, who knew the Wolcotts by name, had told Emmett that he should continue along Route 28 for another eight and a half miles, then take a right onto the dirt road bordered by white cedars. Emmett had measured the distance on the odometer, and though he wasn't certain what white cedars looked like, the road he came upon was lined with evergreens, so he took the turn. But a mile later, there was still no sign of a residence. Luckily, the road wasn't wide enough for Emmett to turn around, so he drove onward and a few minutes later came upon a large timber house at the edge of a lake—beside which was parked Woolly's car.

Rolling to a stop behind the Cadillac, Emmett got out of the Studebaker and walked toward the lake. It was late in the afternoon and the water was so still its surface perfectly reflected the pine trees on the opposite shore and the disparate clouds overhead, giving the world an illusion of vertical symmetry. The only sign of movement was from a great blue heron that, having been disturbed by the closing of Emmett's car door, had taken flight from the shallows and now was gliding silently about two feet above the water.

To Emmett's left was a small building that appeared to be some kind of work shed, because resting nearby on a pair of sawhorses, awaiting repair, was an overturned dory with a breach in its bow.

To Emmett's right was the house overlooking the lawn, the lake, and the dock. Along its front was a grand porch with rocking chairs and a wide set of steps descending to the grass. There would be a main entrance at the top of those steps, Emmett knew, but on the other side of the Cadillac was a path bordered by painted stones that led to a stoop and an open door.

Climbing the steps, Emmett opened the screen and called inside.

—Woolly? Duchess?

Hearing nothing, he entered, letting the screen door slam behind him. He found himself in a muck room with an array of fishing rods, hiking boots, slickers, and skates. Everything in the room was neatly put away except for the Adirondack chairs that were stacked in the middle of the floor. Over a rifle cabinet hung a large hand-painted sign with a checklist entitled CLOSING THE HOUSE.

1. Remove firing pins
2. Stow canoes
3. Empty icebox
4. Take in rockers
5. Take out garbage
6. Make beds
7. Close flues
8. Lock windows
9. Lock doors
10. Go home

Leaving the muck room, Emmett entered a hallway, where he stopped, listened, and called again for Woolly and Duchess. Receiving no response, he proceeded to poke his head into various rooms. While the first two seemed untouched, in the third a cue and several balls had been left on the felt of the pool table, as if someone had stopped a game in midplay. At the hallway's end, Emmett stepped into a high-ceilinged living room with various arrangements of couches and chairs, and an open staircase that led to the second floor.

Emmett shook his head in appreciation. It was one of the finest rooms that he had ever seen. Much of the furniture was in the Arts and Crafts style, fashioned from cherry or oak, perfectly joined and discreetly detailed. Over the center of the room hung a large light fixture that, like the lamps, was shaded with mica, ensuring that the room would be cast in a warm glow once evening fell. The fireplace, the ceilings, the couches, the staircase had all been built larger than normal, but they were in proportion to each other and remained in harmony with a human scale, such that the room seemed at once cozy and generous.

It wasn't hard to understand why this house had maintained such a privileged position in Woolly's imagination. It would have maintained a privileged position in Emmett's, had he had the luxury of growing up in it.

Through a pair of open doors Emmett could see a dining room with a long oak table, and down the continuation of the hallway he could see doors leading to other rooms, including a kitchen at the end. But if Woolly and Duchess had been in one of those rooms, they would have heard him calling. So Emmett headed up the stairs.

At the top of the steps, the hallway led in both directions.

First, he checked the bedrooms to his right. Though they differed in terms of size and furnishings—some with double beds, some with single beds, one with a pair of bunks—they all shared a rough simplicity. In a house like this, Emmett understood, one wasn't meant to linger in one's bedroom. One was meant to join the family downstairs for breakfast at the long oak table, then spend the rest of the day out of doors. None of the rooms showed any sign of having been used the night before, so doubling back, Emmett headed for the other end of the hallway.

As Emmett walked, he glanced at the photographs on the wall, intending to give them only passing consideration. And yet he found himself slowing his pace, then stopping altogether in order to study them more closely.

Though the pictures varied in size, all were of people. Among them were portraits of groups and individuals, children and adults, some in motion, others at rest. Taken separately, there was nothing unusual about them. The faces and clothes were ordinary enough. But taken together, there was something profoundly enviable about this wall of photographs in their matching black frames. And it wasn't due to the prevalence of sunlight and carefree smiles. It was a matter of heritage.

Emmett's father had grown up in some version of this place. As he had written in his last letter, what had been handed down in his family from generation to generation were not simply stocks and bonds, but houses and paintings, furniture and boats. And when Emmett's father chose to tell anecdotes of his youth, there seemed no end to the cousins, uncles, and aunts gathered around the holiday table. But for some reason, for some reason that had never been fully explained, Emmett's father had left all of that behind when he moved to Nebraska. Left it behind without a trace.

Or almost without a trace.

There were the trunks in the attic with their exotic stickers from foreign hotels, and the picnic basket with its orderly arrangement of utensils, and the unused china in the hutch—remnants of the life that Emmett's father had relinquished in order to pursue his Emersonian ideal. Emmett shook his head, uncertain of whether his father's actions should give him cause for disappointment or admiration.

As usual with such puzzles of the heart, the answer was probably both.

Progressing down the hall, Emmett could tell from the quality of the photographs and the style of the clothing that the pictures were moving backward in time. Starting at some point in the 1940s, they receded through the thirties and the twenties all the way into the teens. But when Emmett passed the side table at the top of the stairs, the photographs reversed course and began advancing through the decades. It was when he had returned to the 1940s and was looking with curiosity at a blank space on the wall that Emmett heard the music— music coming faintly from somewhere down the hallway. Passing several of the rooms, he homed in on the sound until he stopped before the second-to-last door and listened.

It was Tony Bennett.

Tony Bennett singing that he would go from rags to riches, if you'd only say you care.

Emmett knocked.

—Woolly? Duchess?

When neither replied, he opened the door.

It was another simply furnished room, this one with two small single beds and a bureau. On one of the beds lay Woolly, his stocking feet extending beyond the end of the frame, his eyes closed, his hands crossed on his chest. On the bedside table were two empty medicine bottles and three pink pills.

With a terrible sense of foreboding, Emmett approached the bed. After saying Woolly's name, he shook him gently by the shoulder, finding him stiff to the touch.

—Oh, Woolly, he said, taking a seat on the opposite bed.

Feeling the onset of nausea, Emmett turned away from his friend's expressionless features and found himself staring at the bedside table. Having already recognized the little blue bottle as Woolly's so-called medicine, Emmett picked up the brown bottle. He had never heard of the medication printed on the label, but he saw that it had been prescribed to Sarah Whitney.

In just this way, thought Emmett, does misery beget misery. For as good as Woolly's sister was at forgiving, she would never be able to forgive herself for this. As he set the empty bottle back down, from the radio came a jazz number, swinging and discordant.

Rising from the bed, Emmett crossed to the radio and switched it off. On the bureau beside the radio was an old cigar box and a dictionary that could have come from anywhere, but leaning against the wall was a framed photograph that could only have come from the empty space in the hall.

It was a snapshot of Woolly as a boy sitting in a canoe between his mother and father. Woolly's parents—a handsome couple in their late thirties—each had a paddle resting across the gunwale, as if they were on the verge of setting out. From Woolly's expression, you could tell he was a little nervous, but he was laughing too, as if someone outside of the frame, someone on the dock, were making a face for his benefit.

Just a few days before—when they had been outside the orphanage waiting for Duchess—Billy had explained to Woolly about their mother and the fireworks in San Francisco, and Woolly, in turn, had explained to Billy about the Fourth of July celebrations his family would have here at the camp. It occurred to Emmett that this picture of Woolly sitting between his parents in the canoe could well have been taken on the very same day that Emmett had lain between his parents to watch the fireworks in Seward. And for perhaps the first time, Emmett had an inkling of why the journey west along the Lincoln Highway had become so important to his brother.

Gently, Emmett returned the photograph to its place on the bureau. Then after taking one more look at his friend, he went in search of a phone. But as he was heading down the hall, he heard a clanging coming from downstairs.

Duchess, he thought.

And the grief that had been welling up inside him was eclipsed by a feeling of fury.

Descending the stairs, Emmett moved quickly down the hallway in the direction of the kitchen, once again homing in on the source of a sound. Stepping through the first door on his left, he entered a room that looked like a gentleman's office, but in disarray—with books pulled from the bookcases, drawers withdrawn from the desk, and papers scattered on the floor. To Emmett's left, a framed painting jutted at a ninety-degree angle from the wall, while behind the painting stood Duchess, haplessly swinging an ax at the smooth gray surface of a safe.

—Come on, Duchess encouraged as he hit the safe again. Come on, baby.

—Duchess, called Emmett once.

Then again, more loudly.

Startled, Duchess checked his swing and looked back. But upon seeing Emmett, he broke into a smile.

—Emmett! Boy, am I glad to see you!

Emmett found Duchess's smile to be as discordant as the jazz number that had come on the radio in Woolly's room; and he felt the same urgent desire to switch it off. As Emmett moved toward Duchess, Duchess's expression transitioned from elation to concern.

—What is it? What's wrong?

—What's wrong? Emmett said, stopping in amazement. Haven't you been upstairs? Haven't you seen Woolly?

Suddenly understanding, Duchess set the ax down on a chair, then shook his head with a solemn expression.

—I saw him, Emmett. What can I say? It's terrible.

—But how . . . ? blurted Emmett. How could you *let* him?

—Let him? repeated Duchess in surprise. Do you seriously think if I had known what Woolly intended to do, I would have left him on his own? I've been keeping an eye on Woolly since the minute I met him. Not a week ago, I went so far as to take away the last bottle of his medicine. But he must have had another one stashed away. And don't ask me where he got hold of those pills.

With all his feelings of impotency and rage, Emmett wanted to blame Duchess. He wanted to blame him, badly. But he also understood that it wasn't Duchess's fault. And rising up within him, like bile in the throat, came the memory of his own assurance to Woolly's sister that all would be well.

—Did you call an ambulance, at least, Emmett asked after a moment, hearing his own voice falter.

Duchess shook his head with an expression of futility.

—By the time I found him, it was too late. He was already as cold as ice.

—All right, said Emmett. I'll call the police.

—The police . . . ? Why would you do that?

—We've got to tell somebody.

—Of course we do. And we will. But whether we do it now or later won't make any difference to Woolly. But it could make a big difference to us.

Ignoring Duchess, Emmett headed toward the telephone on the desk. When Duchess saw where Emmett was going, he scrambled in the same direction, but Emmett beat him to it.

Holding Duchess off with one hand, Emmett picked up the receiver with the other, only to find it silent—the service having yet to be restored for the season.

When Duchess realized the phone was dead, he relaxed his posture.

—Let's talk this through for a second.

—Come on, said Emmett, taking Duchess by the elbow. We'll drive to the station.

Steering Duchess out of the office, Emmett walked him down the hallway, barely listening as Duchess tried to make some sort of case for delay.

—It's terrible what's happened, Emmett. I'm the first to say so. But it's what Woolly chose for himself. For his own reasons. Reasons that we may never fully understand and that we have no real right to second-guess. What's important now is for us to keep in mind what Woolly would've wanted.

When they reached the screen door in the muck room, Duchess turned around in order to face Emmett.

—You should have been there when your brother talked about the house he wants to build in California. I've never seen Woolly so excited. He could just picture the two of you living there together. If we go to the cops now, I'm telling you, within the hour this place is going to be crawling with people, and we'll never get to finish what Woolly started.

With one hand, Emmett opened the screen door, with the other, he pushed Duchess down the steps.

After Duchess stumbled a few feet in the direction of the overturned dory, he suddenly spun around as if he'd had an idea.

—Hey! You see that boathouse? There's a workbench inside it with a whole selection of chisels and files and drills. They were of no use to me. But I bet you could get that safe open in a matter of minutes. After we liberate Woolly's trust, we can go find a telephone together. And once the ambulance is on its way, we can head for California, just like Woolly wanted.

—*We* are not going anywhere, Emmett said, his face growing flush. We are not going to San Francisco or Los Angeles or Tinseltown. My brother and I are going to California. *You* are going to Salina.

Duchess looked at Emmett in disbelief.

—Why on earth would I go to Salina, Emmett?

When Emmett didn't reply, Duchess shook his head and pointed to the ground.

—I am staying right here until I get that safe open. And if you don't want to stick around and help, that's your business. It's a free country. But I'm telling you, Emmett, as a friend: If you leave now, it's a decision you're going to regret. Because once you get to California, you'll realize that a couple of grand isn't going to get you very far. Then you'll wish you had your share of the trust.

Stepping forward, Emmett took Duchess by the collar just as he had at the Whitneys', only this time he used both hands, and he could feel the fabric tightening around Duchess's throat as he rotated his fists.

—Don't you get it? he said through his teeth. There is no trust. No inheritance. No money in the safe. It's a fairy tale. A fairy tale Woolly cooked up so you would take him home.

As if in disgust, Emmett shoved Duchess back.

Tripping over the stones that lined the pathway, Duchess fell on the grass.

542 | AMOR TOWLES

—You're going to the cops, said Emmett, if I have to drag you to the station.

—But, Emmett, there *is* money in the safe.

Spinning around, Emmett discovered his brother standing in the doorway of the muck room.

—Billy! What are you doing here?

Before Billy could answer, his expression transitioned from one of instruction to one of alarm, prompting Emmett to turn back around—at the very moment that Duchess's arm went into motion.

The blow came hard enough to knock Emmett off his feet, but not hard enough to knock him unconscious. Feeling the coolness of blood on his brow, Emmett gathered his senses and rose onto all fours just in time to see Duchess push Billy into the house and slam the inner door.

Duchess

THE DAY BEFORE, after Woolly acknowledged that the notion of a combination had most certainly definitely slipped his mind, he wondered if I wanted to take a walk down to the dock.

—You go right ahead, I said. I think I'll take a moment to myself.

When Woolly went outside, I spent a few minutes in front of Great-grandpa's safe, staring at it with my hands on my hips. Then with a shake of the head, I went to work. First, I tried putting my ear against the metal and turning the dials to hear the clicks of the tumblers like they do in the movies—which worked about as well as anything else you try doing that you've seen in the movies.

Retrieving the Othello case from my book bag, I took out my old man's knife. My idea was to force the point of the blade into the seam between the door and the casing and wiggle it back and forth. But when I put my full weight behind the knife, what gave was the blade, snapping clean off at the hilt.

—Forged, tempered, and burnished by a master craftsman in Pittsburgh, my eye, I muttered.

Next, I went in search of some genuine tools. But after opening every kitchen drawer and rummaging through every closet, I proceeded to the mudroom, where I sifted through every cubbyhole and basket to no avail. For a moment, I considered shooting the safe with one of the rifles, but given my luck, I'd probably be hit by a ricochet.

So I went down to the dock, where Woolly was admiring the view.

—Hey, Woolly, I called from dry land. Do you know if there's a hardware store in the neighborhood?

—What's that? he asked turning around. A hardware store? I'm not sure. But there's a general store about five miles up the road.

—Perfect. I shouldn't be long. You need anything?

Woolly thought about it for a moment, then shook his head.

—I've got everything I need, he said with a Woolly sort of smile. I'm just going to wander around a bit and unpack my things. Then I thought I might take a little nap.

—Why not? I said. You've earned it.

Twenty minutes later, I was roaming the aisles of the general store thinking they must call it that because it generally has everything but what you're looking for. It was like someone had tipped a house on its side and shaken it until everything that wasn't nailed to the carpet came tumbling out the door: spatulas, oven mitts, and egg timers; sponges, brushes, and soaps; pencils, pads, and erasers; yo-yos and rubber balls. In a state of consumer exasperation, I finally asked the proprietor if he had any sledgehammers. The best he could do was a ball-peen hammer and a set of screwdrivers.

When I got back to the house, Woolly was already upstairs, so I returned to the office with my tools. I must have banged away on the face of that thing for about an hour with nothing to show for it but some chicken-scratched metal and a sweat-soaked shirt.

The next hour I spent searching the office for the combination. I figured a wily old moneymaker like Mr. Wolcott wouldn't be so careless as to leave the combination of his safe to the vicissitudes of memory. Especially considering that he lived into his nineties. He must have written it down somewhere.

Naturally enough, I started with his desk. First, I went through the drawers looking for a diary or address book where an important number might be logged on the final page. Then I pulled out the drawers and flipped them over to see if he had written it down on one of the undersides. I looked under the desk lamp and on the bottom of the bronze bust of Abraham Lincoln, despite the fact that it weighed about two hundred pounds. Next, I turned my attention to the books, flipping through their pages in search of a hidden scrap of paper. That endeavor lasted as long as it took me to realize that flipping through all the old man's books would take me the rest of my life.

That's when I decided to wake up Woolly—in order to ask him which of the bedrooms was his great-grandfather's.

Earlier, when Woolly had said he was going to take a little nap, I didn't think anything of it. As I mentioned, he hadn't gotten much sleep the night before, and then he'd woken me at dawn in order to make the hasty exit. So I figured a nap was exactly what he intended to take.

But the moment I opened the bedroom door, I knew what I was looking at. After all, I had stood on that threshold before. I recognized the suggestion of order—with Woolly's belongings lined up on the bureau and his shoes set side by side at the end of the bed. I recognized the stillness—set into relief by the delicate movement of the curtains and the murmur of a news broadcast on the radio. And I recognized the expression on Woolly's face—an expression that, like Marceline's, radiated neither happiness nor sorrow, but which did suggest some semblance of peace.

When Woolly's arm had fallen from his side, he must have been too far gone or too indifferent to bother lifting it up, because his fingers were brushing the floor, just like they had at the HoJo's. And just like then, I put his arm back where it belonged, this time crossing his hands on his chest.

At long last, I thought, the houses, cars, and Roosevelts had all come tumbling down.

—*The wonder is he hath endured so long.*

As I was leaving, I turned off the radio. But then I turned it on again, thinking that in the hours ahead, Woolly would probably appreciate having the occasional commercial to keep him company.

That night, I ate baked beans out of a can and washed them down with a warm Pepsi-Cola, the only things I could find in the kitchen to eat. So as not to crowd Woolly's ghost, I slept on a couch in the great room. And when I woke in the morning, I went right back to work.

In the hours that followed, I must have hit that safe one thousand times. I hit it with the hammer. I hit it with a croquet mallet. I even tried hitting it with the bust of Abe Lincoln, but I couldn't get a good enough grip.

Around four in the afternoon, I decided to pay a visit to the Caddy, in hopes of finding a tire iron. But as I was coming out of the house, I noticed that the rowboat overturned on a pair of sawhorses had a sizable hole in its bow. Figuring that someone had put it there to repair it, I went into the boathouse looking for an implement that might prove useful. Sure enough, behind all the paddles and canoes was a workbench with a slew of drawers. I must have spent half an hour going over every inch of it, but all it offered up was a new assortment of hand tools that weren't going to get me much further than the ones from the general store. Remembering that Woolly had mentioned an annual fireworks display at the camp, I tore the boathouse apart looking for explosives. Then, just as I was about to walk out in a state of moral defeat, I found an ax hanging between two pegs on the wall.

With the whistle of a lumberjack on my lips, I sauntered back to the old man's study, took up a position in front of the safe, and began to swing. I couldn't have made contact more than ten times when suddenly, out of the blue, Emmett Watson comes bursting through the door.

—Emmett! I exclaimed. Boy, am I glad to see you!

And I meant it. For if there was anyone I knew in this whole wide world who could find a way to get into that safe, it was Emmett.

Before I had a chance to explain the situation, the conversation got a little off course—if understandably so. For having arrived while I was in the boathouse and finding no one home, Emmett had gone upstairs and discovered Woolly.

He was clearly rattled by it. In all probability, he had never seen a dead body before, certainly not the body of a friend. So I really couldn't fault him for throwing some blame my way. That's what rattled people do. They point a finger. They point a finger at whoever's standing closest—and given the nature of how we congregate, that's more likely to be friend than foe.

I reminded Emmett that I was the one who'd been keeping an eye on Woolly for the last year and a half, and I could see that he was cooling down. But then he started talking a little crazy. Acting a little crazy.

First off, he wanted to call the cops. When he discovered that the phone was dead, he wanted to drive to the station—and he wanted to take me with him.

I tried talking some sense into him. But he was so tightly wound, he marched me down the hall, pushed me out the door, and knocked me to the ground, claiming that there was no money in the safe, that I was going to the police station, and that, if necessary, he was going to drag me there.

Given the state he was in, I have no doubt that's exactly what he would've done—no matter how deeply he would have regretted it later. In other words, he wasn't leaving me many options.

And fate seemed to agree. Because when Emmett knocked me down, I landed on the grass with my hand practically resting on one of those painted stones. And then out of nowhere, Billy pops up—just in time to draw Emmett's attention in the other direction.

The rock that I had my hand on was the size of a grapefruit. But I wasn't looking to do any serious damage to Emmett. I just needed to slow him down for a few minutes, so he could regain a little perspective before he did something he couldn't undo. Crawling a few feet out of my way, I picked up one that was no bigger than an apple.

Sure, it knocked him to the ground when I hit him with it. But that was more from the surprise than from the force of impact. I knew he'd be back in the swing of things before you knew it.

Figuring if anyone could talk some sense into Emmett, his brother could, I dashed up the steps, ushered Billy into the house, and locked the door behind us.

—Why did you hit Emmett? Billy cried, looking more rattled than his brother. Why did you hit him, Duchess? You shouldn't have hit him!

—You're absolutely right, I agreed, trying to settle him down. I shouldn't have done it. And I swear, I'll never do it again.

Leading him a few steps from the door, I took him by the shoulders and made a stab at talking to him man-to-man.

—Listen, Billy: There's been something of a snafu. The safe is here, just like Woolly said it would be. And I agree with you wholeheartedly that the money's inside of it, waiting to be claimed. But we don't have the combination. So what we need now is a little bit of time, some Yankee ingenuity, and plenty of teamwork.

As soon as I had taken Billy by the shoulders, he had closed his eyes. And before I was halfway through my speech, he was shaking his head and quietly repeating his brother's name.

—Are you worried about Emmett? I asked. Is that it? I promise there's no cause for concern. I barely hit him. In fact, he should be back on his feet any second now.

Even as I said this, we could hear the knob rattling behind us, then Emmett pounding on the door and shouting our names.

THE LINCOLN HIGHWAY | 549

—There, I said leading the kid into the hallway. What'd I tell you?

When the pounding on the door stopped, I lowered my voice in order to speak in confidence.

—The fact of the matter, Billy, is that for reasons I can't go into at this moment, your brother wants to call the authorities. But I fear that if he does that, we'll never get in the safe, there'll be no divvying, and that house of yours—the one for you, and Emmett, and your mother—it'll never get built.

I thought I was making a pretty good case, but Billy just kept shaking his head with his eyes closed and saying Emmett's name.

—We're going to talk to Emmett, I assured him with a touch of frustration. We're going to talk with him all about it, Billy. But for the moment, it's just you and me.

And just like that, the kid stopped shaking his head.

Here we go, I thought. I must be getting through!

But then he opened his eyes and kicked me in the shin.

Isn't that priceless?

A moment later, there I was, hopping on one foot as he ran down the hallway.

—Jeezo peezo, I said, taking off after him.

But when I got to the great room, he was gone.

As God is my witness, even though the kid hadn't been out of my sight for more than thirty seconds, he had vanished into thin air—like Lucinda the cockatoo.

—Billy? I called out, looking behind one couch after another. Billy?

From somewhere different in the house, I heard another doorknob rattling.

—Billy! I called to the room at large, with a growing sense of urgency. I know the escapade hasn't been playing out exactly as we planned, but the important thing is that we stick together and see it through! You, your brother, and me! All for one and one for all!

That's when from the direction of the kitchen came the sound of breaking glass. A moment later Emmett would be in the house. Of that there was no doubt. Having no other choice, I made a beeline for the mudroom where, finding the rifle cabinet locked, I picked up a croquet ball and threw it through the glass.

Billy

AFTER THEY HAD CHECKED IN to room 14 at the White Peaks Motel on Route 28, and Billy had taken off his backpack, Emmett said he was heading out to find Woolly and Duchess.

—In the meantime, he told Billy, it's probably for the best if you stay here.

—Besides, said Sally, when was the last time you took a bath, young man? I wouldn't be surprised if it was back in Nebraska.

That's true, said Billy nodding. The last time I took a bath was back in Nebraska.

As Emmett began talking quietly to Sally, Billy put his backpack back on his back and headed toward the bathroom.

—Do you really need that thing in there with you? Sally asked.

—I need it, said Billy with his hand on the doorknob, because it's where my clean clothes are.

—All right. But don't forget to wash behind your ears.

—I won't.

When Emmett and Sally went back to talking, Billy went into the bathroom, closed the door, and turned on the bathtub faucets. But he didn't take off his dirty clothes. He didn't take off his dirty clothes because he wasn't going to take a bath. That had been a white lie. Like the one that Sally had told Sheriff Petersen.

After double checking to make sure that the drain was open so that the tub wouldn't overflow, Billy tightened the straps on his backpack, climbed on top of the toilet, pushed up the sash, and slipped out the window, leaving no one the wiser.

Billy knew that his brother and Sally might only be talking for a few minutes, so he had to run as fast as he could around the motel to where the Studebaker was parked. He ran so fast, when he climbed into the trunk and lowered the lid, he could hear his heart beating in his chest.

When Duchess had told Billy how he and Woolly had hidden in the trunk of the warden's car, Billy had asked how they had gotten out again. Duchess had explained that he had brought along a spoon in order to pop the latch. So before climbing into the Studebaker's trunk, Billy had taken his jackknife out of his backpack. Then he had also taken out his flashlight because it was going to be dark in the trunk once the lid was closed. Billy wasn't afraid of the dark. But Duchess had said how difficult it had been to pop the latch without being able to see it. *We came this close*, Duchess said holding his thumb and finger an inch apart, *to riding all the way back to Salina without even getting a glimpse of Nebraska.*

Switching on his flashlight, Billy took a quick look at Woolly's watch to check the time. It was 3:30. Then he switched off the flashlight and waited. A few minutes later, he heard the car door open and close, the engine start, and they were on their way.

—·—

Back in the motel room, when Emmett had told Billy that it was probably for the best if he stayed behind, Billy hadn't been surprised.

Emmett often thought it was for the best that Billy remain behind while he was going someplace else. Like when he went into the court-house in Morgen in order to be sentenced by Judge Schomer. *I think it's for the best*, he'd said to Billy, *that you wait out here with Sally*. Or when they were at the depot in Lewis and Emmett had gone to find out about the freight trains to New York. Or when they were on the West Side Elevated and he had gone looking for Duchess's father.

In the third paragraph of the introduction to his *Compendium of Heroes, Adventurers, and Other Intrepid Travelers*, Professor Abernathe says the hero often leaves his friends and family behind when setting out on an exploit. He leaves his friends and family behind because he is concerned about exposing them to peril, and because he has the courage to face the unknown by himself. That's why Emmett often thought it best for Billy to remain behind.

But Emmett didn't know about Xenos.

In chapter twenty-four of his *Compendium*, Professor Abernathe says: *As long as there have been great men who have accomplished great things, there have been storytellers eager to recount their exploits. But whether it was Hercules or Theseus, Caesar or Alexander, what feats these men accomplished, what victories they achieved, what adversities they overcame would never have been possible without the contributions of Xenos.*

Although Xenos sounds like it might be the name of a figure from history—like Xerxes or Xenophon—Xenos is not the name of a person at all. *Xenos* is a word from ancient Greek that means foreigner and stranger, guest and friend. Or more simply, the Other. As Professor Abernathe says: *Xenos is the one on the periphery in the unassuming garb whom you hardly notice. Throughout history, he has appeared in many guises: as a watchman or attendant, a messenger or page, a shopkeeper, waiter, or vagabond. Though usually unnamed, for the most part unknown, and too often forgotten, Xenos always shows up at just the right time in just the right place in order to play his essential role in the course of events.*

That's why when Emmett had suggested it was for the best that Billy stay behind while he went in search of Woolly and Duchess, Billy had no choice but to sneak out the window and hide in the trunk.

—·—

Thirteen minutes after they had left the motel, the Studebaker came to a stop and the driver's door opened and closed.

Billy was about to pop the latch of the trunk when he smelled the fumes of gasoline. They must be at a filling station, he thought, and Emmett is asking for directions. Though Woolly had put a big red star on Billy's map to show the location of his family's house, the map was drawn at too big a scale to include the local roads. So while Emmett knew he had reached the vicinity of Woolly's house, he didn't know exactly where it was.

Listening carefully, Billy heard his brother call out thanks to someone. Then the door opened and closed and they were driving again. Twelve minutes later, the Studebaker took a turn and began moving slower and slower until it rolled to a stop. Then the engine went off, and the driver's door opened and closed again.

This time Billy decided he would wait at least five minutes before trying to pop the latch. Training his flashlight beam on Woolly's watch, he saw that it was now 4:02. At 4:07 he heard his brother calling out for Woolly and Duchess, followed by a screen door's slam. Emmett had probably gone inside the house, thought Billy, but he waited another two minutes. When it was 4:09, he popped the latch and climbed out. He put his jackknife and flashlight back in his backpack, his backpack back on his back, and quietly closed the trunk.

The house was bigger than just about any house that Billy had ever seen. At its near end was the screen door that Emmett must have gone through. Quietly, Billy climbed the steps of the stoop, peeked through the screen, and let himself inside, being sure not to let the door slam behind him.

The first room he entered was a storage area with all sorts of things that you would use outside, like boots and raincoats, skates and rifles. On the wall were the ten rules for *Closing the House*. Billy could tell the list was written in the order in which you were supposed to do things, but he wondered about the last item, the one that said *Go home*. After a moment, Billy decided it must have been put there in jest.

Poking his head out of the storage room, Billy could see his brother at the end of the hallway, staring at the ceiling of a large room. Emmett would do that sometimes—stop and stare at a room in order to understand how it had been built. After a moment, Emmett climbed a set of stairs. When Billy could hear his brother's footsteps overhead, he snuck down the hallway and into the large room.

As soon as he saw the fireplace big enough for everyone to gather around, Billy knew exactly where he was. Through the windows he could see the porch with the overhanging roof, under which you could sit on rainy afternoons and on top of which you could lie on warm summer nights. Upstairs there would be enough rooms for friends and family to visit for the holidays. And there in the corner was the special spot for the Christmas tree.

Behind the staircase was a room with a long table and chairs. That must be the dining room, thought Billy, where Woolly gave the Gettysburg Address.

Crossing the large room and entering the opposite hallway, Billy poked his head into the first room that he passed. It was the study, right where Woolly had drawn it. While the large room had been neat and tidy, the study was not. It was a mess, with books and papers scattered about and a bust of Abraham Lincoln lying on the floor under a painting of the signing of the Declaration of Independence. On a chair near the bust were a hammer and some screwdrivers, and there were scratches all across the front of the safe.

Woolly and Duchess must have been trying to get into the safe with the hammer and screwdrivers, thought Billy, but it wasn't going to work. A safe was made of steel and designed to be impenetrable. If you could open a safe with a hammer and screwdrivers, then it wouldn't be a safe.

The door of the safe had four dials, each of which showed the numbers zero through nine. That meant there were ten thousand different possible combinations. Duchess and Woolly would have been better off trying all ten thousand by starting with 0000 and working their way up to 9999, thought Billy. That would have taken less time than trying to break in with the hammer and screwdrivers. Even better, though, would be to guess the combination that Woolly's great-grandfather had chosen.

It took Billy six tries.

Once the door of the safe was open, it reminded Billy of the box at the bottom of his father's bureau, in that there were important papers inside—just a lot more of them. But under the shelf with all of the important papers, Billy counted fifteen stacks of fifty-dollar bills. Billy remembered that Woolly's great-grandfather had put a hundred and fifty thousand dollars in his safe. That meant that each stack was made up of ten thousand dollars. Stacks of ten thousand dollars, thought Billy, in a safe with ten thousand possible combinations. Closing the door of the safe, Billy turned away, but then turned back again in order to spin the dials.

Leaving the study, Billy continued down the hallway and went into the kitchen. It was neat and tidy except for an empty soda pop bottle and a can of beans that had a spoon sticking straight up out of it like the stick on a candy apple. The only other sign that someone had been in the kitchen was the envelope tucked between the salt and pepper shakers on the table. The envelope, which said *To Be Opened in the Event of My Absence*, had been left there by Woolly. Billy could tell it had been left by Woolly because the handwriting on the envelope matched the handwriting on Woolly's drawing of the house.

As Billy was putting the envelope back between the salt and pepper shakers, he heard the sound of metal hitting metal. Tiptoeing down the hallway and peeking through the door of the study, he saw Duchess swinging an ax at the safe.

He was about to explain to Duchess about the ten thousand

combinations when he heard his brother's footsteps thumping down the stairs. Running back down the hallway, Billy slipped back into the kitchen and out of sight.

Once Emmett was inside the study, Billy couldn't hear what his brother was saying, but he could tell that he was angry from the tone of his voice. After a moment, Billy heard what sounded like a scuffle, then Emmett emerged from the study holding Duchess by the elbow. As Emmett marched him down the hallway, Duchess was speaking quickly about something that Woolly had chosen for himself for his own reasons. Then Emmett marched Duchess into the storage room.

Following quickly but quietly down the hallway, Billy peeked around the doorframe of the storage room in time to hear Duchess tell Emmett why they shouldn't go to the cops. Then Emmett pushed Duchess out the door.

In chapter one of the *Compendium of Heroes, Adventurers, and Other Intrepid Travelers*—after the part when Professor Abernathe explains how many of the greatest adventure stories start *in medias res*—he goes on to explain the tragic flaws of classical heroes. *All classical heroes*, he says, *however strong or wise or courageous they may be, have some flaw in their character which leads to their undoing.* For Achilles the fatal flaw had been anger. When he was angry, Achilles could not contain himself. Even though it had been foretold that he might die during the Trojan War, once his friend Patroclus was killed, Achilles returned to the battlefield blinded by a black and murderous rage. And that's when he was struck by the poisonous arrow.

Billy understood that his brother had the same flaw as Achilles. Emmett was not a reckless person. He rarely raised his voice or showed impatience. But when something happened to make him angry, the force of his fury could come to such a boil that it resulted in *an injudicious act with irreversible consequences.* According to Billy's father, that's what Judge Schomer had said Emmett was guilty of when he had hit Jimmy Snyder: *an injudicious act with irreversible consequences.*

Through the screen door, Billy could see that Emmett was coming to a boil right now. His face was growing red, and having taken Duchess by the shirt, he was shouting. He was shouting that there was no trust fund, no inheritance, no money in the safe. Then he shoved Duchess to the ground.

This must be it, thought Billy. This is the time and place at which I needed to be in order to play my essential role in the course of events. So Billy opened the screen door and told his brother that there *was* money in the safe.

But when Emmett turned around, Duchess hit him on the head with a stone and Emmett fell to the ground. He fell to the ground just as Jimmy Snyder had.

—Emmett! Billy shouted.

And Emmett must have heard Billy because he began to get up onto his knees. Then Duchess was suddenly at the doorway pushing Billy inside, locking the door, and talking quickly.

—Why did you hit Emmett? Billy said. Why did you hit him, Duchess? You shouldn't have hit him.

Duchess swore he wouldn't do it again, but then he went back to talking quickly. He was talking about something called a snafu. And then about the safe. And Woolly. And the Yankees.

When Emmett began banging on the storage-room door, Duchess pushed Billy into the hallway, and when Emmett's banging stopped, Duchess started talking again, this time about the authorities and the house in California.

And suddenly, Billy felt like he had been here before. The tightness of Duchess's grip and the urgency with which he was speaking made Billy feel like he was back on the West Side Elevated in the dark in the hands of Pastor John.

—We're going to talk to Emmett, said Duchess. We're going to talk with him all about it, Billy. But for the moment, it's just you and me.

Then Billy understood.

Emmett wasn't there. Ulysses wasn't there. Sally wasn't there. Once again, he was alone and forsaken. Forsaken by everyone, including his Maker. And whatever happened next rested only in his hands.

Opening his eyes, Billy kicked Duchess as hard as he could.

In the instant, Billy could feel Duchess's grip release. Then Billy was running down the hallway. He was running down the hallway to the hiding place under the stairs. He found the door with the tiny latch right where Woolly had said it was. The doorway was about half the size of a normal doorway and had a triangular top because it had been cut to fit under the staircase. But it was tall enough for Billy. Slipping inside, he pulled the door closed and held his breath.

A moment later he could hear Duchess calling his name.

Billy could tell that Duchess was only a few feet away, but he wouldn't be able to find Billy. As Woolly had said, no one ever thought to look in the hiding place under the stairs because it was right there in front of them.

Emmett

AFTER TRYING THE MUCK-ROOM door and finding it bolted, Emmett ran around the back of the house and tried the door that led into the dining room. When he found that door locked and then the kitchen door too, he was through trying doors. Removing his belt, he wrapped it around his right hand so that the buckle was on top of his knuckles. Then he smashed one of the panes of glass in the door. Using the metal surface of the buckle, he knocked away the remaining shards that jutted from the frame. Sticking his left hand through the cleared pane, he unlocked the door. The belt, he left wrapped around his fist, thinking it might come in handy right where it was.

As Emmett stepped into the kitchen, he saw Duchess's figure at the far end of the hallway turning a corner at a sprint and disappearing into the muck room—without Billy.

Emmett didn't run in pursuit. Understanding that Billy had broken free, he no longer felt a sense of peril. What he felt now was inevitability. No matter how fast Duchess ran, no matter where he ran to, it was inevitable that Emmett would have his hands upon him.

But as Emmett left the kitchen, he heard glass breaking. It wasn't the sound of a windowpane. It was a sheet of glass. A moment later, Duchess reappeared at the other end of the hallway holding one of the rifles.

That Duchess had a rifle didn't change anything for Emmett. Slowly, but unhesitantly, he began walking toward Duchess, and

Duchess walked toward him. When they were both about ten feet short of the staircase, they stopped, leaving twenty feet between them. Duchess was holding the rifle in one hand with the barrel pointing at the ground, his finger on the trigger. From the way he held the rifle, Emmett could tell that Duchess had held one before, but that didn't change anything either.

—Put down the rifle, he said.

—I can't do that, Emmett. Not until you calm down and start talking sense.

—Sense is what I've been talking, Duchess. For the first time in a week. Willing or unwilling, you're going to the police station.

Duchess looked genuinely frustrated.

—Because of Woolly?

—Not because of Woolly.

—Then why?

—Because the cops think you clobbered someone back in Morgen with a two-by-four, and then put Ackerly in the hospital.

Now Duchess looked dumbfounded.

—What are you talking about, Emmett? Why would I hit some guy in Morgen? I'd never been there in my life. And as to Ackerly, the list of people who'd like to put him in the hospital must be a thousand pages long.

—It really doesn't matter whether you did these things or not, Duchess. What matters is that the cops think you did them—and that I was somehow involved. As long as they're looking for you, they'll be looking for me. So you'll have to turn yourself in and sort it out with them.

Emmett took a step forward, but this time Duchess raised the rifle so that the barrel was pointing at his chest.

In the back of his mind, Emmett knew that he should be taking the threat from Duchess seriously. Like Townhouse had said, when Duchess was intent on something, everyone on the periphery was at

562 | AMOR TOWLES

risk. Whether his intentions now were focused on avoiding Salina, or obtaining the money from the safe, or seeing to the unfinished business with his father, in the heat of the moment Duchess was perfectly capable of doing something as stupid as pulling a trigger. And if Emmett got himself shot, what would happen to Billy?

But before Emmett could acknowledge the merits of this train of thought, before he had the chance to even hesitate, out of the corner of his eye he noticed a fedora on the cushion of a high-back chair, and the memory of Duchess sitting at the piano in Ma Belle's lounge with his hat tilted back on his head in that cocksure manner gave Emmett a new surge of anger that restored his sense of inevitability. Emmett would have Duchess in his hands, he would take him to the police, and soon enough, Duchess would be on his way back to Salina, or Topeka, or wherever they wanted to send him.

Emmett resumed walking, closing the gap between them.

—Emmett, said Duchess with an expression of anticipatory regret, I don't want to shoot you. But I will shoot you if you leave me no choice.

When they were three paces apart, Emmett stopped. It wasn't the threat of the rifle or the plea from Duchess that made him stop. It was the fact that ten feet beyond Duchess, Billy had appeared.

He must have been hiding somewhere behind the staircase. Now he was moving quietly into the open so that he could see what was happening. Emmett wanted to signal Billy that he should return to wherever he'd been hiding, to signal him without making Duchess aware.

But it was too late. Duchess had noted the change in Emmett's expression and glanced back to see what was behind him. When Duchess realized it was Billy, he took two steps to the side and rotated forty-five degrees so that he could still see Emmett while training the rifle's barrel on Billy.

—Stay there, Emmett said to his brother.

—That's right, Billy. Don't make a move. Then your brother won't make a move and I won't make a move, and we can talk this through together.

—Don't worry, said Billy to Emmett. He can't shoot me.

—Billy, you don't know what Duchess will or won't do.

—No, said Billy. I don't know what Duchess will or won't do. But I do know that he can't shoot me. Because he can't read.

—What? said Emmett and Duchess together, the one perplexed, the other offended.

—Who says I can't read? demanded Duchess.

—You did, explained Billy. First you said that small print gave you a headache. Then you said that reading in cars made you queasy. Then you said that you were allergic to books.

Billy turned to Emmett.

—He says it that way because he's too ashamed to admit that he can't read. Just like he's too ashamed to admit that he can't swim.

As Billy was talking, Emmett kept his attention on Duchess and he could see that Duchess was growing red. Maybe it was from shame, thought Emmett, but more likely from resentment.

—Billy, Emmett cautioned, whether or not Duchess can read doesn't make any difference right now. Why don't you just leave this to me.

But Billy was shaking his head.

—It does make a difference, Emmett. It makes a difference because Duchess doesn't know the rules for closing the house.

Emmett looked at his brother for a moment. Then he looked at Duchess—poor, misguided, illiterate Duchess. Taking the last three strides, Emmett put his hands on the rifle, and yanked it from Duchess's grip.

Duchess began talking a mile a minute about how he would never have pulled the trigger. Not against a Watson. Not in a million years.

But over Duchess's talking what Emmett heard was his brother saying a single word. Saying his name in the manner of a reminder.

—Emmett . . .

And Emmett understood. On the lawn of the county courthouse, Emmett had made the promise to his brother. A promise he intended to keep. So as Duchess rattled on about all the things he never would have done, Emmett counted to ten. And as he counted, he could feel the old heat subsiding, he could feel the anger seeping away, until he didn't feel angry at all. Then raising the butt of the rifle, he hit Duchess in the face, giving it everything he had.

—.—

—I think you should look at this now, insisted Billy.

After Duchess had hit the ground, Billy had gone to the kitchen. When he returned a moment later, Emmett told him to sit on the staircase and not move a muscle. Then taking Duchess under the armpits, he began dragging him through the living room. His plan was to drag him out of the muck room, down the stoop, and across the lawn to the Studebaker so that he could drive him to the closest police station and dump him at their door. He hadn't gotten more than two steps when Billy had spoken.

Looking up, Emmett could see that his brother was holding an envelope. Another letter from their father, Emmett thought with a touch of exasperation. Or another postcard from their mother. Or another map of America.

—I can look at it later, said Emmett.

—No, said Billy shaking his head. No. I think you should look at it now.

Dropping Duchess back on the floor, Emmett went over to his brother.

—It's from Woolly, said Billy. To be opened in the event of his absence.

A little stunned, Emmett looked at the inscription on the envelope.

—He is absent, isn't he? asked Billy.

Emmett hadn't quite decided how or whether he should tell his brother about Woolly. But from the way Billy said *absent*, it seemed like he already knew.

—Yes, said Emmett. He is.

Sitting on the steps beside Billy, Emmett opened the envelope. Inside was a handwritten note on a piece of Wallace Wolcott's stationery. Emmett didn't know if this Wallace Wolcott was Woolly's great-grandfather or his grandfather or his uncle. But it didn't matter whose stationery it was.

Dated the 20th of June 1954 and addressed *To Whom It May Concern*, the letter stated that the undersigned, being of sound mind and body, left one third of his one-hundred-and-fifty-thousand-dollar trust fund to Mr. Emmett Watson, one third to Mr. Duchess Hewett, and one third to Mr. William Watson—to do with as they pleased. It was signed *Most Sincereliest, Wallace Wolcott Martin*.

As Emmett closed the letter, he realized that his brother had read it over his shoulder.

—Was Woolly sick? he asked. Like Dad?

—Yes, said Emmett. He was sick.

—I thought he might be when he gave me his uncle's watch. Because it was a watch for handing down.

Billy thought for a moment.

—Is that why you told Duchess that Woolly wanted to be taken home?

—Yes, said Emmett. That's what I meant.

—I think you were right about that, said Billy, nodding in agreement. But you were wrong about the money in the safe.

Without waiting for Emmett to respond, Billy got up and walked down the hallway. Reluctantly, Emmett followed his brother back into Mr. Wolcott's office and over to the safe. By the bookshelves was a piece of furniture that looked like the first three steps of a staircase. Dragging it in front of the safe, Billy climbed the steps, rotated the four dials, turned the handle, and opened the door.

For a moment, Emmett was speechless.

—How do you know the combination, Billy? Did Woolly tell it to you?

—No. Woolly didn't tell it to me. But he told me how his great-grandfather loved the Fourth of July more than any other holiday. So the first combination I tried was 1776. Then I tried 7476 because that's one way of writing the Fourth of July. After that I tried 1732, the year that George Washington was born, but then I remembered that Woolly's great-grandfather said that while Washington, Jefferson, and Adams had the vision to found the Republic, it was Mr. Lincoln who had the courage to perfect it. So I tried 1809, the year that President Lincoln was born, and 1865, the year that he died. That's when I realized it must be 1119 because November 19 was the day of the Gettysburg Address. Here, he said, stepping down from the stairs, come take a look.

Pushing the stairs to the side, Emmett approached the safe, where, under a shelf of papers, thousands of brand-new fifty-dollar bills were neatly arranged in stacks.

Emmett ran a hand over his mouth.

One hundred and fifty thousand dollars, he thought. One hundred and fifty thousand dollars of old Mr. Wolcott's wealth had been handed down to Woolly, and now Woolly had handed it down to them. He had handed it down by means of a last will and testament that was duly signed and dated.

There could be no question of Woolly's intent. In that regard, Duchess had been quite right. It was Woolly's money and he knew exactly what he wanted to do with it. Having been found temperamentally unfit to use it himself, in his absence he wanted his friends to use it as they pleased.

But what would happen if Emmett finished dragging Duchess to the Studebaker and dumped him at the police station?

As much as Emmett hated to admit it, Duchess had been right about that too. Once Duchess was in the hands of the cops and it became clear that Woolly was dead, the wheels of Emmett's and Billy's future would grind to a halt. Police and investigators would descend upon the house, followed by family members and attorneys. Circumstances would be studied. Inventories taken. Intentions second-guessed. Endless questions asked. And any turns of good fortune would be viewed with the utmost suspicion.

In another few moments, Emmett would close the door to Mr. Wolcott's safe. That was a certainty. But once the door was closed, two different futures would be possible. In one, the contents of the safe would remain untouched. In the other, the space below the shelf would be empty.

—Woolly wanted the best for his friends, observed Billy.

—Yes, he did.

—For you and me, said Billy. And for Duchess too.

—·—

Once the decision was made, Emmett knew they would need to work quickly, putting things in order and leaving as few traces as possible.

After closing the door to the safe, Emmett gave Billy the task of cleaning up the office while he saw to the rest of the house.

First, having gathered up all the tools that Duchess had assembled—the hammer, screwdrivers, and ax—he carried them outside past the breached dory to the work shed.

Back inside, Emmett went to the kitchen. Certain that Woolly would never have eaten beans out of a can, Emmett put the empty can and Pepsi bottle in a paper bag to be carted out. Then he cleaned the spoon and returned it to the silverware drawer.

The broken pane of glass in the kitchen didn't worry him. The authorities would assume that Woolly had broken the pane in order to get inside the locked house. But the rifle cabinet was another matter. That would be more likely to raise questions. Serious questions. After returning the rifle to its place in the cabinet, Emmett removed the croquet ball. Then he repositioned the stack of Adirondack chairs to make it look like they had toppled over and crashed through the glass.

Now it was time to deal with Duchess.

Taking him under the arms again, Emmett dragged him down the hallway, out of the muck room, and onto the grass.

When Emmett and Billy had decided to take their share of the money and leave Duchess behind with his, Billy had made Emmett promise that he wouldn't hurt Duchess any more than he already had. But every minute that passed increased the risk that Duchess would regain consciousness and pose a whole new set of problems. Emmett had to put him somewhere that would slow him down for a few hours. Or at least long enough for Billy and Emmett to finish their work and be well on their way.

The trunk of the Cadillac? he wondered.

The problem with the trunk was that once Duchess regained consciousness, he would either be able to get out of it quickly or not at all, bad outcomes both.

The work shed?

No. There would be no way to secure its doors from the outside.

As Emmett was looking toward the shed, another idea presented itself, an interesting idea. But suddenly, at Emmett's feet Duchess emitted a groan.

—Shit, said Emmett to himself.

Looking down, he could see that Duchess was moving his head lightly from side to side, on the verge of coming to. As Duchess emitted another groan, Emmett looked back over his shoulder to make sure that Billy wasn't there. Then bending over, he lifted Duchess by the collar with his left hand and punched him in the face with his right.

With Duchess again at rest, Emmett dragged him in the direction of the shed.

Twenty minutes later, they were ready to go.

Unsurprisingly, Billy had done a perfect job of restoring the office. Every book was back on its shelf, every paper in its stack, every drawer in its slot. The only thing he hadn't replaced was the bust of Abraham Lincoln because it was too heavy. When Emmett picked it up and began looking around for a place to set it down, Billy crossed to the desk.

—Here, he said, placing a finger on the spot where the faintest outline of the sculpture's base could be seen.

As Billy waited by the kitchen door, Emmett locked the doors to the front porch and the muck room and then made a final swing through the house.

Returning to the bedroom upstairs, he stood in the doorway. His intention had been to leave everything exactly as he'd found it. But seeing the empty brown bottle, Emmett picked it up and put it in his pocket. Then he said one last goodbye to Wallace Woolly Martin.

As he was closing the door Emmett noticed his old book bag on a chair and realized that the one he had loaned Duchess must be somewhere in the house as well. After checking all the bedrooms, Emmett searched the living room and found it lying on the floor next to a couch where Duchess must have spent the night. Only as he was headed for the kitchen to join Billy did Emmett remember and retrieve the fedora from the high-back chair.

As they walked from the kitchen past the lake, Emmett showed Billy that Duchess was safe and sound.

In the front seat of the Cadillac, Emmett tossed Duchess's book bag and the hat. In the trunk of the Studebaker, he put two paper bags—one with the trash from the kitchen, the other with their share of Woolly's trust. As he was about to close the trunk, he was reminded that just nine days before, he had been standing in the same spot when he received his father's legacies: the money, and the quote from Emerson, which was half excuse, half exhortation. Having come fifteen hundred miles in the wrong direction, on the verge of traveling three thousand more, Emmett believed that the power within him was new in nature, that no one but he could know what he was capable of, and that he had only just begun to know it himself.

Closing the trunk, he joined Billy in the front seat, turned the key, and pushed the starter.

—I had originally been thinking that we'd spend the night up here, Emmett said to his brother. What do you say we pick up Sally and hit the road, instead?

—That's a good idea, said Billy. Let's pick up Sally and hit the road.

As Emmett backed the car in an arc in order to face it toward the driveway, Billy was already studying his map—with a furrowed brow.

—What is it? asked Emmett.

Billy shook his head.

—This is the fastest route from where we are.

Placing his fingertip on Woolly's big red star, Billy moved it along various roads headed in a southwestern trajectory from the Wolcotts' to Saratoga Springs and Scranton, then westward to Pittsburgh, where they would finally rejoin the Lincoln Highway.

—What time is it? asked Emmett.

Looking at Woolly's watch, Billy said that it was one minute to five.

Emmett pointed to a different road on the map.

—If we went back the way we came, he said, we could start our journey in Times Square. And if we hurry, we could get there just as all the lights are coming on.

Billy looked up in his wide-eyed way.

—Could we, Emmett? Could we, really? But wouldn't that take us out of our way?

Emmett made a show of thinking for a second.

—A little out of our way, I suppose. But what day is it?

—It's the twenty-first of June.

Emmett put the Studebaker in gear.

—Then we've got thirteen days to make the crossing, if we mean to be in San Francisco by the Fourth of July.

Duchess

I RETURNED TO CONSCIOUSNESS WITH a sensation of drifting—like one who's sitting in a boat on a sunny afternoon. And as it turned out, that's exactly where I was: sitting in a boat on a sunny afternoon! Giving my head a shake in order to clear it, I put my hands on the gunwales and hoisted myself up.

The first thing I noted, I'll readily admit, was the natural beauty before me. Though I was never much of a country mouse—finding the great outdoors to be generally uncomfortable and occasionally inhospitable—there was something deeply satisfying about the scenery. What with the pine trees rising from the lakeshore, and the sunlight cascading from the sky, and the surface of the water stirred by a gentle breeze. One couldn't help but sigh at the majesty of it all.

But thanks to the ache in my keister, I was brought back to reality. Looking down, I could see that I was sitting on a pile of painted stones. Picking one of them up in order to consider it more closely, I realized that not only was there dried blood on my hand, there was dried blood all down the front of my shirt.

Then I remembered.

Emmett had hit me with the butt of the rifle!

He had burst through the door while I was trying to open the safe. We'd had a difference of opinions, something of a scuffle, and a bit of tit for tat. In the interest of theatrics, I had brandished a gun, waving it in the general direction of Billy. But having leapt to the wrong conclusion about my intentions, Emmett had grabbed the rifle and let me have it.

He may even have broken my nose, I thought. Which would explain why I was having so much trouble breathing through my nostrils.

As I reached up to give my injury a gingerly probe, I heard the engine of a car revving. Looking to my left, I saw the Studebaker, as yellow as a canary, backing up, idling, then roaring out of the Wolcotts' drive.

—Wait! I shouted.

But as I leaned to my side in order to call Emmett's name, the boat took a dip toward the water.

Lurching back, I carefully resumed my place in the center.

Okay, I thought to myself, Emmett knocked me out with the rifle. But then rather than taking me to the police station as threatened, he set me adrift in a rowboat without a paddle. Why would he do that?

Then my eyes narrowed.

Because little Mr. Know-It-All had told him I couldn't swim. That's why. And by setting me adrift on the lake, the Watson brothers figured they would have all the time they needed to get into the safe and claim Woolly's inheritance for themselves.

But even as I was having this ugly thought—a thought for which I will never be able to fully atone—I noticed the stacks of cash in the bow.

Emmett had gotten into the old man's safe, all right, just like I knew he would. But rather than stranding me empty-handed, he had left me with my rightful share.

It was my rightful share, wasn't it?

I mean, isn't that about what fifty thousand dollars would look like?

Naturally curious, I began moving toward the front of the boat in order to do a quick accounting. But as I did so, the shifting of my weight lowered the front of the boat and water began pouring in through a hole in the bow. Retreating quickly to my seat, the bow lifted, and the inrush stopped.

This wasn't just any rowboat, I realized, as water sloshed about my feet. This was the rowboat that was being repaired by the boathouse. And that's why Emmett had loaded the stones in the stern. To keep the compromised bow above the waterline.

The ingenuity of it, I thought with a smile. A boat with a hole and no oars in the middle of a lake. It was like a setup for Kazantikis. The only thing better would have been if Emmett had tied my hands behind my back. Or put me in cuffs.

—All right then, I said, feeling every bit up to the challenge.

By my estimate, I was a few hundred feet from shore. If I leaned back, stuck my hands in the water, and paddled gently, I should be able to make my way safely to solid ground.

Reaching my arms over the back of the boat turned out to be surprisingly awkward, and the water turned out to be surprisingly cold. In fact, every few minutes I had to interrupt my paddling in order to warm my fingers.

But just as I was beginning to make progress, a late afternoon breeze began picking up, such that every time I took a break from paddling, I would find myself drifting back toward the center of the lake.

To compensate, I started paddling a little faster and taking shorter breaks. But as if in response, the breeze blew harder. So much so, that one of the bills flitted off the top of its stack and landed about twenty feet away on the surface of the water. Then off flitted another. And another.

Paddling as fast as I could, I stopped taking breaks altogether. But the breeze kept blowing and the bills kept taking flight, fluttering over the side of the boat, fifty bucks at a crack.

Having no other choice, I stopped paddling, rose to my feet, and started creeping forward. When I took my second little step, the bow dipped an inch too far and water began flowing in. I took a step back and the inflow stopped.

There would be no doing this cautiously, I realized. I was going to have to make a grab for the cash, then retreat quickly back to the stern before too much water had entered the boat.

Steadying myself with my arms before me, I prepared for the lunge.

All it required was deftness. A quick motion combined with a gentle touch. Like when you're removing a cork from a bottle.

Exactly, I thought to myself. The whole endeavor shouldn't take more than ten seconds. But without Billy to assist, I'd have to do the countdown on my own.

At the word *Ten*, I took the first step forward and the boat rocked to the right. At *Nine* I compensated by stepping to the left and the boat lurched left. At *Eight*, what with all the rocking and lurching, I lost my balance and tumbled forward, landing right on top of the cash as water rushed in through the breach.

Reaching for the gunwale, I tried to push myself up, but my fingers were so numb from the paddling that I lost my grip and fell forward again—whacking my broken nose on the bow.

With a howl, I reflexively scrambled to my feet as the freezing water continued to rush in around my ankles. With all of my weight in the front of the boat and the stern rising up behind me, painted stones rolled toward my feet, the bow took another dip, and I went head over heels into the lake.

Kicking at the depths with my feet and slapping at the surface with my arms, I tried to take a deep breath of air, but took a deep breath of water instead. Coughing and thrashing, I felt my head go under and my body begin to sink. Looking up through the dappled surface, I could see the shadows of the bills floating on the water like autumn leaves. Then the boat drifted over me, casting a much larger shadow, a shadow that began to extend outward in every direction.

But just when it seemed as if the entire lake would be subsumed in darkness, a great curtain was raised and I found myself standing on a crowded street in a busy metropolis, except that everyone around me was someone I knew, and all of them were frozen in place.

Sitting together on a nearby bench were Woolly and Billy, smiling at the floor plan of the house in California. And there was Sally leaning over a pram in order to tuck in the blanket of the child in her care. And there by the flower cart was Sister Sarah looking wistful and forlorn. And right there, not more than fifty feet away, standing by the door of his bright yellow car, was Emmett, looking honorable and upright.

—Emmett, I called.

But even as I did so, I could hear the distant chiming of a clock. Only it wasn't a clock, and it wasn't distant. It was the gold watch that had been tucked in the pocket of my vest and that now was suddenly in my hand. Looking down at its face, I couldn't tell what time it was, but I knew that after another few chimes, the entire world would begin moving once again.

So taking off my crooked hat, I bowed to Sarah and Sally. I bowed to Woolly and Billy. I bowed to the one and only Emmett Watson.

And when the final chime sounded, I turned to them all in order to utter with my very last breath, *The rest is silence*, just as Hamlet had.

Or was that Iago?

I never could remember.

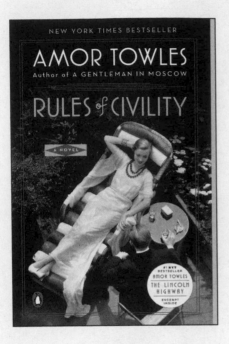
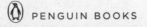

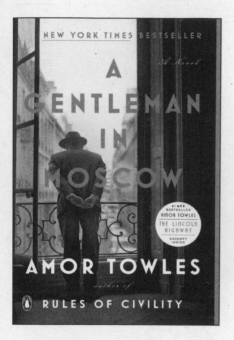